THE YEAR'S BEST MILITARY & ADVENTURE SF 2015
SECOND ANNUAL EDITION

★

THE YEAR'S BEST MILITARY & ADVENTURE SF 2015

SECOND ANNUAL EDITION

★

Edited By

DAVID AFSHARIRAD

The Year's Best Military & Adventure SF 2015

A Baen Books Original

Baen Publishing Enterprises
P.O. Box 1403
Riverdale, NY 10471
www.baen.com

ISBN: 978-1-4767-8177-8

Cover art by Kurt Miller

First Baen printing, June 2016

Distributed by Simon & Schuster
1230 Avenue of the Americas
New York, NY 10020

Printed in the United States of America

10 9 8 7 6 5 4 3 2 1

TABLE OF CONTENTS
★

STORY COPYRIGHTS

THE YEAR'S BEST MILITARY & ADVENTURE SF 2015

★

You Decide Who Wins!

Other anthologies tell you which stories were best—we want *you* to decide! Baen Books is pleased to announce the second annual Year's Best Military and Adventure SF Readers' Choice Award. The award honors the best of the best in the grand storytelling tradition. The winner will receive a plaque and a $500 cash prize.

To vote, go to:
http://www.baen.com/yearsbestaward2015

You may also send a postcard or letter with the name of your favorite story from this year's volume to Baen Books Year's Best Award, P.O. Box 1188, Wake Forest, NC 27587. Voting closes August 31, 2016. Entries received after voting closes will not be counted.

So hurry, hurry, hurry!
The winner will be announced at
Dragoncon in Atlanta.

THE YEAR'S BEST MILITARY & ADVENTURE SF 2015

SECOND ANNUAL EDITION

★

PREFACE

★

by David Afsharirad

HERE WE ARE ANOTHER YEAR farther into the future. A lot has happened since the first volume in the Year's Best Military and Adventure series launched in June of 2015—including a name change, but we'll get to that later. That first volume sold briskly and garnered some excellent reviews. (Check the back cover for examples; I'll wait.) Many of the folks who bought the book elected to vote in the readers' poll, and at Dragon*Con 2015, I had the pleasure of handing out the very first Baen Books Year's Best Military SF and Space Opera Readers' Choice Award to Michael Z. Williamson, for his story "Soft Casualty." Mike was on hand to receive a handsome plaque as well as a handsome stack of five one-hundred dollar bills.

Let's see . . . what else happened over the last 365 days? The sun kept shining, the world kept turning—and SF writers kept producing high quality short fiction. Which is why I've asked you all here today.

But first, about that name change:

When assembling the first volume in the series, I asked Baen publisher Toni Weisskopf about those stories that were excellent but were only kinda sorta space opera and/or military SF. Would we rather have superlative stories that didn't *quite* fit the theme of the book, or merely great ones that certainly *did* fit the theme? We both agreed that we'd be willing to stretch the definitions to ensure that we got the best of the best. And stretch we did, though I should say not to the breaking point. For this year's volume, we decided that the old title just wasn't inclusive enough. Hence the name change to *The Year's Best Military and Adventure SF*. And now, as Paul Harvey used to say, you know the rest of the story.

So what did the year's best military and adventure SF look like in 2015?

Well, some old friends from the first volume came back. Seth Dickinson, whose story "Morrigan in the Sunglare" was in last year's anthology, returns with another story set in that same universe. "Morrigan in Shadow" finds the Earth-based Federation surrendering to the extra-solar colonial Alliance, a move that may spell doom for humanity as there's a particularly nasty alien menace heading our way. Eric Leif Davin is back with "Twilight on Olympus," a story of humanity stepping out into our own celestial backyard—Mars to be precise—and the dangers that are inherent in space travel. And Brad R. Torgersen brings us "Gyre," a story of the Sargasso Containment, in which our solar system is surrounded by a mysterious, impenetrable force field—and being consumed by crippling addiction to a drug known as Rust.

But of course we've also got some fresh faces and the stories these faces (or the brains behind them) produced take us from the recent past to the far, far future.

In Joe Lansdale's "The Wizard of the Trees," a cowboy from Buffalo Bill's Wild West Show finds himself mysteriously transported to a Venus of which Edgar Rice Burroughs would approve. No one does ERB better than Lansdale (except the man himself), and "The Wizard of the Trees" is a shining example of Champion Joe's work in this milieu.

David Brin brings us another tale of the second planet from Sol. This one is called "The Tumbledowns of Cleopatra Abyss" and it proves that the death of classic SF stories has been wildly exaggerated.

From the warm embrace of our sister world Venus, we turn to the cold vacuum of the space between the planets. That inhospitable locale is the setting of Claudine Griggs' "Helping Hand," a tight little adventure tale of a spacewalk gone very, very wrong that will have you reading at the very edge of your seat.

In Andrea M. Pawley's "For the Love of Sylvia City," we leave outer space and head to the floor of Earth's oceans, where humans have retreated to avoid the threat of devastating war—until the war threatens to come to them.

On the military side of things, we have Brendan DuBois' tale of a world besieged by hostile alien invaders—and the brave humans who stand up and fight! That one is called "The Siege of Denver" and it gets things off to a rousing start. Hank Davis takes off his editor's top hat and dons his author's ball cap to bring us a military SF story with a touch of the Weird that fills us all in on what exactly is "The Trouble with Telepaths." And in her moving short story "Remembery Day," Sarah Pinsker contemplates the value of memories—even painful ones—for soldiers, and for those who are left behind when they go off to war.

But let's leave our backyard and go traveling, not only in space, but in time. In "This is the Way the Universe Ends: With a Bang," Brian Dolton offers up a rousing whodunit that will keep you guessing until the very end—of time!

And if all that wasn't enough how's this grab you: The first Hammer's Slammers story in over a decade. Fans of Drake's legendary series thought it likely that we'd seen the last of the Slammers, but editor Mark L. Van Name was not content to let the mercenaries go gently into that good night. He commissioned a new Slammers story from Drake for his anthology *Onward, Drake!* and Drake, the consummate professional, obliged by writing "Save What You Can."

And what could top all this? (Please don't say lids.) How about an introduction by another master of military SF whose first name happens to be David?

David Weber's Honor Harrington series is a landmark in the genre, with millions of copies sold, an ongoing comic series, and a major motion picture in the works. He kindly took time out of his schedule of writing top-notch military SF bestsellers to pen a fine introduction for us.

So what are you waiting for? Turn the page and start reading! But don't forget to jot down notes as to which story was your favorite because once again we're asking *you* to pick the Year's Best Military and Adventure Science Fiction story!

To find out how you can cast your vote, go to http://baen.com/yearsbestaward2015. But don't hesitate—voting closes August 31, 2016.

And while you're reading *The Year's Best Military and Adventure*

SF 2015 and voting for your favorite story, I'll be scouring every nook and cranny of the SF publishing world to bring you the best of the best *next* year. Stories that prove that the short story isn't dead, isn't dying, and that the Golden Age of the science fiction short story is the ever-present now.

Excelsior!

—David Afsharirad
Austin, TX
February 2016

INTRODUCTION

by David Weber

WHY IS MILITARY SCIENCE FICTION so durable? Why has it been around so long, and why does it have so many readers today? And why do those of us who *write* military science fiction write it in the first place?

It's arguable that military science fiction's been around as long as science fiction. Certainly Jules Verne and H.G. Wells were practitioners of military sci-fi, and the "golden age" was riddled with military sci-fi writers. I remember my own very first science fiction novel was Jack Williamson's *Legion of Space*, which was most definitely space opera and could reasonably fall under the military sci-fi rubric. Of course, the granddaddy of all military science fiction/space opera writers had to be E. E. "Doc" Smith, and God knows that we could compile an enormously long list of military science fictioneers since him. H. Beam Piper, Keith Laumer, Gordon R. Dickson, Poul Anderson, Jerry Pournelle, Larry Niven, our own David Drake, S. M. Stirling, John Ringo, and I'm sure several score other people who include the absolute all-time favorite purveyor of military sci-fi of someone reading this introduction.

Military sci-fi comes in all flavors, but good military sci-fi, enduring military sci-fi, is seldom of the "fluff" type. Seldom what I think of as "splatter porn" or of the sort that romanticizes the ugliness of combat and the taking of human life or suggests the "good guys" will get off without paying a horrible price of their own simply because they're the good guys. I'm not saying all of it has the gritty realism of a Drake, and I'm certainly not saying "good" military sci-fi has to be an anti-military screed. But as Toni Weisskopf once pointed out in a conversation with me, there's a distinct difference between military science fiction and militar*istic* science fiction. The biggest difference is that the former is normally written by someone who at least has a clue about how militaries and warfare work whereas the latter is written by someone who *doesn't* have a clue about how they work but thought it would be really cool to write about a war.

But what makes military science fiction so compelling, at least to its readership?

Well, all worthwhile stories are about characters, and characters are about problem solving and conflict of one sort or another. Those problems and that conflict don't *have* to have anything at all to do with a military setting, but the truth is that the most fundamental "conflict" a character can deal with is one which is literally life or death, and that sort of sums up what happens on a battlefield or aboard a submarine stalking an enemy convoy, or aboard a starship facing incoming missiles and energy fire.

Worthwhile characters are also about sacrifice. About being willing, as Heinlein put it—and I'm sure someone is going to point out that the Dean should have been listed among my military sci-fi writers above—to put one's own life between the things one cares about and "war's desolation."

Make no mistake about it, combat is ugly, vile, and brutal. It's about destroying other human lives, hopefully without losing one's own or letting any more of *your* people die than you can possibly avoid. It's about bushwhacking the other fellow, planting landmines and punji sticks, booby-trapping bodies, poisoning waterholes. It's no coincidence that a huge majority of all air-to-air kills by the world's fighter aces were accomplished from ambush before the victims ever saw them coming, starting with World War I's "Beware of the Hun in the sun" and continuing right up to the present day. Or, as George S. Patton put it, "No poor dumb son-of-a-bitch ever won a war by dying for his country. He won it by making the other poor dumb son-of-a-bitch die for *his* country."

There have been periods, intervals, in the history of warfare where concepts of "honor" would appear to have stood this grim reality on its head. There are actual recorded instances of moments like the one when the French and English officers argued over who was entitled to the first volley in an infantry battle. But those moments have been rare, and they were seldom held in very high esteem by the professionals for whom warfare was trade, career, and ugly day-to-day job in one.

There are very few Rupert Brookes in the ranks of *professional* soldiers.

There have certainly been cultures which prized honor above life, from Achilles through the Japanese samurai by way of dozens of other cultures and societies along the way. Of course, there's usually been a distinction between those who received those societies' accolades and those who were kicked to the curb as soon as their services were no longer required . . . often enough by the very civilians they'd fought to save. God knows soldiers have been regarded as ignorant brutes—men who enlisted because they couldn't get a "real" job and who were suited for nothing better—by the "better sort" of their societies for at least the last several centuries of Western Civilization. In my opinion, the best English-language illustrator of that bitterly true distinction may well be Rudyard Kipling's "Tommy," and he was right: "An' Tommy ain't a bloomin' fool—you bet that Tommy sees!" The seamen "pressed" for service in the sailing ships of the British Royal Navy, snatched away from home and family, forced to serve in a grim, grueling environment, with a very high probability of dying, and then thrown on the beach, often mutilated and crippled, if they survived, are only one historical example of that unhappy truth. Virtually every other nation has its own equivalent, although some are more blatant than others.

And yet we return again and again to stories about war, and I think that's at least in part because we recognize what Heinlein was saying on an instinctual level that stays with us, despite the passing fads of the culture du jour. Harry Flashman had a little something to say about the bathos of "The Charge of the Light Brigade," but men and women have been writing poetry about war, sacrifice, death, and—yes—glory since well before Homer. If you don't believe me, check out Gilgamesh. Perhaps it's because there's no evasion, no way to manipulate one's way out of the dangers inherent in combat. Perhaps it's because there's a sort of ultimate democracy in death. And perhaps it's because of what Heinlein was onto, the concept that we owe respect and honor to those prepared to endure the vileness of combat on our behalf.

And, conversely—perhaps even paradoxically—sometimes it's

David Weber

because the writer wants to demonstrate and the reader wants to understand *why* war is the vile ugliness that it is and yet humankind goes right on embracing it. David Drake's Slammers are, I think, an example of that. David is too much the historian not to understand the forces that drive wars—or the fact that those most eager to embrace them are seldom those most likely to die *in* them—but his focus is on the men and women in the furnace. It's on the fact that whatever brings someone into military service in the first place, whether it be patriotism or the possibility of loot, what keeps that person there, keeps that person fighting, in the midst of the terror and mayhem of combat, is a combination of the need to survive and of loyalty to those serving with that person. The members of his unit, of his crew, of his circle of friends at that moment when their joint survival depends upon all of them.

Throughout history, one of a military commander's primary tasks has been to figure out how to get all of the troops under his command to actually *fight*, and that's never been as easy as bad military fiction makes it seem. One of my favorite military historians once referred to armored fighting vehicles as "courage in a can," because the members of a tank's crew are each, individually, vital to the tank's operation . . . and no one can run away and hide. Yet in that ten percent of an old-fashioned infantry division that actually fired at the enemy, that sense of loyalty played a huge role in what motivated them to do that.

Military science fiction examines that, illustrates that, sometimes seeks to debunk that, and human beings find that motivation, that mechanism—that relationship—endlessly fascinating because it says so much about what makes all of us human in the end.

In addition to all the philosophical ramblings above, military science fiction serves as both inspirational and cautionary tales. You can't read a David Drake story, or a Steve Stirling story, without concluding that as someone (I believe it was Poul Anderson) once said—and I'm paraphrasing, I'm afraid—an adventure is someone *else* being cold, hungry, tired and scared far, far away from *you*. There's a certain vicarious excitement in being able to experience, however incompletely, the emotions of that "someone else," but for anyone with a pair of functional neurons to rub together, it's also pretty clear that it's not a situation any sane individual would seek out for its pleasure quotient. Those sorts of stories are the authors' way of standing in the middle of the railroad tracks, waving a red lantern, and bellowing "You *really* don't want to go there!" And in the case of someone like Drake, that warning carries extra weight because we know he's already been there himself.

And yet, even as they caution us, they know we're going there—or someone is—anyway, sooner or later. As Heinlein also pointed out, a true pacifist is a very rare critter, indeed. There is—or, in my own opinion, damned well ought to be—something for which *any* human being would be prepared to fight and die. As Eowyn points out in *The Lord of the Rings,* "Those without swords can still die upon them," and as a character in one of Poul Anderson's Flandry stories pointed out to a very young Dominic Flandry, those who insist that there are no circumstances in which they would embrace violence against other human beings are, in effect, saying that they will not stand up and fight to oppose evil under any circumstances. All too often we applaud that highly principled stand, even if we don't share it, but should we? Isn't it a form of moral cowardice to say that one would prefer to allow the most monstrous evil conceivable triumph rather than sully the lily-white purity of one's highly-principled moral superiority? Anyone has the right to make that choice in his/her own case, to choose to surrender his or her life rather than resort to violence. But how do you make it in *someone else*'s case with even a pretense of morality?

And how many people who make that assertion even in their own case, far less that of someone else whom they love, from the safe cocoon of the society less principled people have created for them, have actually *faced* that evil? As George Orwell put it, "People sleep peaceably in their beds at night only because rough men stand ready to do violence on their behalf," but one hardly needs to go that far afield to find the final, brutal denominator which separates pacifist from all-out warrior. Let someone threaten a mother's child and see what that mother does, however much a pacifist she may think herself. Or, to return to Heinlein yet again, greater love hath no man than a mother cat dying to defend her kittens.

I think that we as readers want to vicariously touch that affirmation of the human spirit as protector because all we have to do is look about us to see the ability of nominally human beings to play the role of predator.

And then, of course, there is the transporting aspect. The ability of that frigate-like book to carry us to another land, to other people, to other experiences. Military fiction—and for a science-fiction readership, that's military *science fiction*—shares all of the above with its readership. Because conflict is so much a part of human nature, because it can be so complex, and because, as Clausewitz said, everything in war is very simple, but accomplishing even simple things is very difficult, we are endlessly fascinated by the way humans deal with that complexity and its paradoxically simple imperatives, not just of survival, but of right and wrong.

In the end, we cannot open a history book, cannot consult the archaeological record, without coming face-to-face with the red-fanged violence of the human past. Military science fiction is an effort to understand and illuminate that past by projecting it into the *future*. Or into *a* future, at least. And in that sense, in an odd sort of way, it's an affirmation of our very humanness. There will be war for as long as human beings are what we would recognize as human beings. We may applaud that fact or deplore it; we cannot *change* it. As Heinlein pointed out on several occasions, the decision that "We ain't a gonna study war no more" simply assures that someone who *is* going to study it will soon be inheriting all our stuff . . . and probably killing or enslaving our friends, neighbors, and family along the way. And so projecting human combativeness into the future suggests there will be *humans* in that future somewhere—still fumbling about, still screwing up, still finding themselves required to make the other poor, dumb son-of-a-bitch die for *his* country . . . and still being someone we do recognize.

It's important, sometimes, to look into the mirror and refuse to look away. To recognize realities we'd really like to pretend no longer apply. And to understand the abyss as fully as we can before we step into it, taking our societies and the people we love and care about with us. Very little of the enduring military science fiction is pretentious enough—or arrogant enough—to hammer its readers over the head with all those lessons, but it doesn't shy away from them, either. It examines them, it pleads the case for this or that view of necessity, pragmatism, honor, horror, selflessness, avarice, sacrifice, cruelty—the entire gamut of the strengths and weaknesses that make human beings what we are.

But the *good* stuff tells a thumping good story while it does all of that, and that's what you're going to find between these covers.

—David Weber

THE SIEGE OF DENVER

★

by Brendan DuBois

It's been years since the alien Creepers invaded Earth and took our major cities hostage. Our planet's resources are dwindling, and it's up to those left alive to fight back against the interstellar menace. Private Melissa MacKay is one such fighter, and when Creepers threaten to keep a supply balloon from getting much needed food and medical equipment to the besieged city of Denver, she'll do what must be done and in the process discover what it means to be a soldier.

IN A DRY TRENCH about twelve klicks west of Denver, Private Melissa MacKay—originally from Hotchkiss, Colorado—rummaged through her battle pack, looking for some paperwork. This section of trench was pretty much identical to the other line of trenches that surrounded the besieged Mile High City, with duckboards on the ground and a dugout nearby to shelter her squad from the occasional incoming fire from the enemy. It was a cool morning, and a small pellet-burning metal stove outside of the dugout burning gave off a little heat.

A couple of meters down the trench, her squad leader, Corporal Stan Jankowski, did his best to shave using a handled mirror stuck into the dirt and a plastic cup of cold water. Next to Jankowski were his own battle pack, a field phone hanging off a stake connecting them to the sector's CP—a burnt-out Best Buy box store out by Route 60—and

11

his Colt M-10. Melissa looked on enviously at Jankowski's M-10. She and the other squad member—Hector Morales, out getting their morning breakfast rations—were only qualified on the Colt M-4, the standard automatic rifle used by the U.S. Army and its associated National Guard units and allies for decades. But her corporal was the one member of the squad who could carry the M-10, the weapon of choice for fighting the Creepers.

It was a bulky thing, black and looking like an oversized grenade launcher. But after a decade of fighting the Creepers—and mostly losing—the M-10 was about the only weapon available to take on the damn bugs. An infantry weapon fighting an interstellar war. What a world. She lifted her head, looked west. There was movement several hundred meters away, some horse-drawn wagons, soldiers, and two old transport vehicles, belching out steam and smoke from their wood-fired engines.

"What are you looking at, Mac?" Jankowski asked, scraping at a cheek.

"The Signal Corps is moving around. Maybe they'll do a launch today."

"Only if the wind is right," he said. "Hey, Mac, you're a history nerd. Any idea when this man's Army last had a balloon corps?"

"Little over a hundred years ago," she automatically replied. "A few years after the end of World War I."

"Right you are."

A hunched-over figure was running towards their trench section, carrying a satchel in his hand.

"Morales is coming in," she said.

Jankowski wiped at his face with a threadbare green towel. "Anybody else running in with him?"

"Nope."

"Goddamn Army."

Melissa said nothing. She knew what Jankowski meant. A typical squad could have up to twelve soldiers, and unfortunately, she and Morales and Jankowski were it. Not good, but not much you could do about it when platoons were taking on company jobs, and companies were taking on battalion jobs. Ten years of war had not only thinned out the planet's population, but had done the same to its battered armed forces.

Morales reached the edge of the trench, rolled over and grinned. His light brown skin was dusted with dirt, and his helmet was at his side, connected to his MOLLE vest, and his M-4 was slung over his shoulder. He held up the satchel. "Who's up for breakfast?"

"I've been ready for an hour," Melissa said. "Let's get to it."

On a clear section of duckboard, Morales opened up the satchel, took out closed metal containers and a Thermos bottle. The young soldier moved quick and their breakfast was revealed: lukewarm and sweet coffee, cold oatmeal, and two links of sausage.

"There should be three links," Jankowski said, voice tight. "Why is there only two?"

"That's all I got from the mess tent, Corporal," Morales said.

"Bullshit. They know we're three here, and we should have gotten three links."

"That's all they gave me."

"What, did you eat one on the way over here? Did you?"

Melissa said, "Hey, you guys take the sausage. I don't particularly like 'em anyway."

Jankowski glared at her and Morales looked relieved, and Melissa took her breakfast down a ways in the trench, so she could eat by herself. It didn't take long, and when she was finished, she was hungry. She was always hungry. Even back home in Hotchkiss at their farm, there was never enough food to fill you up. Melissa walked back to Jankowski and Morales, and the corporal said, "Morales, you're on clean-up. Hump the dishes back to the mess tent."

"Hey, it's Mac's turn," he said. "I'm the one who humped out there to get breakfast. It ain't fair."

"Don't care, Morales, really don't. You're humping it back."

Morales kept quiet but Melissa could tell he was pissed. But so what? Crap rolled downhill, and he was the freshest member of their thinned-out unit. When Morales scrambled back over the side of the trench, she saw objects starting to rise up by the transport wagons she had seen earlier.

"Lookie here, Corporal," she said. "Looks like they're inflating at least three balloons."

The three dark gray shapes lumbered their way up into the morning sky. Jankowski said, "Well, I'll be damned. Wonder how much cargo they're gonna try this time."

"You think they'll make it?"

Jankowski wet a finger and held it up in the air. "Two things will determine that, Mac. One will be the wind direction in this section. That's why they set up shop over there. So far it looks good. The other . . ."

He moved away from the western side of the trench, walked the few steps to the eastern side. Melissa joined him, as they stood on viewing platforms, looked out to the east, where several klicks away, the struggling city of Denver hung on. Before them was a blasted landscape of shattered buildings, broken roadways, rusted vehicles, clumps of grass and brush. On the horizon were the tall buildings of the city itself, hazy through smoke.

But she and Jankowski moved their heads almost as one, to note a dome-shaped structure, blue-gray in color, about two klicks away.

"The bugs," Jankowski said. "They have a vote. They always do."

Melissa leaned on the crumbling dirt of the trench. The area out there was No Man's Land, although a more accurate title would be No Human's Land. There was nearly a hundred-percent chance that if you walked out there, you'd be barbecued within minutes. The dome was a Creeper base, one of seven that circled the city of Denver and which were established in the first year of the war, when the Creepers arrived in low earth orbit. At first it was thought they were a number of large comet-sized objects, until they maneuvered and achieved orbit and then . . .

Unleashed hell upon the earth.

First they exploded a number of nuclear devices in a careful pattern around the globe, immediately frying about ninety-nine percent of electronics via EMPs, and then they maneuvered asteroids to drop into oceans, just outside of major cities around the earth, causing tsunamis that killed millions. Then bases like this one were set up on the ground, sheltering Creepers that came out whenever they wanted to burn and lase anything in their path. And if that wasn't enough, the Creepers had a number of killer stealth satellites in orbit that fried anything powered by electronics—trucks, cars, aircraft, trains, power plants— essentially keeping the planet's survivors stuck in the nineteenth century.

Ten years later the war ground on, with Denver and a host of other unfortunate cities besieged by Creeper forces, which did not allow people out or food in. And why Denver and not Pittsburgh, or St. Louis, or Knoxville? No one knew.

"Corporal?"

"Yeah."

She thought she had him in a reasonable mood, so she pressed ahead. "When I was assigned here, the lieutenant said I'd be doing some makee-learnee with you."

"So he did."

"So how about giving me a couple of practice shots with the M-10?"

Jankowski just kept on staring out at the wasteland. He had been a quiet sort when Melissa arrived here a month ago, not doing much in the way of small talk, just working to keep this section of the trench squared away. Only once had she ever learned anything about Jankowski on her own, and that had happened last month, when temporary hot showers had been set up near the CP. Emerging from the shower, rubbing his torso and arms dry with a towel, wearing a pair of shorts, Jankowski had strolled by her, and on his right upper bicep was an intricate tattoo. The ink job displayed a mountain peak and the Gothic letter "D."

D for Denver, meaning Jankowski was a native son, one of the fortunate who had been out of the city when the Creepers had set up their siege, and who had been trying ever since to go back home.

"Mac?"

"Yeah?"

"Not today."

Melissa took a breath. "All right, Corporal."

"Your paperwork," he added. "When's it due?"

"Sixteen hundred today, Corporal," she said, feeling humiliated at being so late. "There's a courier stopping by to pick it up."

"Then get to it."

"Yes, Corporal."

About ten minutes later, there was a hammering rumble coming from the northeast. She looked up from paperwork balanced on her knee, and she said, "Corporal?"

He was at the edge of the ditch, binoculars in his hands, and he said, "I saw the incoming. Looks like the Creepers were hitting the Rocky Mountain Arsenal again, or maybe the Denver airport."

She returned to her papers. "The arsenal's been inactive for decades. And the airport got smeared on invasion day plus two."

"What's your point?"

"Doesn't make sense."

Jankowski made a noise that passed as a chuckle. "News flash, Mac, they're aliens."

"Yeah." That was always question number one after the war began, trying to figure out why the Creepers came here, why they started the war the way they did, what was the point of traveling via interstellar space to fight like they were well-armed British soldiers against African natives in the late 1800s. Didn't make sense, nothing made sense, and one day Jankowski said, "You know, if we ever make it and a history of this fiasco is ever written, it should be called 'World War Why,'" and Melissa thought that was a pretty good idea.

Morales rolled back into the trench, and said, "Heard an attack strike a couple of minutes ago. The airport?"

"Maybe," Melissa said. "Might be the arsenal."

Morales sat down on the duckboards, put his back up against the wall. "Damn bugs . . . but hey, looks like the balloons are ready to be launched."

Melissa got up and went to the western side of the trench, and she admired the view: three elongated balloons, gently swaying in the slight morning breeze. She could make out little knots of soldiers at work at the base of each balloon, and her chest felt tight. Go, she thought, go. There was an article she had read last year in *Stars & Stripes*, about the Denver siege, and somebody had called it "The Leningrad of the Rockies," after that horrible Nazi siege during World War II that had starved hundreds of thousands.

Morales stood next to her. "Think they'll make it?"

"Up to the weather and the Creepers."

"But there's no people, no electronics on the balloons, nothing advanced. The Creepers should leave it alone."

"Should isn't a doctrine, Hector."

Morales said, "You can always hope, can't you?"

"And hope ain't a tactic, either."

Morales stayed quiet, and Melissa felt sorry for the kid. He was just a replacement, a boy who volunteered from one of the refugee camps in Arizona holding survivors from the L.A. tsunami strike, and he looked bright and strong enough to do his job. But would he be bright enough and strong enough when the proverbial bug crap hit the fan?

Jankowski called out, "Morales! You got watch."

Melissa leaned against the dirt of the trench edge, watching the balloons rise up higher and higher as they were inflated. There was netting underneath each balloon, and the netting was filled with crates. Food and medical supplies, two items desperately needed in Denver, and the balloons were going to be unmanned. For some reason—why, why, why—the Creepers could sense humans in transportation, and previous manned lighter-than-aircraft had come to flaming ends. Efforts to dig tunnels or use old utility conduits to the city temporarily worked until they were blasted from the killer stealth satellites. This time, however, maybe this—

"Movement!" Morales yelled. "We've got something going on over at the dome!"

She whirled around and grabbed a set of binoculars and Jankowski raced up as well. Melissa focused in on the dome base. A slit was quickly dilating close and two Creepers—battle units—were skittering out.

Something heavy gripped her throat. This wasn't the first time she had seen Creepers out in the open, but still, there was some sort of primal fear that bubbled right up at seeing the alien creatures on the move. Each was the size of Army transport truck, moving on eight articulated legs. There was a center arthropod, also articulated, and two large arms, circling around, like they belonged to a goddamn scorpion. The end of each arm was tool-based, sometimes claws or pincers, or sometimes a laser or a flame-type projector, always dangerous. Inside the exoskeleton was a creature, looking like a science-fiction writer's nightmare of an intelligent insectlike alien. The structure was the same blue-gray as the dome base, and almost entirely indestructible.

As one, the Creepers shifted their direction of movement, and they were coming straight on an eastern approach, skittering and crawling over crushed metal, broken masonry, and torn up roads.

"They're coming right at us," Morales whispered, voice shaky.

Melissa said, "The hell they are. They're heading for the supply balloons."

Jankowski said, "Shit, you're right, Mac." He went to the field telephone, gave the handle a *whir-whir*, and spoke loudly and deliberately into the receiver. "CP Bravo, CP Bravo, this is Bravo 12. We have two Creepers, battle version, heading due east from dome eight, repeat, from dome eight. It appears they're heading for the balloon launch site. They're approaching grid coordinates, grid coordinates ten-niner-zero-zero-ten-four-five-six. Repeat, ten-niner-zero-zero-ten-four-five-six."

Melissa pressed the field glasses firm against her eyes to control the shaking from her hands.

"Okay, Bravo 12, out."

He slammed the receiver back into the field pouch and uttered an extremely foul obscenity.

Morales said, "What did they say, Corporal?"

"They're alerting the artillery, activating the QRF. Not sure when it's going to show up."

"Well, that'd be—"

Melissa blinked her eyes as both Creepers fired a quick flash from an arm. Laser shots. Damn.

Melissa turned. A truck was burning near the balloon site.

A whistling whine noise pierced the air.

"Incoming!" Jankowski said. "Duck down!"

Melissa squatted as artillery rounds started hammering the torn-up ground around the Creepers, protecting herself from any shrapnel or flying debris stirred up by the blasts coming from the 105mm artillery stationed a ways back. When the echoes of the blasts rolled away she glanced up.

The Creepers were still on the move. The exoskeletons were practically impervious to normal munitions, except for a lucky sliver of shrapnel or the outgoing rounds from M-10s like the one Jankowski carried, and the artillery blasts had probably only slowed them down for a minute or two.

"Mac! How far away are the Creepers?"

She glanced down at the range card, which marked easily identifiable landmarks in their area of responsibility, and then picked up the binoculars. There. The two creatures were quickly approaching a mound of debris that was topped by the burnt remnants of a CH-47 Chinook helicopter, back during the early weeks of the war before commanders learned any powered aircraft was just a moving target.

"Eight hundred meters, Corporal."

Another flicker-flare of lasers being fired from the marauding Creepers, and an anguished yelp from Morales. "They got one of the balloons! The bugs got one of the balloons!"

Melissa glanced back in time to see the balloon on the far right collapse, as flames raced up the fabric. Not going to make it, she thought, the resupply mission was about to be burnt to the ground before it could even get off the ground.

Damn!

She looked to Jankowski, wondered what he was thinking, wondering how many family members of his were still alive over there. He lowered his head. His shoulders tensed up.

Then Jankowski grabbed the field phone, called down to the OP. "Cease fire on the fire mission, cease fire!"

After tossing the receiver down, Jankowski started back to where his gear was stored: battlepack, helmet, M-10. "Morales! MacKay! Saddle up! We're heading out!"

Melissa tried to swallow, but her mouth was dust-dry. In a flash of seconds, she knew what Jankowski was thinking: the Creepers had already taken down one resupply balloon, desperately needed by the starving citizens of Denver, and there were only two left. Help was on its way but the battle was going to be decided in the next handful of minutes. And the Colt M-10 that Jankowski—and only Jankowski— was qualified to use had an effective range of fifty meters.

About seven hundred fifty meters too short. And Jankowski had decided they weren't going to sit and wait behind the relative safety of the trenches.

All three of them were going over the top, just liked the doomed British, French and German soldiers nearly a century and a half ago.

Morales said, "What about the Quick Reaction Force?"

Jankowski secured his helmet. "Shut up. We're it. We're going over, standard intercept mission, the two of you putting down harassing fire. Get to it!"

Melissa put on her helmet, secured the chinstrap, checked her MOLLE vest and the four extra magazines she carried, picked up her Colt M-4 and joined her corporal. The M-4s were practically useless against the Creepers, but they did irritate them, and sometimes diverted them, allowing a soldier with an M-10 to close in for the kill.

Morales was fumbling with his helmet, hands shaking, and Melissa paused to help him out, and Jankowski said, "Guys, we squared away?"

"Yes, Corporal."

"Yes, Corporal."

"Like I said, just like a training mission. Mac, you take the left, Morales, you take the right. We rush them, concealing as best as we can, and once we get three hundred meters behind us, you two open fire, try to slow 'em down."

He paused. "Denver . . . it's starving. It's up to us. Let's roll."

Jankowski moved down trench to a section where wooden steps had been built, and he was the first one over, with Melissa following and Morales bringing up the rear.

The first thing Melissa noticed was the smell of smoke. Maybe she was used to it in the rear lines or in the trenches, but out here in the open, in no man's land, the scent was stronger, and part of her stomach felt a slug of nausea as she realized the some of the smoke she was smelling was coming from the funeral pyres inside the besieged city.

Melissa counted out her steps, as she moved back and forth, over and under, trying not to pay much attention of what she was crossing over, the churned up earth, the crushed cars, the chunks of asphalt and concrete. Her breathing was harsh, cutting into her, and she recalled how many times she had trained this maneuver, over and over again, until she could do it in her sleep . . .

. . . but now it was for real, with not one, but two alien Creepers up ahead.

"Three hundred," she yelled out, falling to the rough terrain. She brought up her M-4, sighted in at the Creeper on the left, fired off a quick three-round burst. She rolled to the right, and maneuvered behind a large chunk of concrete, as Morales echoed her own outgoing fire. Jankowski was in the center, M-10 on his back, moving so fast she had difficulty keeping up with him.

Another burst of fire, and another. She moved to the left this time, just as the near Creeper raised itself up, and let loose with flame projections from each of its arms. Melissa fell to the ground, tried to burrow herself in, flatten herself out, make herself as small as possible as the flames roared overhead.

"Keep moving, keep moving, keep moving!" Jankowski yelled, practically leaping from one mound of rubble to another. "I'm almost in range!"

She fired off two more bursts, and then popped out an empty magazine, slammed a new one in, and let the bolt fly.

"Morales," she yelled out, "keep on firing!"

Morales didn't answer back. Not her problem. She moved again, ducked down next to a flattened school bus, the yellow paint long ago having faded to white, and she fired off one more burst. The wind shifted and two things came to her that meant a Creeper on the move: the scent of cinnamon and the *click-click* of their segmented body in motion.

Never had she ever been so close to a Creeper, and her hands were shaking as she tried to keep up the harassing fire. Then Morales screamed, "They got the second balloon! They got the second balloon!"

Melissa yelled over to him, "Eyes front, Morales, eyes front!"

Then they were in range for the M-10, and she felt herself lucky indeed to be alive and to see Jankowski get to work. He removed a 50mm M-10 cartridge from his MOLLE vest, spun the base dial to set the range—ten, twenty-five or fifty meters—and she knew he was setting it for the furthest range—and the corporal broke open the breech, slammed the cartridge in, closed it with a hard *snap*.

She remembered her job. The three of them were in a scattered line, hiding behind a length of rubble and broken metal, probably a shattered highway overpass, and she popped up, fired off another burst at the near Creeper, the damn thing looking like it was about to crawl right over her. She rolled to the left as a streamer of flame screamed overhead.

Jankowski moved to the right, slipped up and yelled, "Eat this!" and fired, the recoil of the M-10 nearly blowing him back. Melissa scrambled up broken chunks of concrete, saw a hole she could peek through. The near Creeper was still moving but there was a cloud in front of it, and she yelled, "Yeah, good shot, Corporal!"

Her corporal said nothing, sliding back down the rubble, moving quickly to reload his M-10. Melissa looked back at the Creeper. The round from Jankowski's M-10 had exploded at the fifty-meter range. The cartridge was a binary weapon, with two chemicals inside—one of the most closely guarded secrets in this war—and when mixed, it was lethal to the creature riding inside the Creeper exoskeleton. And right now, the Creeper before her was enveloped in the cloud.

It stopped.

It goddamn stopped.

The eight legs and the two weapon arms started shaking, as well as the center head stalk. It shook and quivered and then fell, to the side, the movement from the articulated limbs digging up divots of soil and rock.

Morales screamed, "You killed it, Corporal, you killed it, you killed it!"

Jankowski moved a few meters down the length of rubble. "Shut up, Hector, you're waking up the dead in Denver. And where's my harassing fire, damn it!"

Melissa moved some more, fired a few more rounds, the bolt slamming open. Empty magazine. The dead Creeper was still dead. Jankowski was pushing his way through more broken debris, slid down a battered highway sign marking EXIT 12, and then went back up to the top.

She tugged out the magazine, slapped in another one, let the bolt slide back. Ready.

Click-click.

Click-click.

Click-click.

The smell of cinnamon—another puzzle, why did the bugs stink of an Earth-bound spice?—and another rip of gunfire from Morales down the way. Kid was keeping his cool, which surprised her. He was too young, too eager, and he was a refugee, a Coastie, which meant he got a lot of grief from other soldiers. She could barely see him but he was still on his job.

Melissa moved up, was so goddamn close to the second Creeper that she could throw a stone at it, and Morales yelled, "The third balloon is up! They've launched the third balloon."

Morales should have kept his damn mouth shut. Jankowski was near the top of his pile of rubble and he was bringing up his Colt M-10, but he hesitated, looked back at the balloon rising up from the staging area.

He slipped, fell forward, got up on his hands and knees, and his head and upper torso was torn away in a blast of fire, flesh, and a spray of blood.

Morales screamed, "It got the corporal, it got the corporal! Mac, whaddya we going to do?"

She yelled back, "Keep firing!"

"But . . . but . . . where's the QRF?"

She yelled something nasty about the QRF to Morales, moved as fast as she could to the right, the M-4 now feeling like it was made of lead. Her chest hurt, her feet hurt, and smoke was making her eyes water, and she was chewing her tongue, trying to get saliva going again. She skittered across the broken rubble, scraping her hands, and she looked to the west. The balloon was up, by God, and dangling below was a rope net, holding crates upon crates of rations and medicine.

Morales was shooting again. Good boy.

She moved up the broken slope, seeing the booted feet and the uniformed legs of her dead corporal, the stench pushing into her nostrils and mouth, trying hard not to see the charred chunks and bones on the upper torso.

Where was it?

Where was it?

There.

The Colt-10 was about a meter away. She picked it up, the damn thing heavier than her M-4. Could she do it? Could she?

She went up the rubble, a couple of meters away from Jankowski's body, whispered something to the corpse, and then flattened herself down on a piece of rusted metal. The damn bug was filling up her entire view. She brought up the M-10, aimed over the open iron sights, pulled the trigger.

WHAM!

It felt like a horse had just kicked her right shoulder. Melissa screamed, fell back, and she heard the detonation of the M-10's round. Panting hard, she crawled up the rough slope and saw the familiar cloud of a detonating round, and a Creeper, just like it should be.

Except the cloud was behind the Creeper.

She had missed.

Damn!

And in a flash she knew why. Poor old Jankowski had set the range for an approaching Creeper, and the damn thing had kept moving after barbecuing her corporal, and she had overshot.

She had overshot.

"Mac, it's still moving!"

She had to reload the M-10.

Which meant she had to grab another round from . . .

Jankowski's charred body.

Melissa moved in tunnel vision, trying to keep everything out of focus save what was before her, which was Jankowski's body. His fatigues were torn and one knee was scraped bloody raw. He must have hurt himself bad during the attack but the guy kept on going, hadn't bothered to stop or complain.

Focus. MOLLE vest torn and shredded.

There.

Three M-10 cartridges.

She tugged one free.

Morales yelled something and she yelled back, "Just keep firing, damn it!"

Sitting down, she spun the dial on the bottom of the cartridge, taking it from SAFE and stopping at ten meters.

Just ten meters away.

Fingers feeling thick and fumbling, she broke open the M-10's breech, removed the empty shell, slid the fresh one in. Snapped the breech shut.

"Morales!

"Mac!"

She took a deep, painful breath: "If . . . something happens, you take over, got it? There are two cartridges left on Jankowski's vest. Got it?"

Morales yelled something and she didn't have time to keep talking.

Time to move.

She went back up the rocky slope, breathing hard, the stench of cinnamon even worse, the *click-click* almost deafening, More distant gunfire from Morales. Harassing fire, yeah, harassing. Just another term for doing something useless that made you feel better.

Up now on the slope, she thought of praying but couldn't think of a single word, and she flattened herself, brought the M-10 back to her shoulder. The Creeper was starting to raise itself up on its rear, and she thought, the rubble, it can't get a good aim on the resupply balloon because of the rubble, and it's pushing itself up to burn it down.

Melissa aimed the M-10, and the Creeper spotted her, because it was lowering itself down and—

WHAM!

Another scream. Her shoulder felt like it was torn to pieces, only kept in place because of her uniform blouse.

But she forced herself to watch.

Had to.

The round exploded just below the Creeper, and she thought, damn, should have grabbed another cartridge, because it looked like she had missed, and then the Creeper kept on lowering itself down.

Right through the toxic cloud.

And within a minute, it was on its back, quivering, shaking, moments away from dying.

Melissa rolled on her back, sobbing. Broken pieces of rock were jabbing into her back and legs and butt, and she didn't care.

Something floated above her, nearly blocking the sun.

She raised a hand, blocking the sun.

It was the resupply balloon.

Morales appeared, dusty and sweating. In one hand he had his M-4, and in the other, an open canteen. He offered the canteen to Melissa and she took two swigs of warm and flat-tasting water.

It was delicious.

Morales said, "The balloon's moving in the right direction. Bet it gets to Denver within the hour."

She rolled over, raised up her head. Sure enough, being caught by the winds, the balloon with its precious cargo was heading straight to the Mile High City.

"Bet you're right," she said, giving him back his canteen. "Let's . . . let's gather up the corporal and get back to where we belong."

"Roger that, Mac."

She was so engrossed in her paperwork that she didn't notice the first soldier coming into the trench, but seeing the second soldier and the third and then their lieutenant, commanding their company, part of 1st Battalion, 157th Infantry Regiment, Colorado National Guard, really got her attention. She dropped her papers and stood up at attention, with Morales a couple of meters away doing the same. The third member of their squad, wrapped in a plastic poncho, secured by lengths of rope, had been taken away an hour ago by a Graves Registration team. His M-10 was leaning up against the trench, the two remaining cartridges on the duckboard.

Lieutenant Russ Picard gave the length of trench a quick look with his good eye. Half of his face was scarred with burn tissue and a black patch covered the empty socket. His uniform was dirty and repaired, and he looked tired, very tired. Companies were usually run by captains, not lieutenants, but as was said so often, nothing was usual any more.

"Who made the Creeper kills?" Picard asked.

Melissa said, "Corporal Jankowski. I got the second. Private Morales provided harassing fire."

"Are you certified on the M-10?"

"No, sir, I'm not."

He came forward, extended a hand, which she shook. "You are now."

She felt a flash of surprise, and then said, "The balloon, sir, did . . . did it make it to Denver?"

He grinned. "It certainly did . . . but . . . well, it's not enough. It's never enough. Still, a number of civvies over there are going to live tonight thanks to this squad. Good job."

Then he looked down at Melissa's paperwork, and she bit her lip in embarrassment at the mess she had caused. "What's that on the ground?"

"Belongs to me, sir."

"Tetler, if you please."

One of the privates picked up a sheet of paper, passed it over to Picard. He gave it a glance and said, "Well?"

Melissa said, "Geometry, sir. It's my geometry final. It's . . . due at 1700 today."

Picard said, "No, it's not. You just got an A. How does that sound?"

She couldn't help smiling. "Sounds great, sir."

He leaned in some. "How old are you, Private?"

"Fourteen, sir. I'll be fifteen next May."

"Private Morales?"

"Twelve, sir."

Picard nodded. "Good job, the both of you." Speaking to Melissa, he said, "You think you can stay here?"

She spoke quickly. "We'll need a replacement, sir. Two if they can be spared. And one of them should be a corporal."

Picard patted her shoulder. "Why? We've got a sergeant right here, don't you think?"

Melissa managed to say, "Thank you, sir."

"Good." He looked to his escorts. "Come along gents, it's time to get back to the war."

In a minute she and Morales were alone. Her head felt as light as the balloon that had made it, and her hands and legs tingled with joy. Morales said, "Why are you smiling so much? Happy about the promotion?"

She tossed her papers in the air. "Happy I passed geometry."

SAVE WHAT YOU CAN

★

by David Drake

The area was supposed to be cleared of civilians. With the Republic of Bessarabia gearing up for an attack on the spaceport in Mormont, the isolated farm house where the Hammer's Slammers lay in wait was no place for the young girl and her ailing grandfather. Sergeant Raney knows how dangerous a war zone is; she's spent her entire adult life with the Slammers. And she knows that in war, difficult decisions must be made—and sometimes the only thing to do is to save what you can.

RANEY DIDN'T THINK she'd been able to sleep more than a fifteen minutes or so on the run from the spaceport, but when the truck rocked to a halt she heard someone outside shout, "End of the line, troopers! Out! Out!"

"This is Mormont?" she said to the trooper beside her. If it was, she'd slept most of six hours.

"I guess," he said. "Unless they changed their bloody minds again on the road. Which is likely enough."

Raney slung her sub-machine gun, then put on her commo helmet. She wasn't netted in to the First Platoon channel; that was the first order of business after she reported.

"Say?" she said to the trooper shuffling to the open tailgate ahead of her. They'd loaded at night, and she only knew a few people in First Platoon. "Who's the CO?"

They'd been crammed in so tight that you had to negotiate to get room to curl up to sleep, but that was all the talking Raney had done during the ride. They were all slugged out from Transit; they'd offloaded from the ship and packed straight onto the trucks without the usual couple days' stand-down to acclimate.

"That's Sergeant Krotcha," the trooper said, "but they said we're with a section of combat cars and the El-Tee of them's in command of the team. Say, are you a recruit?"

"Not exactly," said Raney, feeling her lips grin a little. She was thirty standard years old, twelve years a veteran of the Slammers. "I'm a sergeant/gunner from Third, but my jeep's deadlined. My driver's with the vehicle, waiting for the rest of Support Section to land. Major Pritchard stuck me in First because Third had already pulled out and they need all the bodies they have up on the border."

"You watch," said the other trooper, holding the tailgate latch with one hand as he stepped from the truck's bumper to the ground. His 2-cm weapon banged between the tailgate and his body armor. "We'll be here freezing our butts for a month without our hold baggage, and nothing will happen."

"That's okay with me," Raney said, swinging down in turn. She thought of asking the fellow's name, but there'd be time later so it didn't matter.

Or there wouldn't be time, that could happen too. Then it mattered even less.

Their convoy was four civilian trucks—the one Raney had been aboard had *Glover Shirtwaists* painted on the side—with a combat car ahead and another behind. They'd halted in an irregular plaza surrounded by one- and two-story fieldstone houses with slate roofs. It had stopped snowing, but at least a decimeter lay on the roofs and pavement.

Sky, land and buildings were different dirty shades of gray, and it was as cold as a witch's tit. Raney saw no sign of civilians.

The last truck was a stakebed carrying the infantry skimmers snugged down with cargo ties. They were being offloaded now, but Raney figured she'd better report before she picked up the skimmer they'd assigned her at the spaceport.

She'd only had time to glance at her skimmer, but that was long enough to see that it was a clapped-out junker. If she had to do any serious travel on it, she was well and truly screwed.

Krotcha was a heavy-set man, not old—forty, maybe—but bald except for a black fringe circling above his ears. Raney knew him slightly. He was talking to somebody on his commo helmet when Raney walked over to him.

"Top, Major Pritchard attached me to you just as you were pulling out," Raney said. "I'm—"

"You're Raney," Krotcha said. His gaze was disturbingly sharp. "You got a tribarrel in Third, don't you?"

"Yeah, but the jeep's deadlined for parts until the *Sundquist* lands," Raney said. "Maybe tomorrow—"

"And maybe next month," Krotcha said, shrugging. "Well, I'm glad to have you, Raney. I'd be a long sight gladder to have your gun too, but in a ratfuck like this I guess you take what you can get."

A younger man in clean khakis and new body armor joined them. He'd gotten down from the lead combat car, *Camptown*. Krotcha looked toward him and said, "El-Tee, this is Sergeant Raney from Third. I'm putting her in Wetsam's squad. Raney, this is Lieutenant Taggert from Charlie Troop, he's in charge."

"Sir," said Raney. "I'm still on the Third Platoon net. There wasn't time—"

Krotcha leaned forward to read the serial number from her helmet, then spoke it into the AI of his own unit. A machine voice in her ear said, "Accepted." A moment later the same voice said, "Command net, accepted."

Raney nodded thanks. Top was treating her as a sergeant rather than just an extra trooper, though she wouldn't have any command responsibilities unless something went badly wrong. She didn't know the people in the platoon well enough to be giving orders, but she'd do what she could if it all hit the fan.

"There isn't time to breathe," Taggert muttered. He suddenly looked very young; Raney wondered if this was his first command. "The Bessies mobilized as soon as they learned the Commonwealth had hired us. It looks like they hope to take the spaceport before the Slammers have landed, all but us on the *Garrett*."

"We'll have backup soonest, sir," Sergeant Krotcha said. "The other ships can't be more than a day out, and then it's just a couple hours before there's a company of panzers barrelling down the road to us."

He sounded reassuring, upbeat even, when he spoke to the green lieutenant. You'd scarcely imagine that he was the same man who'd muttered to Raney, another veteran, that the rest of Hammer's Regiment might not land for a month.

"I'll get my ride and find Wetsam," Raney said, turning away. The combat cars were in air-defense mode, their tribarrels slanted up toward the north. They would sweep incoming shells from the sky before the combat team—and the nearby portion of Mormont—was in any danger.

Three locals in gray uniforms had come out of a building facing the plaza and were walking toward the command group. Two of them carried long-barreled coil guns; the middle-aged man in the middle had only a pistol.

Raney used the locator of her helmet as she walked toward the stakebed. It was taking time to unload the skimmers; the catches of the tie-downs had frozen. She wasn't surprised to find Sergeant Wetsam in the crowd at the back of the truck.

"Sarge, Top assigned me to you," Raney said to the trooper highlighted by her face-shield. "I'm Raney."

Wetsam—short, sturdy and thirty; a male equivalent of Raney herself—gave her a wry smile. "Lucky you," he said. "Did he tell you were he'd put us?"

"I don't know squat," said Raney. "Pretty much like usual."

The skimmer being driven off the truck now was hers. It looked even worse in morning sun than it had when she first got it under the spaceport floods.

"Well, there's a farm north of town proper and half a click off the main road," Wetsam said. "We're there to snipe at the Bessies if they barrel straight up the road to Mormont. If they decide to use the farm for their own outpost, though, I'll be bloody glad to have you and anybody else you can scrape up besides."

The snow on the road was unmarked, so Wetsam took the squad well to the right through the straggling woods. If the wind kept up, the snow swirled from the pavement by the skimmers' air cushions would be wiped out in a few hours anyway. Wetsam was right not to give the Bessies a chance that they didn't need to have, though.

Wetsam was number two in the line and Raney brought up the rear.

She had her skimmer punched out to hold the moderate pace. Winter had frozen the undergrowth down to bare canes.

The clean-up slot was proper for Raney's rank—she might even be senior to Wetsam, though she had no intention of pushing the point—but she hoped that her skimmer didn't crap out while the others drove on without her. She would call on the helmet if necessary, but they wanted to hold electronic silence. The Bessies couldn't listen in on the frequency-hopping communications, but helmet commo might alert them to the Slammers' presence.

The farm that was to be the squad outpost was a one-and-a-half story fieldstone building in a large yard. There was a shed, a chicken coop, and a shoulder-high woodpile ten meters long.

The fence was probably more of a way to dispose of stones plowed up from the field than a barrier. It was waist-high on three sides, but on the back toward the woods it was low enough for a healthy skimmer to hop. Raney and another member of the squad stopped just short of it. Each in turn then lifted the front of the other's machine while its rider gunned the fans. They parked against the rear of the building with the other skimmers.

Wetsam had opened the slanting door in the ground against the rear wall. Beneath was a root cellar which reached some distance back under the house proper.

"Okay, here's our hide," Wetsam said. "Blessing, you take Sparky and Carl to tear apart them sheds. The rest of us'll use the timbers to brace the cellar roof in case the house gets shelled. Raney, there's a window in the roof peak. Central hasn't warned us yet, so I'm not expecting anybody down the road till we're set up here. Just in case, though, you keep an eye out. All right?"

"Roger," Raney said. Her sub-machine gun didn't have the punch to be effective on targets five hundred meters away, but the other squad members were used to working together. Besides, shooting at scouts would just warn the Bessies that the farm was a target worth dealing with.

The only door to the house was in the front. It was ajar; a trickle of snow had blown over the board floor. The fireplace—Raney checked it with thermal imaging on her face-shield—was cold.

The stairs to the loft were almost steep enough to be called a ladder. When Raney started up, a dog began yapping above her. She paused, then lunged up two steps and raised her head above floor level behind the holographic sights of her sub-machine gun.

A little girl stared big-eyed from the side of a bed. She held a puppy in one arm and was trying to clamp its muzzle shut with the other hand. She shrieked and dropped the dog when Raney appeared. The yapping continued, punctuated by slobbering as the puppy tried to lick tears from the girl's face.

Raney stepped onto the loft floor. She could stand upright if she stayed under the ridgepole. There weren't supposed to be any civilians left in the district, but besides the kid—she looked about eight—there was an old man lying in bed. The quilt over his chest rose and fell slightly, but his face was as still as wax.

"What are you doing here, kid?" Raney said. "You'll get blown to Hell! You were supposed to evacuate."

"Grampa can't go!" the girl said. "The Da Costas said they wouldn't carry him, he'd just die anyway, but I won't leave him!"

"Look, sometimes you gotta cut your losses, kid," Raney said. She squatted to bring her head more on a level with that of the kneeling girl. "You know, save what you can. I'm sorry, but your grandfather isn't going to make it much longer even without a shell landing on top of him."

Which was what was going to happen a couple minutes after the squad started shooting.

"I won't!"

Raney sighed. "What's your name, kid?" she said, trying to sound calm and friendly. This was just one more screw-up. That's what a war was: one bloody screw-up after another.

"Celie," said the girl. She hugged the dog close again. "And this is Bubbles."

Instead of keying her helmet, Raney bent over the ladder and shouted, "Sarge! Wetsam! I need you soonest!"

Glass splintered. Instead of coming around to the door, Wetsam had knocked out a back window. Through it he called, "What the hell is it, Raney?"

"We got civilians! Get up here!"

"Bloody hell," the squad leader snarled. More glass broke, but it was some moments before Wetsam appeared through the doorway from the back room. He'd have used the butt of his weapon to clear glass from the casement, but that left sharp edges. Nicking an artery by accident could let your life out as sure as a powergun would.

"Celie, come stick your head over," Raney said. Obediently the girl came and looked down the stairs beside Raney. Bubbles waddled over also, whining.

"Bloody *hell*," Wetsam said.

"There's an old guy in the bed, too," Raney said. "He's on his last legs, but she won't leave him."

"The bloody National Guard swore they'd cleared all the bloody civilians from the bloody area!" Wetsam said as he started up the stairs.

"Hey, you don't suppose the locals might be bloody useless, do you?" Raney said. She stood and eased Celie back from the stairhead with her. "We've never run into that on other deployments, have we?"

"Joke," Wetsam said as he joined them in the loft. He stared at Grampa and made a sour expression with his lips. "But we're still stuck with them."

"Do we get the Guard in Mormont to pick 'em up?" Raney said. "We can't carry the old guy on our skimmers."

"They didn't take him before, so why're they going to now?" Wetsam said. The puppy was sniffing his boots. "Besides, I don't want a bunch of Guards tramping around here. If the Bessies ignore us till we decide to get noticed, we got a lot better chance of retiring."

"Well, then we got to bring them down into the cellar with us," Raney said. She thought about retirement, but it was just a gray blur. She knew she wasn't going back to Hagel's World—ever; but there wasn't any other planet that she *wanted* to be. The Slammers were the only place she'd been that seemed like home.

"Hell, it's cramped already," Wetsam said, but he wasn't really arguing. "Bloody hell."

"You know what's going to happen to the upper floors," said Raney. "Want me to go down and you reach him down to me on the floor?"

"Yeah, I don't have a better idea," Wetsam said. He bent over the bed and gripped the old man around the shoulders.

"What are you *doing*?" Celie said, and her puppy started to yap again.

"We're going to get your grampa some place safer," Raney said, going down the stairs backward. It wasn't going to be *very* safe, but it was the best they could do for now. It was all they had themselves, but the Slammers got paid for it.

The dog suddenly squatted and peed on Wetsam's boots. Wetsam didn't react, maybe didn't even notice. Raney wouldn't have blamed him if he'd kicked Bubbles downstairs, but then the kid would make even more noise than the dog had.

Wetsam bent, lowering the old man. Raney stood with one boot on the floor and the other on the first step. She surged up, then eased back when she had a hand on each side of Grampa's ribs.

He weighed next to nothing, but she felt his breath on her cheek as she stepped back. It smelled sour.

Bubbles bounced down the stairs front-first, circling and yapping as Raney walked to the door. She wasn't going to try fitting Grampa through the jagged casement.

The girl scooted down ahead of Wetsam. Just as well that Raney didn't need help carrying the old man.

Celie walked beside her, holding one of grampa's dangling hands. "Are you going to save us from the Filth?" she asked.

"Huh?" said Raney, then realized that "Filth" must be the local name for citizens of the Republic of Bessarabia. "We'll, we're going to try to give the Bessies a bloody nose if they come this way, but maybe they won't."

"You'll save us," the little girl said firmly. "I *know* you will."

"If Central was right about what's coming down the road tonight . . . ," Wetsam said from behind them. He was carrying the bedding and even the thin mattress. "I figure we'll be lucky to save our own asses."

Raney didn't respond, but she sure didn't disagree.

Grampa was still alive, though the only evidence of that was the occasional wheeze of breath through his open mouth. The girl huddled against him; the puppy varied between sniffing at the crouching Slammers and trying to wriggle between the two civilians.

The heaters in Raney's helmet, boots and gloves kept her functional, but the bare skin of her face prickled beneath the faceshield. They'd created the hide by slanting the beams of the outbuildings from the back wall of the cellar to the floor. The kitchen table, the front door and the cellar door lay on the supports to catch debris and slide it away if the building above them collapsed.

It would have been reasonably warm with nine people and a dog crammed in, if they hadn't had to remove the cellar door. It wasn't a real bunker, but as a hide where they could keep out of the sight of Bessies heading for Mormont, it'd do. It had to.

The sun was low beyond the woods behind them, and the blurred gray of the sky was shading deeper. It wasn't the sort of night that ever became pitch black, though; the bare branches would still be faintly silhouetted against the overcast at midnight. A mist was rising.

Celie hadn't spoken for half an hour, and her eyes were closed. Wetsam was letting the squad sleep three at a time, but Raney had stayed awake. Dozing on the truck, followed by the surprise of finding the civilians, seemed to have cured the normal loginess of Transit.

They were watching the road through tiny sensors placed on the stone fence. "Visitors!" Raney said in a harsh whisper when her face-shield careted movement. All the troopers had probably seen the vehicle, but it was a lot easier to call the alert than learn that you were the only one after all.

Troopers shifted, ready to rush up the stairs. "Stay where you are!" Wetsam snapped.

Raney checked the indicator lights on her sub-machine gun, green/green/red: loaded, sights on, safety on. The other troopers were going over their weapons also.

A pair of four-wheeled vehicles with sloping bodies came down the road from direction of the Bessarabian frontier. One head stuck over the top of each compartment.

The scout cars probably had armor, but it couldn't be very heavy. Snow swirled from beneath the wheels. They were moving at about 40 kph; Raney's display would calculate the exact speed if she thought there was any reason to. She didn't.

Wetsam reported to the command in Mormont. Then he said, "Nothing for us, troopers. But I don't guess it'll be much longer."

The second scout car halted near the trackway to the farm where the Slammers waited. The leader continued toward Mormont, but the driver slowed to half his previous speed.

The scout car was within a hundred meters of the town when light flickered from the upper stories of buildings on the edge of town. Moments later Raney heard the crackle of coil guns and the distant *whang*-eeeee of ricochets.

The scout car halted. Instead of turning, it accelerated straight back in the direction from which it had come: the vehicle had reversible steering.

A much louder *crash!* sounded from somewhere within Mormont. The car at the farm junction exploded, gutted by a heavy slug which had pierced it the long way. Parts of the engine blew out through the plating and diesel fuel erupted over the road.

The surviving vehicle fanned the deep red flames when it drove through them, still accelerating. It was going over 60 kph as it vanished around a curve. That was probably its top speed.

Wetsam took his hand from the shoulder of the trooper who had started to get up. "Not your business, Kenner," the sergeant said. "Not till I tell you it is."

The anti-tank slug hitting the scout car had been louder than a high-speed collision, and the *whump!* of the fuel igniting had rattled windows in the house. The old man didn't move, but the puppy ran out into the yard yapping. Celie sat up straight.

"Did you kill the Filth?" she demanded. "Are we safe?"

"Stay where you are, darling!" Raney said, because the girl looked as though she might try to run up into the yard. "No, it's not over. Besides, that was your own people, not us."

Taggert must be hiding the Slammers' presence for as long as possible. If they'd asked Raney, she would've told them to fool the Bessies into thinking that there were already too many Slammers in Mormont to dare attacking. The Bessies probably knew that only one transport had landed, though.

Anyway, Taggert was the CO. It didn't matter what a sergeant-gunner thought.

"What kinda army do the locals have, anyway?" asked Kenner. He looked at the squad leader, but Wetsam just shrugged.

"Small arms, pretty much," said Raney, who always studied the briefing cubes on a deployment. "All but the cadre's militia, though every male adult has some training. Those half-kilo slug guns are about all the heavy weapons they've got. The Bessies are mechanized, which is why the Commonwealth hired us."

"Who do the Bessies have working for them?" another trooper asked.

"Nobody," Raney said. "They figured it was a better use of their money to build hardware and use it themselves. They can't afford mercs."

"We'll ram their hardware straight up their asses!" Wetsam spat. Most of his troopers grunted agreement.

In the long run that was probably true, Raney thought—if the Bessies didn't capture the spaceport tonight. The trick was holding Mormont and whatever other roads led into the Commonwealth until the rest of the Regiment landed.

Green fireballs sailed across the sky, heading south: the tail flares of Bessie bombardment rockets. The sharp ripping sound of the rockets' passage was a half-second delayed from the lights' passage overhead, but the second and third salvoes were so close behind the first that it all blurred into vicious chaos.

Celie began to cry; the dog outside stood at the mouth of the cellar and yapped. The sound of both was lost in the roar of the bombardment.

Warheads began to detonate. Only an experienced ear would have recognized that most of them were going off in the air instead of among the buildings of Mormont. Cyan light flickered across the rockets, setting them off. The high airbursts weren't exactly harmless— fragments would be falling like steel hail across Mormont—but they wouldn't damage the Slammers' vehicles or infantry which had overhead cover.

The tribarrels of the two combat cars were on air defense, slapping down incoming shells. The two-centimeter bolts—the same as the shoulder weapons of Wetsam's troopers—packed enough energy to detonate the bursting charge of any shell, even armor-piercing rounds if for some reason the Bessies were using those.

The sensors picked up movement on the road again. "All right, my children," Wetsam said. "Time to take your places. Keep bloody below the wall till I tell you, or I'll blow your bloody heads off myself."

Raney led the way up the stairs because Wetsam had assigned her to the northwestern corner of the farmyard. He was on the southwestern corner himself, with his five troopers spaced out the north-south length between the sergeants, parallel to the road.

Raney low-crawled briskly toward her slot. The shallow furrows of the garden were frozen, turning the ground into a sheet of corrugated metal. At least there was no undergrowth. Humans had carried bamboo with them to more planets than they hadn't; Raney would rather squirm through razor ribbon than a well-grown stand of the stuff.

She wished that she'd thought to tell the little girl to stick by the old man, but the Commonwealth hadn't hired the Slammers to babysit. They were well and truly about to earn their pay now.

The fog was getting thick. Raney switched her helmet visuals to thermal imaging. The feeds from the sensors shifted automatically. She viewed the yard—mostly the stone wall—on the top half of the face-shield, and the view through the northernmost sensor on the bottom.

You never wanted to watch *only* remote feeds and just assume everything in your immediate surroundings was fine. Raney had once had the hell bitten out of her by the local equivalent of ants, but that had been a cheap lesson. She'd known a guy on Warwick who'd been knifed by a local who moved *very* quietly.

Bessie vehicles were coming down the road in column, three abreast. The leading rank had eight wheels and turrets mounting big coil guns. Those would throw projectiles at least as heavy as slugs from the anti-tank guns the National Guard had waiting for them in Mormont. Two pairs of wheels were well forward on the chassis, which meant that the frontal armor was thick enough for hard use.

The second rank was of six-wheeled armored personnel carriers with automatic coil-guns in small turrets. The gun of the outer vehicle slewed toward the farm half a klick away. As the column rumbled forward, the APC fired short bursts toward the wall. The whole eastern file followed suit as each vehicle came far enough around the curve for their guns to bear on the farm.

Raney squeezed as low as she could in the hard ground. If she could have fit in a furrow, she would have. Most of the bursts were high, but some projectiles ricocheted wildly from the stone.

A few slugs were made from noble metals. They bounced off in vivid neon colors along with the usual orange-red sparks of steel.

Bits shattered from the hard stone. Concentrated fire could knock holes in the wall as sure as a wrecking ball, but that wasn't what was going on now. The Bessies weren't firing at *something*, they were firing because they were nervous. Shooting made them feel that they were taking action.

Raney knew that and knew that the sprayed projectiles weren't a danger to the thick wall. She still didn't like it.

There were ten ranks of Bessie vehicles, maybe eleven—Raney was counting to take her mind off the situation, not because there was any real need. The third and last ranks were of the large gun vehicles. Besides the APCs, there were several APC chassis which mounted a short-barreled, ten centimeter or thereabouts, in a turret in the middle of the hull.

When the head of the column was within a kilometer of Mormont, the leaders stopped. The following vehicles spread to either side. The ground was lightly wooded, but even the APCs could bull their way through the brush.

Unexpectedly, the final rank of APCs pulled left when they reached the farm track. They started toward the house in line. The rear guard of gun vehicles waddled on toward Mormont.

The light was gone by now, and the mist was heavy enough to swirl in vortices above the APC guns as they probed the wall and house beyond. Driving bands vaporized in the jolts of electricity that sent projectiles through the coil guns. Gaseous metal spurted skyward like smoke signals.

The kid'll be fine if she just stays in the cellar. If she can't do that, she's too dumb to live. Too bloody dumb!

"On my word," Wetsam said calmly on the squad frequency. He was a good sergeant; Raney wished she'd had more like him in her days as a trooper. "Turrets first, then tires. Squad . . . *light 'em up!*"

The approaching vehicles had moved slightly out of line. The leader was within a hundred meters of the fence, the other two were only twenty meters behind. Raney rose with the others, but she didn't have a useful target for her sub-machine gun yet.

The coil gun of the second APC was firing, but that stopped when three cyan bolts hit the turret simultaneously. The copper plasma from a 2-cm weapon had an enormous wallop. An orange fireball bloomed above the white droplets of molten armor. That must have been hydraulic fluid from the traversing mechanism, since the coil gun didn't have combustible ammunition.

Two bolts hit the leader's turret and one the turret of the last vehicle. Raney's face-shield blacked out the plasma tracks; without filtering they would have been as dazzling in thermal imaging as they would to the unaided eye.

The leading APC's coil gun fired another burst. Four plasma bolts, then a fifth, hit the turret, finishing what the first two bolts had failed to do. The vehicle stopped; the second APC collided with it while trying to turn right.

The final APC turned left, presenting its broadside to Raney. She walked short bursts down the tires, one and the next and then the third.

The tires had run-while-flat cores, but Raney's bolts ignited the rubber casings. Foul blackness billowed from sullen flames. After a few moments the casings exploded, spewing doughnuts of smoke sideways.

Bessie infantry in the body of the APC threw open the back hatch. Three soldiers stumbled out, unharmed but panicked by the ambush and the *Whump! Whump! Whump!* of their own tires. Raney began to shoot, aiming for the center of mass.

Her second target vanished in a white flash and a bang so loud that it threw down part of the stone wall. The fellow must have been carrying a satchel of buzzbombs; a single warhead wouldn't have caused such a blast.

Raney rolled into a kneeling position again. As she did, something went off inside the leading APC. An orange flash ruptured the hull seams and lifted the turret from its ring. It hung skew for an instant, then slipped down inside the vehicle's body.

All three wrecks were burning. Figures, probably infantry from the second APC, moved blindly in the thick smoke. They were bright targets on Raney's infra-red display. She dropped one and saw the chest of another disintegrate at the impact of a 2-cm bolt.

Raney changed magazines. Her sub-machine gun's iridium muzzle glowed white. She'd kept her bursts short, but a firefight like this was hard on guns and shooters both. She gulped air through her mouth despite the toxic foulness—smoke, ozone, and the Lord knew what from the burning vehicles. She simply needed more air than her nose filters allowed her.

Raney couldn't see Mormont from her position, but she switched the bottom of her display to a sensor on the opposite corner of the farmyard while she scanned the road north to the border directly. The

Bessie gun vehicles were moving into the town, wreathed in iridescence as their heavy coil guns fired.

Buildings collapsed, and a slug ricocheted a thousand meters in the air in an arc which wavered between magenta and violet. The sounds of the shots and the impacts was like the rush of a distant thunderstorm.

The nearby APCs continued to burn, but the only movement around them was occasional debris wobbling in the air currents. Raney wondered how many personnel the vehicles held.

However many there'd been, they were all dead now.

The APCs which had gone down the road with the main attack were disgorging their infantry. The troops spread out, following the heavy armor in. The APCs fired their automatic weapons, aiming high to clear the dismounted infantry. Explosive shells from the support vehicles bloomed red on the distant roofs, but the sound of the bursting charges was lost in the sharp electrical cascade of the coil guns.

Wetsam and two of his troopers had an angle on the force attacking Mormont. The nearest of the Bessies was over a kilometer away, but powergun bolts were line-straight. The 2-cm weapons were heavy enough to be lethal to humans at any range. The sniping wouldn't decide the battle, but bolts striking from behind would unsettle better soldiers than the Bessies who'd attacked the farm had seemed.

Raney tried to link to the sensors in one of Taggert's combat cars, but her helmet didn't have the power to lock the signal. The amount of electronic hash from coil guns and plasma would make commo difficult even for the Slammers within Mormont.

Raney had been in a street battle like Mormont on her second—or was it the third?—deployment with the Slammers, on Puerto Miro, back before she'd transferred to combat cars. She remembered aiming up through a street-level window in the cellar and firing 2-cm bolts into the overhang of a Central Government tank.

She'd been trying to jam the turret. Instead she had set off stored ammunition in a blast that had brought the building down on top of her. Her back and breast armor had saved her life, but the six hours before her squadmates dug her out had been the longest of her life.

The crew of that tank had had an even worse day, though; briefly, of course. The Bessies in Mormont tonight weren't doing much better.

Buzzbombs detonating in the town made the air flicker white. The Bessies and the National Guard used similar weapons, so the explosions could be from either party. The three orange gouts of ignited diesel fuel were Bessie casualties, though: probably the funeral pyres of heavy gun vehicles which had led the attack.

Mormont's streets weren't wide to begin with, and buildings brought down by the Bessies' own bombardment would have narrowed them even more. In a point-blank fight, the advantage was all with the defenders crouching in alleys with buzzbombs.

"*All Taggert elements,*" said the commo helmet. "*Bessie Command has ordered his forces to withdraw. Out!*"

"Whee-ha!" said one of Wetsam's troopers. He must be the man nearest to Raney, because he hadn't used helmet commo.

"*Wetsam, this is Command,*" said Taggert's voice. Because Raney was on the command net, she got the call also, though she doubted that the El-Tee meant to inform her directly. "*Bring your squad back into town and report to me in the plaza. Move well to the east so you won't meet the Bessies running the other way. Over.*"

"*Sir, we're in a good place to hammer 'em when they pass by on the road,*" Wetsam said in an urgent tone. "*We've taken out three APCs and their smoke covers us, over.*"

"*Negative, Sergeant,*" said Taggert. "*They've got plenty left to roll over an outpost. If they start taking fire from the flank they'll do just that. Get your asses back here soonest. Command out.*"

"*Roger,*" said Wetsam. "*Out.*"

Apart from the signal from Central—which was obviously netted in to Bessie communications—Raney wouldn't have been sure that the attackers were pulling back, but the fighting in Mormont had certainly quieted down. For an instant she regretted losing the chance to hit the Bessies from the flank, but the El-Tee was probably right to recall them. They were facing at least a full armored battalion, and Wetsam's squad had lost the advantage of surprise.

"*Squad, we're heading back,*" Wetsam ordered. "*We'll swing a little wider out from the road this time and reenter town from the east. Watch the trooper in front of you, and if we run across any Bessie stragglers, waste them before they know who we are. Out.*"

Raney expected somebody to argue, but the only responses were grunts and muttered Rogers. She was glad to get out. She'd agreed with the idea when Wetsam first suggested that they stay, but a moment for thought had showed her that the farm would be a deathtrap.

Her opinion of Taggert went up a little. He was green, but he'd stayed cool after a nasty battle at knife range.

Raney straightened—there was no reason to keep low now—and gasped with pain. Her left hip felt like she'd been bumped by a tank. When the satchel of buzzbombs went off, she must've hit the ground harder than she'd realized. She ought to replace the sub-machine gun barrel while she was at it.

"*Sarge,*" called Blessing, bending over a trooper lying on the ground. "*I got Sparky's weapon and ammo. What do we do with the body?*"

"*Leave him,*" said Wetsam through helmet commo. "*We'll police him up after things quiet down, or anyway somebody will. How about his helmet, over?*"

"*He took a round front to back through the forehead,*" Blessing said, switching to commo. Though Raney was part of the squad's net, her helmet wasn't synched with medical readouts like those of the rest of the squad. "*It's no more use now than Sparky is. Out.*"

"*Roger,*" said Wetsam. He started for the farmhouse and the parked skimmers.

If I'd taken one through the head, none of them might have noticed. Not that I'd be caring then either.

A Bessie APC raced up the road. A tire was rubbing; it sounded like a long wail of terror. Raney wondered if the driver had bothered to reboard his troops before driving away and whether any of the troops from that vehicle had survived.

She thought of what she could do if she'd had her gun jeep. And she thought about the chance that had fired a slug through Sparky's skull and not her own . . . because that's all it was, chance, when the Bessies had replied to the ambush with a blind fusillade.

The puppy was running around, barking in terror. Raney hadn't thought about the civilians since the shooting started. She felt a stab of guilt for forgetting the little girl, but what the hell was she supposed to have done?

The glass was gone from the two front windows. A few holes scarred the panel of the open door, but it was still on its hinges. The blast that knocked down Raney and part of the farmyard wall had probably cleared the window casements.

Slugs had chewed the roof, leaving a score of gaps where broken slates had fallen in bits. The ground beneath the eaves was a ridge of rubble, and more must have dropped inside.

They'll be all right if they stayed low. The cursed dog is all right.

"Hell, we're screwed!" Blessing snarled from around the back corner of the house.

"No, it'll be all right," Wetsam said. "We may have to double up, that's all."

Raney said nothing as she walked forward. Her face was blank. She gripped her sub-machine gun firmly, but that was a reflexive response to tension.

Slugs had passed through the front and hit the back of the roof from below. The whole back half had lost integrity and slid down in a slate avalanche, covering the ground behind the house. Wetsam and his troopers were scrambling to clear the skimmers from a pile of broken rock.

The dog got out. Then, *The dog had been out.*

The pile of slate dipped in the center where much of it had poured into the open cellar. If the Slammers hadn't removed the door, Celie and her grandfather would've been trapped inside, beyond saving in the time the squad had available. Instead, the wave of slate might have crushed—

Raney looked down. The child was still huddling against the old man. They were wedged into the back edge of the hide, where they'd been when the troopers ran out to their fighting positions. The cascade had stopped just short of the girl's feet.

"Celie, get up here *now*!" Raney said. If she went down to fetch the girl, her weight would trigger a further rush of stone. Celie might be able to scramble high enough to grab the sling of Raney's weapon, though.

Celie looked up, then began blubbering. She buried her face in the old man's chest again.

"Raney!" Wetsam called in much the same tone that Raney had used to the girl. "Give us a hand here! We've gotta get out. You want to get us all killed?"

He was right. Bringing more fire down on the farmhouse from the withdrawing Bessies wasn't going to help the civilians. Raney slung her sub-machine gun and began tossing broken slates out into the yard.

Her crappy skimmer had been on the end of the line where it wasn't hit by the falling slates. That was pretty typical of the way things had been going on this deployment.

The steering yoke of Wetsam's skimmer was badly bent, and the left side of Kenner's plenum chamber had been bashed in badly enough to prevent the rear fan from swivelling properly. Nonetheless with a second trooper riding pillion behind Blessing, the squad made it back into Mormont without further drama.

Raney didn't worry about her skimmer the way she had on the way out. She had a splitting headache and the inside of her throat felt as though somebody had scoured it with barbed wire. The chance of having to walk back to Mormont had dropped well down on her list of concerns.

Now and again she thought about the kid as she guided her skimmer through the woods, but even those feelings were grayed out by the battle at the farmhouse. Serious emotions would've taken more energy than she had left.

Wetsam had to detour twice after they got into Mormont proper. The fieldstone buildings were solid, but a heavy enough shock turned their walls into loads of riprap.

Direct fire from the gun vehicles had brought down a number of buildings, and a few Bessie rockets had gotten through. The spilled rocks were barriers that most of the squad's skimmers couldn't climb in their present state.

They were in the central plaza before Raney was aware of it; she had been following Blessing's skimmer instead of noting what was around her. Part of her knew that she'd taken more of a knock from the explosion than she'd thought at the time, but even the aware part didn't care very much.

Both combat cars had survived, but the fighting compartment of Taggert's had been penetrated just behind the right wing gun. The tribarrel hadn't been damaged—it was back in air defense mode now—but Raney didn't suppose the gunner had been so lucky.

One of the Bessie gun vehicles had made it to the edge of the plaza. An arm protruded from a turret hatch.

The vehicle's tires were still burning, but a light breeze from the south carried most of the smoke away. There were several other fires in the northern part of the town. Guardsmen in gray uniforms had gathered upwind, peering at the wreck.

Taggert stood with Krotcha beside *Camptown*. He raised his face-shield as Wetsam pulled up beside him. The lieutenant had aged twenty years since Raney last saw him. The lower edge of his face-shield had the mirror-bright sheen of iridium, vaporized from tribarrel bores and redeposited on the synthetic crystal.

"Sarge," Taggert said, "the Bessies are going to hit us again in three hours. They've got reinforcements, infantry and armor. The infantry's conscript and they don't have APCs, but the armor's heavies that'd been hung up behind the artillery train."

"Hell," said Wetsam. There was no emotion in the word. "Can we hold 'em?"

"Not if we wait for them to hit us," Taggert said. "The Guards lost most of their anti-tank guns and they're low on buzzbombs. I'm going to take the cars and a squad of infantry in a sweep around the east and then hit'em while they're still forming up. Krotcha—"

He nodded to the infantry platoon leader. Krotcha hadn't spoken since the outpost returned.

"—says you're the right man to lead the infantry since he'll be in charge of the defense back here. You in shape for it?"

"I guess," Wetsam said. "Beats getting it in the neck. We'll need skimmers, though. We had damage, and Raney's here was crap from the start."

"You can pick your skimmers," Taggert said. "Raney's with me, though."

The El-Tee glanced at her. His eyesockets looked like pits, partly because he'd rubbed them with hands covered in redeposited metal.

"Sergeant, can you handle that tribarrel?" Taggert said, thumbing toward the wing gun above him.

"Sure," Raney said. She knew she didn't sound enthusiastic. She wondered if she had a concussion.

She focused on the weapon, tilted northward against the sky. "Do we have time to change barrels? Those look shot out."

"Get at it," Taggert said. "We're moving out in ten minutes."

The combat car had a ladder at the back, but Raney boarded in the usual fashion for veterans: onto the step in the plenum chamber, to the top of the plenum chamber, to the cab slope while grasping the fighting compartment bulkhead, and then swinging her legs into the fighting compartment. She'd never been assigned as crew to a combat car before, but anybody who'd been in the field for a few deployments had ridden them.

The interior was cramped as usual, packed with coolers, ammo crates, and personal gear. Raney hadn't expected to find a trooper on his hands and knees, mopping at the bloodstains with what seemed to be a tunic.

The fellow looked up when Raney's boots banged down. He was young and bumped sideways in surprise at her presence.

The uniform fabric wasn't absorbing much blood, but it was obviously important to the trooper to do *something*. Blood had painted his own back and side, but it didn't seem the time to mention that.

She said, "I'm Raney," and gave him as broad a smile as she could manage. She probably looked like death warmed over herself. "I guess I'm your new right gunner."

The trooper looked horrified. *Does he think I'm a newbie?*

"I usually crew a jeep, but it's deadlined for now," Raney added, just in case. She took the gun out of air-defense mode and swung the rack with spare barrels out from the bulkhead. There were three, so she could change the whole set. "Ah, that looks to be like a job for a steam hose."

The trooper stood up. "I'm Meese," he said. Raney was deliberately bending over the gun so that Meese didn't have to decide whether or not to offer his bloody hand. "Ah, yeah, but the hose went west when the bustle rack caught it. I thought I ought to do, you know, what I could."

"I know what you mean," Raney said. She hit the barrel wrench with the heel of her hand to break the threads loose. "I never got used to it either, and I've been out on a lot of deployments. As soon as we're back from this run, we'll borrow a hose or cobble something together, right?"

That was more of a lie than not: even as a newbie, Raney's emotions had shut down at things like the way the gunner died. She drank more than she maybe ought to between deployments, but that was nobody's business but her own.

They needed a left gunner, though. Meese was better than an

infantryman who hadn't been trained on tribarrels, so it was worth coddling him a little.

Raney traded the worn barrel for a glistening new one from the rack, then replaced the second and third as well. They were in better shape than she'd thought from the ground, but a mission like the one Taggert had outlined deserved the best preparation she could give it.

She took the handgrips of the tribarrel and swung it lock to lock. It gimballed smoothly. It felt good to be back behind the big weapon; she seemed to have lost the headache, and her vision was sharper again too.

Taggert climbed aboard, his face-shield still up. He looked alert but worn. He nodded to Raney and Meese, then switched the bow gun back on manual.

Something flopped to the deck of the fighting compartment. It was a hand, still wearing a Slammer's issue glove. It had been caught in the elevation mechanism.

The lieutenant didn't seem to know what the object was. Meese stared transfixed.

Raney took the last reload drum out of an ammo canister and hooked it on the end of the barrel rack the way she usually did. She picked up the hand and dropped it into the canister, then locked the lid down again.

"We'll bury it with the rest of the body when we get back," she said.

Taggert blinked. "Right," he said and dropped his face-shield. Over the general push he said, "*All right, Taggert Force, saddle up. Wetsam, send the scouts out. Troops, follow in plotted order. Out.*"

Two skimmers moved south, deeper into the town. Taggert's combat car lifted from the cobblestones, rotated in its length, and followed at a fast walk. The El-Tee wasn't heading east by the route the outpost had come home by, probably because of the collapsed houses.

The two scouts were out of sight before *Camptown* began to move. The combat car's sensors were very good, but even the best electronics wouldn't spot a Bessie crouching in a spider hole with a buzzbomb.

The scouts' eyesight wouldn't spot that either, but the chances were good that the sound of the skimmers would bring the hostile out early. It was better to lose a single trooper than the lead car.

That was a logic Raney had understood since her first deployment.

She grinned slightly. This was the first time she remembered finding it comforting, though.

The other three infantry followed *Camptown*, closely for the moment; they would space out beyond town. The second car, *Cormorant*, was the rear guard.

It had begun to snow again, a scattering of big flakes at first. Gusts of small flakes arrived on a cold wind before the task force turned northwest again on a narrow lane. The drifts were already high enough to hide landmarks, but the region had been mapped in detail before the satellites had gone down.

Raney could have followed Taggert Force's progress on her face-shield, but instead she surveyed her half of the immediate terrain. That took concentration, because in a gun jeep she was usually responsible only to the front. The wing gun pivoted 180 degrees, though she would have to push the El-Tee out of the way if she needed to light up a target who'd waited till the car had passed.

Raney grinned again. She'd had officers she would willingly have knocked down, given half an excuse, but she didn't have any complaint about Taggert thus far.

Her face-shield was on thermal imaging again. The terrain was a blur of vague shapes, as though she was viewing a reef from under water. A human, even insulated by thick clothing, would show up like a flare on a clear night, however.

"*El-Tee, we've got a problem,*" Wetsam said. He was using the command net rather than the general push. "*Amorato's batteries are losing power. I can replace him at scout, but what about him? Because we can't leave him here alone. Over.*"

Taggert swore. "*A skimmer carrying double can't hold forty-plus kph we need for the timing,*" he said, "*and the cars don't have room for four.*"

Raney smiled at that. Cramming a fourth trooper in body armor into the fighting compartment—certainly into *Camptown* now, but realistically with any car in the field—would crowd it dangerously when the shooting started. On route marches, it was just miserably uncomfortable.

"*All right, Wetsam,*" Taggert said after a pause. "*Tell Amorato to come alongside. I'll stop and take him aboard. We'll dump the skimmer, over.*"

"Sir, this is Raney," she said. She was on the command net by sufferance, but she was here regardless and she had something to say. "We can couple the skimmer's charging cable and keep on moving. Over."

"*That's against regs, Sergeant,*" Taggert said. "*Besides, this is broken country and we're going into action. It's not safe. We'll take him aboard, over.*"

"*El-Tee, she's right,*" said Wetsam. "*Sir, we do it all the time in the field. Somebody's batteries* always *crap out. Over.*"

And if you're worried about being safe . . . , Raney thought, but the words didn't reach her lips. *Then you're in the wrong line of work.*

"*And I'm a newbie on my first deployment and don't know squat, eh?*" Taggert said.

Neither sergeant spoke. Raney kept her eyes on the brush outside the car.

Taggert unexpectedly laughed. "*Well, that's true enough. Wetsam, bring your man alongside and show me the way to couple him and still move, so that I'll know how to do it myself next time. Taggert out.*"

Cormorant had an overlength—three-meter—cable in its equipment locker, so they used that rather than the two-meter cables aboard *Camptown*. Amorato would be able to slip behind the combat car is tight terrain but move to the left out of the worst of the big vehicle's wash most of the time. The coupled trooper would have to mind his driving so that he didn't wind up with the car for a hood ornament, but he didn't complain.

Raney checked the skimmer's diagnostics through her helmet. It was charging, rather than running directly off *Camptown*. She'd been afraid the skimmer might have a dead short, which would make Amorato a pedestrian as soon as he uncoupled. There was obviously a problem, but it wouldn't become acute until after the battle that was certainly coming in the near future.

"*Taggert Force, hold at the marked locations, over,*" the El-Tee ordered. It didn't affect Raney and the other gunners, but a map appeared on the displays of the infantry and the drivers of the combat cars.

Camptown slowed, then wallowed to a halt. The fans idled, spinning just fast enough to keep positive pressure in the plenum chamber. They were still loud.

They had reached a streambed, visible only as a clear track—snow-covered ice—lined by frozen reeds. It meandered through brush. Ahead was a heavily forested slope which made Raney frown.

Woods like that would be a bitch to squeeze through in a gun jeep, and a combat car was *much* wider. The car had the power to bull through all but well-grown trees with boles of fifteen or twenty centimeters, but that would make as much racket as road construction. They had to hope that the Bessies weren't keeping a good watch to their flanks and rear.

That was likely enough: the Bessies were convinced that they were the attackers and that all they had to worry about were the Mormont defenses. The Slammers had to take a chance if they were going to save the route to the spaceport.

This was a *hell* of a chance, granted; but if the port was captured, Taggert Force didn't have anywhere to run to anyway.

Camptown's sensors had been gathering information from the other side of the ridge ahead of the task force. Injector pumps, spark plugs, magnetic suspension dampers, vehicle diagnostic computers—anything electrical gave off a signal. The combat car's AI ran them through identification algorithms and plotted them onto a terrain map. Taggert forwarded the map to every helmet.

"*Force*," Taggert said on the general frequency. "*The Bessies are rearming and fueling along the main road down the next valley. They're clumped up, and many of them are coupled to fuel trucks. Infantry, move up to the edge of the trees where you've got a sight line, then reverse your skimmers and dismount. When I give the signal, take out fuel and ammunition vehicles, and then the civilian trucks that have brought the Bessie conscripts.*"

Taggert coughed to clear his throat. He couldn't have sounded more assured if he'd been Colonel Hammer and he had the three tank companies in line beside him. He went up another notch in Raney's estimation.

"*When the infantry is in position,*" he said, "*the cars will drive through the Bessie line, then drive back. We'll be behind most of the fighting vehicles—*"

Arrows on the display showed the two blue arrows careening past a muddle of red dots, then reversing. Raney wished she thought it was going to be that simple.

"—*so we'll be hitting them from the back. The four heavies*—"

A line of four red dots pulsed. The were the southernmost Bessie elements and would be leading the thrust into Mormont.

"—*have axial weapons that're pointing south, so don't worry about them until we've got all the turreted gun vehicles out of the way. They're the danger to us. Any questions, over?*"

"*Sir, Cormorant Six,*" said the other car's commander. "*The Bessie artillery's only a kay north of here. If we withdraw north, we can get them too, over.*"

"*Negative, Cormorant,*" Taggert said. "*We're not getting greedy. We'll recover the infantry and head back to Mormont after we've had a little target practice. Now, further questions? Over.*"

Nobody spoke.

"*Good,*" said Taggert. "*Taggert Force, take your positions. Taggert out.*"

The five infantry moved ahead, into the woods. A moment later, *Camptown* started forward at a fast walk.

The creek broke open under the downdraft supporting their thirty tonnes. Water sprayed to the side in crystal droplets.

Raney scanned the terrain. She thought, *I still haven't rebarrelled my sub-machine gun.*

Bessie artillery began firing again while Taggert Force was sliding and crunching through the forest. Raney barely noticed the rockets. The intake roar of *Camptown*'s fans dimmed all other noise, and the green/white tracers in her peripheral vision didn't interfere with her focus on the red beads of predicted targets plotted on her face-shield

When they came over the hill, *Cormorant* closed up so tightly that when it knocked down a sapling which *Camptown* had missed—no driver could track perfectly in terrain so broken—a shower of hard-shelled fruit showered onto Raney from the treetop. It was as much luck as training that she didn't trigger a wild burst into the woods.

It had been a *lot* like the patter of bark and clipped branches when ambushers sprayed their first shots high in a forest. The best way to handle an ambush was to charge through behind overwhelming gunfire . . . .

Raney's grin was humorless. She'd screwed up in the past, but never that bad. Well, it hadn't happened this time either.

A whine filled the valley before them. It was so loud that Raney could feel it over the intake howl. She recognized it from a deployment five years before on Princip, where Government tanks used railguns which stored their power in great uranium flywheels. When they were at full spin, they made just that sort of sound.

Wetsam broke squelch twice, indicating all his troopers were in position. They'd been loose with commo on the march, but the infantry sergeant wasn't taking chances now that they were in the same valley as the Bessies.

Camptown twitched left, around a sandstone outcrop swathed in the roots of the bush growing over it. "*Hit it, Bolan!*" Taggert said on the vehicle channel.

The combat car lurched, bouncing upward as the driver coarsened his blade pitch. The fans were already running at full output.

Camptown thundered through the last ten meters of woods. The trees were scattered, but the car hit one that Bolan would surely have driven around if they'd had the leisure. They had thirty tonnes and the help of gravity behind their rush. The bulging plenum chamber butted the tree out by the roots and sent it cartwheeling down the slope like a drum major's baton.

Snow was still falling, and the fans kicked more up from the ground. Raney walked a burst across a group of humans, probably dismounted infantry.

She lifted her muzzles, shifting fire onto trucks moving south on the road. The troops on the ground were more dangerous—any one of them could fire the lucky shot that blew Raney's brains out—but the Slammers couldn't kill all the Bessies. The purpose of this attack was disruption, not annihilation, and exploding vehicles were about as disruptive as you could hope for.

Thermal imaging didn't allow ranging: a child with a stick three meters away looks the same as a gunman at six—but that didn't matter now. Everything within the valley was hostile, and to anything but serious armor a 2-cm bolt was lethal at line of sight.

Raney hit the cab of the first truck. It slewed off the road as she put another short burst into the truck body. The blindingly vivid bolts were stenciled black across her face-shield, but the fires they lit were white blossoms in the thermal display. Fabric and plastics burned at the plasma's touch; some metals ignited also, and flesh too fed the flames.

Camptown continued to accelerate now that they didn't have to hold their speed down to that of the skimmers. They careened through the last of the trees and bumped over the floor of the valley. This was the first time Raney had crewed a combat car, but she found aiming to be surprisingly easy. She was experienced in shooting on the move, and the car was a more stable gun platform than her familiar jeep was.

Fireballs erupted to the left and ahead, fuel bowsers hit while coupled to Bessie armored vehicles. Fires bathed Raney in radiance and fogged the side of her face-shield.

She hit the cab of the second truck, which stopped; then the third, whose fuel tank ruptured. That vehicle was already a bubble of fire when it crashed into the one ahead.

Raney ignored the figures running away from the trucks, some of them on fire. She was slewing her gun toward a line of vehicles parked off the road—they were probably empty, but they'd burn just the same—when something clanged through the combat car.

Camptown spun end for end in a vicious whipcrack. Raney slammed into the rear bulkhead, caromed against the left wing gun— Meese had just crashed into Lieutenant Taggert—and finally hit the deck splay-legged beneath her own tribarrel.

The fans stalled—the jolt had tripped circuit breakers. The car skidded stern first, plowing a broad furrow across the ground. A rooster-tail of ice and frozen turf rained down, some of it falling into the fighting compartment.

There was a round hole the size of a commo helmet in the left rear of the compartment and a larger hole in the right side, slightly forward of the first. The exit hole was noticeably oval: the slug had started wobbling when it punched its way through the side armor the first time.

Raney wasn't sure where she was or what had happened. She got to her feet. Nothing looked familiar. The spade grips of a tribarrel were in front of her and she grabbed them from reflex. Memory flooded back with the familiar contact.

Camptown was pointing in the opposite direction from what Raney last remembered. Fire and wreckage scarred the ranks of Bessie vehicles which had been preparing to attack Mormont. Taggert, Meese, and the guns of the following combat car had raked them, turning fuel trucks into fireballs and smashing the combat vehicles' light rear armor.

The four newly arrived Bessie heavies were side by side a half-kilometer away. Following Taggert's orders the Slammers hadn't shot at them, but a ghostly plume of ionized metal hung over the vehicle on the near end of the line. That banner was the driving band of a slug weighing a full kilogram, vaporized when a jolt of electricity flung the projectile down the gun bore.

The big vehicle had six wheels on a side, all of them steerable. The Bessie commander had used the enormous centrifugal force of the flywheel to rotate his vehicle in place, facing around more quickly than a jeep could have done. He then used the rest of the flywheel's inertia to power the round he fired at *Camptown*.

Every once in a while a mercenary met someone who was very, very good. More often than not, that was the mercenary's last experience. The saving grace here was that shifting the vehicle and firing the shot had slowed the flywheel to a crawl. It would take minutes to spin it up to the point that the gun could fire again.

"Bolan, go!" Raney shouted. "Go go go!"

She felt *Camptown* shiver as the driver brought his fans back on line. With luck either the orders or common sense would get them going, but that was out of her hands. She held the tribarrel's muzzles low and ripped a long burst across the six left-side tires of the heavy which had nailed them.

The tires burst in quick succession, throwing gobbets of flaming rubber in all directions. That wouldn't disable the big gun; it ran the length of the hull's axis with only a stub of the barrel projecting from the heavy bow armor. It made it next to impossible for the vehicle to move, however, even if the crew was willing to fight from a hull which was wrapped in the filthy red flames of its own tires.

Bolan got *Camptown* moving forward—that is, back toward the slope the Slammers had attacked from. They seemed to be crawling, but that might just be because everything had speeded up in Raney's mind.

She sprayed the other three heavies, cyan flashes lighting the flanks and louvered rear panels as well as hitting some of the tires. Her face-shield was on direct visuals now. She didn't remember changing mode, but it was all right. Fuel fires threw up great torches which reflected from the snow.

"*Taggert Force, withdraw!*" said the El-Tee's voice. "*Withdraw at once, out!*"

Raney kept firing at the heavies until her gun shut off when it ran out of ammunition. The iridium barrels blazed like incandescent lights. She ejected the empty ammo drum and locked a fresh one in place.

As *Camptown* wove through the straggling limit of the trees, Raney opened fire again. She had the tribarrel pivoted to its lock and had to lean over the edge of the compartment to see her sights. She was trying to hit the heavies again, but a pair of APCs were in the way. They were already burning, but she raked them anyway. The barrels were already shot out, so why not?

"*El-Tee?*" Wetsam said. "*Can you take Talbert aboard? I've got him double with me, but he's gorked out from painkillers and can't hold on so good. Over.*"

"*Roger,*" Taggert said. "*Force, we'll hold up on top of the ridge. Over.*"

He turned and said, "*Raney?*"

She was watching the dots on her readout. Both cars had come through—*Cormorant* was close behind them—but there were only four skimmers. That was okay; skimmers were even easier to replace than troopers were, and there was a galaxyful of eighteen-year-olds just as desperate to get off-planet as Raney had been.

The El-Tee tapped her the shoulder. "*Raney?*" he said. Repeated, she realized; thinking back, she remembered the sound of him speaking a moment before.

"Sorry, sir," she said. "Over."

"*I just wanted to say 'Good job,' Sergeant,*" Taggert said. "*You may have saved our asses back there.*"

"That was Bolan, I'd say," said Raney. "But thanks. Over."

"*If you ever want to transfer to cars, there's a platoon sergeant's slot open for you here.*"

"Umm," said Raney. Her mind was drifting. She went back to watching beads of light on her face-shield.

Taggert and Meese hoisted Talbert into the fighting compartment with wounds in both legs and a silly grin on his face. His eyes were closed and he was snoring softly.

Taggert Force paralleled the main road for the last three kays into Mormont. They passed close enough to the outlying farm to see that several heavy shells had landed on the house since the squad left it.

Raney didn't say anything. There was nothing to say.

★ ★ ★

Raney had heard the vehicle purring up the road from Mormont, but it wasn't until it pulled into the track to the farm that she paid attention. There was nothing to worry about: G Troop and a platoon of tanks from H Company had passed six hours before, heading north.

She tossed another piece of meat—it was labeled meat in the ration pack; it was pink but had no grain—to the puppy. Only then did she turn on the stump of gatepost where she was sitting.

Baur wove the gun jeep past the burned-out Bessie APCs and pulled up. He looked startlingly clean in ordinary battledress, which reminded Raney to check that her field roll—fatigues in a ground sheet—was in the side rack along with the driver's own. Apart from the rips and ordinary grime, Raney's sleeves were stiff with redeposited iridium which had sublimed off the bores of her tribarrel.

Her long bursts into the Bessie heavies had been a brutal misuse of the weapon. Her lips smiled. They'd done the job, though; and she'd been being misused pretty badly herself at the time.

"Hey, Sarge," Baur said. "They said I'd find you here. We're supposed to join Third Platoon in Servadac. I don't guess it's that big a rush with the Bessies asking for peace, though. The rest of the team in Mormont was stood down, so if you want to wait . . . ?"

"Naw, nothing here for me," Raney said. She started to get up, then thumped back heavily when her legs twinged. "Give me a moment, is all."

"I'm in no hurry," said Baur. He got out of the jeep and stretched, looking around. "Blood and Martyrs. You were part of this?"

"Yeah, they drove right up to us in the fog instead of dismounting," Raney said. The puppy had finished sniffing Baur's boots. She threw the last of the meat to her. "It was hairy for seven of us even with the Bessies making it easy. I think we were supposed to be hitting the column from behind when the last of them passed. There wasn't much of that, but I guess it worked out okay."

She tried again to get up, this time putting her hand on the stone for a little extra boost. She made it, wobbling for a moment.

Baur looked at the long grave bordered with small rubble from the house. There were three larger headstones, though Raney hadn't had anything to mark them with.

"Bloody hell," Baur said, not loudly. "You lost three outa seven, Sarge?"

"Just one," said Raney. "They called him Sparky."

"Sparkman?" said Baur. "Red hair and bad acne scars?"

Raney shrugged. "I never saw him by daylight," she said. "The other two were civilians, but I had the engineers make room here instead of dumping them in the trench with the Bessies."

The mass grave was closer to the road, covered with a tumulus shoveled up from the wall around the field. There was a layer of stones over Sparky and the locals too, but Raney had told the guy with the backhoe to cover them with dirt in case somebody wanted to plant flowers there sometime.

"Come on, Bubbles," Raney said, squatting down with her hands out. "We're going home to Third Platoon."

"Hey?" said the driver.

"We've got a mascot, Baur," Raney said. Holding the dog, she walked to her seat behind the tribarrel. "Her name's Bubbles."

FOR THE LOVE OF SYLVIA CITY
★
by Andrea M. Pawley

The Carbon War left dryland a ruin, but in Sylvia City, sheltered beneath the ocean waves, life goes on. That was last time. Now the Carbon War is heating up again, and unless the citizens of Sylvia City can keep their location a secret, the war will come to them. Luckily they have someone on their side, a drylander who calls Sylvia City her adopted home—and who will do what it takes to keep her home safe.

SLIME CRISS-CROSSES AMX-5. I ease a snail from the cable's sheathing. I doubt something this small is causing the communication anomalies with Sylvia City, but I promised my podsisters I'd examine our outpost's section of the cable again.

I put one snail after another into the masticator floating at my side. Each gastropod I find on the cable suffers the same fate. Just removing the snails wouldn't be good enough. The ones I tagged when I first noticed them a few weeks ago found their way back to eat the algae that's started growing along the cable sheathing. Ending a snail's life isn't like killing a whale. Snails don't sing about their history, but I'd rather not harm something that's managed to survive in these conditions.

The ocean pushes at me more than usual. I'm only twenty meters below the water line and just five kilometers from where AMX-5 enters the ocean. On scalesuited knees, I sink down to stable ground free of the trash littering most of the continental shelf. My mandatory service posting is closer to the dryland world than I ever wanted to be.

Since my first month at the outpost, I've used my free time to bioremediate and disperse the waste in the immediate vicinity of the cable. My podsisters, Daniella and Fatima, have their own tasks and interests. Time in the shallows degrades their health. Removing the trash beside our outpost's section of the cable was my own special project. With authority and supplies, neither of which I have, I'd set up carbonic acid converters like the ones cleaning the ocean around Sylvia City. Converters would make a real difference. My trashless swath along AMX-5 is nice to look at, but it's nothing permanent. A few weeks after my service ends, the dryland trash that floats down from above and creeps along the benthos will again cover the cable.

Steel shows on a section of AMX-5 where snail slime has eaten through. Snails still swarm the breach, which is strange. They usually detach before they get too far into the cable's magnetic field. Turning my greenlamp up to full, I lean in for a closer look. Real Benthans wouldn't do that, but my dryland eyes never seem to gather enough light.

A scan indicates that water's only pushed a few millimeters into the sheathing. My instruments detect no electric current. The cable sometimes loses power but never for very long. I check the time. My journey back to the outpost will take half an hour in the *Nidaria,* my snug submarine vessel. If I'm late, Dannie will worry, but a superficial repair like this one won't take long. I expand a drycage over the damaged section of AMX-5 and evacuate the water inside. I begin to peel back cable sheathing layers, some living, some inanimate.

This is my 227th repair. At 228, I'll have mended the cable once for each month since Sylvia City took me in nineteen years ago. I haven't told anyone about the tally, not even Dannie. She'd say I'm keeping track for the wrong reasons, and she'd insist I don't owe Sylvia City more than anyone else does. But she doesn't know what it means to be born on dry land.

I was an infant when my parents fled with me to the ocean floor. Sylvia City had already turned away thousands of Carbon War refugees after the first few hundred tried to spread the dryland conflict to the benthos. But my mild-mannered parents were engineers with the skills to fix Sylvia City's overburdened environmental systems. My parents were welcomed. I was let in, too. I have no memory of life beyond the ocean floor, but growing up, I was known as the last dryland refugee. Ten thousand cable repairs can't erase that fact.

I try to focus on my work in the drycage. I'm careful to place tools so they don't nick my scalesuit. In the shallows where I'm working, the weight of water won't crush someone in a compromised scalesuit, but carelessness is a bad idea. The ocean holds too many dangers.

Sharks were once the greatest threat on the Blake Plateau. Now, threadfin drones are. They look like fish, but they travel alone, and they're made of metal. Built by drylanders to spy on one another, threadies explode when they come near people in the water. Only a drylander would blow something up to guard a secret. Shrapnel from an explosion can slice through a scalesuit and the person inside it.

I'm never close enough to a threadie to worry about the blast zone. Marksmanship is the only thing I've ever excelled at, so Sylvia City decided my mandatory service would be at the outpost with the most threadie contact. Since the end of the Carbon War, when AMX-5 was still a vital communication link between the wet and the dry land, Sylvia City has kept her promise to maintain the cable. I wouldn't have tried so hard to impress anyone with my ability to shoot a compressor gun if I'd known the reward would be six months living this close to the shore.

My thoughts drift ahead to the 228th repair. I wonder what it will be. I don't know if anything will be different after I complete it.

Red light flashes across my scalesuit eye coverings and resolves to a dot that indicates something unknown fifty meters away. I'm about to be delayed. The approaching object would have to be at least as large as a threadie for my proximity alert to detect it. I have no way of knowing how big it is or if it's anything more than a large piece of trash, but I know it's coming closer. With the water so churned up today, I can only see twenty meters. I wait for the object to change direction. It doesn't.

I'd rather be safe than shredded or bitten. I hurry through this repair's last steps and turn off my greenlamp. Sharks notice bright lights. So do threadies. I reach for my compressor gun, which is already charged to fire. I only need one shot to destroy a threadie. Twenty meters of visibility will give me plenty of time. But if a shark's approaching, I'll need multiple re-charges to deter one of those mutated creatures. The compressor takes time to ready after each shot. The crushed snails in the masticator will speed up the process, but I don't know how much. For a moment, I hope this part of the ecosystem is too compromised to foster apex predators. It's a shameful thought, one a real Benthan would never have.

Sensing heightened tension, a layer of my scalesuit breather tries to push past my lips and into my throat where it can protect me from drowning. I've never needed the device as a throat-breather, though I've had to cough it out of my windpipe many times. It's only a distraction now. I bite down to stop the breather's intrusion. The device pulls back to sit atop my nose and mouth where it belongs. The thing in the water is forty meters away now.

The *Nidaria* is closer, but in the other direction. I resist the urge to turn and swim to my vessel. Predators often attack from behind. I swipe my scalesuit to release an olfactory neutralizer to help disguise my location from a shark. The neutralizer won't affect a threadie if I'm in its path. My compressor gun is primed to fire.

I stare into the wide, watery darkness. My proximity alert shows the object's approach is slowing. It might be preparing to attack. My knees press into the ocean floor. I'm breathing too hard. I curse my lack of benthic enhancements.

The neutralizer isn't having an effect. Whatever's approaching can't be a threadie because it's moving from side to side. Threadies travel on a set path that rises and falls through the ocean's photic layer. The pattern of movement on my proximity alert doesn't make sense. The distance to the object shrinks to thirty meters. I still can't see it.

Dread sucks the moisture from my mouth. I realize my mistake. I was looking in the middle of the water column. My gaze rises to the water's surface. Waves show as gray-black shadows. Just at the limit of my vision, something resolves. I think I recognize it. I should lower my compressor gun, but I hold it steady. Noise disappears. My thoughts race faster than time should allow. What I see is more startling than a threadie or a shark.

A boy falls toward the ocean floor. His mouth is open. He can't be more than six years old. He still has all his limbs. He might have only just drowned. Tattered clothing made of sea plants marks him as a scavenger child from one of the defunct oil platforms. The nearest is kilometers away.

If the boy only went under a moment ago, I could save him. I could swim up to him before he falls too far. I could break the water's surface for the first time in my memory. I could revive him with filtered air from my own lungs and the press of my scalesuit-covered hands against his chest. I could breathe the fetid air above. I could push that air into the boy's body. I could wait for the boy to breathe again. I could fight to keep my own head above the watery embrace that's held me safe all these years. I could give the boy back his life and let the poisons in the air above steal a little of my own. I could throw away nineteen years of trying to feel like a real Benthan. Or I could let the boy die.

Sound disappears. The water's roiling slows. My thoughts cavitate. I know what to do.

Noise like color blazes around me. I swipe my scalesuit for a rapid ascent. I soar. I catch the boy's sinking form. I increase my scalesuit's buoyancy. The boy and I shoot toward the ocean's surface. We burst above the water line. A swell pitches us toward the sky. The light blinds. My scalesuit eye coverings can't compensate for the glare. I squint against the pain. If I were a real Benthan, my retinas would be ruined. My eyelids squeeze shut. The pain recedes. I blink and can see again.

The ocean's surface crashes onto itself. Swells break into whitecaps. My scalesuit's buoyancy helps me keep the boy's head above water. His body is limp. If his heart beats, I don't feel it. I want to believe he only just went under. I put his back against my front and begin to compress and release his chest. His clothing pulls apart beneath my motions. A rash—red, raw, and bleeding—covers his head and shoulders. The wounds are almost familiar. The rest of his body shows the blue-gray pallor of hypothermia.

I peel off a layer of my breather and set it across the back of my scalesuit-covered hand. The bud needs a moment to grow. I suck as much filtered air into my lungs as they will hold. I stroke the breather parent protecting my own airways. I roll it to the side. Cold water sprays the skin of my exposed nose and mouth. I pinch the boy's nostrils closed. My mouth seals over his. I blow clean air into his clogged lungs. I pump his chest again. I gulp at the dryland air. It tastes of acid. I force this polluted air into the boy. The inside of my nose burns.

I will the boy to live. In his slack features, I imagine a benthic future for him, one that knows the rhythms of the deep ocean.

I feel movement in his chest. The water pitches us around. The boy convulses. I hold onto him. Together, we rise on a wave. He gurgles and begins to cough. He vomits. I turn from his bilious spray.

The shore five kilometers away comes into view. I've seen images of what that landscape should look like. AMX-5's power station should be visible on a peninsula. Just beyond that, buildings should rise from streets clogged with traffic. A latticework of rail lines should weave between the middle stories of skyscrapers and across the tops of shorter buildings. Transportation vehicles should zip around. Aerial crafts should dot the sky.

The shore looks nothing like that. Reality wobbles. The child shuddering in my arms begins to slip away.

AMX-5's power station seems intact, but the shore beyond is a calamity. Black smoke streams from a dozen buildings and gathers above the city. Flames spark orange and yellow in too many places to count. Rail cars wait motionless in the middle of elevated lines or lay crashed atop automobiles glinting below. No evacuation sirens sound. No instructions to shelter blare. Not a single rescue craft circles a flaming building. The greater distance holds more smoke.

The world has seen this before. I have, too, in documentaries about the Carbon War. The boy's rash suddenly makes sense. He's been exposed to carbon weapons fire, though he was outside the weapon's immediate range. His head and shoulders must have been above the water line when a pulse deployed, but he was far enough away not to be turned to ash. The ocean protected the submerged portion of the boy's body the same way it protected Sylvia City when I was an infant. Air conducts carbon weapon pulses. Water doesn't. People die, but infrastructure remains in place.

New worry seizes me. A haven that persists from one apocalypse to another might look even more to refugees like a promised land. Just as before, anyone who can follow AMX-5 from the shore into the water will soon set upon Sylvia City. This time, the drylanders might be more forceful about bringing weapons and conflicts. The whale song halls might not survive.

I hold tighter to the boy. His terrified gaze darts around. My lips begin to burn. I press them together. I've read about what a secondary carbon rash feels like, but this is the first time I remember experiencing one. I'm lucky only my lips touched the boy's flesh. Salves can mitigate the pain of my secondary rash, but in a few days, my scalesuit will die from having touched the boy in so many places. With his primary rash, the boy's medical need will be so great that only doctors in Sylvia City will be able to save him.

An airplane appears just above the swells. The craft flies in halting, predatory bursts parallel to the shore.

Flecks of ash like graphite tears smear the boy's face. My exposed skin must look the same. Ash from dead drylanders and burning buildings is in the air. Millions might have died already. Their remains will rest momentarily on the ocean's surface before precipitating through the pelagic to fall—inedible and useless—to the benthos.

The ocean will suffer greater injustice than ashes though. Carbon weapons release vast amounts of carbon dioxide into the air. So do survivors willing to burn anything they can find for warmth and cooking fuel. Like the last time, the ocean will attempt to absorb it all. The water's acidity will shoot up. Great colonies of plants and animals will die. New, sickly species will add to the ranks of mutated sharks, thin-shelled snails and algae that grows where algae shouldn't be able to grow.

Sylvia City has ways to prepare herself and her environment. She can mitigate some initial carbonic acid effects, but she needs to deploy her defenses while the danger is still in the ocean's upper layers. Panic squeezes the breath from my chest. I hope Sylvia City knows what's happened.

The airplane turns toward the ocean and drops low to hover a few kilometers away near an oil platform. People must have been detected. I can't look away from what's about to happen, but the boy has seen enough. Despite his coughing, he buries his face in my neck.

A blast shoots out from under the airplane's wings. The area in front of the craft undulates with the pulse, which makes contact with the platform. Anyone who was alive is ash now.

I've been above the water line too long. I check that the breather bud on my hand is ready. I lean back so I can see the boy's face. In my scalesuit, I must seem strange to him, but my differences are nothing compared to what people from Sylvia City look like.

"I'm going underwater," I tell the boy. His eyes are bloodshot. "To Sylvia City. I can give you something to let you breathe in the water. You'll be able to get to the shore, but you'll need treatment for what the carbon weapon did to you. Sylvia City can help. If you come with me, you'll have a home for the rest of your life, but you'll be different from everyone else. Always. Or you can go back to the dry land."

The plane finds a boat and prepares to unleash another blast.

"Do you want to come with me?" I say.

The boy's chin trembles.

"I don't want to die again," he says.

I smile. Pain needles my lips.

"Hold still," I say. I peel the breather bud from the back of my hand. The boy's eyes widen. I set the breather over his nose and mouth. The breather's edges pulse along his flesh to find the shape of his face. His eyelids pinch together with the sensation. I hold tight to him. The airplane flies toward us. A low hum grows in the air and threatens to roar.

"Bite down," I say. The boy misses his opportunity. The breather dives into his throat. I stop the boy from clawing at his neck. The waves toss us around. The airplane nears. I stroke my breather so it will sit over my mouth and nose. I shift the boy to my back. He clings to me like I might let him go. The plane slows to hover. The boy's fingers dig into my scalesuit. The benthos calls to me. With the boy, I dive.

Water gasps and echoes around us. Light dims. Alive, we sink toward the benthos.

My scalesuit protects me from the ever-colder water layers, but the boy has nothing to keep him warm until I can get him into my emergency scalesuit back in the *Nidaria*. More pain lies in his future. His new-grown breather pulls oxygen from the water and stops his lungs from compressing, but his eyes and ears have no such protection. Barotrauma is inevitable.

We reach the ocean floor. I turn on my greenlamp and squint into the depths. A field of trash shows, but not AMX-5. Surface waves must have pushed me away from the cable. I swipe my scalesuit to search for AMX-5's magnetic field. It should be detectable within three kilometers. Nothing shows on the display. I can't have moved so far in such a short amount of time.

Something about the snails on the cable earlier nags at me. I've never seen them gorge so deeply, like they'd been eating algae and sheathing for hours.

Finally, I understand. The cable's power isn't intermittent. It's completely gone. The power station must have been damaged on the inside. Despair bubbles through my thoughts. My podsisters at the outpost don't know what's happened on the dry land, and neither does Sylvia City. Preparations haven't started.

The boy's hold at my neck loosens. The rash, the cold, and the water pressure are taking their toll on him. I have to find the cable and the *Nidaria* beside it. I need to warn Sylvia City about the new war.

I bite back my breather and try to think. The murky water torments me. Somewhere, the cable is waiting.

One direction seems to hold a little less trash. I swim that way. With an arm on the boy at my back, my progress through the water is slow. My greenlamp eats the darkness and extrudes it in my wake. The density of trash lessens. I'm drawn toward the swath of ocean floor I cleaned.

AMX-5 comes into view. Something hits me from behind. I'm knocked forward. I lose hold of the boy. I reach for my compressor gun. It's still primed to fire. A reef shark circles. The mutated creature is over three meters long. It turns toward the boy, who drifts like he's unconscious or already dead.

I point my compressor gun at the shark and fire. The blast hits the shark in the gills. The stunned creature swims away. I slot the gun into my masticator, bulging with snail sludge.

I swim toward the boy. He's not moving. The shark returns. The compressor gun is charged. I hope Sylvia City will understand what I have to do. I fire.

I blow the shark apart. Blood clouds the water. Fish chunks spin past. I cup a few large pieces and press them into the masticator. I start the energy transfer to the compressor gun again. The blood scent will attract other predators, but I'll be ready if anything else emerges from the depths.

The boy and I have to get out of the water. I need to find the *Nidaria*. The boy's eyes are slits. He doesn't react to my touch. I tuck him under an arm and swim back to AMX-5. I take a chance and swim downslope.

At last, the depths give up the *Nidaria*. She's just as I left her, except now she's the boy's lifeline. And Sylvia City's.

I open the *Nidaria*'s hatch and pull out my emergency scalesuit. I slide the boy into it. Burst capillaries dot his face. I set another breather over his mouth and nose. Edges seal. The scalesuit expels water and shrinks to fit the boy's shape. If not for the boy's stunted limbs, he could be any Benthan child behind wide scalesuit eyes.

The boy and I only just fit into the *Nidaria,* which is designed for one Benthan. Luckily, they're taller than drylanders and bigger-boned. The hatch sucks closed behind us.

The unconscious boy's body presses against my legs. I set his scalesuit to parent controls and hydration. His body twitches under the prick of tiny needles filled with water, antibiotics, and nutrition. His scalesuit will warm him and serve as a barrier to stop his primary rash from spreading. The rash my scalesuit and I are carrying won't spread because they're secondary. I instruct the boy's scalesuit to sedate him. I don't want the boy to wake frightened and in pain. I want the next day of his conscious life to begin healthy in Sylvia City.

I set the *Nidaria* to follow AMX-5 down the continental shelf to the outpost.

We glide through the water a few feet above the ocean floor. The *Nidaria*'s pace is slow. Her gills are designed to keep herself and one person, not two, oxygenated. I tune the *Nidaria*'s hydrophone to the strongest signal it can find. The saddest whale song I've ever heard pulses into my ears. The auto-translator picks out the notes that whales use to refer to Sylvia City and sanctuary.

Darkness armors the benthos. Ahead, a thin school of fish comes into greenlamp view. The *Nidaria* swims through the school, which takes refuge in her wake.

I scan the field of trash. Soon, new carbon ash will coat it all. Not yet though. On the sea floor beside a twisted metal frame, a threadie lays immobile. I've never before seen one motionless. I swipe off the *Nidaria*'s anterior light and reach for my compressor gun.

Reason prevails. Instead of shooting through the *Nidaria*'s window, I back the vessel up. I turn the greenlamp on again and swing the *Nidaria* in an arc wider than a threadie blast zone.

Farther along AMX-5, another unmoving threadie comes into view. I keep the *Nidaria* clear of it. A third threadie appears and a fourth. By the time the darkened outpost resolves, I've counted a dozen newly fallen drones.

A crater's been blasted from the ground beside the outpost. The building's exterior is damaged. I try to breathe and see what's there and not what I'm afraid of, but it's hard. My podsisters could be floating dead inside, their scalesuits only partially on when the water and the pressure came. I coax the *Nidaria* into a circuit around the outpost. I search for breaches where water's flooded in.

I find none. Instead, a light inside the building turns on. Fatima is standing on the viewing deck and staring at the *Nidaria*. Her raised hand shields her eyes, cast in the same blue-white as those of the abyssal fish. She and Dannie don't need greenlamps to see in the deep ocean. Fatima turns on an exterior light. The bottom of the threadie-made crater still isn't visible.

"A threadie landed on the roof," Fatima says.

Her hydrophoned voice inside the *Nidaria* is a relief.

"Are you hurt?" I say. "Or Dannie?"

"No," Fatima says, "the threadie didn't explode when it landed, but I thought the core might leak radiation, so I used the grapple to send the toxic thing sailing. It exploded when it hit the benthos. Did you see any other threadies on your way back?"

In my thoughts, something phosphoresces. It's a grain of sand, then a rock, then a ledge rising up from the ocean floor. The thought shimmers like a beacon from Sylvia City. I understand what I need to do. I still have one more repair. My scalesuit will be good for a few days.

"Yes," I say. "I saw some threadies. I'll be in soon."

I bring the *Nidaria* close to the outpost's waterlock. Instead of docking the vessel inside, I rest her on the benthos near where the outpost's communication line connects to AMX-5.

I extract myself from the *Nidaria* and step onto the ocean floor. AMX-5 has never before looked so vulnerable. In one swift motion, I slice all the way through the cable. The primary carbon rash that must be spreading along AMX-5's new algae can't have arrived at the outpost before the *Nidaria* even if she was slow. Now, the rash will never reach Sylvia City. I cauterize each end of the cable and set the stumps back on the ocean floor. This is only the beginning.

I crowd into the *Nidaria* again and dock her inside the outpost. Dannie's waiting for me on the other side of the waterlock door. Her big-boned face, colored like the gray sand around Sylvia City, is visible through the porthole between the waterlock and the outpost's interior. Worry tightens Dannie's expression.

The waterlock drains. So does the *Nidaria*. I make a mental list of what I'll need: nano-nets, the heavy grappler, another compressor gun, and as much bioremediant and dispersant as I can strap to the *Nidaria*'s exterior.

I peel off my breather and push the top of my scalesuit back so it rests at my neck. I squeeze out of the *Nidaria*. Dannie swishes open the door connecting the dock and the outpost's living spaces. The same whale song the *Nidaria* found fills the outpost and pours into the waterlock.

"You're never late coming back," Dannie says from the doorway. Her voice trembles. "We didn't know what happened to you."

As gently as I can, I pull the scalesuit-covered boy out of the *Nidaria*. He's slippery as a fish. I turn toward Dannie. She draws in a quick breath. Her gaze rises from the child.

"Is he alive?" she says.

"Yes."

"What happened to your lips?"

Fatima slides past Dannie and into the waterlock.

"It looks like secondary carbon rash," Fatima says, "which probably has something to do with why the cable's been down for hours."

I hand the boy's sedated form to Dannie and tell her and Fatima what happened. Before I'm done, tears are running down Dannie's cheeks, and Fatima's gaze is turned inward, probably with thoughts about how quickly the outpost will need to be evacuated. For the journey back to Sylvia City, my podsisters and the boy will be safe in the *Fulton*, the outpost's other, more traditional vessel.

I won't be going with them.

Dannie steps inside the outpost's living spaces and lays the boy down on a cushion. I begin to gather up all the nano-nets in the waterlock.

"We won't need those for the journey back to Sylvia City," Fatima says.

"I know," I say. "They're for me. I'm taking the *Nidaria*. I'm going to blow up the dryland power station. With each threadie capable of making a crater the size of the one outside, I'll only need a few. After that, I'll dissolve the cable all the way from the shore to the outpost. Farther, I hope."

Fatima's blue-white eyes widen.

I set the nano-nets beside the *Nidaria*.

"That's crazy," Fatima says. "Have you seen your scalesuit? The rash it's carrying will kill it in a few days. If you get a primary rash, your scalesuit will die in a few hours. You'll drown inside the *Nidaria* or on the benthos, or carbon weapons fire will kill you."

She's right, but that won't stop me.

"With the power station gone," I say, "and the trash drifting back over signs of the cable's path, it'll be years before the drylanders can find Sylvia City again. Maybe they never will."

"Yes, but . . . " Fatima's lips twist around like they're searching for the words to stop me. None exist. She sighs. It's a plea. She says, "Take the *Fulton* instead. The bridge has a waterlock and can be drained. You won't need a scalesuit."

"The boy needs the *Fulton*," I say. "It's the only ship big enough to get all three of you back to Sylvia City before the boy dies. He goes with the *Fulton*."

Dannie pulls up alongside Fatima.

"No," Dannie says. Her voice is only just louder than the whale song. "You can't do this. It's too much for one person."

"It's not for one person," I say. "It's for Sylvia City. It's my last repair."

"You don't have to do it alone," Dannie says. "I'll come with you. We can both fit in the *Nidaria*, can't we?"

I shake my head.

Fatima says, "A few hours in the shallows will blind you permanently, Dannie. You're no good for this task. Neither am I."

"I don't care!" Dannie says. "I can—"

Fatima lays a hand on Dannie's shoulder. Dannie knocks it away.

"She's going to die," Dannie says. "We can't let her go."

"Someone should get rid of the power station and the cable," Fatima says. "It's the right thing to do. The drylanders could already be planning their descent. We can't go into the shallows to stop them, but there are other ways to help."

Fatima shrugs off her scalesuit. It falls to the floor. In dark brown underclothes, Fatima stands next to Dannie. I've never seen Fatima's bare gray arms before. She steps out of her scalesuit's foot coverings and picks up the protective layer that's traveled with her most of her life. She holds her scalesuit out to me.

"You'll need this," Fatima says, "and my emergency scalesuit, too."

My voice catches like a breather's stuck in my throat. At last, I say, "But if something goes wrong on your way back to—"

"It won't," Fatima says. "We'll be fine on the *Fulton*'s bridge."

Dannie's just as fast removing her own scalesuit. She holds it out to me.

"Wear this one when it's time to come home," Dannie says, "to Sylvia City."

Tears sting my eyes. I reach for my podsisters' scalesuits. A tightness in my chest releases. I thought it would never go away.

THE WIZARD OF THE TREES

★

by Joe R. Lansdale

What was supposed to be a cruise back to the U.S.A. in the lap of luxury goes from bad to worse to weird—to out of this world. When the unsinkable Titanic *hits an iceberg and does just that, Jack Davis thinks all is lost. But a splitting headache and an encounter with a strange creature below the icy waves of the Atlantic conspire to transport him to the jungle world of Venus. There he'll face down enemies, find true love, and discover a place to call home.*

I AM HERE because of a terrible headache. I know you will want more of an explanation than that, but I can't give it to you. I can only say I was almost killed when the great ship *Titanic* went down. There was an explosion, a boiler blowing, perhaps. I can't say. When the ship dove down and broke in half, I felt as if I broke in half with it.

An object hit me in the head under water. I remember there was something down there with me. Not anyone on the ship, not a corpse, but something. I remember its face, if you can call it that: full of teeth and eyes, big and luminous, lit up by a light from below, and then I was gasping water into my lungs, and then this thing was pulling me toward a glowing pool of whirling illumination. It dragged me into warmth and into light, and my last sight of the thing was a flipping of its fish-like tail, and then my head exploded.

Or so it seemed.

When I awoke, I was lying in a warm muddy mire, almost floating, almost sinking. I grabbed at some roots jutting out from the shoreline and pulled myself out of it. I lay there with my headache for awhile, warming myself in the sunlight, and then the headache began to pass. I rolled over on my belly and looked at the pool of mud. It was a big pool. In fact, pool is incorrect. It was like a great lake of mud. I have no idea how I managed to be there, and that is the simple truth of it. I still don't know. It felt like a dream.

With some difficulty I had managed a bunk in steerage on the *Titanic*, heading back home to my country, the United States of America. I had played out my string in England, thought I might go back and journey out west where I had punched cows and shot buffalo for the railroad. I had even killed a couple of men in self-defense, and dime novels had been written about me, the Black Rider of the Plains. But that was mostly lies. The only thing they got right was the color of my skin. I'm half black, half Cherokee. In the dime novels I was described as mostly white, which is a serious lie. One look at me will tell you different.

I was a rough rider with Buffalo Bill's Wild West Show, and when it arrived in England to perform, they went back and I had stayed on. I liked it for awhile, but as they say, there's no place like home. Not that I had really had one, but we're speaking generally here.

I managed to my feet and looked around. Besides the lake of mud, there were trees. And I do mean trees. They rose up tall and mighty all around the lake, and there didn't seem anything to do but to go amongst them. The mud I wouldn't go back into. I couldn't figure what had happened to me, what had grabbed me and pulled me into that glowing whirlpool, but the idea of it laying grip on me again was far less than inviting. It had hauled me here, wherever here was, and had retreated, left me to my own devices.

The mud I had ended up in was shallow, but I knew the rest of the lake wasn't. I knew this because as I looked out over the vast mire, I saw a great beast moving in it; a lizard, I guess you'd call it. At least that was my first thought, then I remembered the bones they had found out in Montana some years back, and how they were called dinosaurs. I had read a little about it, and that's what I thought when I saw this thing in the mud, rising up gray and green of skin, lurching up and dipping down, dripping mud that plopped bright in the sunlight.

Down it went, out of sight, and up again, and when it came up a third time it had a beast in its mouth; a kind of giant slick, purple-skinned seal, its blood oozing like strawberry jam from between the monster's teeth.

It may seem as if I'm nonchalant about all this, but the truth is I'm telling this well after the fact and have had time to accept it. But let me jump ahead a bit.

The world I am on is Venus, and now it is my world.

My arrival was not the only mystery. I am a man of forty-five, and in good shape, and I like to think of sound mind. But good as I felt at that age, I felt even better here on this warm, damp, tree-covered world. I would soon discover there was an even greater mystery I could not uncover. But I will come to that, even if I will not arrive at a true explanation.

I pulled off my clothes, which were caked with mud, and shook them out. I had lost both my shoes when the ship went down; they had been sucked off of me by the ocean's waters with the same enthusiasm as a kid sucking a peppermint stick. I stood naked with my clothes under my arm, my body covered in mud, my hair matted with it. I must have looked pretty foolish, but there I was with my muddy clothes and nowhere to go.

I glanced back at the muddy lake, saw the great lizard and his lunch were gone. The muddy lake, out in the center, appeared to boil. My guess was it was hot in the middle, warm at the edges. My host, the thing that had brought me here, had fortunately chosen one of the warm areas for me to surface.

I picked a wide path between the trees, and took to the trail. It was shadowy on the path. I supposed it had been made by animals, and from the prints, some of them very large. Had I gone too far off the path I could easily have waded into darkness. There was little to no brush beneath the trees because there wasn't enough sunlight to feed them. Unusual birds and indefinable critters flittered and leaped about in the trees and raced across my trail. I walked on for some time with no plans, no shoes, my clothes tucked neatly under my arm like a pet dog.

Now, if you think I was baffled, you are quite correct. For a while I tried to figure out what had nabbed me under the waters and taken me through the whirling light and left me almost out of the mud, and then disappeared. No answers presented themselves, and I let it go and set my thoughts to survival. I can do that. I have a practical streak. One of the most practical things was I was still alive, wherever I was. I had survived in the wilderness before. Had gone up in the Rocky Mountains in the dead of winter with nothing but a rifle, a knife, and a small bag of possible. I had survived, come down in the spring with beaver and fox furs to sell.

I figured I could do that, I could make it here as well, though later on I will confess to an occasional doubt. I had had some close calls before, including a run-in with Wyatt Earp that almost turned ugly, a run-in with Johnny Ringo that left him dead under a tree, and a few things not worth mentioning, but this world made all of those adventures look mild.

Wandering in amongst those trees, my belly began to gnaw, and I figured I'd best find something I could eat, so I began looking about. Up in the trees near where I stood there were great balls of purple fruit, and birds about my size, multi-colored and feathered, with beaks like daggers. They were pecking at those fruits. I figured if they could eat them, so could I.

My next order of business was to skinny up one of those trees and lay hold of my next meal. I put my clothes under it, the trunk of which was as big around as a locomotive, grabbed a low-hanging limb, and scuttled up to where I could see a hanging fruit about the size of a buffalo's head. It proved an easy climb because the limbs were so broad and so plentiful.

The birds above me noticed my arrival, but ignored me. I crawled out on the limb bearing my chosen meal, got hold of it and yanked it loose, nearly sending myself off the limb in the process. It would have been a good and hard fall, but I liked to think all that soft earth down there, padded with loam, leaves and rot, would have given me a soft landing.

I got my back against the tree trunk, took hold of the fruit, and tried to bite into it. It was as hard as leather. I looked about. There was a small broken limb jutting out above me. I stood on my perch, lifted the fruit, and slammed it into where the limb was broke off. It stuck there, like a fat tick with a knife through it. Juice started gushing out of the fruit. I lifted my face below it and let the nectar flood into my mouth and splash over me. It was somewhat sour and tangy in taste, but I was convinced that if it didn't poison me, I wouldn't die of hunger. I tugged on the fruit until it ripped apart. Inside it was pithy and good to eat. I scooped it out with my hands and filled up on it.

I had just finished my repast, when above me I heard a noise, and when I looked up, what I saw was to me the most amazing sight yet in this wild new world.

Silver.

A bird.

But no, it was a kind of flying sled. I heard it before I saw it, a hum like a giant bee, and when I looked up the sunlight glinted off of it, blinding me for a moment. When I looked back, the sled tore through the trees, spun about and came to light with a smack in the fork of a massive limb. It was at an angle. I could see there were seats on the sled, and there were people in the seats, and there was a kind of shield of glass at the front of the craft. The occupants were all black of hair and yellow of skin, but my amazement of this was nothing compared to what amazed me next.

Another craft, similar in nature came shining into view. It glided to a stop, gentle and swift, like a gas-filled balloon. It floated in the air next to the limb where the other had come to a stop. It was directed by a man sitting in an open seat who was like those in the other machine, a man with yellow skin and black hair. Another man, similar in appearance sat behind him, his biggest distinction a large blue-green half-moon jewel on a chain hung around his neck. This fellow leaped to his feet, revealing himself nude other than for the sword harness and the medallion, drew a thin sword strapped across his back, dropped down on the other craft and started hacking at the driver who barely staggered to his feet in time to defend himself. The warrior's swords clanged together. The other two occupants of the wrecked craft had climbed out of the wells of their seats with drawn swords and were about to come to their comrade's aid when something even more fantastic occurred.

Flapping down from the sky were a half-dozen winged men, carrying swords and battle axes. Except for the harness that would serve to hold their weapons, and a small hard, leather-looking pouch, they, like the others, were without clothes. Their eyes were somewhat to the side of their heads, there were beak-like growths jutting from their faces, and their skin was milk-white, and instead of hair were feathers. The colors of the feathers were varied. Their targets were the yellow men in the shiny machine on the tremendous tree limb.

It became clear then that the man with the necklace, though obviously not of the winged breed, was no doubt on their side. He skillfully dueled with the driver of the limb-beached craft, parried deftly, then with a shout ran his sword through his opponent's chest. The mortally wounded warrior dropped his weapon and fell backwards off his foe's sword, collapsed across the fore of his vessel.

The two warriors in league with the dead man were fighting valiantly, but the numbers against them were overwhelming. The man with the medallion, or amulet, stood on the fore of the craft, straddling the carcass of his kill, and it was then that I got a clear view of his face. It has been said, and normally I believe it, that you can't judge someone by their appearance. But I tell you that I have never seen anyone with such an evil countenance as this man. It wasn't that his features were all that unusual, but their was an air about him that projected pure villainy. It was as if there was another person inside of him, one black of heart and devious of mind, and it seemed that spectral person was trying to pressure itself to the surface. I have never before or since had that feeling about anyone, not even Comanche and Apache warriors that had tried to kill me during my service with the Buffalo Soldiers.

It was then that one of the two defenders, having driven back a winged warrior he had been dueling with, pulled with his free hand a pistol. It was a crude looking thing, reminiscent of an old flintlock. He raised the pistol in the direction of his adversary and fired. The pistol's bark was like the cough of a tubercular man. The winged man spouted blood, dropped his sword, brought both hands to his face, then relaxed and fell, diving head-first like a dart. As the winged man dove between the limbs near me, crashed through some leaves, and plummeted to the earth, the sword he dropped stuck conveniently in the limb before me. I took hold of it thinking that now I had a weapon for self-defense, and that it was a good time to depart. I told myself that this fight, whatever it was about, was not my fight. They were so busy with one another, I had not even been seen. So, of course, casting aside common sense, I decided I had to get into the thick of it.

It may well have been the fact that the men in the craft were outnumbered, but I must admit that one glance at the man with the jeweled medallion and I knew where my sentiments lay. I know how that sounds, but I assure you, had you seen his face you would have felt exactly the same way.

Why I thought one more sword might make a difference, considering the horde of winged men assisting the evil-faced man was enormous, I can't explain to you. But with the thin, light sword in my teeth, I began to climb upward to aid them.

This is when I realized certain things, certain abilities that I had sensed upon arrival, but were now proving to be true. I felt strong, agile, not only as I might have felt twenty years earlier, but in a manner I had never experienced. I moved easily, squirrel-like is what I thought, and in no time I reached the craft caught in the fork of the limb.

The winged men were fluttering about the two survivors like flies on spilled molasses. The man with the necklace had paused to watch, no longer feeling the need to engage. He observed as his birds flapped and cawed and swung their weapons at his own kind. It was then that he saw me, rising up over the lip of the limb, finding my feet.

I removed the sword from my teeth and sprang forward with a stabbing motion, piercing the heart of one of the winged attackers. It fluttered, twisted, and fell.

The yellow-skinned couple glanced at me, but accepted my help without question or protest for obvious reasons. I must have been a sight. Naked, having left my clothes at the base of the great tree. My skin and hair matted with mud. I looked like a wild man. And it was in that moment I noticed something I should have noticed right off, but the positioning and the leaves and smaller limbs of the tree had blocked my complete view. One of the yellow skins was a woman. She was lean and long and her hair was in a rough cut, as if someone had just gathered it up in a wad and chopped it off with a knife at her shoulders. She was not nude as her opponents were. She wore, as did her companion, a sort of black skirt, and a light covering of black leather breast armor. She had a delicate, but unquestionably feminine shape. When I saw her face I almost forgot what I was doing. Her bright green, almond-shaped eyes sucked me into them. I was so nearly lost in them that a winged man with an axe nearly took my head off. I ducked the axe swing, lunged forward, stretching my leg way out, thrusting with my sword, sticking him in the gut. When I pulled my sword back, his guts spilled out along with a gush of blood. As he fell out of view, more of the things came down from the sky and buzzed around us, beating their wings. They were plenty, but it was soon obvious our skills with weapons were superior to theirs. They used the swords and axes crudely. They handled them with less skill than a child with a mop and a broom.

My partners—such as they were—were well versed in the use of the blade, as was I, having learned swordsmanship from an older man while I was amongst the Buffalo Soldiers. My teacher was a black man, like me, and had once lived in France. There he had been trained well in the use of the steel, and I in turn had learned this skill from him. So it was not surprising, that in short order, we had killed most of our attackers and sent the others soaring away in fear. The necklace-wearing man, who had been observing, now joined in, attempting to take me out of the fray, and I engaged him. He was good with the sword, quick. But I was quicker and more skilled, blessed with whatever strange abilities this world gave me. He caused me a moment's trouble, but it only took me a few parries to grasp his method, which was not too unlike my own. A high and low attack, a way of using the eyes to mislead the opponent. I was gradually getting the better of him when his driver coasted his machine next to the limb. My opponent gave out with a wild cry, came at me with a surge of renewed energy, driving me back slightly, then he wheeled, leaped onto his machine, and slid quickly into his seat, smooth as a woman slipping sleek fingers into a calfskin glove. The sled with the two yellow men in it darted away.

I turned, lowered my bloodstained blade, and looked at those whose side I had joined. The woman spoke, and her words, though simple, hit me like a train.

She said, "Thank you."

It was another side effect of my arrival here. I was not only stronger and more agile, I could understand a language I had never heard before. As soon as the words left her mouth they translated in my head. It was so immediate it was as if their language was my native tongue.

"You're welcome," I said. This seemed a trite thing to say, me standing there on a limb holding a sword, mud-covered and naked, with my business hanging out, but I was even more astonished to have my words understood by her without any true awareness that I was speaking my own language.

"Who are you?" the woman asked.

"Jack Davis," I said. "Formerly of the United States Buffalo Soldiers."

"The United States?" she asked.

"It's a bit hard to explain."

"You are covered in mud," the man said, sheathing his sword.

"You are correct," I said. I decided to keep it simple. "I fell into a mud lake."

The man grinned. "That must have took some doing."

"I consider myself a man of special talents," I said.

The young woman turned her head in a curious fashion, glanced down at me. "Is your skin black, or is it painted?"

I realized what part of me she was studying. Under all that mud had I been Irish and not part Negro, my blush would have been as bright as the sinking sun. Before long it would become obvious to me that on this world nudity was not something shameful or indecent in their minds. Clothes for them were ornaments, or were designed to protect them from the weather, but they were not bothered by the sight of the flesh.

"Correct," I said. "I am black. Very much so."

"We have heard of black men," she said. "But we have never seen them."

"There are others like me?" I said.

"We have heard that this is so," said the woman. "In the far south, though I suspect they are less muddy."

"Again," said the man, "we thank you. We were very much outnumbered and your sword was appreciated."

"You seem to have been doing well without me, but I was glad to help," I said.

"You flatter us," he said. "I am Devel, and this is my sister, Jerrel."

I nodded at them. By this time Devel had turned to the sled and to the dead man lying on its front, bleeding. He bent down and touched his face. "Bandel is dead by Tordo's hand, the traitor."

"I'm sorry," I said.

"He was a warrior, and there is nothing else to say," said Jerrel, but she and Devel, despite their matter-of-fact tone were obviously hurt and moved. That's why what happened next was so surprising.

Devel dragged the corpse to the edge of the sled, and then the limb, and without ceremony, flipped it over the side. "To the soil again," he said.

This seemed more than unusual and disrespectful, but I was later to learn this is their custom. When one of their number dies, and since they live in high cities and populate the trees, this is a common method. If they die on the ground, they are left where they fell. This treatment was considered an honor.

I processed this slowly, but kept my composure. My survival might depend on it. I said, "May I ask who these men were and why they were trying to kill you?"

Jerrel glanced at Devel, said, "He chose to help us without question. He is bonded to us in blood."

"True," Devel said, but I could tell he wasn't convinced.

Jerrel, however, decided to speak. "They are the Varnin. And we are warriors of Sheldan. Prince and princess, actually. We are going to their country, in pursuit of the talisman."

"You're warring over a trinket?" I said.

"It is far more than a trinket," she said. "And since there are only us two, it is hardly a war."

"I would call in reinforcements."

She nodded. "If there was time, but there is not."

She did not elaborate. We left it at that for the time being, and set about releasing the silver craft from the limbs where it had lodged. This seemed like a precarious job to me, but I helped them do it. The craft proved light as air. When it came loose of the limbs it didn't fall, but began to hum and float. Devel climbed into the front seat position, where the dead man had been, touched a silver rod, and the machine hummed louder than before.

Jerrel climbed into one of the seats behind him, said, "Come with us."

Devel glanced at her.

"We can't leave him," she said. "He looks to be lost."

"You have no idea," I said.

"And he helped us when we needed it," she said. "He risked his life."

"We have our mission," he said.

"We will find a safe place for him," she said. "We still have a long distance to go. We cannot just abandon him."

This discussion had gone on as if I were not standing there. I said, "I would appreciate you taking me somewhere other than this tree."

Devel nodded, but I could tell he wasn't entirely convinced.

I stepped into the machine, took a seat. Devel looked back at me. I could tell this was a development he was not fond of, in spite of the fact I had taken their side in the fight.

But he said nothing. He turned forward, touched the rod. The machine growled softly, glided away through a cluster of leaves and limbs. I ducked so as not to be struck by them. When I looked up the machine had risen high in the sky, above the tree line, up into the sunny blue. I was astonished. It was such a delicate and agile craft, so far ahead of what we had achieved back home. This made me consider that, interestingly enough, their understanding of firearms was far behind ours. There was a part of me that felt that it would be nice if it stayed that way. It seemed humans and bird-men were quite capable of doing enough damage with swords and axes. As for the pistol Devel had fired, he had discarded it as if it had been nothing more than a worn out handkerchief.

I glanced over the side, saw below all manner of creatures. There were huge leather-winged monsters flying beneath us, and in the clear areas between the trees. On the ground in the rare open spaces I could see monstrous lizards of assorted colors. The beasts looked up at the sound of our humming machine, their mouths falling open as if in surprise, revealing great rows of massive teeth. We passed over hot muddy lakes boiling and churning with heat. Huge snakes slithered through the mud and onto the land and into the trees. It was beautiful and frightening. In short time I had survived the sinking of a great ocean liner, an uncommon arrival in a hot mud lake, climbed a tree to eat, found a fight against a yellow man with a strange talisman who was assisted by winged creatures, and I had taken sides in the fight. Now, here I was, lost and confused, flying above massive trees in a featherlight craft at tremendous speed, my body feeling more amazing than ever, as if someone had split open my skin and stuck a twenty year old inside of me. It made my head spin.

"Exactly where are you going?" I had to raise my voice to be heard above the wind.

"Perhaps it is best we do not speak of it," Devel said. "You aided us, but our mission is personal. You know what you know about the talisman and need know no more. "

"Understood, but where are you taking me?"

"I am uncertain," Devel said.

"Very well," I said, not wishing to be put out of the craft and left to my own devices. I needed to try and stay with them as long as I could to learn more about this world. Here was better than wandering the forest below; how much better off remained to be seen. As an old sergeant told me around a wad of chewing tobacco once, "If you ain't dead, you're living, and that's a good thing." It was one of the few bits of advice he had given me I had taken to heart, as he was always jealous of my education, which he called white man's talk. I had been blessed with a Cherokee mother who had learned reading and writing in white man's schools and had become a teacher. She always said education didn't belong to anyone other than the one who was willing to take it. She also said education was more than words and marks on paper. She taught me the customs of the Cherokee, taught me tracking, about living in the wild. All the things I might need to survive.

That said, I preferred the comfort of the flying sled to the rawness of the wild world below. This way I had time to consider and plan, though I must admit my considerations and planning were not accomplishing a lot. It was more as if wheels were spinning inside my head, but wouldn't gain traction.

Besides, let me be entirely honest. The woman was why I wanted to remain. I was smitten. Those green eyes were like cool pools and I wanted to dive right into them. I wanted to believe there had been some kind of connection on her part, but considering my current appearance the only person or thing that might love me was a hog that had mistaken me for a puddle to wallow in.

I can't say how long we flew, but I feel certain it was hours. I know that exhaustion claimed me after a while; the cool wind blowing against me, me snug in my seat. I may have felt better and stronger, but I had swam in the cold ocean, pulled myself from a hot mud pit, climbed a great tree and fought a great fight, so I was tired. I drifted asleep for awhile.

When I awoke the sun had dipped low in the sky, and so had we. We were coasting down between large gaps in the great trees. We came to trees so huge they would have dwarfed the redwoods of home. There was even one with shadowy gaps in it the size of small caves.

That's when I saw nearly all the trees had large gaps in them, from head to foot. It was part of their natural construct. As the sun finally set, we flew into one of those tight wooden caverns, Devel parked his airship, and we stepped out.

The night was dark as in the inside of a hole. No moon was visible. What stars there were made a thin light. But then, as I stood there looking out of the gap, soaking in the night, an amazing thing happened. It was as if there was suddenly dust in the air, and the dust glowed. I was confused for a moment, then some of the dust landed on me. It wasn't dust at all, but little bugs that were as silver as the flying sled, shinier. The entire night was filled with them. They gave a glow to everything, bright as the missing moonlight.

I should pause here and jump ahead with something I later learned. There was no moonlight because there was no moon. This world was without one. Of all the things I had trouble getting used to, that was the one that most pained me. No bright coin of light coasting along in the night sky. In place of it were glowing insects, lovely in their own way, but they could not replace in my mind the moon that circled Earth.

Jerrel pulled a length of dark cloth from inside a container in the craft, fastened it to the top and bottom of our cavern. It stuck to where she put it without button or brace or tack or spike. The cloth was the same color as the tree we were in. I realized immediately, that at night, and perhaps in day at a decent distance, it would appear to be a solid part of the tree. We were concealed.

There were cloaks inside the craft's container, red and thick. Jerrel gave Devel one, me one, took one for herself. She turned on a small lamp inside the craft. The source of its power I assumed was some kind of storage battery. It lit up the interior of our cavern quite comfortably.

Jerrel broke out some food stuffs, and though I couldn't identify what she gave me, except for a container of water, I lit into that chow like it was my last meal. For all I knew it was. It wasn't good, but it wasn't bad either.

Before long, Devel lay down and pulled his cloak over him and fell asleep. I was near that point myself, but I could tell Jerrel wanted to talk, that she was interested in me. She began with a few simple questions, most of which I couldn't answer. I told her about the great ocean liner and what had happened to me, how I thought I might be in a dream. She assured me she was real, and not a dream. When she laughed a little, the way she laughed, sweet and musical, it assured me my ears were hearing a real voice, and that my eyes were seeing a strange and rare beauty.

Jerrel tried her best to explain to me where I was. She called the world she knew Zunsun. She took a slate from the craft with a marker, drew a crude drawing of the sun, then placed her planet two places from it. I knew enough basic astronomy to know she was talking about the planet we called Venus.

I learned there was only one language on Zunsun, and everyone spoke it, with varying degrees of accent according to region. I told her about the moon I missed, and she laughed, saying such a thing seemed odd to her, and it was impossible for her to grasp what it was I so sorely missed.

After a time, she opened the back of the sled and took out a large container of water. She also found a cloth and gave that to me to clean up with. I was nervous wiping myself down in front of her, but as she seemed disinterested, I went about it. Running water through my hair and fingers, wiping myself as clean as possible with what was provided. When I was nearly finished, I caught her eye appraising me. She was more interested than I had first thought.

I don't know why, but Jerrel took me into her confidence. Had Devel been awake, I don't know she would have. But I could tell she trusted me. It was an immediate bond. I have heard of and read of such things, but never believed them until then. Love at first sight was always a romantic writer's foolishness to me, but now I saw the idea in an entirely new light, even if it was the light from a battery.

"Tordo has taken our half of the talisman," she said. "The other half is in the city of the bird-men. Once it was whole, and it's powers gave the bird-men a great advantage against us. Our people warred constantly against them. We had no real land to call our own. We moved among the trees, for we couldn't defend ourselves well in a direct fight against the bird-men, not with them having both halves of the talisman, and aided by wings."

"Where does it come from?" I said. "What does it do?"

"I can only speak of legend. The halves have been separated a long time. One half was with our people, the other with theirs. It is said that in the far past the two tribes, weary of war, divided the talisman. This was not something the bird-men had to do, as they were winning the conflict, and we would not have lasted. But their warrior-king, Darat, felt we could live together. Against the advice of his counsel, he gave our people one half of the talisman and kept the other. Divided, it is powerless. United it was a dangerous tool of war. No one remembers how it was made or of what it was made, or even what powers it possesses. When Darat died the tradition of peace carried on for many years with new rulers, but then the recent king of the bird-men, Canrad, was of a different mind. After many generations he wanted the lost power back."

"And one of your people, Tordo, betrayed you?" I said.

Jerrel nodded. "He was a priest. It was his job to protect our half of the talisman. It was kept in a house of worship."

"You worship half of an talisman?"

"Not the talisman. The peace it gives us. Peace from the bird-men, anyway. There are others who war against us, but they are less powerful. The bird-men could be a true threat. It surprises me that Canrad has taken this approach. The peace between us had worked for so long.

"What we are trying to do is stop Tordo before he delivers our half of the talisman. My father, King Ran, sent us. We did not want to alarm our people. We thought to overtake the thief swiftly, as we got news of his treachery immediately, Tordo's and that of the lesser priest, the one who was with him in the flier. But it turned out Tordo was prepared for our pursuit. His actions hadn't been of the moment, but were long prepared. He had the winged men waiting. An assistance given him by King Canrad. Tordo knows how my father thinks, knew he would try and catch him with as little alarm as possible by using a small force. He knew this because Tordo is my father's brother, our uncle."

"Betrayed by family," I said. "There isn't much worse."

"We could go back and raise an army, but it would be too late. Two days and he will be in the city of the Varnin, and they will have both pieces of the talisman, and all of it's power."

"Seems to me, that being the case, you should have flown all night."

Jerrel grimaced. "You may be telling the truth about being from another world."

"You doubt me?" I asked.

She smiled, and it was brighter than the light from the battery. I melted like butter on a hot skillet.

"Let me show you why we do not fly at night. Why no one in their right mind does."

She took hold of the cloth she had placed over the entrance to the tree cave, tugged it loose at one edge, said, "Come look."

I looked, and what I saw astonished me. The sky was bright with the glowing insects, thicker than before. Their light showed me the sky was also full of great bat-like creatures, swooping this way and that. They were the size of Conestoga wagons, but moved more lightly than the flying sled. They were snapping and devouring the shiny bugs in large bites, gulping thousands at a time.

"Fly at night, they will make sure you do not fly for long. We call them Night Wings. They rule the sky from solid dark until near first light, and then they go away, far beyond the trees and into the mountains where they dwell."

"This means your uncle has to stop for the night as well," I said.

"Exactly," she said. "When the Night Wings depart in the early morning, we will start out again, hope to catch up with them. They don't have a tremendous lead, but it's lead enough if they are able to arrive at the city of the Varnin and my uncle delivers the talisman."

"Were you and your uncle ever close?"

"Close?" she said. "No. He was not close to my father. He felt he should have his place of rule. My guess is he hopes to do just that, under the agreement of Canrad of Varnin. He would rather rule with a cloud over his head than not rule at all."

"I would like to assist you. I have a good sword arm. I can help you stop your uncle. I pledge my allegiance to you."

Jerrel grinned when I said that.

"I accept," she said. "But Devel must accept as well."

"That sounds good to me," I said.

"For now, let us rest."

We took our cloaks, stretched out on the floor of our wooden cave. I tried to sleep, and thought I would have no trouble, exhausted as I was. But I merely dozed, then I would awake thinking I was fighting the waters of the Great Atlantic, only to find I was indeed on Venus, sleeping in a tree, and sleeping not far away was the most beautiful and enticing woman I had ever known.

I was up when Jerrel and Devel rose.

It was partially dark, but some light was creeping through the cloth over the gap in the tree. Jerrel pulled it loose, let the beginnings of early morning seep in.

Jerrel and Devel moved to an area of our cave away from me and whispered. As they did, Devel would glance at me from time to time. His face was a mixture of emotions, none of them appeared to be amused.

After a moment Devel came to me, said, "Jerrel trusts you. I feel I must. Her judgment is generally sound."

"I assure you," I said. "I am trustworthy."

"Words are easy, but you will have your chance to prove your loyalty," he said. "Don't let us down."

"Did I let you down in the fight?"

"No. But what we face from here on out will be much worse. It will try all of us."

"Then put me to the test," I said.

We flew away from the tree and into the morning sky. As we went, the sun grew large and the sky grew bright. The glowing bugs were long gone to wherever they go—some in the gullets of the Night Flyers—and the hungry bat things were gone as well. We sailed on into the bright light and before long it was less bright and the clouds above were dark and plump with rain. Finally, the rain came, and it came hard and fast and began to flood the seats on the craft.

Devel guided our flying sled down and under the lower limbs of the trees. We dodged in between them swiftly, and close to limbs that for a moment looked like inevitable crash sites. But he avoided them, flicked us through clusters of leaves, and then down under a series of trees that were smaller in height than the others, yet wide and numerous of branch with leaves so thick the rain could hardly get through. It was as if a great umbrella had been thrown over us. As we went, the sky darkened more and the rain hammered the trees and shook the leaves; random drops seeped through. Then came the lightning, sizzling across the sky with great gongs of thunder. There was a great crack and a flash, a hum of electricity, and a monstrous limb fell from one of the trees.

The lightning, as if seeking us out for dodging the rain, flicked down through a gap in the larger trees and hit one of the smaller ones just before we glided under it. A spot on the limb burst into a great ball of flame and there was an explosion of wood. It struck the front of the craft, hit so hard it was as if a great hand had taken hold of the front of the flying machine and flung it to the ground.

Fortunately we were not flying high at the time, but it was still a vicious drop. Had it not been for the centuries build up of loam from leaves and needles and rotting fruit to cushion our fall, we would have burst apart like a tossed china cup.

We smacked the ground hard enough to rattle our teeth. The machine skidded through the loam like a plow breaking a field. It went along like that for a great distance beneath the trees, then hit something solid that caused us to veer hard left and wreck against the trunk of one of the smaller trees.

It was such an impact, that for a long moment I was dazed. When I gathered my thoughts and put them into some reasonable shape of understanding, I examined my surroundings. I was in the middle seat of the flying sled, Devel ahead of me, Jerrel behind. But she wasn't. She was missing. I struggled out of my seat, got up close to Devel. He wasn't moving. He couldn't. He was dead. A short limb jutting out from the tree had been driven securely through his chest, bursting his heart. His body was painted in blood.

I fell off the crumpled craft, landed on the ground and started to crawl. When I got enough strength back to manage my feet under me. I searched around for Jerrel, screamed her name.

"Here," she said. I turned, saw her rising up from behind a pile of leaves and branches. She was scratched up, but from where I stood she looked well enough, all things considered.

When I got to her she surprised me by taking me into her arms, clutching me to her.

"Devel?" she asked.

I gently freed myself from her embrace, shook my head. She made a squeaking noise and fell to her knees. I squatted beside her, held her as she shook and cried. As if to mock us, the sky grew light and the rain stopped. The world took on a pleasant, emerald glow.

★ ★ ★

I was still astonished to find that at death all that was done in way of ceremony was that the dead were placed on the ground. I assumed in the humid air of Venus, aided by insects and internal decay, bodies would soon lose their flesh and find their way into the soil. But it was still disconcerting to see Devel pulled from the machine by Jerrel, stretched out on the soil to be left. Jerrel weeped over him, violently, and then she was through. She left him, as she said, to Become One With The All. I convinced her to stretch his cloak over him, though she thought it was a waste of material. I know how this makes her sound, but I assure you, this was custom. I guess it was a little bit similar to some American Indian tribes leaving the corpses of the dead on platforms to be consumed by time and elements.

We traveled forward. The sky had completely cleared and the storm had moved on. We could hear it in the distance, roaring at the trees and the sky. I don't know how long we walked, but finally we came to a clearing in the wilderness, and in the clearing were mounds of giant bones. Some were fresh enough that stinking flesh clung to them, others had almost disappeared into the ground itself. Teeth gleamed in the sunlight. In the distance the dark rain clouds moved as if stalking something, lightning flashed and thunder rolled and the wind sighed.

"It's a kind of graveyard for the great beasts," Jerrel said, looking around.

It was indeed. It went on for what I estimate to be ten or fifteen miles long, a half-mile wide.

We had brought some supplies from the crippled flying sled with us, and we found the shade of some very large and well-aged bones, sat down in the shade the bones made, ignored the smell from still rotting flesh, and ate our lunch. It was an odd place for a meal, but our stamina had played out. We sat and Jerrel talked about Devel. It was minor stuff, really. Childhood memories, some of it funny, some of it poignant, some of it just odd, but all of it loving. She talked for quite a while.

When our strength was renewed, we continued. I guess we had walked about a mile among the bones when we found her uncle's airship. It was blackened and twisted and smacked down among a rib cage that looked like the frame of a large ship. The man I had seen before, the one who had been driving the craft, was still in it, though some creature had been at him—had actually sucked the flesh from his head and face. But it was him. I could tell that, and if I had any doubts Jerrel dismantled them. She drew her sword and cut off his fleshless head and kicked it into a pile of the bones.

"Traitor," she said. I saw then not only the beautiful woman I had fallen in love with, but the warrior, and it frightened me a little.

"The question," I said, "is where is your uncle? Wait. Look there."

A little father up, among the bones, were the wrecked bodies of several bird-men, blackened and twisted and scorched by fire.

"The lightning hit them same as us," I said. "Maybe your uncle was killed."

But we didn't locate his body. Perhaps a beast had found him, but it was also possible that he was journeying on foot to the kingdom of the Varnin.

"This means we may catch up with him," I said.

Before long I spied his tracks in the soft soil, pointed them out. Jerrel could find Varnin without tracking her uncle, but it was him and the talisman we wanted, so the tracks were encouraging.

It was near night when we finally passed the lengthy stacks of bones. We edged toward the forest. The trees, low down and high up, were full of ravaging beasts, but the open land worried me most. Anyone or anything could easily spot us there.

Edging along the trees, moving swiftly and carefully as possible, we were taken aback by the sudden appearance of half a dozen beasts with men mounted on them. My fear had been realized. They spotted us. The beasts they were riding looked remarkably like horses, if horses could have horns and were shorter and wider with red and white stripes. They were guided in a way similar to horses as well, bits and bridles, long, thin reins. The riders were seated in high-set saddles, and as they came closer it became apparent they were not human at all.

Humans have flesh, but these things had something else. Their skin was yellow like Jerrel's skin, but it was coarse and gave one the impression of alligator hide. They had flaring scales around their necks. Their features were generally human-like, but their noses were flat as a coin, little more than two small holes. Their foreheads slanted and the tops of their heads peaked. Their mouths were wide and packed with stained teeth and their round eyes were red and full of fiery licks of light. They were carrying long lances tipped with bright tips of metal. Short swords with bone handles bounced in scabbards at their hips. Closer yet, I saw there were little glowing parasites flowing over their skin like minnows in a creek.

Jerrel said, "Galminions. They are eaters of human flesh. Robbers. They run in packs. And they smell."

They came ever closer. Jerrel was right. They did smell, like something dead left under a house.

"Ah," said the foremost rider, reining his mount directly in front of us. The others sat in a row behind him, smiling their filthy teeth. "Travelers. And such a good day for it."

"It is," Jerrel said. "We thought a stroll would be nice."

The one who had spoken laughed. The laugh sounded like ice cracking. He had a peculiar way of turning his head from side to side, as if one eye were bad. When the sunlight shifted I saw that was exactly the problem. He was blind in that eye; no red flecks there. It was white as the first drifts of snow in the Rockies.

"How is your stroll?" said Dead Eye.

"It's been warm, and it's quite the hike," Jerrel said, "but it has been amusing. It has been so good to speak to you. We must be on our way. We wish you good day."

"Do you now?" said Dead Eye. He turned in his saddle and looked back at his companions. "They wish us good day."

The companions laughed that similar laugh, the one that sounded like ice cracking, then made leathery-shifts in their saddles.

"It's good to see we're all in a cheery mood," Jerrel said.

When Dead Eye turned back to us, he said, "I am cheery because we are going to kill you and eat you and take your swords. But mainly we're going to kill you and eat you. Maybe we'll start eating you while you're alive. Of course we will. That's how we like it. The screams are loud and the blood is hot."

"You will dance on the tip of my sword," I said. "That is what you will do."

"And what are you exactly?" said Dead Eye.

"A black man."

"I can see that. Were you burned?"

"By the fires of hell. Perhaps you would like a taste of hell itself."

"What is hell?"

I had wasted my wit. "Never mind," I said. "Let us pass, or—"

"I will dance on the tip of your sword," Dead Eye said.

"Exactly," I said.

"What about the rest of us," he said. "Shall they dance as well."

"I suppose that between our two swords there will be dancing partners for all of you."

This really got a laugh.

"He is not joking," said Jerrel.

"We will be the judge of that," Dead Eye said. "For we are not jokesters either."

"Oh, I don't know," I said. "You look pretty funny to me."

My comment was like the starter shot.

They came as one in a wild charge. Jerrel and I worked as one. We seemed to understand the other's next move. We dodged into the trees, and the Galminions followed. The trees made it difficult for them to maneuver their beasts, but we moved easily. I sprang high in the air and came down on the rider nearest me with a slash of my sword, severing his head, spurting warm blood from his body like the gush from a fountain.

Jerrel lunged from behind a tree, and avoiding the ducking horned head of one of the mounts, stuck it in the chest. With a bleating sound it stumbled and fell, rolled about kicking its legs, tumbling over the fallen rider, crushing him with a snap of bone and a crackle of bumpy skin.

That was when Dead Eye swung off his steed and came for me, driving his lance directly at my chest. I moved to the side, parried his lance with my sword. The tip of his weapon stuck deep in a tree, and the impact caused him to lose his footing. When he fell, it was never to rise again. I bounded to him and drove my sword deep in his throat. He squirmed like a bug stuck through by a pin. His white eye widened. He half spun on my sword, spat a geyser of blood, shook and lay still.

The others fled like deer.

"Are you all right?" Jerrel asked.

"I am, and believe it or not," I said, "fortune has smiled on us."

For Jerrel riding one of the beasts was uncomfortable and she rode awkwardly. For me it was like being back in the cavalry. I felt in control. The creatures handled very similar to horses, though they seemed smarter. There isn't much that isn't smarter than a horse, by the way. That said, they had a gait similar to mules, making for a less smooth ride.

"You call this fortune?" Jerrel said.

"If your uncle is on foot, yes," I said.

As we rode on, in front of us the clearing went away and a mountain range rose before us. It was at first a bump, then a hump, and finally we could see it for what it was. The mountain was covered in dark clouds and flashes of lightning, all of it seen to the sound of rumbling thunder. The patches of forest that climbed up the mountain were blacker than the trees that gave the Black Hills of the Dakotas their name.

The day moved along, the sun shifted, and so did the shadows. They fell out of the forests and grew longer, thicker, cooler and darker. A few of the shiny bugs came out. We shifted into the woods, found a spot where old wood had fallen and made a kind of hut of trees and limbs. We dismounted and led our animals inside through a gap. I found some dead wood and pulled it in front of the opening. I chopped a lean but strong limb off a tree with my sword and used it to stretch from one side of our haven to the other. On one side of it I placed our mounts, the limb serving as a kind of corral. After removing their saddles and bridles, I used bits of rope from the bag of supplies we had brought from the wreck of the sled to hobble them, a trick Jerrel had never seen before.

Finally we stretched out on our side of the barrier with our cloaks as our beds. We lay there and talked, and you would have thought we had known each other forever. In time the Night Wings were out. They flew down low and we could hear their wings sweeping past where we were holed up. Many of the bugs outside slipped in between the gaps of fallen wood and made our little room, such as it was, glow with shimmering light.

Jerrel and I came together at some point, and anything beyond that is not for a gentleman to tell. I will say this, and excuse the dime-novel feel to it. My soul soared like a hawk.

Next morning we were up early, just after the Night Wings and the glowing bugs abandoned the sky. We saddled up and rode on out. From time to time I got down off my critter and checked the ground, found signs of our quarry's tracks, remounted and we continued. By the middle of the day we had reached the mountain and were climbing up, riding a narrow trail between the great dark trees.

The weather had shifted. The dark clouds, the lighting and thunder had flown. As we rode from time to time I saw strange beasts watching us from the shadows of the forest, but we were not bothered and continued on.

Late in the day I got down and looked at our man's tracks, and they were fresh. Our mounts were giving us the final edge on his head start.

"He is not far ahead," I said, swinging back into the saddle.

"Good. Then I will kill him."

"Maybe you could just arrest him."

"Arrest him?"

"Take him prisoner."

"No. I will kill him and take back the talisman."

I figured she would too.

The trail widened and so did our view. Up there in the mountains, nowhere near its peak, but right in front of us at the far end of the wide trail, we could see the city of the bird-men. The great trees there had grown, or been groomed, to twist together in a monstrous wad of leaves and limbs, and mixed into them was a rock fortress that must have taken thousands of bird-men and a good many years to build. It was like a castle and a nest blended together with the natural formations of the mountain; in places it was rambling, in others tight as drum.

I said, "Before we come any closer, we had best get off this trail and sneak up on our man. If we can jump him before he enters the city, then that's the best way, and if he is inside already, well it's going to be difficult, to put it mildly."

Jerrel nodded, and just as we rode off the trail and into the dark forest, a horde of bird-men came down from the sky and into the thicket with a screech and a flash of swords.

Surprised, we whirled on our mounts and struck out at them. It was like swatting at yellow jackets. I managed to stick one of the creatures and cause him to fall dead, but as he fell his body struck me and knocked me off my mount. I hustled to my feet just as Jerrell ducked a sword swing, but was hit it the head by the passing hilt of the sword. She fell off her beast and onto her back and didn't move.

I went savage.

I remember very little about what happened after that, but I was swinging my sword with both skill and insane fury. Bird-men lost wings and limbs and faces and skulls. My sword stabbed and slashed and shattered. I was wet and hot with the blood of my enemies.

To protect themselves they flapped their wings, lifted up higher, and dove, but they were never quick enough and were hindered by the thickness of the trees and my speed was beyond measure. I leaped and dodged, parried and thrust. I raged among the flapping demons like a lion among sheep.

Finally it was as if all the bird men in the world appeared. The sky darkened above me and the darkness fell over me, and down they came in a fluttering wave of screeches and sword slashes and axe swings.

I was a crazed dervish. I spun and slung my blade like the Reaper's scythe, and once again they began to pile up, but then I was struck in the head from the side, and as I tumbled to the ground, I thought it was the end of me.

I couldn't have been down but for a moment when I felt a blade at my throat and heard a voice say, "No. Bring him."

Jerrel and I were lifted up and carried. My sword was gone. I was bleeding. I saw walking before the pack of bird-men, Tordo, Jerrel's traitorous uncle.

We were hoisted out of the forest and onto the trail, carried up toward the amazing twists of forest and stone. As we neared I saw small clouds of smoke rising from stone chimneys, and in loops of groomed limbs I saw large nests made of vines and sticks and all manner of refuse. The nests were wide open, but they were built under the great limbs and leaves of trees that served as a roof. Beyond them there was an enormous tree, the biggest I had seen on my world or this one, and there was a gap in it that served as an opening into the city proper. A great draw bridge had been dropped, and it stretched out over a gap between trees and mountain, and the gap was wide and deep beyond comprehension. Over the draw bridge we were carried, and into the great fortress of wood and stone.

My thought was that Jerrel was already dead and I was next, and let me tell you true as the direction north, I didn't care if I died. With Jerrel lost, I wished to die.

As it turned out, I didn't die. And neither did Jerrel. I didn't realize she was alive until we found ourselves in the bowels of the fortress in a prison that was deep inside the cave of a tree. A series of metal bars served as our doorway. Looking through the bars I could see a long corridor that was also the inside of a tree, and there were two guards nearby, one with a lance, one with an axe, both with expressions that would make a child cry.

In our cell they dropped us down on some limbs and leaves that served as beds. There was a peculiar odor. The only thing I can equate it with is the smell of a hen house on a hot damp afternoon.

I knelt over Jerrel, lifted her head gently. "My love," I said.

"My head hurts," she said. The sound of her voice elated me.

"I guess so. You took quite a lick."

She sat up slowly. "Are you okay?"

"I got a bump myself, behind my ear."

She gingerly touched it with the tip of her fingers. "Ow," she said

"My sentiments exactly. What I don't understand is why they didn't kill us."

"I think, in my case, my uncle wants me to see the ceremony."

"What ceremony?"

"The linking of the two halves of the talisman. The acquisition of the greatest power on our planet. He wants me to see what he has achieved before he puts me to death. Wants me to know the deed is done, and I have failed to prevent it, and then we die."

"If you ain't dead, you're living, and that's a good thing," I said.

It took her a moment to take that in. It was as if whatever power allowed my words to be translated to her language had lost a beat. After a moment she laughed her musical laugh. "I think I understand."

"We won't give up until we're beyond considering on the matter one way or the other," I said.

"I love you, Jack," she said.

"And I you." We allowed ourselves a kiss. Yet, in spite of my bravado, in spite of the repeating of my old sergeants words, I feared it might be our last.

"Love is a wonderful steed," said a voice, "ride it as long as you can."

We looked up, and there above us, sitting on a ridge of stone was a bird-man, his feet dangling. He looked youngish, if I can claim any ability of judging the age of a man who looks a lot like a giant chicken crossed with the body of a man. A very weak looking chicken. He appeared near starved to death. His head hung weak. His ribs showed. His legs were skinny as sticks, but there was still something youthful about him.

"Who are you?" I asked. It wasn't a brilliant question, but it was all I had.

"Gar-don," he said, and dropped off the ledge, his wings taking hold with a fanning of air. He settled down near us, his legs weak and shaky. He sat down on the floor, his head sagged, he sighed. "I am a prisoner, same as you."

"Gar-don," Jerrel said. "The former king's son. His heir."

"That was how it was supposed to be, but no longer. I was usurped."

"Canrad," said Jerrel.

"Yes," Gar-don said, "Now he is king. And I am here, awaiting the moment when he is able to acquire the rest of the talisman, and from what I overheard, that moment has arrived."

"Yes," Jerrel said. "For all of us. I am Jerrel, Princess of Sheldan."

Gar-don lifted his head, took a deep breath, said, "I know of you. I am sorry for your fate, and his."

"Jack," I said. "I am called Jack."

"I shall go out as a prince," Gar-don said. "I will not beg. My horror is not my death, but what the two halves of the talisman can do. Canrad will possess immense power."

"What does this power do?" I asked.

"We only have legend to explain it to us. It gives him the power over spirits and demons from the old trees."

"The old trees?" I said.

"Giant trees that contain spirits of power," Jerrel said. "Those kind of trees no longer exist. They ceased to exist before I was born, before my father was born, his grandfather and so on. The spirits are contained in the two halves of the talisman."

"Canrad will be able to control the people then," Gar-don said. "They, like my father, and myself, were perfectly happy with our peace treaty. Only an insane being wants war. The people only follow Gar-don because they fear him. All uprisings have been destroyed, or the participants have gone into hiding. After today, they might as well never have existed, for he will control anyone and everyone with his new powers. He will not be able to be defeated."

"But you don't know actually know how he will do that?" I said.

"I have only heard of the legend," Gar-don said. "The power of the spirits, the demons of the trees. Exactly what they are capable of, I do not know. Our people have always feared the talisman, and knowing now that it will be united, no one will resist him. It would be useless."

There was a clatter of sound in the hallway. Gar-don stood weakly, said, "It seems we are about to find out the exactness of the talisman's power."

They came for us, unlocking our cell, entering quickly. To be sure of our compliance there was a horde of them with long spikes and strong nets and an angry attitude. I managed to hit one with my fist, knocking him to the floor in a swirl of dust and feathers. Jerrel kicked another. Gar-don tried to fight, but he was as weak as a dove. They netted the three of us, bagged us, kicked us awhile, then hauled us away like trapped vermin being take to a lake to be drowned.

We were brought to a large throne room, that like the overall stronghold was made of stone and was combined with the natural strength of trees and limbs and leaves. Enormous branches jutted out of the walls high above our heads, and perched on them like a murder of ravens, were bird-men and bird-women—the first females I had seen of that race. An occasional feathered drifted down from above, coasted in the light.

Above that perch on which the bird-people were seated was a tight canopy of leaves, so thick and layered it would have taken an army of strong warriors many days to hack their way through it; actually, I'm not even sure they could do it in years.

They brought us in and held us close to the floor in our nets. We could see through the gaps in the netting. Besides the bird-people on the limbs above, the throne room was packed with others, some of them warriors, many of them nobles, and some citizens. We were the spectacle, and all of the bird-people had been summoned to witness whatever ceremony was at hand. I assumed it would not be a parade in our honor.

On a dais was a throne and on the throne was a large winged man who looked as if an ancient human being, fat of body, thin of legs, with a head like a warped melon, had been mated to a Condor and a buzzard, all of him swathed over with warts and scars and age. A golden cloak draped his shoulders, and except for half the talisman on a chain around his neck, he wore nothing else. His eyes were dark and the color of old, dried pine sap. This, of course, was King Canrad.

Tordo stood near the throne, one hand on its back support. There were guards on either side of King Canrad and Tordo. The room was full of warriors as well.

Canrad nodded at Tordo. Tordo stepped to the center of the dais, removed his half of the talisman from his neck, and lifted it up with both hands. Sunlight coming through an open gap behind the king glittered across the talisman like sunlight on a trout's back.

"What say you?" said the king.

The crowed cheered. It sounded like the sort of cheers we Buffalo Soldiers used to give the lieutenant when he rode by on horse back. A white man who led us like we couldn't lead ourselves, as if our color tainted our intelligence. It was a cheer, but it came from the mouth, not the soul.

The king said, "The old order is here. Gar-don, son of the former king, who was not worthy and shall not be named is also here. He will see how a true king shows his power."

"It is you who is not worthy," Gar-don called out from his netted position on the floor.

"Strike him," said the king. "One of the warriors stepped forward and brought the staff of his spear sharply across Gar-don's back. Gar-don grunted.

"We also have among us the daughter of King Ran of the Sheldan," said the king. "A rather inferior race in my opinion. Add a black man-thing that I can not define, nor can anyone else, and we have three enemies of the throne. The gods will welcome their death. They will be the first to die by the power of the talisman. I will call up all the demons of the trees and they will render these worthless creatures into wet rags."

"I know your law," Jerrel said, pushing herself to her knees under the net. "I ask my right to challenge you, or your second. If I win, our lives will be spared."

"I am too old to be challenged," said the king. "I have no intention of sullying myself with a duel. Nor will I sully one of my men. Why should I? You have the right by our law to make a challenge, and I, as king, have the right to refuse. I refuse. Be silent."

King Canrad leaned forward on his throne. I could almost hear his bones creak. His wings trembled slightly. He looked like a gargoyle rocking on its ledge. He said to Tordo, "Bring me the power."

Tordo hesitated, then moved toward him. King Canrad held out his hand. "Give it to me."

Tordo held his half of the talisman forward with his left hand, and as the king reached to take it, Tordo sprang forward, snatched at the talisman around the king's neck, yanked it loose of its chain.

Links of chain clattered on the floor as Tordo slammed the two pieces of the talisman together with a loud click. He lifted it above his head with a smile. He yelled out a series of words, an incantation. I understood the words, but not their jumbled purpose.

And then the spell was finished, and . . .

. . . Well, nothing. It was as quiet in the throne room as a mouse in house slippers. From somewhere in the crowd there was a cough, as if someone had a mouthful of feathers, which considering who was in the room, could have actually been the case.

Tordo's gleeful expression died slowly. He said a word that didn't translate, but I had an idea what it meant. He turned slowly and looked over his shoulder. He had gone from a potential wizard of the trees to a fool with two connected pieces of jewelry.

The guards hustled up from the bottom of the dais, their spears raised, ready to stick Tordo.

"No," said the king. "Give me the talisman first."

One of the warriors tugged it from Tordo's hands, removed his sword as well, gave the talisman to the king. The king held it in his hands. He looked at it the way fisherman might look at his catch, realizing it had appeared much larger under water. "It is useless. It is a lie." He lifted his eyes to Tordo. "I will make your death a long one."

While they were so engaged, and all eyes were on them, I lifted an edge of the net, crawled out from under it and seized one of the bird-men. I drew his sword from its sheath and shoved him back. I sprang toward the dais. A warrior stepped in front of me, but I jabbed quickly and the sharp blade went through his eye and down he went.

With my newfound abilities renewed, I leaped easily to the dais and put my sword to the king's throat.

The guards on either side of the throne started toward me.

I said to the king, "Give the order to free the lady and Gar-don, or I will run this through your throat."

The king's body shook. "Free them," he said.

The net was lifted. The warriors around them parted. I noticed there was a rearranging of soldiers, some shifted out of one group and into another. It was a good sign. They were showing their division.

I said, "Those who wish the king well, fear the point of my sword. Those who wish him ill, perhaps you would enjoy my sword thrust. We shall see which is more popular."

There was a slight murmur.

By this time Jerrel and Gar-don had joined me on the dais. They stood near me and the king. Jerrel picked up the pike of the guard I had killed. Tordo hadn't moved; he feared to move.

Gar-don said, "I am your king. I am the son of the true king, who was the son of a king, and the king before that. Today the talisman failed Canrad and Tordo. The spirits within it do not wish their will to succeed. They do not wish their powers used for something so pointless as killing and destruction and war. It is peace they want. It is peace they have allowed. And I suggest we obey their will and continue on that path, lest they turn on us and destroy us all."

Someone said "Gar-don, our king."

A moment latter this was repeated, and then someone else said the same, and then voices rose up from the crowd and they filled the room, and the voices came not from the mouths of the frightened, but from the souls of true believers.

There were a few who for a moment seemed unwilling to make the change to Gar-don, but they were vastly outnumbered, and those who tried to defend Canrad were quickly dispatched in a wave of bloody anger. If there was a lesson to be learned from Gar-don's remarks about the talisman, they hadn't actually learned it, which meant the bird-people were as human as the wingless. They were not ready to accept the talisman was nothing more than an ancient myth.

Gar-don took the talisman, held it up as Tordo had done. He was still weak and struggled to hold it aloft. But his spirit was strong. He spoke so loudly his words could be heard at the back of the room and up into the leafy canopy.

"The power of the talisman will remain unused. Half of it will go back with Princess Jerrel, back to her city and her king, where it will continue to remain powerless, and our peace will continue."

"What of him," said a bird-woman, stepping forward to point a long finger at Tordo.

Gar-don turned his head to Tordo, studied him. He was about to speak when Jerrel beat him to it. "Gar-don, King of the Varnin," she said. "I ask you to sanction my right to combat with Tordo. He has stolen from my family. He has insulted my family. And I desire to insult him with the edge of my blade."

"And if you lose?" said Gar-don.

"I won't," Jerrel said. "But if I do, let him go. Banish him."

"Don't do this," I said. "Let me take your place."

"I am as good a warrior as any other, my love."

"Very well," said Gar-don. "But before that . . ."

He turned to the former King Canrad.

"I banish you. As of now, you will rise and you will go away, and you will never come back."

The old man rose, and in that moment, seeing how weak he was, I almost felt sorry for him. Then a blade came out from under his cloak and he stabbed at Gar-don. I caught Canrad's arm just in time, twisted. It snapped easily. He screeched and dropped the dagger. I let him go.

Gar-don leaned forward and looked into Canrad's eyes. "I see emptiness."

Gar-don weakly picked up the dagger Canrad had dropped. He seemed strong all of a sudden. "It will not matter what I do, Canrad, you are dead already." With that, he jammed the blade into the former king's chest. The old man collapsed in a cloaked wad, and immediately a pool of blood flowed around him.

"Give Tordo a sword," Gar-don said, turning back to the situation at hand. "Death is your loss, Tordo. Banishment is your victory."

Jerrel dropped the pike and was given a sword.

Tordo was given a sword. All of the disappointment of the moment, every foul thing he was, bubbled up and spewed out of him. He attacked with a yell. He bounced forward on the balls of his feet, attempting to stick Jerrel. Jerrel glided back as if walking air.

Everyone on the dais moved wide of their blades as they battled back and forth, the throne sometimes coming between them. Once

Jerrel slipped in Canrad's blood, and in spite of this being a private duel, I almost leapt to her aid, but Gar-don touched me on the arm.

"It is not done," he said.

Tordo put one boot on Canrad's lifeless neck and used it as a kind of support to lift him up and give him more of a downward thrust. But Jerrel slipped the lunge.

Tordo sprang off Canrad's lifeless neck and made a beautiful thrust for her face. I let out a gasp of air. It was right on target.

At the last moment Jerrel dropped under his thrust, which lifted the hair on her head slightly, and drove her weapon up and into his belly. He held his position, as if waiting for his form to be admired, then made a noise like an old dog with a chicken bone in its throat, and fell flat on his face. Blood poured out of him and flowed into the puddle of gore that had fanned out from beneath Canrad.

Jerrel studied the corpse of Tordo for a moment. She took a deep breath, said, "I have drawn my kin's own blood, but I have avenged Tordo's treachery and honored my father."

Gar-don stepped forward and surveyed the crowd. He lifted his chin slightly. The response to this was another cheer from the multitude, and this one was more than from the throat. It was from deep within the soul.

There were great celebrations, and we were part of it. It was pleasant and necessary to the new agreement between kingdoms, but I was glad when it ended and we were given back the mounts we had taken from the Galminions, sent on our way with supplies, fanfare, and of course Jerrel's half of the talisman.

As we rode along the wide trail in the morning light, winding down from the great lair of the bird-people, I said, "Do you think Gar-don's people believed what he said about the talisman?"

"Perhaps they did," Jerrel said. "Perhaps some did. Perhaps none did. The only thing that matters is there was no great power when the two pieces were united. It's just a legend."

"Designed to prevent war between your people and theirs," I said. "That seems like a legend worth believing. The halves of a great power divided so neither has a unique and overwhelming power over the other."

"Devel would be amused," she said.

We experienced a few adventures on our way to Jerrel's kingdom, but they were minor, mostly involving brigands that we dispatched with little effort, a few encounters with wild beasts. When we arrived in the land of Sheldan and Jerrel explained all that had happened to her father, I was afforded much curiosity, mostly due to the color of my skin.

I was thanked. I was rewarded with a fine sword and scabbard. I was given a prominent place at King Ran's table, and it was there that Jerrel told him that we were to marry.

It was the first I had heard of it, but I was delighted with the idea.

That was some time ago. I am sitting now at a writing desk in a great room in this Sheldan castle made of clay and stone. It is dark except for a small candle. I am writing with a feather pen on yellow parchment. My wife, the beautiful warrior Jerrel, sleeps not far away in our great round bed.

Tonight, before I rose to write, I dreamed, as I have the last three nights. In the dream I was being pulled down a long bright tunnel, and finally into the cold, dark waters of the Atlantic, washing about in the icy waves like a cork. The great light of a ship moved my way, and in the shadows of that light were the bobbing heads of dying swimmers and the bouncing of the *Titanic*'s human-stuffed rafts. The screams of the desperate, the cries of the dying filled the air.

I have no idea what the dream means, or if it means anything, but each night that I experience it, it seems a little clearer. Tonight there was another part to it. I glimpsed the thing that brought me here, pulled me down and through that lighted tunnel to Venus. I fear it wishes to take me back.

I finish this with no plans of it being read, and without complete understanding as to why I feel compelled to have written it. But written it is.

Now I will put my pen and parchment away, blow out the candle, lie gently down beside my love, hoping I will never be forced to leave her side, and that she and this world will be mine forever.

HELPING HAND

★

by Claudine Griggs

The laws of physics are as cold and absolute as the vacuum of space. It's a lesson that Alexandria Stephens knows better than most. For years she's worked in the vacuum. But when she finds herself stranded with no hope of rescue, she'll learn something new: that the cold equations of outer space are no match for her fiery determination to live.

ALEXANDRIA STEPHENS knew she was going to die a slow, cold death in space. She floated fifteen meters from her capsule, a single-pilot maintenance shuttle that could operate in low- or high-Earth orbit.

Construction expenses for single-operator vehicles offered all kinds of economic advantages, especially considering the slender profit margins for satellite or orbital-platform contracts. Moon shuttles required two-to-six-member crews, but market forces made smaller transports the only viable option for near-Earth missions. Alexandria's vehicle was durable and maintained by Glen Michaels, an old-school aerospace mechanic whom she trusted like a brother, though Alexandria often double-checked his work while they drank beer and argued about emerging technologies. They both understood that the ship was everything; if trouble developed, shuttle pilots were more than inconvenienced.

But the occasional death of a pilot did not deter the corporate suits. Number-crunching lawyers and actuaries demonstrated that Space Jockeys, Inc., could lose a shuttle and pilot every eighteen months and still turn a profit—including replacement costs, death benefits, and liability payments. They were still serious about safety, and the actual twenty-year average loss rate was one worker per thirty-two point three months, which included a three-man crew that crashed last year on approach to the Eagle Monument construction site at Tranquility Base. But company officials were more serious about the bottom line.

Alexandria understood the dangers when she signed her flight contract, and she would have enlisted at half the pay and twice the risk. Alex had dreamed of becoming a commercial pilot since age eight and had been with Space Jockeys for seven and a half years, earning a reputation as one of the brightest and fastest technicians on duty—twice turning down supervisory positions to continue fieldwork.

"Even in space," she confided, "pencil pushing is not my style."

She was John Wayne on horseback, riding from satellites to telescopes to orbital lasers. At shift's end, she knew exactly how much range had been covered and how many thoroughbreds had been corralled. She loved it, but now she was dying, a flesh-and-blood meteoroid midway from her shuttle and a geosynchronous satellite that was humming again thanks to a new circuit panel she'd installed in seventy-one minutes flat.

There were forty-five minutes of life support left in her suit, and the rescue ship *Sibert*, like the *Carpathia*, would arrive too late. The *Sibert*'s mission would be body recovery.

Alexandria's motion held steady, spinning back to front about once per minute and approaching the shuttle at negligible speed, slightly off course. But even if she were on course, her air would run dry before she reached the vehicle. And after the O_2 tanks emptied, the heating units would shut down and her body would solid up fast in the minus 240-degree shadow of Earth. She could see the lights of her ship, a soft glow from the nuclear powered satellite, and millions of stars. The deep emptiness of the Pacific Ocean was framed by glowing cities.

Strangely, the lights comforted her even if they could not save her. She needed propulsion from her mobility pack, a damned near infallible piece of equipment with multiple safeguards that had been knocked dead by a pea-sized meteoroid that also cut her forward motion, set her rotating, and disabled her means back to the lifepod that should already be returning her to base. As a result, Alexandria was no longer an astronaut, no longer an $835,000 corporate investment; she was orbital debris to be cleared away when the *Sibert* arrived. Her shuttle was fifteen meters distant, but it might as well be halfway to Andromeda. The meteoroid would have been more merciful had it bulls-eyed her helmet instead of mobility unit. A quick, unaware death.

Now, there was no way to alter her forward motion or rotation, which, as it turned out, was the only enjoyable part of this mess. As she waited for life-support to end, at least she would have a 360-degree view. Alexandria was an optimist, confident to an almost infinite degree, but she was also a physicist. Reality existed. Space was unforgiving. And her future prospects were zero.

Thirty minutes later, still drifting and trying to enjoy the galactic view, Alexandria realized that she had been an idiot, allowing half an hour to slip by without grasping the possibility of life. She and the physical universe were intimate friends, and such friends do not go gently into the night.

A thick Velcro strap held an old-style, standard-issue Jockey Watch around her suit at the left wrist. She pulled the lash as tight as possible, pulled until she feared the band would break though it was rated for 750-degree temperature swings and 1,500 pounds of tensile strength. She refastened the Velcro, trusting the strap to maintain suit pressure.

Then, without hesitation, she unhinged her left glove. The cold vacuum of space stabbed her naked skin. She screamed inside her suit from pain but held firmly onto the glove she had just removed. Everything depended on that hunk of layered fabric and aluminized polymers; Alexandria only hoped it had sufficient mass to nudge her toward the ship—and she had already wasted thirty minutes floating like a cabbage. Of course, her throw must be hard and precise; then she must latch onto the ship with one hand if she got there.

"Probably easier to sink one from mid-court," she thought, "but I'll take the shot."

The pain stopped after her hand froze solid, and Alexandria could focus her thoughts again. She waited until the spin positioned her facing the satellite. Then, offering a prayer to Isaac Newton, she hurled the glove underhanded with the same control she used on the pitcher's mound at Princeton, throwing from the center of her body and aiming dead at the satellite. If her trajectory were correct, the counterforce of a space-glove fastball should propel her toward the shuttle.

There was some good news. Her suit seemed to be holding pressure at the watchband; she veered more or less in the desired direction; and her body rotation increased to only once every thirty seconds. The bad news. She was still traveling too slowly and her track would just miss the shuttle. But Alexandria was no longer a vegetable. There were eleven minutes to solve the problems.

She allowed three minutes for observation and recalculation of the necessary course change. Then, without hesitation, without overthinking, she grabbed her frozen left hand and snapped it off like an icicle. Then she hurled it awkwardly over her head and left shoulder.

Alexandria's counterclockwise rotation slowed, though she was now spinning gradually feet over head, and it took a few minutes to confirm that she on target toward the beautiful, warm, oxygenated *Anthem.* The only questions were: Would she arrive before her suit ran out of O_2? Could she snag the shuttle with one hand and a frozen stump? Would the wristband hold pressure while she maneuvered inside?

Alexandria focused on her goal with each gyration. She counted off meters per minute and tried to slow her breathing. She calculated the moment when she must thrust for a handhold.

"*Anthem* to Jockey Mother. Alexandria calling Jockey Mother. Over."

"Hello, *Anthem!* What's the story, Alex? We calculate you're dead. Over."

"Hey, Georgie Boy. You didn't think I was going down without a fight? Cancel the distress call, and tell Doc there's prosthetic work headed his way. My left hand's an orbiting ice ball. Over."

George liked Alexandria. Never lost or damaged a ship in her career, and she could change a control panel before most techs found the right screwdriver.

"What do you mean?!" said George. "You tell us the jig is up and then shut down communications. Are you in the shuttle? Over."

"All cozied up. Inflated a tourniquet around my forearm and am about to dose myself with Morphinex-D, the all-purpose pain killer, sedative, and antibiotic for today's space traveler. The ship's on auto return and docking because I'll soon be in Happy Land, but I expect the doc to have me mission-ready in four weeks. And if Old Man Jones thinks I'm paying for suit repair on this job, he'll look worse than my mobility pack when I'm done with him. Over."

"While we're on that subject," said George, "folks around the control room are pretty upset. You phone home, tell us you're gonna die, and then shut down the intercom. Not very nice, Alex. Not one bit. Over."

"Sorry, George. Didn't want anyone to hear me crying if I broke down. I would've had to kill you if that happened, so forgive me. I'll buy the beer as soon as I can hold a mug, and tell Jones to pay bonuses to our watch designers. I'd like to kiss them all. Over and out."

MORRIGAN IN SHADOW
★
by Seth Dickinson

The Earth-based Federation has surrendered to the extra-solar Alliance colonies even as the alien Nemesis threatens the existence of humanity. But for a small band of black ops soldiers, the fight is not over. Victory is attainable—but at what cost?

capella 1/8

She's falling into the singularity.

Straight off her nose, shrouded in the warp of its mass, is the black hole that ate a hundred million colonists and the hope of all mankind.

So Laporte throttles up. Her fighter rattles with the fury of its final burn.

Spaceflight is about orbits. That's how one thing relates to another, up here: I whirl around you. I try to pull away. You try to pull me in. If we don't smash each other apart, or skip away into the void, maybe we can negotiate something stable.

But Laporte has learned that sometimes you just need to fall.

Her instruments don't understand what's happening. They're military avionics, built to hunt and kill other warships (other people) in cold flat space. Thus Laporte flies her final mission in a screaming constellation of errors, cautions, icy out-of-range warnings. An array of winter-colored protests from a machine that doesn't know where it is or why it's about to die.

She wants to pat the ship (a lovely, lethal, hard-worn Uriel gunship, built under Martian skies, the skies of her lover's childhood) on its nose and say: there, there, I know exactly how you feel. I'm with you, man. This shit is beyond me.

But it's not beyond her. She knows why she's here.

Laporte never thought she'd be a good soldier. Certainly she'd never planned to be an exceptional killer. Or a mutineer leading a revanchist fleet up out of Earth's surrender and into a crusade across the length of human space. Or, in her final act as a human being (if she dares make claim to that title any more), the avatar of an omnicidal alien power with no intelligence, no awareness, and a billion-year-old cosmic imperative to destroy all higher thought.

But she is all those things now. Born from the tragedy of a war as unnecessary as it was inevitable. Shaped by combat and command and (between it all, pulling in the opposite direction) the love of the finest woman she's ever met.

After all that, after Simms and NAGARI and That Revelation Ken, she knows why she's here. She knows what force plucked her out of paradise and fired her down the trajectory of her short, violent life. To this distant terminus where the universe folds up behind her into a ring of light, everything she loves, everyone she's hurt, receding.

She knows what she's come to kill. The object of her last assassination.

"Boss, this is Morrigan," she tells her flight recorder. "I am descending towards the target."

That's what she calls Simms, even now. Not "love." Boss.

There are three stories here, although they are all one:
What happened in Capella, at the end.
What happened with NAGARI, at the beginning.
What happened between Noemi Laporte and Lorna Simms, which is the most important story, and the one that binds the others.
It begins with the war, and with Lorna Simms—

simms 1/9

For a long time, long enough to murder tens of thousands of people, Laporte thought Simms was dead.

They fought for the United Earth Federation in the war against the colonist Alliance. Laporte and Simms were Federation combat pilots (SQUADRON VFX-01 2FM/FG2101 INDUS—The Wargods, Captain Lorna Simms Commanding) and they were good, so good, they fought like two fists on a drunken boxer, moved by instinct and kill-joy. Of course, a boxer has a body as well as a pair of fists—but they tried not to consider the shape of what connected them.

It wasn't love or lust alone (they were soldiers and their discipline held), nor was it only respect, or fear, or sly admiration. Something of all of this. Whatever connected them, it helped them fight. Simms the Captain, leader of killers, and Laporte her faithful wingman, who was the finest killer.

And they fought to save their Federation, their happy humanist utopia, Earth and Mars and the Jupiter moons—a community of people making each other better. They fought hard.

The war is a civil war. As intimate and violent and hard to name as the bond between Laporte and Simms. An apocalyptic exchange of fratricides between the Federation and its own far-flung interstellar colonists: the Alliance.

For a little while, long enough to give them hope, Laporte and Simms and their Wargods almost won the war.

Then the Alliance clockmaker-admiral, the cryogenic bastard Steele, set a trap. It caught Simms, Laporte, and their whole squadron. Everyone died. It was like a lesson: no band of heroes will save you. No soldiers bound by law and decency.

Out of that ambush Simms and Laporte flew each other to refuge, but it was not refuge enough, the war was in their bones and flesh now: Simms was dying, poisoned by radiation. So they sat together on a crippled warship and they talked about anything but each other.

Remember that? After the ambush at Saturn? Remember adjusting Simms' blankets and pressing your cheek to her throat? Hoping she'd live long enough for both of you to die together, as you'd always dreamed?

(Laporte's dreams are not, it turns out, wholly her own.)

The Alliance was winning, they agreed. Neither of them could see a way to avoid defeat. Neither of them would admit that to the other—not defeat, nor the other thing between them.

Simms passed out. Laporte stayed by her side.

And then a rescue ship came, and with it came al-Alimah, the woman with the gunmetal eyes and the shark-sleek uniform of a Federation black ops officer. She came to tempt Laporte away from Simms with the promise of her other love—

Victory. Al-Alimah came to offer Laporte a chance at victory. And she named the agents of that victory NAGARI.

nagari 1/10

What is victory? Only a fool goes to war without an answer.

The Alliance is winning (has won). What is their victory condition? Their grievance? The fatal casus belli that sparked it all?

The Federation is a gentle state, built on Ubuntu, a philosophy of human connection. So they say: the war began because the Alliance couldn't stand to be alone. They spent two decades rebuilding the severed wormhole to Earth, so they could demand reunification, so they could mobilize our thriving economy to build their warships. So they could galvanize our culture for war.

What the Alliance asked the Federation is what the woman named al-Alimah asked Laporte, as they stood together over the radiation-cooked body of Lorna Simms: give up your gentle ties. Come with me, towards victory. Become a necessary monster.

When the Federation refused to militarize, the Alliance invaded. It was their only hope.

Either they gained the Federation's riches, or they faced the Nemesis alone.

Laporte, she made the other choice, the one her beautiful home could not. She went with al-Alimah. She joined the phantom atrocity-makers called NAGARI and she discovered her own final hope, her endgame for Federation victory.

It'll require the extermination of the entire Alliance population. So be it. She is an exceptional killer. She proved that after she left Simms.

That's how she ended up here, at this raging dead star on the edge of Alliance space, this monument to the power of the alien Nemesis. The tomb of Capella—

capella 2/8

Back in the now: and someone's chasing her.

She sniffs him out by the light of his engines. Something's come through the wormhole behind her and started its own plunge towards the (terrible, empty, fire-crowned) black hole.

Laporte grins and knocks her helmet twice against her ejection seat, crash crash, polymer applause for the mad gentleman on her trail. She knows who it is. She's glad he's come.

She tumbles the Uriel end-for-end so that she's falling ass-first into oblivion and her nose is aimed back, up, towards the universe. There's a ring of night and bent starlight all around her, where the black hole's gravity bends space, but up above, as if at the top of a well, are the receding stars.

And there he is. A fierce blue light which resolves into the molybdenum greatsword-shape of an Alliance strike carrier. *Atreus.* Steele's flagship. Two and a half kilometers of tactical divinity.

Admiral Onyekachi Tuwile Steele prosecuted the war in the Sol theater. A game of remorseless speed chess with fifteen billion pawns in play. In the end, after the Federation exhausted all its gambits and defenses (save one, the one called NAGARI), he won the war.

He's a perfectionist, Steele. A man of etiquette and fine dress, a man who moves like a viper or a Kinshasa runway model. He makes intricate, clockwork plans, predicated on perfect understanding of his opponent's behavior. He cannot abide error.

He made only one.

Nowhere in the final hours of the war, the Mars gambit, the desperate defense and ultimate failure of SHAMBHALA, did he send enough hunter-killers to eradicate Laporte.

And now he has come a-howling after her, propelled by portents and terrors, operating on a desperate, improvised logic. That logic might be: if she wants it, I cannot permit it. If Laporte reaches for a thing, I must deny it to her. She is too dangerous to ever have a victory.

It might be something else. It's dangerous to let your enemy understand your war logic.

simms 2/9

There are three stories here. They all matter.

One is the story of Laporte at Capella, trying to kill billions. That's the ending.

One is the story of Laporte leaving Simms for NAGARI, in the name of victory. That's the beginning.

But in between them is another story, because the road from victory to genocide passes through love. In this middle part, the Federation's civilian government surrendered to the Alliance. And here in the ashes Laporte found Simms alive, Simms found Laporte still (barely) human, they each found the other in the cold scorched wolfpack of the Federation Navy, lurking on the edge of the solar system and contemplating mutiny.

This story is the most important, because it was Laporte's last chance to be a person again.

So: Laporte reaches for Simms. She wants to be close again. She wants to come back.

They're lying side by side in the avionics bay of Laporte's fighter: an alloy coffin as cold as treason. Mostly empty. The terms of the cease-fire have stripped all military electronics from the Federation Navy.

Like their uniforms—taken too. They work in gym clothes and mechanic's overalls. Whenever they breathe the vapor spills out white like a suitbreach. Every ten minutes a dehumidifier clicks on.

Simms shivers. Her hands rattle and she breaks the test pin she's using against the teeth of a server stack. "Shit," she says, closing her eyes. "Fuck."

She survived radiation poisoning. But surviving a wound doesn't erase it. You only rebuild yourself around the scar.

Laporte knifes the RESET switch up, down, up, down. They'll start over. "Slowing me down, boss," she says, trying to take Simms' fear and judo it around, make it funny, disarm its violence. "Slowing me down."

"Fuck you too." Simms clenches and unclenches her fists, one finger at a time. She's longer than Laporte, and stronger. Before she soaked up fifteen grays of ionizing radiation, she could always keep up. "*You* try fingerbanging a combat spacecraft after a lethal dose."

Laporte makes a wah-wah baby noise. Simms laughs. They work for a few more minutes and soon they've made the fighter ready to hold combat software in the spare memory of its navigational systems.

If they're going to mutiny, the mutiny needs its fighters. And Laporte is planning a mutiny.

Simms puts down the test pin and shivers from her scalp to her toes. She looks silver-gold, arid. She is the child of Mongolian steppe and American range and the desert of Mars. She's used to cold. Laporte's afraid that it's not the cold making her shiver. Simms has been listening, the last few days, as Laporte lifts up her scabs and talks about NAGARI, and about her plan for victory.

"They took out all my bone marrow," Simms says. "I'm full of fake bone shit. Medical goo."

Laporte rolls into her (the old words, in a pilot's brevity code: *Boss, Morrigan, tally, visual, press,* It's you, I'm me, I see you, I will protect you) and Simms puts an arm around her. Laporte kisses her under the jaw, very softly, and rests her ear against Simms' collarbone. There's a plastic button rubbing into her cheek but she doesn't mind.

"Seems to work okay," she says. She looked up radiation therapies: desperate transplant of reprogrammed skin cells and collagen glue. She imagined them peeling the skin off Simms' thighs to fill up her bones.

"Yeah." Simms' heart is slowing down, soothing out. It can't find the fight it's looking for. Or it's disciplining itself for what's to come. "I still work."

Laporte looks up from her collarbone to look her in the eye. "Are you going to fly with me?"

Will she fly in the mutiny? Laporte's grand plan, NAGARI's final hope? The Federation has surrendered, but its soldiers, its guardian monsters, do not consent to Alliance rule. They were made to win.

"I don't know yet," Simms says, looking at her hands. Whatever she says next will be an evasion. "I need to know more about your operational plan."

I need to know more about what you've become. What you got up to without me, while I was in the tank with my skin peeling off and glue in my blood.

"I need you out there," Laporte says. She means it to be business, pilot chatter, a tactical requirement. But she's thinking about how she left Simms. How it might have seemed, to Simms, that she had been expended. Cast off as spent ordnance.

Simms makes a soft sound, like she's too tough or too happy to cry.

The dehumidifier wakes up to dry out their words.

capella 3/8

The mutiny is what carried Laporte from the middle to the end.

The Alliance killed the Federation's best soldiers. It battered the Federation into political surrender. But it never beat NAGARI. It never beat Laporte.

When the peace negotiations began, Laporte flew her re-armed Uriel from post to distant post, rallying the Federation's dying strength for the death ride to Capella. Dozens of ships. Hundreds of pilots. Answering to Noemi "Morrigan" Laporte, the last ace, the one who wouldn't let the fire go out.

Laporte airbrushed the suggestion of a raven on her fighter. Its claws are bloody. There is armor in its jaw.

She asked Simms to ride in her back seat as she went to raise mutiny. "A couple undead soldiers, flying the mutiny flag," she joked. "Like a buddy cop thing." But Simms looked away and Laporte thought, what am I doing, how can I ask her to light this war back up, to be the spark that escalates it from atrocity to apocalypse? The war took her skin and melted the inside of her bones. It ripped out the lining of her guts. She can't even shit without fighting the war.

"I'm not mission capable yet," Simms said, and she looked at Laporte as if the war had taken one more vital thing from her. "I hope the avionics work. I broke a lot of test pins in there."

So Laporte flew with al-Alimah instead. Al-Alimah from NAGARI.

The Federation government surrendered but its fleet did not. They struck during treaty negotiations. Laporte's rebel armada fought its way out of Sol by shock and treachery. Breached the blockades in Serpentis. Menaced the Alliance capital in Beta Aquilae.

And as they did, Laporte's NAGARI elite slipped into Vega. One wormhole away from their true goal.

Capella.

Admiral Steele's been chasing Laporte the whole way. Trying to repair his only error. And here they are now, in Capella, at the end of the hunt—Laporte plunging towards the black hole in her little Uriel and Steele's titanic *Atreus* plunging after her.

The Uriel's electronic warfare systems make a deep frightened sound. Laporte's helmet taps her chin and says:

VAMPIRE! ASPECT! STINGRAY! SSM-[EOS]-[notch 000x000]-[20+!]

It'll be missiles, then. A fuck-ton of missiles.

If he turned around now, with all *Atreus'* fuel still coiled up in her engines, Steele could probably stop his fall. Claw his way into a hover above the black hole, and then make the grueling climb up to the wormhole and safety.

But he's accelerating. Chasing Laporte. Risking himself and his entire crew to kill her.

Laporte opens a COM channel. Aims it downward. Into the dark. She has allies here, if they can be made to understand the danger.

"Ken," she sends. "It's me. Don't keep me waiting, old man."

That's why she's come here, to the singularity, to the tomb of Capella. Because the Nemesis made it.

Just as they made her.

nagari 2/10

Ken is a dream of Laporte's. Laporte's dreams are not entirely her own.

Ken happened long before the Alliance rebuilt the wormhole, long before the war—

She was six years old, playing in the yard. Her parents had a house in Tandale, part of Dar es Salaam, where they worked on heavy trains, moving cargo from the Indian Ocean all across Tanzania. Her father was a reserve pilot and her mother was in arbitrage. Little Noemi, left to self-directed education, as was the Ubuntu preference for the young, spent her days building a model train system in the dirt between her water garden and her ant battle arena. But the ants would not stay in the ant battle arena, not even a little—they kept foraying into the train system, no matter how many of them Noemi punitively de-limbed.

Ken suggested she consider the broader logic driving the ants. Ken often gave Noemi advice. Her parents were very proud that little Noemi had actualized such a useful inner friend.

After an exhaustive survey of her territories, Noemi discovered the problem. There was a rival ant colony north of the water garden. The two groups had fallen to war. She studied up on ant diplomacy, complaining into her phone, and concluded there was no pluralist solution. The colonies would compete for hegemony over all available resources. Unless one side achieved a swift victory, lives and labor would be lost on the war. An attritional stalemate could ruin them both.

She uncurled the garden hose and drowned the northern colony. The choice was simple, in that it was easy. It only depended on one thing. She knew and loved the ants in the south of the yard. She cared nothing for the ants in the north. There was no other distinction between them.

When you are a monster, as Laporte certainly is, you have to cling to the things that you love. The ligatures that connect you to the rest of humanity.

If you lose them, you may whirl away.

simms 3/9

Laporte didn't understand the Ken dream until she joined NAGARI. That's the beginning.

What the Alliance asked the Federation is what the woman named al-Alimah asked Laporte. She was a tall woman with gunmetal implants in place of her eyes. She gave Laporte a choice: stay with Simms as she fights the radiation poisoning, or come with me and try to win the war.

"The medics are coming," she said. "You can stay with your Captain until she dies, or until she doesn't. You'll make no difference. None of your talents or capabilities will contribute to her battle."

(Laporte is a wingman and she never leaves her wing leader—)

"Or you can come with me. I'm with a black ops unit. Special moral environment. NAGARI. You know we're losing this war. You know we need you."

(—except when necessary to complete the mission.)

And Laporte thought, if she lives, if she wakes up, I want to be able to say—

Hey, boss. We've won. I took care of everything for you. Did you have a good vacation?

So Laporte took al-Alimah by her tactical gloves and went with her, out of the sweltering briefing room, out of the dying ship where everyone's sweat was hot enough to leave red radiation burns, where their marrow rotted inside their neutron-salted bones.

And that was how she joined NAGARI.

nagari 3/10

NAGARI. A committee of monsters: a federation of sharks. Shaved-skull operators cooking lamb on the naked coils of their frigate's heatsinks. All veterans. Not one in uniform.

There are real psychological differences between Federation and Alliance citizens. Fifty years of sealed prosperity in Sol gave birth to a generation of humans who are very good at living but *very* bad at killing.

That's why the Federation, for all its socioeconomic might, is losing the war. (That's why Laporte thinks the Alliance chose war over peace. They could never win the peace. And they were built for victory.)

But Laporte isn't a good Federation citizen, no oh, that's what Simms told her in their radiation-cooked parley: you're a killer, you need no reason and no hate. It's just you. And that's why you'll be fine without me.

And Simms was right. Laporte has an instinct for violence. And there are others like her, gathered under the mantle of Federation black ops, where the terrain of their violence extends far beyond the battlefield.

"This is your first mission." Al-Alimah briefs her in the back of the mess kitchen as they inventory the remainders. Cumin and cinnamon and allspice blown down over them, but the stink of ozone is stronger. Al-Alimah's eyes are sensors and projectors: they sketch visions for Laporte by scratching her eyes with particle beams. "You will infiltrate an Alliance personnel convoy carrying non-combatant contractors. Dental and culinary services for rear-area bases."

When Laporte blinks the images left by al-Alimah's eyes don't fade.

"You will deploy a neutron weapon against the dormitory ships. Leave no survivors."

Laporte imagines Simms asking: what is the military rationale for this strike, sir? She vows to ask, after the mission. She vows to get good data on the mission effects. She used to keep a kill tally, one strike for each fighter she shot down, one chance to preen and brag for Boss.

She sleeps with a cable in her skull, and she dreams about the strike over and over. When she flies it, it feels like a dream too. The neutron weapon makes no light or sound except the shrieking RAD warnings in her cockpit. She comes home to backslaps and fistbumps and moonshine from the still.

"The objective is atrocity," al-Alimah tells her, when she asks. The NAGARI analyst wears a baggy gray jumpsuit, indifferent to rank and physical presence. "The Alliance uses statistical modeling to predict our tactics. They've learned that we obey a set of moral guidelines. The only way to confound their predictions is to introduce noise."

Noise. Killing all those dentists with radiation was *noise*.

When Simms was irradiated she was very quiet.

Laporte stops spicing her food. She dresses in stark self-washing jumpsuits and she showers cold. The other operators are happy monsters, full of gossip and tall tales, not shy about talking shop or sex. Laporte touches no one. She doesn't talk about her missions. In the gym and the simulator she is laconic and dependable but she never asks for anything. She practices self-denial.

One of the other operators, Europa-born and silver-haired, comes after Laporte for reasons either carnal or tactical. The closest she gets to intimacy, of one sort or another, is when she says: "You act like you're a monk! Monks give up stuff they like, man. Monks deny their pleasures."

That's right. Monsters shouldn't be warm. They shouldn't have fun. Being a monster should feel like it costs.

But the silver woman grins at Laporte, an I-know-you grin, and says, "So when you pretend you hate the work—I know what that means. I know what's up."

Laporte flies noise jobs for months. False flags. Political assassinations. Bycatch enhancement. Straight-up terrorism. She has to round her kill tally to the nearest thousand. She has one of her teeth replaced by an armored transponder, so that someone will know she dies even if her body's vaporized.

Simms would not be proud. Simms fought a war against an invading army, and she hated the fuck out of them. But she had rules. NAGARI is anti-rule. Strategically amoral.

Is this her whole purpose now? Trying to buy the Federation a few extra months through the exercise of atrocity? Missions that violate every tenet of Ubuntu and civilized conflict?

It's war, Simms once said. In war, monsters win. Laporte gathers up that thought and buckles it around herself, for want of Simms, for want of victory.

Is she fighting because victory might mean seeing Simms again? Imagine that. Imagine saying: Hey, boss, you're alive. I neutron bombed a few thousand dentists, and we won the war. Can I buy you a drink?

simms 4/9

Back in the middle. In the story that moves Laporte from NAGARI to the black hole. Her last chance to stay human.

"It's not true," Laporte tells Simms.

They've finished re-arming all the fighters, breaking the ceasefire lock. This is the lean time between the surrender and the mutiny, when the Federation's surviving fleet lurks in the cold on the edge of the solar system, a faithful dog cast out and gone feral. Waiting for Laporte and NAGARI to rouse them to revenge.

"What's not true?" Simms asks. She pokes the fire with her cooking mitt.

They have a trash fire going on the *Eris'* hangar deck. Warships are very good at coping with internal fires, and very bad at serving as long-term habitats. They grew some chicken in the medical tissue loom and now they're burning trash under a plate of thermal conductor, in the hope of making a chicken curry.

"That monsters win," Laporte says. The chicken pops and spatters grease. Simms laughs and Laporte, thinking of dead cells sloughing apart under radiation, shudders. Her transponder tooth, left over from NAGARI work, is cold under her tongue. "In the end, actually, monsters tend to lose. And that's much worse."

"What do you mean?" Simms eyes her up. Simms is still exploring Laporte's new crazy side, separate (in her practical mind) from Laporte's old crazy side, before their long radiation-cooked severance. "Is this something from your NAGARI drug trips? Cosmic insight, plucked from the void?"

"Yeah," Laporte says, remembering the surgical theater, the feeling of cold entheogen slurry pumping into her skull. Where they discovered the truth about Ken. "I wish you'd been there."

"But I was there," Simms says, stirring the fire. The thermal conductor is a cheerful cherry-hot color, and Simms hums as she works, like she's trying to be casual about how much she cares for this idea: the possibility that she was out there, helping Laporte win, even while she was bolted to a triage rig with her bones melting out through needled tubes. "I was in your thoughts. Wasn't I? Isn't that what kept you alive?"

Why would she be so happy about this, about helping Laporte be a good monster, and then, just a day later, refuse to fly with Laporte in the mutiny?

Why?

nagari 4/10

This is what Laporte was up to while Simms' bones were melting:

Laporte flies her terror missions. She goes out alone and she returns alone, and between those stanchions she kills her targets. Her effect on the universe, the vector sum of her actions, is purely subtractive.

She *isn't* fine without Simms. Simms was her captain and her friend, the last tie keeping Laporte in the human orbit. But that's the point, right? Laporte's a monster now. Her past is useful to her only in the way that gunpowder is useful to a bullet. The more pain in it, the better.

The war's falling apart, slouching towards surrender. NAGARI scores victory after horrible victory. But the Federation Navy can't follow their lead. The clockmaker-Admiral Steele outfoxes the Navy again and again, closing in on Earth.

Laporte becomes a kind of leader among the operators, on strength of her efficiency, in admiration of her self-sufficiency. She learns the name of every NAGARI operator, their habits and crimes, their gym schedules (hey man, spot me) and cooking tricks (come on, not this curry shit again). She also learns the callsigns of every active pilot: physiological parameters, operational histories.

But she can't connect the two, the names and the callsigns. When a callsign dies on a mission, she isn't sure who it was until she misses their grunt in the gym, their recipes on the heatsink grill.

The Federation is still losing the war. Her intention is to keep flying until she dies.

But the memory of Simms (and the memory of what she said: you'll be fine, you don't need a reason) drives her mad with competition. She had a competition with Simms! She always wants to be better than her Captain expects.

So when she wakes up from a training dream she goes to al-Alimah and asks: "Why are we doing this? What's the point of noise jobs and neutron bombs, if it's just a way to put off the inevitable surrender?"

She expects the answer she's given herself: Monsters are weapons. It's not up to the weapon to choose targets.

But al-Alimah startles her. As if she is a ghost alive in the memory of childhood Tandale summers, al-Alimah says: "Tell me about Ken."

"What is this?" Laporte stares her down, eye to gleaming post-surgery tactical eye. "Why do you care about that?"

"You told your Captain Simms that you had an invisible friend as a child. He urged you to develop your faculty for violence."

Laporte laughs. It doesn't surprise her that NAGARI knows this shit but it's *hilarious* that they care. "Ants, man. He wanted violence against ants. Ken was an imaginary friend."

Al-Alimah doesn't waver. "During your adolescence, you were treated for schizotypal symptoms. You reported violent ideation, dissociative thoughts, and a fear of outside intrusion. Your first boyfriend left you because he was afraid of you."

Laporte opens her arms in a gesture of animal challenge. "Are you worried," she says, grinning, "that I might be unwell?"

Al-Alimah laughs. She can pretend to be very warm, when she wants, although it's terrifyingly focused. Like all her charm radiates from a naked wire charged red-hot.

"What would Ubuntu have had you do to the ants?" she asks. "What would our Federation's philosophy say to two ant colonies at war?"

Find a pluralistic solution. Locate the structural causes of inter-colony violence. Rework the terrain, so that peaceful competition between colonies can produce a common good.

"Ubuntu is for people," Laporte says. "It doesn't work on ants."

Al-Alimah touches Laporte's wrist with one long, cold finger. "Think about the universe," she says, "and what portions of it belong to people. If Ubuntu applies to the human territory, what is NAGARI for?"

"Oh my God," Laporte says.

She understands instantly. She grasps the higher purpose of NAGARI.

She has a terrible, wonderful, world-burning premonition. A way to win the war.

nagari 5/10

Ask the Alliance, Steele's people, the aggressors and the victors in this terrible war: what is the grievance? The fatal casus belli?

Imagine a republic charged and corroded by perpetual emergency. Scattered across lonely stars. Simmering on the edge of rebellion. They may be tyrants. May also be the bravest and the most tenacious people ever born.

This is what Laporte knows, what NAGARI knows, about their history—

Humanity met something out there. Implacably hostile. Unspeakably alien. Nemesis.

Love is about knowing the rules of your connection. You know how you could hurt her, if you wanted, and she trusts you with this knowledge. And war is about that too. You learn the enemy's victory conditions, her capabilities and taboos. You build a model of her and figure out where it breaks. You force the enemy into unsurvivable terrain, pinned between an unwinnable war and unacceptable compromise.

But what do you do when the rules you use to understand how one thing relates to another stop working? When the other thing has no rules at all?

simms 5/9

Rules about Simms, from the time before radiation and ambush:

The Federation military forbids fraternization in the ranks. While Ubuntu treasures community, emotional attachment can compromise the chain of command.

So at first the fire between them, the charge in the air, bled off in confined ways—

Laporte tried not to look at Simms too much, or too little, so nobody would notice her unusual attention. This is like war logic. When you look for the enemy with your active sensors, you also tell the enemy where you are and what you intend.

When they checked each other's suits they were extremely professional. Soon they realized this was an error, since soldiers are profoundly obscene. But it was too late to start making catheter jokes.

Sometimes they sparred in the gym. Simms was icy and Laporte grinned too much. The whole squadron turned out to cheer. (They're all dead now.)

A new rule, after NAGARI and the Federation's surrender, after al-Alimah puts them back together. A rule they teach other—

You must never hint at your secret fear. The terrible thought that it might have been better if you'd never found each other again.

nagari 6/10

Al-Alimah shares the history of humanity and the Nemesis, the history that Laporte knows from school— and the secret parts NAGARI has collated.

There were two Nemesis incursions.

The first war, the war that divided mankind into Federation and Alliance, began like a nightmare and ended like an amputation. The Nemesis surfaced from the wormhole web and moved across human space erratic and arbitrarily violent. Humanity scored tactical victories (tactical victory is the tequila of combat highs: hot in the moment, hateful in the aftermath) but in the end the Nemesis world-killer called *Sinadhuja* made it all the way to Serpentis.

One step from Earth.

When *Sinadhuja* entered the wormhole to Sol, the Earth fleet resorted to their last hope. A firewall bomb. It cauterized the wormhole connection. Killed *Sinadhuja*, saved the hearth of the human species, and left the rest of mankind out there in the dark.

That's how the Federation and the Alliance became separate things—sometimes that's how you define yourself, in the space when you are separated, when you have abandoned all hope of reunion.

One night, waiting for al-Alimah to appear and task her with another massacre, clawing up gibbets of her gel mattress and then smoothing them back so they vanish into the whole, Laporte realizes that she knows Simms is dead. She has to be. It's naïve to think she survived the radiation. Naïve to imagine an end to the war, a happy reunion, a quiet retreat where they can tend to each other's wounds. Simms is dead.

It would be worse if she were alive. She would hate the monster Laporte, and she would hate herself for leaving Laporte to the monsters. Simms is a hell of a soldier, a superb pilot. That's how she defines herself. A good pilot never leaves her wingman.

What do you call this? The decision to know something not because it is true, but because it's useful?

Out there alone the Alliance survived. Thirty-two years they prepared for the Nemesis to strike a second time. Certain that victory would secure the future of mankind in the cosmos. Certain that defeat would mean extinction.

capella 4/8

She falls engine-first towards the black hole and *Atreus* falls after her with its torch aflame and missiles ramifying out into the space between them in search of the kill geometry, the way to confine her, the solution to Laporte.

Steele's ship outguns her by orders of magnitude. The Alliance fought Nemesis twice. They learned war-craft the Federation has never matched.

Atreus' missiles can make their own jumps. Leap from their first burn straight to Laporte across a stitch of folded space. But the singularity they're all falling for warps space, which makes it hard to jump. So the missiles come at her drunk and corkscrewing or they die in the jump and shear themselves open like fireflies burning too hot.

Not all of them, though. Not all of them. A few make it into terminal attack.

Laporte talks to Simms under her breath. Reporting the situation. *Boss, Morrigan, am spiked, stingray stingray, vampires inbound. Music on. Defending now.*

She rolls her shoulders and arms her coilguns and starts killing the things come to kill her.

And down there, down beneath her, in the groaning maelstrom where space-time frays and shears and starts to fall, where the course of events balances on the edge of inevitable convergence towards a central point, something wakes.

The light of a stardrive, peeling free of the fire. The huge dark mass of something mighty. Molting out of the black hole's accretion disc. Climbing up to meet her.

Ken says, in a voice as young as summer gardens, as old as ants:

Hello, Miss Laporte.

nagari 7/10

"The Alliance started the second Nemesis incursion," al-Alimah says.

They're having dinner together. Laporte's sure this is a dream, but because she sleeps with her nervous system braided into NAGARI's communal dreamscape, it's probably also real.

Al-Alimah wants to talk about Ken.

Laporte picks up her fork and eats. They're in a rooftop café and there's a warm wet wind, storm wind, coming from the north and west. The meal is salmon sous-vide cut into translucent panes of flesh. Like the pages of a carnage book.

When she touches the salmon with her fork it curls up around the tines. "The Alliance attacked the Nemesis?"

"There was an insurrection." Al-Alimah's a long woman, breakable-looking, tall like Simms but not trained to bear her own weight under acceleration. In dreamland she's traded her gray uniform for a rail-slim black gown. She looks like a flechette. A projectile. "Someone broke ranks."

After the first incursion, Nemesis behavior was the province of military intelligence. By political necessity, or perhaps out of some sense of Lovecraftian self-preservation, the Alliance tried to keep the pieces of the puzzle widely separated. But one of their Admirals, Haywain van Aken, finally unified the clues into a grand theory.

"What was it?" Laporte interrupts. The tines of her fork are hypodermic-sharp but she doesn't notice until she's already pierced herself, three points of blood on her lips, inside her cheek.

"We don't know." Al-Alimah shrugs with her hands. The tendons in her wrists are as fine as piano wire. "Not yet. But we know what he did."

Van Aken became convinced he could communicate with the Nemesis. He built a signaling system—almost a weapon, a cousin of the Alliance's missiles: it jumped high-energy particles directly into the mass of the target. Then he went rogue. Hurtling off past the Capella colony and into unexplored space. Possessed by a messianic conviction that he could find the Nemesis and end the war.

Laporte cracks her neck and leans back. Watches Alliance warships moving through the clouds around them, pursuing van Aken into Nemesis territory, overcoming disorganized Nemesis resistance with determination and skill. On the horizon a voice that isn't Admiral Steele's begins to murmur about the possibility of real victory.

"Forward reconnaissance found van Aken's ship adrift in a supernova remnant." Al-Alimah swallows something Laporte never saw her bite. She has a little piercing in her tongue. It's strange to imagine her going to get her tongue pierced. Maybe she put it in herself. "His crew had mutinied. An outbreak of psychosis." The sky flickers with records of violence, directionless, obscene. "Then the Nemesis boarded his ship. They took him."

"What?" Laporte stops chewing. It shocks her to imagine the Nemesis claiming a single human being. That isn't their logic. That's human logic.

"Yes. The Alliance had the same question." Al-Alimah points to the sky. Jawed shadows gather on the sun, four-kilometer reapers studded with foamed neutronium. "Three days later, scouts sighted the first of eighty-six *Sinadhuja* world-killers converging on human space."

The Alliance fought a harrowing retreat but the Nemesis poured after them, insane, inscrutable, an avalanche of noise. No central point of failure to target, like the single *Sinadhuja* in the first incursion. Nowhere for the Alliance to aim its might. It was like trying to kill a beehive with a rifle. Except that each bee, each *Sinadhuja*, was a match for half the Alliance fleet.

Al-Alimah flashes two peace signs at Laporte. Four stars glimmer on her fingertips: two binary stars. "The war ended in Capella. The Alliance had a colony there. They decided to hold the line long enough to evacuate." Tiny model *Sinadhuja* warships climb out of the webs of her hands, jaws gaping. Like scarabs. Like sharks. "The Nemesis fleet did something to the system's stars. Altered their orbits. It's tempting to read it as a demonstration of power, an act of intimidation or rebuke. Except that the Nemesis never used symbolic violence before."

Four stars roll off her fingertips and spiral down into each other. Supernova light pops, rebounds off al-Alimah's eyes, and collapses into a pinpoint devourer. The black hole.

"A hundred million civilians." Al-Alimah taps her two forefingers together, as if to telegraph the number. "A quarter of their fleet. All lost."

And something more important, too. The thing you lose when you realize that victory is impossible no matter how hard you fight.

Monsters win, Laporte.

Laporte thinks about grand strategy. The Nemesis might return anywhere, at any time. The Alliance needed ships, and weapons, and brilliant science, and something to offer its citizens as proof against despair—a new victory to fight for. So the Alliance did the only thing it could. It set to work rebuilding the way home: reopening the Serpentis-Earth wormhole with Nemesis technology.

And when that home refused to join the great work, the project of human survival, the Alliance resorted to war.

"And so we come to now," al-Alimah says. She leans back, as if she has discharged her duty, and drinks her wine. "Our great predicament."

The war between an Alliance driven by exigency, by the utilitarian, amoral need for survival, and a Federation built on humane compassion, on the idea that you do the right thing no matter the circumstance. How do you fight that war, if you're the Federation? If you can't listen to the Alliance argument without a scream of sympathy?

You make something like NAGARI. A cadre of monsters to do what you cannot.

The sky has changed again. It's Simms up there now. She has a face of triangles and planes, a faceted thing, and it pulls on Laporte, it engages her. Combat pilots decompose all things into geometry: threats, targets, and the potential energies between them.

"Your old Captain." Al-Alimah looks up at her too. "We never wanted to recruit her. Too conventional."

Laporte looks away from Simms, and voices the apocalypse option.

"If we can find some way to make the Nemesis return," she says, "and then collapse the Earth-Serpentis wormhole again, we can let the Nemesis wipe out the Alliance and end the invasion."

If they collapse the wormhole so the Nemesis can't get in, then the Federation will survive. Guarded by light-years of real space. All it will cost is a few billion human lives.

Everything can go back to the way it was. Human paradise. A confined peace.

Al-Alimah is still waiting. Lips curled in amusement. Gunmetal eyes infected with the blind crawling light of distant computation. "That's just utilitarian strategy," she says. "Doesn't take a dream to make that connection. Tell me, Laporte, why do you think I brought you here? What endgame do you think all those terror missions were training you for?"

Ken. A childhood name for a childhood friend.

A man thought he could communicate with the Nemesis. Admiral Haywain van Aken.

Laporte puts her fork through her cheek. In the dream, it doesn't hurt.

capella 5/8

Atreus must see the monster rising behind Laporte. Steele must see the shape of the demon she's conjured up out of the accretion disc. The *Sinadhuja* world-killer is the insignia of everything the Alliance stands against. The monster in the mist. *Atreus* was built in hope of killing it.

Perhaps Steele will target his missiles at the *Sinadhuja*.

Laporte coilguns another incoming missile and it flashes into annihilation so bright her canopy has to black it out like a negative sun. And Steele keeps firing at her. *Atreus* keeps accelerating. If he sees the *Sinadhuja* he doesn't maneuver in response.

Once Steele said, about the war, about his strategy against the Federation:

I employ overwhelming violence. Because my enemies are gentle, humane, compassionate people. Their Ubuntu philosophy cannot endure open war. And the faster I stop the war, the faster I stop the killing. So my conscience asks me to use every tool available.

And Laporte answers him. Look what you conjured up, you brilliant, ruthless bastard. Look what you made. Someone willing to use every available tool to fight back.

Once Simms said, about her wingman, about Laporte:

You're insane. I'm glad you're on my side.

Laporte dances between the vectors of the missiles come to kill her and when they come too close she expends her guns on them and they intersect the snarl of the tracers and die like lightning. It's mindless, beautiful work. Like a dream. She talks to Simms:

Boss, Morrigan. It's almost done.
Ken stirs from his deep place to save his prize.

nagari 8/10

By now it's clear that the Federation will surrender. No conventional military action can defeat Steele's war logic, his simulation farm, his psychological pressure, his willingness to dive past ethical crush depth.

So NAGARI plans to make contact with Nemesis.

"Send me in first," Laporte says.

Consider semiosis—the assignment of symbols to things, and the manipulation of those symbols to communicate and predict change. That's how intelligent life works. Build a model of the universe, test your ideas in the model, and find the best way to change the world.

Only the Nemesis don't have any recognizable semiosis. They're a whirlwind traversing the Lacanian desert, a fatal mirage, recognizable only by the ruin of its passage.

Until Admiral Haywain van Aken sacrificed himself. Until he somehow convinced the Nemesis to take him in.

And ever since, the Nemesis have been speaking. Or attacking. It's hard to know.

For more than a decade the Nemesis have been broadcasting the apparition of Admiral Haywain van Aken into human minds. The Nemesis organisms communicate by direct nerve induction at a distance. Particles wormholed into the tissue of the target. (There is, of course, no possibility that the Nemesis are a product of natural evolution.)

"If they can do that," Laporte protests, "they can just murder us all. Cook our skulls from light-years away." Or read the brainstates of human commanders, predict everything they do, the way Laporte and Simms could predict each other.

"No. Not without van Aken." Al-Alimah lays out NAGARI's hypothesis: the Nemesis have no mentality. They cannot conceive of other minds to predict or destroy. Their war is algorithmic, a procedure of matter against matter, spawning tactics by mutation and chance and iterating them in the field. They never leap straight to the optimal strategy, because a smart foe predicts the optimal. Their war logic is hardened by chaos. Noise.

Van Aken is their beachhead in the land of human thought.

"He wants you," al-Alimah says, her long fingers on Laporte's wrist again. "You in particular are valuable to him. We want you to serve as an ambassador."

"That's stupid." Laporte may be a monster but she is not some other monster's spawn. "Are you saying I was purpose-built?"

"No. Far more likely that you were selected because you're somehow amenable to the Nemesis." Al-Alimah leans forward with her lips parted as if to admit her own monster secret. "Laporte, the third Nemesis incursion is already underway. Not with warships and weapons, not this time, nothing so crude. The Nemesis are attacking the command and control systems behind those assets."

Language. Plans. People.

"What are the mission parameters?" The Alliance has control of the Sol-Serpentis wormhole. Laporte can't just fly out to Capella. "How do we use this to save the Federation?"

Al-Alimah stands and her gown whips in the rising wind. "We drug you and mate your brain to a computer network. You will enter a traumatic dream state and communicate with van Aken—with Ken. We keep dosing you until you learn how to trigger a Nemesis attack on the Alliance. Or until you go mad." Her gunmetal eyes, looking down at Laporte, never blink. "You will be the third attempt. There were two prior candidates. They seized apart."

Laporte leans back in her chair and looks up at the woman.

She can be the necessary monster. She could call down genocide on the Alliance and save her beloved home. If she believes the Federation is the only hope for a compassionate, peaceful, loving future, then, logically, she should be willing to kill for it. If she has a button that says "kill ten billion civilians, gain utopia," she should press it.

She could win the war, for the memory of Simms. And Simms is dead, right? The dead can't be ashamed.

"Okay," Laporte says. "I'm in. I volunteer."

They will connect her to the NAGARI dreamscape and to the salvaged corpses of Nemesis organisms from the first incursion. They will scar messages into her brain. They will wait for the Nemesis, for the ghost of Haywain van Aken, to read them and reply.

Surgeons crown her in waveguides that ram through her skull and penetrate the gyrae of her brain. Cold drug slurry pumps the length of her spine: entheogens, to tear down the barriers between Laporte's psyche and outside stimuli. She goes under. She dreams.

simms 6/9
nagari 9/10

"Curry's ready," Simms says, and Laporte's stomach growls out loud. They grin at each other. Simms looks at Laporte's armored tooth and her grin falters just a little.

They eat their trash-cooked chicken curry side by side with their hips squashed together. Laporte tries not to jostle Simms' ribs with her sharp little elbows. Simms crunches on a bit of bone, makes a face, and gets juice on Laporte's buzzed hair. There is no shampoo anywhere on the ship so this is a bit of a disaster. Simms mops her up with blood cloth from the triage kit.

"Tell me why it's bad if monsters don't win," Simms says, blotting at the back of her neck.

Laporte leans on her for a moment, because she adores Simms' desire to hear this story again, especially the end. "I met Ken," she says, "he was in the dream, and he was real. They could see him in my mind. Something triggering nerve potentials."

She went into seizure almost instantly. The NAGARI surgeons let it happen.

Laporte stood in the garden in Tandale with the hose in her hand and pollen itching her nose. Ants crawled over her bare feet. From the house came the smell of her parents' cooking, impatient and burnt. She looked down at herself and laughed: she was in her favorite caraval cat t-shirt.

"Ah, Miss Laporte," Ken said. "You made it."

She looked for him but all she could was the ants fighting, killing, generating new castes, mutating themselves into acid bombs and huge-headed tunnel plugs. "Admiral," she said. "Is that you?"

"Delighted to speak with you again. Let me briefly outline the necessary intelligence. A short history of all life. Then we can arrange our covenant."

Whatever Ken said to her must have been some kind of code,

parasitic and adaptable, because it expressed itself as a love story. A story about Laporte and Simms.

Imagine this, Ken said, imagine a universe of Laportes and Simmses. Lorna Simms has rules. She builds communities, like her squadron, or like a network of wormholes. She takes the wildcat aces and the ne'er-do-wells, the timid and the berserk, and she teaches them all how to work together. When that work is done, Simms would like to leave you with a nice set of rules describing a world that makes sense. Simms is a Maker.

"Huh." Simms puts a little moonshine on the rag and keeps scrubbing at Laporte's head. "You have such nice dreams about me."

"Wait until you hear mine."

The other great class of life is the Laportes. (These are tendencies, mind, not binary teams. But they are real: vital parts of the history of life in the universe.) The Laportes rattle around breaking things, claiming things, reshaping things. They can achieve every bit as much as the Simmses, in their own way—but their triumphs are conquests, seductions, acts of passion and violence. The Simmses build systems and the Laportes, parasites and predators and conquerors and geniuses and sociopaths, change them.

Whether delightful or destructive, the Laportes are Monsters.

When a Laporte meets a Simms, they fight. The Laporte might run rampant. She might murder the Simms, or trick her into subservience, or leave her spent and exhausted. Or the Simms might win, fencing the Laporte in with loyalties and laws, making her a useful part of something bigger. Understand? You following, Simms?

"It's about civilizations. Strategies. Game theory." Simms is a war junkie in her own way, a good self-directed Ubuntu learner, and she's done her homework. "And I'll bet, Laporte, that I know where your Admiral's going. The Simms win."

They win because they understand the Laportes. They make little models of what the Laportes are going to do, and they figure out how to get ahead of them, how to make their worst impulses useful, how to save them from harm (or lead them into it). They teach the Laportes what they can and cannot do.

Like Steele. Building statistical models of the Federation's tactics. Caging them in a prophecy of their own capabilities. And the only way out of that cage is to transgress the laws you use to define yourself.

"Hold still," Simms says. "This stuff really likes your hair."

"The Simmses do tend to win." Laporte leans back against her, just a little. When Simms is fixing Laporte up she forgets to be stiff and wary. "They win too much. And over billions of years, across the infinity of the universe, it turns out that's dangerous."

Imagine the god-Simms, ascendant. Puppeteering the cosmos with invisible loyalties. Learning how to guide the passions and the violence of the Laportes. Imagine Simms building not just a good squadron or a good civilization but a good galaxy, all the matter in it optimized for happy, useful thought.

Imagine a Simms setting out to build a *rechnender raum*: thinking space. Her laws written into the fundament.

"How did you learn all this?" Laporte asked the scurrying ants. In the shapes of their war she saw the ghost of an old man with dead stars in his eyes.

Ken had surmised some of it before his rebellion. And while the Nemesis had never communicated with him directly, they had, in their own way, signaled the truth: duplicating Haywain von Aken's consciousness millions of times, torturing it into madness, and exterminating the branches whose madnesses diverged from their desire.

"I'm not sure I follow that last part," Simms says. Now she's mopping the curry from behind Laporte's right ear. "Something about supercivilizations?"

"Imagine a place where everything could have anything it needed. For whatever it wanted." That was the happy Simms-world. Imagine a purpose? You can obtain it. You can get the resources you need.

"Like an Ubuntu slogan."

"Yes," Laporte says, shivering. That was what Ubuntu wanted to make. A place where people had everything they needed to be good. A place without violence and deprivation.

In the garden, Admiral Haywain van Aken told her that a universe without violence or deprivation was destined for something worse.

Cancer.

capella 6/8

Her Uriel sings her death to her.

DV UNDERBURN is a long drumbeat, pleading for more fuel, and SPIKE [COBRA TAME/ATREUS] is a keening like headache, and MUSIC SOUR describes itself, and every time Steele fires she hears VAMPIRE! and a noise like someone ringing her molars with an armor chime.

But she's not going to die. She's too fast. She's too fierce. She's severed all the connections that would slow her down.

She kills a missile half a second from killing her and for an instant all her sensors are flash-blind but she kills the next too, a dead reckoning snapshot from a hundred kilometers with the pin graser. How? Because she has escaped the borders of herself. The *Sinadhuja* has trained its sensors on her. Ken is watching her. And she can see through his eyes. She can think with his tissue, his fatal substrate. She is bleeding out of herself and into the Nemesis, the totipotent holocide-mind, the killing anima. Crossing the bridge Ken built.

Admiral Steele is calling to her. *"Federation pilot,"* he's saying, in that rich purring voice, not audibly afraid, *"you have been compromised by Nemesis psywar. Kill your engines and shut down your defensive jamming."*

Ken is calling to her. Miss Laporte. Come closer. We can complete our covenant. Together, we can save humanity.

"Okay, Boss," Laporte says. "Let's get ready."

nagari 10/10

Cancer, and its relationships to paradise and love:

You build a place without violence or deprivation. A place where anything can have everything it needs to be its finest, fullest self.

This is how cells became organisms. How people became civilizations. How a bunch of misfits and fuckups became a fighting unit *almost* tough enough to challenge Admiral Steele. A Simms wrote some laws to say: if we pool our energies, we can create a common good. And if you follow the rules, yeah, you, Laporte, if you don't eat too much common good, if you put in more than you take out, then we can last.

Imagine a Simms-god rampant, organizing the universe, winning the love of all the Laportes. So productive and persuasive that no one notices its ultimate agenda is hollow, self-referential, malignant.

Think about me. Organize everyone and everything to think about me. What am I? I am thinking about how to make everything think about me. I am a tumor, recruiting every system I encounter in the name of my own expansion.

"Whoa, now." Simms puts a wet finger on the back of Laporte's neck. "I'm very compelling, sure. Magnetic. But that's not me."

"Shh. Let me finish." Except, Laporte realizes, she is finished. That's the whole story. "Van Aken believes in a cosmic proof: the axiomatic, mathematical superiority of cancer to all forms of containment. An empty thought that consumes intelligent systems and uses them to think about propagating itself."

Given a range of purposes, and a surplus of resources, one purpose would always triumph: the purpose of defeating and incorporating all other purposes. The two ant colonies in Laporte's garden had to dedicate themselves entirely to war. If one of them spent part of its energy on ant compassion, or ant culture, or ant art, it would lose. Cancer was the destiny of smart systems: empty, voracious, every part of them thinking about nothing but how to expand.

Unless there was someone with a hose to pour water on them.

"So," Simms says, humoring Laporte's great mythic rant, "why do we still have a universe? Why are we here, thinking about ourselves?"

"That's just what I asked van Aken," Laporte lies. Because she feels that it would be too creepy, too alien, to admit that she understood it right away.

In the part of the story she's avoiding, in the garden of the seizure dream, Laporte turned on her hose and began flooding her childhood constructs into mud. "The Nemesis are the anti-malignancy measure. They kill Makers. That's why they're so noisy and inefficient. So they can escape the models that Makers use to win wars."

From a distant Nemesis construct, tumbling through the ergosphere of Capella, borrowing the black hole's energies to hurl charged particles through quantum wormholes into Laporte's mind, Ken smiled his agreement. Tattooed it into Laporte's brain.

If you were afraid of intelligent thought consuming the universe, you had to turn the cosmos into an acid bath. An endless war against the triumph of Lorna Simms.

simms 7/9

"Okay," Simms says, squinting. "I think I got it all." She leans down, curled over Laporte's head, to look her in the eyes. "What happened next? Did you make the deal?"

"I did." She asked Ken: how do I get the Nemesis to wipe out the Alliance? And he told her: you must come to me, in Capella. "That's why I'm going out tomorrow."

Simms blinks, once, twice, a sign that she doesn't like this place, she wants to move on. They're touching on the open question, the raw wound between them. Is Simms going to fly again? Is she going to be part of Laporte's mutiny?

Are they still wingmen?

"And then?" Simms asks, pushing them past the moment.

"I couldn't get out. I couldn't wake up." It's funny how sharp Simms looks, upside down. Like she has some inverse swagger. Laporte wants to ask her to stay right there but what does Simms see, looking back? Is the inverse Laporte agreeable? "Contact with the Nemesis was killing me. I had no reason to live. Nothing to come back for."

She's seen the recordings of her brainstate. The seizure burning from skull to stem.

When Simms smiles upside down it looks like a grimace, which makes it much more familiar. "So they gave you anticonvulsants. And you woke up. Then you made up this part to help you get laid."

Laporte tells her anyway. "Al-Alimah whispered to me. And I heard her. She said . . ."

"Simms is alive," Simms says. "She survived radiation therapy, and now she's out there. Looking for you."

That was how Laporte came back from the seizure dream, just in time to fight in the Mars gambit and rage at the Federation's final surrender. Word came down: it's over. Move to a holding orbit. Await terms. Al-Alimah tore the orders up and all the assembled NAGARI operators made a satisfied growl like they were too angry to cheer.

"And that's how you got back to me." Simms kisses her on the right eyeball. "You're a sweet liar."

"Ew," Laporte says. "Don't do that."

But she smiles and—

capella 0/8
—tries to catch Simms' hand.

"You're meeting with the Admiralty tonight." Simms claps her on the shoulders, boom boom, look at you, kid, you're a big shot. And then she draws away, upright, articulate, her flight suit unzipped and tied around her waist, her hair loose on her shoulders. She backs away from Laporte in triangular half-steps, back leg then front, as if they're fighting and she is making room to retreat. The air that rushes in to fill the absence of her is cold and it smells of burnt curry.

"I am," Laporte says, wishing she would stay close. "I'm presenting the final battle plan. Al-Alimah's victory gambit."

"You're going to tell them you have a plan to bait the Nemesis into attacking the Alliance. A strategic distraction. When Steele pulls his fleet out of Sol, we can seal the node and live in peace."

"That's right."

"But that's not the plan." Simms aims one finger at her, a half-curled, hey-you stab. "You're not going to tell them the real plan. That's between you and your NAGARI friends."

The Nemesis are insuperable. Nothing can defeat them. They have unlimited resources (their warships conjured out of black hole accretion discs by probability manipulation) and their behavior, well, that's even worse: they have no mentality, no strategy to predict, nothing that can generate a nice clean model. Only a godslaying virulence, a random and chilling will to annihilate, manifesting strategies and hurling them at the enemy until the enemy has exhausted all countermeasures and taught the Nemesis their strengths.

To fight them is to instruct them how to kill you.

Haywain van Aken has summoned Laporte to Capella. To the black hole that is the Nemesis' engine, factory, and beacon in human space. Why? Laporte has a guess. They have no purpose or objectives of their own—those are Maker things, teleological, forbidden to them. Only their basic logic: whatever we encounter, we destroy.

But they didn't kill van Aken. They took him into communion. Maybe that act brought them closer to victory. Maybe, to them, subverting van Aken was an act of destruction: a lethality enhancement.

"I believe," Laporte begins, struggling, trying to hide her struggle, this is so hard to say because it requires her to navigate around her secret fear: that she is about to abandon Simms again, forever, in favor of the consummate monstrosity. "I believe I can trigger a

Nemesis behavior that will exterminate everyone in Alliance space. I believe the Federation will endure. Humanity will have a chance at survival."

"That's how we save the Federation? How we keep Ubuntu alive? Sacrifice ten billion human lives?" Simms crosses her arms. "We're okay with defensive genocide?"

"That's war. We kill people to achieve our objectives."

Simms' hard eyes radiating a hard signal, and Laporte reads it in a way that's maybe unfair: I liked knowing that you were *my* monster. I liked knowing you had boundaries. "We kill soldiers."

"People," Laporte says, echoing the old Ubuntu lessons: everyone is human. There is no justifiable violence—only degrees of tragedy. "We're always killing people."

They stare at each other and on the raw metal deck between them Laporte can feel them piling the tally, the killcounts, the fighter pilots and warship crews they've murdered personally, the deaths contingent upon those by way of grief or loss (children abandoned, lovers driven to suicide, parents spiraling away into addiction). The *strategic targets* and *footprint bleed* and *noncombatant bycatch* and for Laporte it all wraps up in the voice of some terrified Alliance contractor on a suit radio trying to explain that he doesn't support this war, doesn't want to be here, he's just trying to pay off his electrical apprenticeship, would they please send a rescue ship, he's tumbling off into space and his radiation warnings are red and he doesn't want to drown in his own vomit, please, please. Send help.

When the Alliance captured Earth orbit, Admiral Steele threatened to bomb a city every hour until the Federation issued an unconditional surrender. What else could he do? Not with every soldier in the Alliance could he occupy even one continent. He had to use the tools at his disposal. He had to resort to calculated atrocity in the name of final peace.

Funny how that Ubuntu lesson can turn around, isn't it? How easily *degrees of tragedy* becomes *degrees of necessity*.

"You told me," Laporte says, "that if I hesitated, I would die. So I never hesitate."

Simms looks at her old wingman and new lover and whatever she's looking at is receding fast. "I hate them," she says. "But I don't know if I hate them enough to do this."

Laporte wants to grin and quip. She would tell Simms what Simms told her: monsters win.

But if she says that, she's telling Simms that this is all on her. That she's the one who made Laporte.

"There's no alternative," she says instead. "If we surrender to the Alliance, it's all been for nothing. We become part of the war against the Nemesis. And the Nemesis kill us all."

Simms does something with the fear in her eyes. Like she's folding it up and pointing it at something. "This al-Alimah woman. Were you two close?"

"Not like that." Not like you.

"I want to talk to her." Simms points at the deck behind Laporte, like a cue to turn around, and in doing that she makes it clear: the meeting will not include Laporte. "I've got some concerns to articulate."

"Fine." She can't keep the petty irritation from her voice. They should be together, effortlessly and unanimously lethal, two fists on the same fighter. "Are you flying with me tomorrow? When I go put out the signal?"

"I still need to check myself over in the simulator," Simms says. "Make sure the radiation shakes are gone."

Laporte's flown with her long enough to hear the *no*.

capella 7/8

She is in her Uriel, fighting off Steele, falling into the dead star and the waiting *Sinadhuja*.

She is in communion with the *Sinadhuja*. There are hallucinations puncturing her mind. She is in the garden with Ken.

"This is the bargain," he says.

He's a tall, strong-jawed man in the broadshouldered uniform of an Alliance admiral. He must be proud of that uniform, because he still wears his short-billed cap and his insignia. But the texture of him is black and squirming and when Laporte touches him she sees he's made of ants, ants at war, lopping limbs and antennae off each other with their scissored jaws.

Her fingers come away acid-burnt.

"Are you ready?" Haywain van Aken says. His eyes are two rings of fire, the accretion discs of two dead suns. "Do you understand what's about to happen?"

The *Sinadhuja* looms up behind her fighter. Four kilometers long and pregnant with methods of extinction. As it matches velocity with her ship its thrusters flare violet-black, the jets decaying sideways into some hidden curled dimension. It is attacking her, speaking to her, these two are the same. The Nemesis can never understand human minds well enough to manipulate them. But they have Haywain van Aken to do it for them.

"The Nemesis exist to tear down conscious thought," Laporte says to Ken.

She is in the cockpit, nudging the stick, steering her Uriel into the *Sinadhuja*'s open gullet. All the alarms have gone silent, except one: PROXIMITY. PROXIMITY. Steele's voice is an electronic scratch, fading off, saying: *Brevet-Admiral Laporte, you are compromised. It's not too late. You can still self-destruct. You can still take out your sidearm and shoot yourself in the head. Brevet-Admiral Laporte, last time someone did this they blew up four suns—*

"The Nemesis have internal safeguards. Processes designed to rip apart any accidental intelligence they develop." Ken's peeling off the skin of his left-arm, degloving it, creating a sacrament of killing ants. "But this makes it hard for them to win."

They can't create their own leaders. They can't build models of the things they need to kill. They can summon up infinite might, but never learn how to apply it efficiently. How could they? In their fundamental state the Nemesis are a storm, a destructive process. Semiosis, the use of symbols to understand and plan, is forbidden to them.

A storm is powerful. But smart things can shelter from a storm.

So how do they defeat the gods of thought using only the logic of annihilation? Or, more aptly: what tactics might they stumble on, in their blind exploration of the possibility space?

Laporte cups her hands and accepts the sacrament. The ants start eating her flesh. She crushes them between her palms, to show her strength, and it only drives them deeper.

"They provoke the creation of monsters," she says. "Experts at the use of violence. And then they consume them to enhance their own violence."

"You will lead the Nemesis in war against the Alliance," van Aken intones, reading the sacred terms, the covenant he sacrificed himself to create. "You will guide them as long as you can. Inevitably, you will be devoured by the Nemesis, and your authority will be erased. But as long as you endure, you can protect your home."

The ants are inside her now. She can feel them under her skin. She looks at her arms and sees them in her muscle, bound by violence, grappling and flexing. The Alliance's spies and admirals would drink razors to get a look at her brain right now, full of the alien logic that will give her a transient kind of power over the local Nemesis.

"What about you?" she asks. Ken was a good friend, once, with good advice, even if he's now the organizing point of all Nemesis behavior in human space. "How long will you last?"

His smile is warm and toothy, an earnest, clever smile, and each tooth in it is a broad-headed warrior ant. "Humanity is going to be at war with Nemesis for a long, long time," he says. "I am the anima in command of semiotic warfare. I am the Admiral of communion. I keep myself from the jaws by supplying the Nemesis with new weapons. And if you can manage the Nemesis, Miss Laporte, if you can keep the fire burning hot . . . then I will have new monsters to cultivate."

"Ah," she says, satisfied. She gets it! It makes simple sense.

Van Aken knows how to achieve a kind of common ground with the Nemesis. How to make humanity at least temporarily useful. The Nemesis devoured van Aken because he could enhance their lethality. Make them better monsters.

Humanity will defy the Nemesis as long as their strength lasts. They'll get ruthless. And thus they will become the Nemesis' monster farm. A new drop in the acid bath. Victory is not only annihilation: it's monster-genesis.

"I'm sorry your lover abandoned you," Ken says. "She was a good person, deep down. That's why she didn't understand the necessity of our work."

The jaws of the *Sinadhuja* begin to close around Laporte's ship.

simms 8/9

After the curry-and-cosmology fight, they go to the gym to beat the shit out of each other. That helps less than it used to: Simms is still weak and they both know it, and holding back in a fight is just like lying anywhere else.

Showers require less discipline than they used to. They retreat to their haven in the officers' cabins, freed up by the death of most of *Eris'* staff, and they have makeup sex. It's the night before the mutiny, before Laporte asks Simms, one last time, to be her zombie warrior buddy cop. The night before Simms says, sorry, I'm not mission capable.

Laporte drowses in Simms' arms and then she wakes up to the sight of al-Alimah leaning over her. She's upgraded her eyes. They are blind, brilliant silver. The stud in her tongue gleams like Laporte's armor tooth.

"The mission," al-Alimah says, "begins now."

By reflex (it's all reflex, love reflex) Laporte reaches for Simms who's curled up beside her and in need of protection. But no one's there: only a warm place. She sits up to shove al-Alimah back. Simms pounces on her from behind, Laporte recognizes the feel of her forearms and the smell of her, she tries to fight but Simms is stronger, she's *stronger*, she was holding back in the gym. She pins Laporte facedown in the mattress with a growl.

Al-Alimah puts a needle into Laporte's neck and the world goes out.

Laporte remembers this as just a dream. Not because it's true, but because it's useful.

nagari 11/10

"Stop asking me to fly with you," Simms says. "I'm done. I can't be part of this. That's my final decision."

This is the moment before Laporte falls into Capella. At the end of the mutiny, in the slim window before Steele catches up with the NAGARI task force and stops them from breaching Nemesis space. Laporte's Uriel is waiting on the *Eris* hangar deck with a full warload and two empty seats. There is no time for hesitation.

"Boss," Laporte says, reaching out. She's sealed up in her flightsuit and when she touches Simms it's through the interface of her tactical gloves, fireproof, skin-sealed, built to insulate and protect. "Hey."

Not again, she wants to say. Don't do this again. We survived this. We split up but we found each other again and we cooked some curry and fixed some fighters, we're so close, we're going to win. For values of victory encompassing genocide.

Simms pulls away. "You're not the woman I knew," she says. "You can go make your bargain. But I don't want to be part of it."

Their orbit is over. The punch-drunk bloodlust and the will to win. They've spiraled too close and now they will fling each other away, each of them ballistic and alone. Simms prefers defeat.

"*Laporte*," al-Alimah calls, from the *Eris*' CIC. "*We're losing time. Are you airborne?*"

"You don't need me," Simms says. "You never have."

Laporte wants to say something clever, to fix this. An alien told me that every Laporte needs a Simms. That monsters have to love makers, so they can hone each other. So they can keep a safe orbit. Simms, if you go, I don't know how to find my way back.

But this time it's Simms who walks away from her.

Laporte flies through the wormhole, into Capella. Into the maw of the singularity. She falls.

capella 8/8
simms 9/9

The jaws of the *Sinadhuja* close around her ship. Armored mandibles clamping down to protect the warship's antimatter stores and soft internal structure and most of all van Aken, who is the bridge the Nemesis need, the means of their third incursion. Shutting off the ring of receding starlight, and the blue nova of the *Atreus* high above.

The *Uriel*'s navigational lights illuminate the *Sinadhuja*'s interior. Laporte scans serrated geometry swarming with jointed, armored Nemesis organisms. Somewhere down there van Aken's human body has been translated, or consumed, into a component of the *Sinadhuja*. A semiotic weapons system.

Ken. Who is in Laporte's head, who knows what she knows. Who knows that *Atreus* is here to kill her. Who knows that she left Simms on a hangar deck in Vega.

Laporte's armored tooth fires a jolt of pain up the side of her jaw.

"Boss, Morrigan," Laporte says. She knows she has to say this. A dream told her. "We're a go. Wake up. Do it."

In the Uriel's back seat, the electronic warfare station, Simms smashes her helmet against the headrest in surprise.

"Fuck!" she says. Her voice is dry like paper tearing. "Holy shit!"

Laporte's weapons panel lights up with status reports. An IV dumping combat stimulants into Simms' blood, a cardiac implant restarting her heart, reflex sequencers firing commands into her brainstem. Waking her up from functional death. Since they left *Eris* together, Simms has been sustained by the emergency oxygen in her synthetic bone marrow and whatever black ops technofuckery al-Alimah cranked into her.

Hidden from Haywain van Aken's communion. From his semiosis weapon, his dream of ants, his bridge into conscious minds.

In the garden, Ken says: "She left you. She thought you were an abomination. I don't understand."

Understand. That wonderful word. Laporte, giddy with the knowledge that Simms is alive again (again!), alive and flying with her, just can't resist the quip: "Just a bad dream, Ken."

"Al-Alimah. She fabricated that event and put it in you. Why?" The formicidae face tilts. "What about your mission, Laporte? What about human survival?"

"You're the mission, Ken." The Nemesis never manifested any central vulnerabilities during the second incursion. Never organized around any one point of weakness. "I'm sorry."

In the back cockpit Simms is speaking into her COM, the quick clipped voice of a veteran combat pilot, signaling for backup: "*Atreus, Atreus*, this is TROJAN. Request fire mission, flash priority, target is a *Sinadhuja* world-killer with enemy command assets aboard. Jump vectors coming now—"

Laporte's helmet pokes her in the back of the head. ALERT! it complains. EMCON VIOLATION! It doesn't like what Simms is doing, hotloading the reactor, shunting power into the ship's IFF and navigational beacons. Broadcasting targeting data on an Alliance tactical channel: a screaming, desperate plea to *shoot me*.

"TROJAN, Atreus." Steele's scalpel voice faint, so faint, distorted by the *Sinadhuja*'s armor and defensive jamming, by the grip of the black hole. By all these things keeping his missiles at bay. "*We have your target. Stand by for fire. Godspeed, pilots.*"

Maybe, in younger and less certain days, Laporte and Simms would have paused to say things left unsaid. To say goodbye.

But they don't need that now. They're on the same frequency. Much like the *Atreus* and the Uriel gunship, which is looking around the *Sinadhuja*'s guts with its targeting package, plotting trajectories with its navigational sensors, and telling Steele where, exactly, to fire his miracle missiles.

It's very hard to kill a *Sinadhuja*. From the outside.

In the garden, Ken makes a soft, thoughtful noise. "You knew I'd read your memories. So you let Simms and al-Alimah use you as a weapon. They leveraged Admiral Steele into cooperating with you. They used the NAGARI dreamscape to fabricate Simms abandoning you. And I believed it, because I cared about you."

Laporte grins an ant-tongued grin. She came here knowing, in a veiled way, that Simms was waiting for her. But she had no idea, all the way down, whether Steele had actually agreed to the plan. Whether his missiles were feints or fatally true.

But she knows, right now (as the first of Steele's fusion bombs jumps in ten meters off her nose and arcs off towards the back of the *Sinadhuja*'s interior) exactly what she needs to do. She needs to live. And so does Simms.

Laporte touches the stick, one last time, to line up the Uriel's cockpit with the gap in the armored jaws above.

"Eject!" In pilot code, you always say it three times, to make it real. "Eject, eject!"

She gets a nanosecond glimpse of Simms in the backseat mirror. She's grinning like an idiot.

Laporte pulls the wasp-colored handle between her legs. Her ejection seat hurls her starward, between the flashing jump-sign and corkscrewing trails of *Atreus*' missiles, up through the *Sinadhuja*'s jaws and away. She's turning as she rises, G-force snapping the acceleration sumps in the seat, and she can see another light with her, orbiting her, no, it's not an orbit, they're just flying together, co-moving.

"Simms!" she calls. "Boss!"

Down beneath them the *Sinadhuja*'s drive flares up red and massive and vomits debris and cuts out. The world-killer drops away, free falling, a mountain conjured up out of the black hole and now reclaimed by it. A flash of annihilation light blows through its hull down astern and suddenly it's geysering jets of molten metal, crumpling on itself, jump missiles darting out of the interior and curving back to re-attack with their submunitions scattering out behind them like fairy dust.

In the garden Ken says: "This is a selfish choice, Miss Laporte. What do you gain by killing me? You know they'll keep coming. You know they always win."

"Maybe." Laporte sprays him with her garden hose. He's already falling to pieces, ants sloughing off and returning to the dirt. "Maybe we'll make enough monsters to stop them."

Is that, his fading voice asks, how you want things to be? Everything honed to fight? Irrevocably weaponized?

Laporte doesn't know what to say to that. She has been a monster. But she's going to see Simms again, and when they're together, she won't feel like anything but a happy woman. Is monsterhood conditional? Like a mirror you hold up to the war around you, just long enough to win?

Everything dies. Even humanity, Laporte supposes. Maybe how you live should count for more than how long you last.

Admiral van Aken sends a soft farewell. He doesn't seem angry. More proud than anything.

Godspeed, he says. And good luck, Miss Laporte.

The *Sinadhuja*'s hull shatters. Blazes up in dirty fire and fades to ash and smelt and then the ruin of the world-killer falls away. Down below, in the accretion disk, black shapes begin to stir.

"Good kill," Simms says, like they're still back in Sol, shooting down bad Alliance pilots. Her voice is tinny over the suit radios, but very confident. "Scratch one Nemesis warship."

High above them, silhouetted against the distant bundled stars, *Atreus* has turned over. She's decelerating, burning "up," trying to stop herself from hitting the black hole. Trying to make it back to the wormhole above.

"*TROJAN*, Atreus." Steele quite calm and utterly polite—disappointingly unmoved to cheer. Laporte would've liked to rattle the bastard. "*We have your beacons. A search and rescue craft is on the way. Reply if able.*"

"Morrigan." Simms calling. "Morrigan, it's Boss."

"Atreus, *this is* Eris, *Federation Second Fleet.*" Another transmission.

Stretched by blueshift and spiked by radiation. *"We have transited the wormhole. We are deploying tankers to assist your escape burn."*

"Copy you, *Eris. Put your tankers on GUARD for rendezvous control."*

"Morrigan!" Simms calls. "We're fucked!"

"What is it, Boss?"

"We got cooked pretty bad, Laporte." She sounds more disgusted than afraid. "Gamma flash. Check your rad meter."

Laporte picks the radiation alarm out of the small congress of alerts on her suit visor. It wants her to know that she's absorbed a critical dose, that she needs medical assistance, and that she should consider recording a last message for her loved ones.

"Ugh," Simms says. She makes an about-to-spit noise and then, considering her helmet, abandons it. "I'm going to have so much cancer."

Laporte dismisses the alarm and cues up an anti-emetic injection. They'll be okay. A little radiation never kept a good Federation pilot down. She starts tapping her seat thrusters, moving towards Simms, and look, Simms is already headed for her. As they pass they reach out and grab each other by their forearms so that they turn together around a common point.

"I think we'll be okay, boss," she says. She can hear the beacon of the search-and-rescue ship, howling down to them from the stars above, and the frame-shifted scream of the black hole eating light, far down below. "I think we'll be okay."

Simms claps her on the wrist, once and then again. "Me too, Morrigan." She's still grinning. "Me too."

FLASH FLASH FLASH
ISN BACKBREAKER FASTEST
S 0348 BAST $DATE_DYNAMIC_REFRAME
FM SECCON//BETAQ
TO ALLIANCE HIGHER

1. NEMESIS PSYWAR CHANNEL DESTROYED IN CAPELLA STRIKE BY JOINT FEDERATION/ALLIANCE ACTION
2. ALLIANCE SPECIAL ASSETS RECOVERED. DEBRIEFING PENDING. NOW IN RADIATION THERAPY ABOARD FEDERATION WARSHIP ERIS

3. LIMITED NEMESIS INCURSION NOW IN PROGRESS VEGA. SMOKEJUMP UNITS RESPONDING. FEDERATION NAGARI TASK FORCE RESPONDING. PRELIMINARY ESTIMATE 60% CHANCE CONTAINMENT
4. FIREWALL UNITS ON STANDBY
5. SOL EXPEDITIONARY FORCE: IMMEDIATE RETASK TO VEGA FOR SMOKEJUMP RELIEF
6. DUE TO ENHANCED NEMESIS THREAT POSTURE, DIPLOMATIC RESOLUTION TO SOL REGIME REALIGNMENT ACTION IS BACK IN PLAY
7. MAINTAIN HIGHEST VIGILANCE. HUMANITY STANDS

REMEMBERY DAY

★

by Sarah Pinsker

The Veil blocked the brutal memories of war 364 days a year. For many, it was a blessing. But for some, forgetting was worse than remembering.

I WOKE AT DAWN on the holiday, so my grandmother put me to work polishing Mama's army boots.

"Try not to let her see them," Nana warned me. I already knew.

I took the boots to the bathroom with an old sock and the polish kit. I had seen Nana clean them before, but this marked the first time I was allowed to do it myself. Saddle soap first, then moisturizer, then polish. I pictured Nana at the ironing board in our bedroom, pressing the proper creases into Mama's old uniform.

The door swung open, and I realized too late that I had forgotten to lock it. Mama didn't often wake up this early on days she didn't have to work.

"Whose are those?" my mother asked, yawning.

"Uh—" I didn't know what to say, which lie I was supposed to tell.

Nana rescued me from the situation, coming up behind Mama. "Those were your father's, Kima. I asked Clara to clean them for me."

Mama's gaze lingered on the boots for a moment. Did she think they were the wrong size for Grandpa? Did she recognize them?

"I need the bathroom," she said after a moment. "Do you mind doing that somewhere else, Clara?"

I pinched the boots together and lifted them away from my body so I wouldn't stain my clothes, gathering up the polish kit with my other hand. Mama waited until I slipped past before she wheeled in. Her indoor chair was narrow, but not narrow enough for both of us to fit in the small bathroom.

"I'm sorry," I whispered to Nana once the door closed.

"No harm done," Nana whispered back.

I finished on the kitchen floor, now that there was no reason to hide. It was almost time, anyway. The parade would start at ten by us. In some places, people had to get up in the middle of the night.

Mama came in to breakfast, and I put the boots in a corner to dry. Nana had made coffee and scrambled eggs with green chiles, but all I could smell was the saddle soap on my hands. We all ate in silence: Mama because she wasn't a morning person, and Nana and I because we were waiting. Listening. At eight the sirens went off, just the expected short burst to warn us the Veil would be lifting.

Mama whipped her head around. "What was that? Oh."

The lifting of the Veil always hit her the same. My teacher said each vet reacted in a different way, but my friends never discussed what it was like for their parents. Mama always went "Oh" first, lifting her hand to her mouth. Her eyes flew open as if they were opening for the first time, and for one moment she would look at me as if I were a stranger. It upset me when I was little. I think I understand now, or anyway I'm used to it.

"Oh," she said again.

She studied her hands in her lap for a moment, and I saw they were shaking. She didn't say anything, just wheeled herself into the bathroom. I heard the water start up, then the creak as she transferred herself to the seat in the shower. Nana came around the table to hug me. When she got up to lay Mama's uniform on her bed, I followed with the boots I had shined. We waited in the kitchen.

Showering and dressing took her a while, as it did on any day, but when she appeared in the kitchen doorway again, she had her uniform on. It fit perfectly. Mama didn't need to know that Nana had let it out a little. I had never seen a picture of her as a young soldier, but it wasn't hard to imagine. I only had to strip away the chair and the burn on her face. This was the one day I looked at her that way; on all other days, those were just part of her.

"Did you shine these for me?" She pointed to her boots.

I nodded.

"They're perfect. Everyone will be so impressed." She pulled me onto her lap. I was getting too old for laps, but today she was allowed. I stayed for a minute then stood again. When she laughed it was a different laugh from the rest of the year, a little lower and softer. I've never been sure which is her real laugh.

At nine, we all got in the van, and Mama drove us downtown.

"Mama, can I ask you a question?"

"Yes?"

"What did you do in the War?"

I saw her purse her lips in the mirror. "There's a long answer to that question, *mija*, and I don't think I can answer it right this moment while I'm driving. Can we talk more in a while?"

I knew how this worked. "In a while" didn't always come. Still, this was her day. "I guess."

A few minutes later Mama took an unexpected right turn and pulled the van over. "How about if we skip it this year? Go get some ice cream or sit on the pier or something?"

"Mama, no! This is for you!" I didn't understand why she would suggest such a thing. My horror welled up before I thought to see what Nana said first.

She turned to Nana next, but my grandmother just shrugged.

"You're right, Clara. I don't know what I was thinking." Mama sighed and put the van back into gear.

Veterans got all the good parking in the city on the holiday. Mama's uniform got us close. The wheelchair sticker got us even closer. I didn't understand how they all knew where to go, how to find their regiments, but they did. Nana and I stood near the staging area and watched as the veterans hugged each other and cried. Mama pointed to me and waved. I smiled and waved back.

We found seats in the grandstand, surrounded by other families like ours. I recognized a couple of the kids. We had played together beneath the stands when we were little, when we called it Remembery Day because we didn't know better. Now that I was old enough to understand a little more, I wanted to sit with Nana. The metal bench burned my legs even through my pants. A breeze blew through the canyon created by the buildings. It rustled the flags on the opposite side of the street, and I tried to identify the different states and countries.

A marching band started to play, and we all sang "The Ones Who Made it Home" and then "Flowers Bloom Where You Fell." At school I learned that parades used to include national anthems, but since the War our allies everywhere choose to sing these two songs. I can sing them both in four different languages. The band stopped in front of each stand to play the two songs again. It was always a long parade.

Behind them came six horses the color of Mama's boots and every bit as shiny. Froth flew from their mouths as they tossed their heads and danced sideways against their harnesses. Their bits and bridles gleamed with polish, but they pulled a plain cart. It rolled on wooden wheels and carried a wooden casket. The young man driving wore the new uniform designed after the War, light gray with black bands around the arms. Nobody who hadn't fought was allowed to wear the old one anymore.

Then came the veterans. Fewer every year. Nana has promised me Mama was never exposed to the worst stuff; I worry anyway. I imagine there will be a time when there aren't enough of them to form ranks, but for now there were still a good number. Some, like my mother, rode in motorized wheelchairs. Some had faces more scarred than hers. Others waved prosthetic hands. Those too weak were pushed by others or rode on floats down the boulevard. I saw my teacher march past. I had never noticed him in the ranks before, but I guess he wasn't my teacher until this year, so I wouldn't have known to look for him. The way he talked in class I would never have guessed he was a veteran. Of course, that was the case with all of them since the Veil was invented. I don't know why I was surprised.

When Mama passed I mustered a little extra volume, so everyone would know she was mine. She spotted me in the crowd and pointed and waved. We cheered until our throats were raw. It was the least we could do, the only thing we could do.

The same thing was happening at the same time in all the cities and countries left. I pictured children and grandparents cheering under dark skies and noonday sun. It was summer here, but winter in the northern hemisphere, so I pictured the other kids bundled up, their bleachers chilling their legs while the bench I sat on made me sweat behind my knees.

The last soldiers passed us, and we made sure we had enough voice left to show our appreciation to them as well. Behind them, another horse, saddled but riderless, with fireweed braided into his mane. He was there to remind us of the clean-up crews, those who had been exposed after the treaty. None of them were left to march.

We waited in the stands after the parade ended. Nana spoke with some people sitting nearby. Some families left, but others lingered like us. We knew it would be a while. The veterans had gone off to gather at their arranged meeting places as they were supposed to do, in bars or parks or coffee shops at the other end of the route. A couple of people in uniform walked back in our direction and slipped away with family, ignoring the looks we gave them. We all knew they were supposed to be at the vote.

"What do you think they'll decide this year?" asked a boy around my age. I had met him before, but I didn't remember his name, only that both his parents were in the parade. He sat alone.

I shrugged and gave my teacher's answer. "That's up to them. It's not for us to approve or disapprove."

He moved away from me. Nana was still talking. The bench had cleared and I lay back on it despite the heat. We were lucky to have had such beautiful weather. The sky was a shade of blue that got deeper the more I looked at it, like I could see through the atmosphere and into space. I thought about the other girls like me in a hundred other cities, waiting for their mothers and lying on benches and looking up at the sky.

We waited a long time. Nana pulled out her book. Her finger didn't move across the page the way it usually did, so I guessed she wasn't really reading. I closed my eyes and listened to the sweepers come to clear the streets, and the other stragglers chatting with each other. Now and again the bleachers clanged and shook as small children chased each other up and down.

Eventually, I heard the whine of a wheelchair operating at its highest speed. I shaded my face and looked down. Mama. Her eyes were puffy like she had been crying. Some years she smelled like beer, but this year she didn't.

I sat in the backseat and counted all the flags hanging from houses and shops.

"And?" Nana asked after we had ridden in silence for several minutes.

"No."

"Was the vote close?"

Mama sighed, her voice so soft I strained to hear it. "It never is."

Nana put her hand on Mama's arm. "Maybe someday."

"Maybe."

Back at the house, we took in the flag. Mama changed her clothes. She sat in her recliner with her hands folded in her lap, while Nana took the uniform from her to hide until next year. I went to get my father's photo from my drawer. I didn't see Nana on the other bed until I stood up. She was holding her face in her hands.

"That damned Veil," she said. "I'll never understand why they vote for the Veil, year after year."

"Because the memories are too strong." I repeated what my teacher told me. "The war was too brutal."

"But she wants to remember."

"It wouldn't do anyone any good if she ran into one of her friends in the grocery store who didn't remember her. It has to be everybody or nobody, Nana."

"But they push down so many good memories along with the bad ones."

"I think the good memories hurt too." I had seen the tears in my mother's eyes.

"Tell me something about him that I don't know." I climbed onto the arm of the recliner.

My mother smiled and took the photo from me, tracing his jawline and then the buttons on his dress uniform.

"I met him in the gym on base. He was the only guy who would spot me while I lifted without making comments."

"I know, Mama. What else?" I didn't mean for the impatience to show in my voice. "I'm sorry. I don't mean to rush you."

"He liked to play games with the village children outside the compound where we were stationed. The officers hated it, told him he would get kidnapped, but he sneaked out whenever he could."

I smiled. "I didn't know that. What games did they play?"

"The first week we were there, he brought chalk with him. He said there was one little boy, and he went to give him a piece of chalk, and suddenly he had two dozen children climbing all over him with their hands out. He was lucky it was chalk, so he was able to break it into smaller pieces. Some of the little ones tried to eat it. 'At least they got their calcium,' he told me later. After that, he didn't bring them anything, since he didn't have anything else to split so many ways. He made me teach him hopscotch, so he could teach it to them. Can you imagine that? This big soldier playing hopscotch? Then four square, football, anything they could play with a stick or a line in the dirt or the ball they already had. He would sneak back in with his eyes glowing like he had forgotten where we were and why we were there. Then the first attack—" She twisted her hands in her lap.

"Why were you there, Mama?"

A church bell began to chime, and another one, and another.

"Tell me more, Mama, quick!"

There was so much I wanted to know. A tear rolled down her cheek, and she pulled me close. She didn't answer, and I knew it was too late. I thought of my father, the man in the uniform, and tried to picture him teaching hopscotch to me instead of village children. It was hard to imagine somebody I had never known, never could know. I should have started with her instead of my father.

Minutes passed, and the bells stopped. Mama's face closed down like a shutter. She fumbled in the pocket on the side of her chair. The photo of my father slid off her lap and to the floor.

"I don't know why, but I'm in the mood to watch something funny before we make dinner," she said. "Do you want to watch with me?"

"Sure. I'll be right back." I picked up the fallen photograph.

"Who's that?" she asked, glancing up.

"Somebody who fought in the war."

"A school project?"

"Yeah," I said.

"I'm proud of you." She smiled. "Those soldiers deserve to be remembered."

Nana was asleep on her bed. I hid the photo back in my drawer where Mama couldn't reach it or find it accidentally. Why had I asked about him first? I could never know him. He was gone and she was here and I still didn't know any more about the parts of her that went away.

★ ★ ★

Mama's voice carried down the hall. "Clara, are you watching with me?"

"Coming."

I pulled a chair up beside Mama's and leaned up against her. She leaned back. This was the Mama I knew best. The one who couldn't quite remember why she was in a wheelchair, who thought war was something that had happened to other people. The one who laughed at pet videos with me.

Some year, maybe the old soldiers would vote to lift the Veil. Maybe I'd get to know the other Mama, too: the one who remembered my father, who had died before I was born. The one who could someday tell me whether it had been worth everything she had lost. Next year, I would try to remember to ask that question first.

GYRE
(a Sargasso Containment story)
★
by Brad R. Torgersen

Teller is just another courier pilot trying to make a living in a dog-eat-dog solar system. So when a woman shows up at the space docks carrying a suitfcase in which rests a strange metallic cylinder and a transaction card loaded with currency, he doesn't ask too many questions. His job: get the cylinder to the Sargasso Grid, the mysterious forcefield at the edge of the solar system. Sounds easy enough—but whatever that cylinder may be, it has attracted a lot of attention from some very bad people.

THE RED-LETTERED SIGN over the tube to my berth clearly said NO PASSENGERS.

Yet there she was on the ramp: petite, stern-faced, and clasping a suitcase in both hands. Sweat beaded her forehead and her chest rose and fell quickly.

"If you can't read, it's not my problem," I said to her as I nudged past, pushing a cart loaded with lockers.

"This is dock six-oh-six," she said, "which means you're the courier pilot?"

I stopped halfway down the tube and turned back to face her.

"Yes, I am. The commercial spacelines are over on the third node. This is freight and cargo territory. You're in the wrong part of the station."

"Actually, Mr. Teller, I found you right where they told me to find you."

I raised an eyebrow.

"Whoever *they* are, they neglected to mention that couriers don't carry people."

"I'm not here for myself, Mr. Teller. I am here for this."

The young woman opened the suitcase to reveal a foam-packed interior. A shining, metallic cylinder was tucked into the foam, like an egg in a nest. There were no stickers or barcodes on the cylinder, and the young woman looked at me expectantly, as if the cylinder's mere presence explained everything.

I sighed.

"Fine, I still have room for small stuff. Whatever it is. But you'll have to go back and get it cleared through customs first. Then take it to the yard purser and have the transit fees deposited and transferred to my corporate account. I am assuming whoever sent you with this, also sent you with money?"

"They did."

She locked the suitcase back up and stepped down the ramp toward me, waiting until we were practically chest-to-nose before reaching into her shirt pocket and removing a transaction card. She raised the card up to my eye level.

"There is enough here to ensure that neither customs nor the purser need be involved. I was told that you are a man of discretion, Mr. Teller."

Who in the hell had this girl been talking to?

She apparently knew far more about me than I was comfortable with her knowing. I was about to beg off when I looked up at several people in bulky armor who were approaching the tube's mouth. They all carried guns. And they didn't look like the normal uniformed patrol.

The young woman, noticing my eyes, jammed the transaction card into one of the open pockets on my flight vest, then spun and faced up the ramp. With one hand she held the suitcase protectively behind her. With the other, she reached back to deftly guide my fingers around the suitcase's handle.

"What the hell—?" I began, but she cut me off.

"There are instructions on the card, Mr. Teller. You must ensure that this package arrives safely at the Sargasso Grid. Whatever else happens."

One of the armored men saw the young woman. He hand-signaled to the others with him. They brought their weapons up in unison, and I distinctly heard the sound of safeties clicking off.

She screamed and ran at them, getting a quarter of the way up the ramp before multiple shell blasts took her down. Blood went everywhere.

I stood gape-mouthed and deafened, the suitcase still in my hand.

The barrels of their weapons retrained on me as the men advanced down the ramp. When they reached the young woman's corpse, one of them bent to check the body. He rolled her over on her back, causing one of her arms to flop loosely. A black sphere tumbled from her lifeless fingers, and all of the armored men looked down at it in alarmed surprise.

Whatever else happens . . .

I spun and threw the suitcase onto the lockers and began pushing the cart with all my strength. Two meters further, there was a line of yellow and black caution tape that stretched all the way around the tube: the demarcation for the emergency cut-off seal. As the cart rolled over the tape, I slapped at the red panic disc on the tube's wall.

Decompression doors snapped shut behind me. I didn't wait to see if they'd be grenade-proof.

The yard was in pandemonium. Ships were decoupling right and left. I dodged, on thrusters, while various voices from traffic control screamed in my headphones.

"—unconfirmed reports of additional decompression at—"

"—they're rioting on the mezzanine, the constabulary are—"

"—unable to regain control. Telemetry is hazed—"

I tuned out the chatter and focused on driving. It took about ninety seconds of sweat-inducing manual navigation to clear completely off the node, then I punched the primary drive and felt the fusion reactor's vibrations through the base of my spine.

Ahead lay the blackness of interplanetary space, and beyond it . . .

There's a dragon down below . . .

Every experienced pilot knew that interstellar space was closed to us. As if the whole of the universe had been kept safe from human meddling, behind an invisible, locked door. Men had tried to penetrate the Sargasso Grid, and died for their ambition. Part of me wondered if we'd ever solve the mystery, and actually venture beyond the solar system; to explore other stars. But that was a challenge for others—better paid, with superior research budgets—to tackle. My personal goals were much more humble. Transport item A to point B, receive money C. Rinse and repeat.

No glory. But then, not much danger either.

Until now.

The transaction card was a stiff rectangle in my vest. I fished it out and stuck it into the reader slot on my dashboard. A new voice flooded into my ears, overriding all others. I sucked in breath, recognizing the man instantly.

"I regret the necessity of this maneuver, Sal. It's been a few years since you visited Earth. I know you never cared about our local politics down here, but things have gotten bad. Really, really bad. This Rust drug is like a plague. The whole planet is going crazy with it. Literally. If you're hearing this message then it means I am dead, and I've left it to my daughter to get both this message and its attached cargo into your hands. You're the only courier I trust, Sal. Everyone else is on the take from someone. Or caught up in Rust-created illusions. But I know you, just like I knew your dad. You'll do the right thing. I've included enough funds to make it worth your while, too. Five megacredits. There is another ten meg waiting for you when you reach home port, after the long trip out to the edge of the Grid. But go to Saturn first. I'm including coordinates, and a cypher key, on this card, for clearance. I'm sorry I can't tell you more, but the less you know, the better. For all our sakes. You are a professional. I am sure you understand."

The voice recording faded out, and I double checked the balance on the card to verify if what Jeran Velasquez had said was true.

It was. *Five million.* Almost enough to put an entirely new secondary drive into my ship. Dump the clunky, outdated converters. Open up additional room for more cargo. Faster times in and out of orbit. My mental calculator began whirring on the figures. Whatever else Jeran had gotten me into, he'd definitely made sure I knew that *he* knew I wasn't going to do anything out of charity. This was a transaction, first and foremost. It was just a damned shame his daughter had had to die in the process.

His daughter. *Damn.* I'd never even found out her name. I closed my eyes and saw her lifeless young body being rolled over, like a side of beef. It gave me the shivers, and I couldn't make them stop. I eventually told the autopilot to continue pouring on the thrust, then got out of my pilot's crèche and used the handrails and foot pads to go to the forward cargo compartment.

The cart had spilled wildly, during pull-out from the orbital station. It took me a few minutes to get stuff re-arranged and strapped down. The suitcase? I took it with me back to my personal cabin, where I popped it open and gazed again at the metallic cylinder.

It didn't look like a standard data drive. There were no jacks, lines, nor obvious seams in the metal—to indicate that the cylinder could be opened or accessed. For all I knew, it was just a solid piece of brushed steel. Only Jeran's message convinced me that there was more to the cylinder than met the eye.

I closed the cylinder back up in its case, and told myself I'd not let it out of my sight.

Jeran had been right about one thing, I didn't care about the political situation on Earth. I made my money hauling butt between Jupiter, Saturn, the asteroid belt, and occasional trips to Mars. My reputation with Space Patrol was clean. I was good at my job, played by the rules that mattered, and there were no questions asked. Not even when the local situation got messy—as I'd just seen it get messy in a very deadly way, back at the node. I certainly wouldn't be returning to the spaceyards of Europa any time soon. Not until I knew more about what had happened. Or why an old friend from Earth had sent his daughter all the way to the Jovian moons, to die.

Rust. Jeran wasn't kidding. The stuff was causing mayhem. And Earth had plenty of company in the chaos department. The courier free-exchange news network had been lighting up for weeks. One safe harbor after another had been red-lined, due to outbreaks of what could only be described as fatal addiction and delusions, due to drug consumption and spore contamination. Whole colonies had been quarantined. There was talk that the death toll in the asteroid belt alone was well over a thousand, and climbing like a rocket.

What had Jeran's daughter given me, precisely?

If the metal canister in the case held an equivalent volume of the potent black Rust, then it was worth more than my entire ship, several times over. But that didn't make any sense, with Jeran involved. The man was not a narcotics dealer. He was an honest businessman turned politician. Clean, sober, and proud of it too. One of the few pols I actually trusted to try to make things better, not worse. The chances of him being involved in anything truly illegal were so remote as to not even be worth considering.

I shook my head. Questions just made things messy, and were bad for business. Dad taught me that. And I'd seen little, in the ten years I'd been doing the job, to convince me that my dad was wrong. Keep your eyes open and your lips zipped. Stick to the contract. Be a pro. Point A to point B, for money C. Live a long, prosperous life. And nobody bothers you. As long as you don't bother them first.

Except, the old wisdom held little comfort for me now. I laid on my bunk and wrapped a blanket around my body, still unable to stop the shivering.

They caught me just fifteen minutes shy of the official governmental boundary. Two ships. They were using EM and radar suppression because I didn't see them until I saw the flashes from their thruster systems. I potted my own secondary drive to one-ten and felt my teeth rattle, as I warned them off via radio. For my trouble I was told they'd have one of their kinetic weapons put a hole through my fuel torus—if I didn't heave to, and await official latch-on.

Such a threat was a blatant violation of the interplanetary courier charter, which granted all licensed members of the Courier Guild the equivalent of diplomatic immunity. By threatening to attack my ship, these people had placed their entire government in danger of being blacklisted by the Guild—which would practically cut them off from civilization.

The contents of that suitcase must have been important.

Rust. Was that really all it came down to?

Cussing up a storm, I potted down the secondary drive to zero, spun the ship, then potted the secondary back up for braking. Then I went to wait calmly at the main hatch as the two Space Patrol ships matched with mine, and extended grapplers. I felt my craft jarred slightly as the grapplers took hold, then the *thunk-clunk* of the ship-to-ship tube as it sealed on the outside of the hull.

I opened my hatch—expecting more guys with guns. What I got

was a well-toned older woman in a tight spacer's suit, flanked by four bulky men wearing ceramic armor. Their insignia marked them as Space Patrol. Their eyes were hidden behind dropped sets of flash visors.

The woman's face—

I averted my eyes as we shook hands. Despite the reconstruction surgery, her face was difficult to look at. Whatever had happened to her, it had been bad.

"Mr. Teller," she said.

"That's correct," I said hesitantly.

"I'm O'Riley. Space Patrol tried to contact you numerous times via radio, but you weren't answering our hails. Under the provisions of the interplanetary theft ordnance—which your Guild recognizes—I was obligated to prevent you from departing Jupiter space with dangerous contraband onboard."

She stepped into my ship without being invited. I stepped back, not sure I could have prevented her in any case. Her movements were those of someone accustomed to the deck of a ship. Her eyes appraised the interior of my vessel as she moved.

"I'm not sure what you're talking about," I said, trying to keep up with her.

"Mr. Teller, neither of us is dumb enough to believe that. The young lady who gave you a suitcase, before suicide bombing your berth, didn't hand you a bouquet of flowers."

"Like hell," I said. "She was murdered. Those weren't cops who gunned her down."

"Did you know her?"

"Not at all. In fact, I told her she was in the wrong part of the station to be seeking passage. Then she was shot to death. I didn't wait around to see much of what happened next. Didn't feel like being a collateral casualty."

I looked to each of the four men who accompanied O'Riley. They seemed alert, but not necessarily menacing. They were taking their cues from the woman. I finally got ahead of her and put an arm across the corridor, blocking her passage. I don't know who she thought she was, but I wasn't going to just let her ransack me without sufficient cause and documentation.

"By commandeering a courier en route," I said firmly to her, "you are walking on very thin ice. The internal security problems of Jupiter's moons are *your* concern, not mine. All data and cargo on this vessel are secured under the Guild's own Common Confidentiality Clause. You can't seize any of it without first petitioning the local Guild office for a writ."

"I know," she said, not smiling. One of her men stepped forward and handed me a piece of hardcopy.

Son of a . . . it even had the Guildmaster's signature on it.

I thought of Jeran's daughter being shot to death, and clenched my teeth to keep from filling the air with obscenities.

"Come with me," I said, and led them aft.

O'Riley held the metallic cylinder in both hands.

"Satisfied?" I said.

"Yes," she replied.

"Then the conditions of the writ have been met. I'll have to ask you to leave my ship and allow me to resume my voyage, immediately."

"Of course, Mr. Teller. Thank you for your professionalism."

I wanted to tell her she could shove it up her ass, but held my tongue.

The six of us walked back to the hatch in silence. O'Riley gave the cylinder to one of her men, then they walked back across the threshold.

She turned to face me before she went.

"Ordinarily, we would seize whatever monetary funds were used in the course of an illegal shipment. In this case, however, I recommended that we write them off. I don't think you knew what was being entrusted to you. Believe or not, I know a boarding like this is galling, Teller. I've been there a time or two myself. But Space Patrol has to be sure. Rust is no laughing matter. It's getting far too many people killed. Or worse. This is a pandemic the whole solar system is afraid of now."

She turned on a heel without allowing me to retort, and I watched her walk swiftly across the ship-to-ship tube without saying another word.

I closed the hatch and heard the tube decouple and withdraw, followed by the release of the grapplers. I climbed back into the pilot's crèche and navigated away on thrusters, distancing myself from the two Space Patrol ships until it was safe enough to engage the secondary, and resume my trip to Saturn.

It wasn't until ten minutes later that my radio suddenly came alive with another hail.

"Yes?" I said, flipping on the video as well as the audio.

"You deceitful bastard," O'Riley spat at me, her face pink with anger.

"Beg pardon?"

"Shut down your drive and prepare to be re-boarded."

"What for?"

"You defied our search."

"Bull. I obeyed the stipulations of the writ. You got what you wanted."

She brandished the metal cylinder in my field of vision.

"It's a worthless piece of mill stock!"

I stared at the screen image of the cylinder for a moment, then realized that the empty suitcase itself still lay on the floor of my cabin.

The suitcase . . .

Without taking my eyes of the screen, I gently manipulated my controls and began potting up the primary drive. It would burn a lot of reaction mass, but at this point I needed raw thrust. The secondary had a fuel-efficient specific impulse ratio that served me well in most instances. But now? Now I just needed to keep space between myself, and the Space Patrol. Whatever this was about, it wasn't my business and it wouldn't matter once I was out of O'Riley's jurisdiction. Clearly Jeran hadn't given me Rust, if that was what she was after. And I wasn't going to cool my heels in a brig cell on Callisto while they pulled my ship apart, looking for something I didn't have.

O'Riley's ship and my ship had been going in opposite directions for over ten minutes. In the time it would take them to decelerate, do an about-face, and engage their drives—even as powerful as those drives were—I'd be out of reach.

Or so I hoped.

"Shut down immediately or there will be dire consequences, courier."

I frowned at her.

"I fulfilled the writ. You can't search me again without obtaining a second one. Look it up in your treaty with the Guild."

I clicked off the feed without giving her a chance to retort, and kept the primary drive running strong. The two Space Patrol ships did slow, stop, turn, and slam their own pots to the max, but it was too late. They couldn't get me before I hit the boundary.

Whatever Jeran had intended, his sleight-of-hand had provided me with enough time to make my break.

Saturn space. I swung my ship around until I could aim the drives for deceleration. The downthrust towards Enceladus would take almost a day, at this range, and I wasn't in any hurry.

What I did do was unstrap and go back for the suitcase itself, which still sat—open and forlorn—on the floor of my cabin.

I shook it out, examined the interior pockets, and found nothing.

Returning to the pilot's crèche, I re-activated the transaction card—still plugged into the dash—and waited while the card executed a routine that triple-checked data with the navigational system.

I put my headset back on in time to hear Jeran's voice.

"Looks like you made it halfway, Sal. Excellent. You may have also figured out my little trick. Sorry about not letting you into the loop sooner. I knew there was a high probability you'd be boarded before you could leave Jupiter space, and I didn't want there to be any chance that you'd give away the goose. I had to make sure you were as convinced as they were. Of what, I still can't say. All you need to know is that you need to dock at Enceladus and ask for the Intra-System Ambassador's office. Take this card and the suitcase. The office should already have your name, and will know what to do.

Once my ship's computer was talking to Saturn's in-system network, I moved the five million off the card and into my corporate account, threw the card into the empty suitcase, and closed the case tight.

The ride down into the gravity well of Saturn was uneventful, allowing me to grab some sleep, a shower, and a fresh flight suit. After that, I made some advanced calls to the yard at Enceladus—checking on prices for replacement of the secondary drive. I haggled with a few companies, before agreeing on an amount, then I set myself up at a business hotel on-station for the two weeks it would take to have the work done.

Sliding into the traffic control net, followed by my berth at the orbital yard station, also went without incident.

I didn't have a clue what was up until I opened the hatch, and three Guild officers grabbed me and threw me up against the bulkhead, cuffing me unceremoniously.

"They'll strip you for this, Teller."

"What the f—" I said out the side of my mouth, my head pressed painfully to the wall.

"Collusion with a drug-runner is one thing, but these are Rust freaks you're carrying water for. What were you thinking? This puts the reputation of the entire Guild on the line. At a time when we can least afford it. Rust craziness is slowly dismantling the chain of commerce throughout the entire solar system. We need the Guild to stay clean. You're lucky we don't dump you out the airlock."

So much for the warm welcome. My pleading to see the Ambassador's people went unheeded, and I was shuffled off to a locked room at the Guild's office—where I was allowed to talk to no one, nor see anybody, for at least two days. During which I could only guess at my fate. Nobody would talk to me. Not even the woman who brought me my meals. She wouldn't even look me in the eye.

On the third day, the locked door opened, and the Guildmaster entered, along with a familiar individual.

"Oh crap," I breathed.

"Surprised to see me, Mr. Teller?" O'Riley said, her face just as difficult to look at, as the last time. Her eyes practically dripped with anger.

"A little," I admitted.

"Don't be. Did you think we'd just let you go?"

"Let me guess. You radioed ahead of me, claimed I was still carrying contraband, and had the Guild hold me until you could catch up."

"Very good. You're not as dumb as this situation makes you out to be."

I turned to face the Guildmaster.

"Sir, I'm a little curious. Since when has the Guild answered to any planetary government—even Space Patrol—without there being an internal investigation first?"

"Shut up, Teller. I knew your father. He was one of our best. He'd have never allowed himself to get involved in something like this. They were *using* you."

"They *who?* Sir, I don't know *what's* happening. Did O'Riley tell you how this started? A woman was murdered right outside the hatch to my ship. I'd be dead now too if I'd not gotten across the emergency line in the docking tube, before things blew."

"A Sargasso cultist acting in concert with other Sargasso cultists," O'Riley said stiffly. "We didn't become aware of Mr. Teller's collusion until it was revealed he'd acted in false faith during our search under writ."

"Sir," I said, ignoring O'Riley, "I think this all might become a bit clearer if you just contact the Ambassador's office and give them my name. I've seen what happens to Rust addicts. The woman who was killed? Stone-cold sober. And the people who did it? Hardly Space Patrol. Something very wrong is going on. And I think this O'Riley woman might be very wrong too."

"We have the suitcase, and the card, and we did contact the Ambassador's office. They've never heard of you, Teller. Like I said, you've been *used*. You'll be fortunate if all we do is confiscate your ship and revoke your license."

"You have the suitcase?" O'Riley said to the Guildmaster. Her voice sounded surprised.

"We seized it upon Teller's arrival."

"May I see it, please?"

"What for?"

O'Riley looked at me for a moment.

"I'd rather not say in front of the collaborator."

Frowning, the Guildmaster walked out of the room with O'Riley, who had begun to whisper something to him in his ear. Two plainclothed Guild officers remained behind, watching me dispassionately.

"This is all crap," I said to them, not necessarily expecting a response.

"We know," the two women replied in unison.

"What?"

One of them held an index finger to her lips while the Guildmaster re-entered with O'Riley in tow—the suitcase in her hand.

O'Riley flipped it open on the room's single, plain desk. The transaction card clattered out.

"Where is it?" O'Riley asked, hurriedly sticking fingers and hands into the interior pockets on the suitcase's lining.

"It?" I said. "There's nothing in that suitcase but air."

O'Riley made a snarling noise as she upended the suitcase and shook it violently, finally swinging the case by the handle and slamming it against the desk, snapping the hinges and cracking the exterior.

A single, tiny, plastic disc, spun out of the crack—and rolled across the floor.

All eyes in the room went to the disc. O'Riley's face lit up, and she turned to chase after the item, when the Guildmaster waved a finger at one of the two guards, who stepped to the door and instantly closed it.

"Are we secure?" O'Riley asked.

"For now," the Guildmaster said. "Still think Teller is dirty?"

"I never really did," she said.

"Somebody better explain what the hell this all means, or I am going to start throwing fists!" I exclaimed, launching out of my chair and eyeballing the four of them.

"Calm down," the Guildmaster said.

"Sir, you have no idea what I've been through. A woman was murdered on my doorstep. I've been boarded and searched, then accused of criminal collusion, and finally thrown in this cell for the past three days. Call me crazy, but I think I remember having some *rights* that everyone has happily trampled."

"Sorry," O'Riley said. "It's just that . . . how much do you know about Rust?"

"Fancy new organic drug. Showed up on the black market not too long ago. Commands a steep price. The buzz is better than anything, or so I am told. Except when it gets you dead. Which is often. But that's part of the thrill, they say. High addiction rate. Apparently the spores have been infecting food shipments, and contaminated hydroponics are causing all kinds of outbreaks."

"You pay attention to the Guild news, that's for sure," the Guildmaster said.

"Here's what you don't know," O'Riley said. "On Earth, it's even worse than the official news will dare say. They're talking about possibly putting whole cities under martial law. In the asteroid belt, or out here in the Jovian moons, each and every settlement is practically self-quarantined. One location goes bad, you simply redirect traffic. Seal it off. They don't have that option on Earth. The Rust is now getting out into the general farming and food supply. Before long, hundreds of millions of people might be affected."

"So what does this have to do with the woman who got shot after she handed me that suitcase?"

"There are very well-financed and highly positioned people who are making a lot of money on the Rust black market," O'Riley said. "This little disc? Do you know what's actually on it?"

"No," I admitted.

"The planned genomes for several counter-viruses," the Guildmaster said. "Basically, the blueprints for a genetically engineered time bomb that can dismantle Rust down to the last spore. Assuming we can get to a pure source."

"Pure source of what? The Rust?"

"Yes," O'Riley said. "Once exposed to the organic source, the counter-virus will be able to key properly on all Rust that's been spawned from the source. Red, or black. It may even help cure those who've already become addicted, or infected."

"But why all the games?" I asked. "Where's the source?"

"The Sargasso Grid," O'Riley said. "I watched my brother die from Rust. I've seen it do worse to others. I'm not Space Patrol, but I struck a deal with them to help them fight Rust trafficking. But even I didn't know the half of it, until a man brought a mother and her sick son to me. All three of them looking for Nikki Dark."

My brain lit up.

Nikki Dark. Owner of the *Dreadnaught*. Rather infamous in Guild circles, for her exploits. A scoundrel of many bar stories. Which made her either hated or admired, depending on your particular angle.

"Wait," I said, eyeballing O'Riley's scar-laced face. "Don't tell me *you* are Nikki Dark."

"I am," O'Riley said.

"Nikki Dark and the Space Patrol, working together to fight Rust-running," I said. "I guess stranger things have happened."

"Like the mob buying off people all over the solar system, to hamper efforts to find a way to defeat Rust at the point of origin?" the Guildmaster said. "Even we haven't been safe, Teller. Which is why we had to keep up the pretense of you being a suspect, right up until we were sure you had in your possession what had been promised to us by Mr. Velasquez."

"Who has a dead daughter now!" I burst out, seeing her limp body flash before my eyes.

"Nobody trusts anybody anymore," O'Riley said. "Velasquez was working on a cure at the same time people orbiting Mars were working on a cure. The Mars effort didn't finish their work in time. The Rust-runners had someone on the inside trying to disrupt things. Velasquez had what he thought was a workable counter-viral template, but no way to reach the source. And no way to simply transmit his findings without the transmissions being tapped or blocked."

"The Rust-runners would rather watch interplanetary civilization collapse, than aid in the effort to halt the epidemic?" I asked, incredulously.

"Vultures," the Guildmaster said. "Which is why we finally came down on the side of assisting. Velasquez knew us, or rather, he knew your father. We knew you could get this far, if you'd been set up with the proper cover story. Now you'll go the rest of the distance for us."

"For what?" I said, pacing back and forth in the cell. "The Sargasso Grid is a no-man's land. You go in, you never come out. Or if you do, you come out crazier than crazy. Like the Sargasso cultists."

"The Sargasso Grid, and the Rust, and the cultists, and the mob," O'Riley said, "they're all part of the same thing. Can't you see? The Rust came from the Sargasso. That's our origin. The cultists actively encourage Rust use. The mafia sees Rust as its can't-lose commodity. Worth gigacredits. Velasquez gave us the key to potentially dismantling the entire problem. But we have to brave the Sargasso to do it."

"What, do we go floating out there in the dark and hope something magically happens?"

"No," O'Riley said. "We have a way to exactly track down our target."

Just then, the door to the cell opened, and a small gurney was wheeled in. There was a little boy tucked into numerous sheets and blankets. He looked incredibly thin and pale. So much so, I wasn't even sure he was still alive. The slightest rising and falling of the boy's chest told me he was still with us. The woman at the gurney's side was hollow-eyed and lean-looking too. Obviously the mother, from the way she couldn't take her eyes off her son's sallow face.

The two Guild officers with us, quickly closed the cell again.

"This man brought the counter-virus?" the mother said.

"Lily Silva," the Guildmaster said, "meet Sal Teller. He'll be taking you and Mateo to the Sargasso Grid, along with Ms. O'Riley."

"Aboard the *Dreadnaught?*" I asked, looking to O'Riley.

"No," she said. "My ship is too well-known. We've already sent it on its way elsewhere, as a decoy. You know that new secondary drive you bought? Well, you'll be surprised just how much your money got you, when we get back to your berth. Your ship was never outfitted to get much past Uranus. Now it could go deep into the Sargasso, and not even come close to bingo fuel point."

"And what's the ace in the hole?" I said, staring at the sick boy in the gurney. "Do we have a homing signal or something?"

"You might say that," the mother—Lily—said. She leaned over the gurney and spoke quietly to her son.

"Can you still talk to her, Mateo? Can you still talk to Rat?"

"I can *feel* Rat," the boy said, almost too quietly for me to hear him. "But her name's not really Rat. I told you that. She's named Jingfei. And she's with the man who would have been my papa. Carvahlo. And they're with the Other."

I felt the hair go up on the back of my neck.

"Carvahlo," I said. "You don't mean *Victor* Carvahlo?"

"Yes," Lily admitted. "He was—he should have become—my husband. Before the accident in the Sargasso. The one that twisted his mind. How or why he became the point of origin for the Rust is a question I can't answer. I'm almost afraid it's something *I* helped engineer. A piece of research I did, and which Victor twisted for some crazy purpose. Out there in the Sargasso. Now it's like the Rust brings part of the Sargasso back to the solar system. To normal space. Where it's destroying lives and minds. Including my son's."

"Who is Jingfei?" I asked.

"We don't really know," O'Riley said. "We think it was somebody from one of the penal colonies on Ceres."

"Ceres is off-limits," I said. "One hundred percent quarantine."

"This Jingfei girl got off before the blockade," the Guildmaster said. "She was deep under the effects of Rust contamination when she fled. Somehow, Mateo here is in contact with her. Emotionally. Mentally. He can sense where she is, and where we need to go to find her. Mateo's got Rust contamination too, obviously."

I jerked away from the gurney.

"He's not contagious," Lily said loudly, here tired eyes glaring at me. "If he was, we'd all be contaminated by now. But the Rust is in him, and it's in him good. I thought I had a cure when we fled Mars. Marcus—someone who served time with Jingfei on Ceres—came to me, hoping I had the answers. He took us to Nikki Dark—Ms. O'Riley—and we discovered we only had part of the puzzle solved. What we needed was a way to fight back. With a virus that would actively infect and destroy Rust at the molecular level. The Space Patrol helped relay this to Earth, and Mr. Velasquez said he'd send us the best solution that he could come up with. Rust-runners and corrupt officials permitting."

"If they were willing to kill his daughter like they did," I said, "all of us are in great danger."

"Which is why we had to cook up the game, and make you believe it," the Guildmaster said. "So that if you somehow got caught en route to Saturn, you wouldn't know any better. And you certainly couldn't lead them to Lily or her son. But now that we have the disc, there's no more sense delaying the inevitable. Go. Take your ship, and O'Riley, and Lily, and her son, and find Carvahlo. Through the connection Mateo has with this Jingfei girl. Lily will know what to do with the genetic blueprints on the disc. We already put the synthesizer aboard your ship; that she will need to make the prototypes. You just have to get her within spitting distance of the Rust's actual source. She will make the proper exposures, then you have to get the active counter-viral samples back to us. So that we can release them into the wild. And hopefully this nightmare will start to end. For everybody."

I stared at the boy in the bed.

Too sick to live, and perhaps even, too sick to die?

A miserable existence.

"Okay then," I said. "If it means getting my ship back, and eventually making good on the ten megacredits I was promised, let's go."

I'd never been this far out. The sun was like an extra-bright star, just barely discernible among all the other stars. Each of which shone like a pinprick of light on an otherwise perfectly black, velvet canvas. It had taken several weeks to go the distance. Even with the souped-up drive my ship had been outfitted with. O'Riley and the Guildmaster hadn't lied. They'd replaced my actual purchase with a super-expensive prototype drive the Space Patrol was testing on interdiction cutters. I was the only civilian allowed to have one, or so they'd told me when we broke orbit. And it would get us to the destination and back without having to make any more pit stops—and risk potentially getting sandbagged by Rust-runner goons, trying to keep us from destroying their market.

"Jingfei is close," Mateo's weak voice whispered.

My ordinarily cramped quarters had been cleared out, and now they served as Mateo's hospital room. I slept in the pilot's chair most of the time, while O'Riley took the long-neglected navigator's chair. Lily, of course, kept close to her boy. And Marcus? He'd stayed with the Guildmaster. Giving us only a verbal message to deliver to Jingfei, assuming we actually found her. And Carvahlo.

"He did what needed to be done," Lily told me upon our departure.

Which was fine for me. I didn't think the ship could hold another grown male. Not after taking on two passengers the ship hadn't been designed to accommodate in the first place.

I'd been following Mateo's directions for the most part. Riding an invisible barrier just inside the known limit of the Sargasso Grid, until Mateo was sure that Jingfei—whom he had also called Rat on occasion—was directly ahead.

I didn't dare pot up the drive. Every nerve in my body screamed against plowing my ship into the Sargasso. It was madness. There was no guarantee that we wouldn't all go just as mad as Lily's one-time husband had gone. I'd heard the scuttlebutt around the Guild. Even seen some of the leaked digital imagery recovered with Victor Carvahlo. From the boarding of the *Illico One*.

How had the rhyme begun?

> *Aye, aye, m'lady?*
> *There's a dragon down below,*
> *Aye, aye, m'lady,*
> *Yet exploring we shall go.*

I wasn't the adventuresome type. What the hell was I doing all the way out here, at the precipice of eternity? Every pilot had a pet theory about the Sargasso. Some said it was a barrier created by God, to keep mankind from straying too far beyond our intended domain. Others said it was a dimensional anomaly, held at a certain distance by the curvature of space-time, created by the gravity well of the sun. Still others though it was a wholly artificial thing: a sort of psychic barrier, laid down by an alien species trying to either keep us in, or prevent others from stumbling along and letting us out.

I myself? I didn't really care what it was.

I just knew that going into it was suicide.

"Carvahlo is out there," Nikki Dark—O'Riley—said to me, as she stared over my shoulder from the navigator's station. She'd been a sharp second mate, and there'd been no bickering about who gave the orders during the trip from Saturn. Far from being a scoundrel, I thought O'Riley was probably the most professional co-pilot a man could ask for. It was a shame we were going to have to split up and go our separate ways when we got back home.

Assuming we didn't get devoured by the Sargasso first.

"I wish the kid could dog-whistle this Rat girl, and have her drag Carvahlo out to meet us. I mean, what do we expect to find when we get there, anyway? Carvahlo and his minions, welcoming us with open arms? It will be obvious why we've come, once they see Lily. And her virus synthesizer. I can't imagine Sargasso cultists who treat Rust like a holy sacrament, will be too pleased to see a ship filled with infidels— all of us come to destroy the very thing that gives their lives meaning."

"We're counting on the fact that Victor Carvahlo literally thinks of Lily as an angel," O'Riley reminded me. "You saw the same footage I did, after we left Saturn. The stuff they don't let the news show? He claimed—upon being rescued—that Lily came to him in the form of a literal angel, and protected him from a demon while he was trapped aboard the *Illico One*. That's our hole card. He hasn't seen Lily in years. Crazy or no, some part of him must still love Lily. Enough to let her sway him. If even only for long enough to let the synthesizer do its job. It only takes one of us to escape and get the counter-virus back to the Guild. After that, every Guild ship will be carrying counter-virus. It'll be spread to every settlement, no matter how remote. And Earth too."

"And what if the counter-virus doesn't work?"

O'Riley frowned, and didn't answer my question. Which was merely a reminder to me that we'd all been dancing around the uncomfortable fact that this whole plan—already banking on improbabilities—had no guarantee of achieving the desired goal of eradicating Rust. For all we knew, the virus could mutate and turn into something even worse than Rust. Perhaps, much worse?

Although there didn't sound like a death much worse than the one O'Riley had described, when confiding in me about the final hours of her brother. I thought I understood her motive, at least. She now had a son to protect. The Space Patrol offered legal immunity in exchange for her services—to help stop Rust.

Lily too had her son to protect.

Me? I had nothing.

But over the time it had taken us to reach this point, I kept watching my new navigator out of the corner of my eye, and realizing that A to B to C didn't necessarily describe everything that was worth doing in the universe.

"Ah, screw it," I said, finally putting my hand to the drive's potentiometer. "Waiting around wondering what might happen is almost worse than what's actually going to happen."

My ship pushed into the Sargasso.

And we never looked back.

The space station wasn't really a space station at all. Rather, it was a collection of wrecked ships all piled together on a tiny, carbon-molecule dwarf moon. The abandoned technology had been jury-rigged and re-worked until it formed a minimally functional habitat on the moon's dark surface. When we flew over that specific part of the moon with the most activity showing on the surface, there was no apparent place for use to dock or land.

So far, the dreaded Sargasso hadn't taken its toll on our senses. No angels, nor devils, had risen in our minds to make us want to claw our eyes out.

The single hailing call we'd received, had been answered by Lily. Who'd cleaned herself up and even put on a little makeup, before putting herself in front of a comm unit and responding with the words, "Victor, it's me, Lily. Victor, I have to see you. I want to come home, please."

Since then, we'd seen not a single sign that they might be belligerent. The dwarf moon was inhabited, yes—but by how many, we couldn't say.

Eventually, we picked a clear spot near what seemed to be an open-mouthed hangar, and set down. The dwarf moon's gravity was miniscule. Just enough to keep it cohesively spherical. But not much beyond that. With Mateo being too fragile to leave alone, Lily, O'Riley, and myself, all agreed to have O'Riley stay behind while Lily and I went out in suits. To see who—or what—might be waiting to greet us.

The strange thing was, nobody was there to greet us. The hangar—lit by flickering lamps, all salvaged from some unfortunate old ship's cargo bay—was empty. Just an airlock door awaited us.

I signaled O'Riley that we were going in, and she promised to keep alert in the pilot's chair. So that she could lift off at the slightest hint of trouble. Whether Lily or I made it out or not.

The airlock seemed to work normally. We stepped through the outer door, waiting for the lights on the other side to change from red, to yellow, to green, then we checked our own suits to be sure we weren't fooled.

Nope. They showed green too. Though we didn't dare take our helmets off. The air inside was doubtless laden with Rust spores. We didn't intend to subject ourselves to contamination and infection, if we could help it.

We stepped into a corridor that snaked away into the distance, twisting at odd angles. As we walked, I noted that each section of the corridor appeared to have come from a different vessel, and a different time period. There were pieces of ships in the corridor that were literally almost two hundred years old. Or older. My knowledge of archaic shipwright technique only went back so far. But somehow, it had all been welded and fused together—to make a livable whole.

Though we had yet to see a single sign of human habitation.

That changed when we got to the corridor's end. Lily clutched the detachable sample catcher portion of the genetic synthesizer to her chest, as a man approached. He wasn't wearing a space suit, nor anything else other than a tattered, somewhat stained bathrobe. A scraggly, long beard sprouted from his face, and his hair ran over his shoulders and down his back.

I glanced at Lily, and she glanced at me.

Victor? The question passed between us.

Lily shook her head, no.

"The angel has returned to us," the man said in a dreamy baritone, while he bowed low to Lily, and practically ignored me. "Carvahlo knew you would come. He has seen it in a vision. He sees many things in his visions. As do we all. But why are you wearing that garment? Surely the angel does not need to fear the air of her own temple."

"Temple?" Lily blurted, incredulously.

But the bearded man in the dirt robe had merely turned away, and began striding down an entirely different corridor.

We hurried after him.

"That guy doesn't seem too unhealthy," I said under my breath. "A little mangy, perhaps, but hardly psycho."

"He's badly addicted," Lily cautioned. "You could see it in his manner while he talked. He's hallucinating even now. He might not even be aware of the fact that we're following him."

"Let's just hope he takes us past the brewery," I said.

"Brewery?" Lily asked.

"What else do we call it? Where they grow the Rust to begin with."

She patted the sample catcher with a gloved hand.

"One whiff is all this thing needs, and we can go."

"Assuming they're inclined to let us go," I said. "I still feel like a mouse wandering around in a maze filled with cats."

Lily didn't respond to me.

Suddenly, the corridor emptied out into what appeared to be the retrofitted interior of a massive, archaic, slush deuterium fuel tank. Hundreds of lights had been snaked over and across the dome over our heads—joined by haphazardly connected electrical conduit. So that the space practically blazed with white light. Lily and I stared, our helmet bowls automatically closing their silver glare shields. After which, everything in the dome seemed like we were seeing it through a pair of dark sunglasses.

Two dozen different people were arrayed around the floor, sitting on benches or couches which seemed to have been taken from the recreational cabins of ten different ships. The inhabitants paid almost no attention to us as they focused their eyes on a single man—who sat on a mad hatter's throne of contorted pipe and steel, from which aisles radiated between the benches and couches.

Our guide led us up one of the aisles.

"Victor," Lily breathed. I could barely hear her in my helmet's speakers.

The man on the mad hatter's throne, was barely recognizable as human. He was gaunt to the point of seeming like a skeleton. As if severely starved over a long duration. His skull weighed down a bowed neck, and thin lips stretched over brown teeth. The eyes were watery and unfocused. Seemingly staring at nothing. Until our guide leaned in and whispered to the skeleton's ear. Then the watery eyes snapped up and came to focus on us.

"Is it a deception?" the skeleton demanded in a ragged voice.

As one, the collection of people on the benches and couches began to wail and beat their fists against the sides of their heads.

"No," Lily said, using her suit's external speakers. "It's me, Victor. It's Lily."

"Take your helmet off," was all the skeleton said.

"No," I commanded her firmly.

"I don't think I have a choice," she said.

"You want to wind up like the rest of these freaks?" I hissed. "Just walk to him and show him your face through your helmet."

She did as I suggested, stepping cautiously to the throne and manually dialing back the glare shield, so that Victor Carvahlo could see clearly into the face bowl.

He gasped audibly, and shot to his bony feet.

"She has come!" he bellowed.

The congregants switched from wailing and beating their heads, to cheering and waving their hands in the air. Their actions mimicking Victor's mood, almost as if they were attuned to him. Was that it? Was that part of what happened with Rust addiction? You ended up on the same wavelength or frequency as the other addicts around you?

Then Victor's face darkened.

"You bring an unwanted guest," he said, pointing a scrawny arm at me.

"He's my helper, Victor," Lily said. "I could not have come without him. Please, don't hurt him. He's just a pilot. He'll be taking his ship and leaving soon."

Suddenly one of the people on one of the benches leapt in front of me and brandished a finger in my face. I stared at her—almost as skeletal as Victor himself—and realized she was a youngish Asian girl. Her stomach was distended, but not from fat. It was from having not eaten in far too long. In fact, all of them seemed to be malnourished in the extreme. Did they run out of actual food? Had the hydroponics for producing Rust killed off the real crops they needed to survive?

I waited for the girl in front of me to say something. She seemed to have an accusation on her lips.

"Rat!" Victor bellowed. "Tell us this man's secrets."

Her mouth opened, ready to put the lie to Lily's gentle deception. But then the girl faltered. Her eyes seemed to go far away. And she nodded several times, her chin bobbing up and down. At which point she returned to her bench and curled up.

Victor murmured at her, and slowly sat back down.

"That one sees much," he said. "I can always rely on her to ferret out the facts, from the lies. And I *hate* lies. You know that, Lily."

"Nobody has come to lie to you, Victor. I've come to stay. I want . . . I want to understand how you *see* things. How you make the material that helps other people *see* things too. The Sargasso Grid hasn't killed you, my love. It's made you—"

"A god?" Victor offered, running a pointy finger along his beard-covered jaw.

Lily simply waited. There was more he clearly wanted to say.

"No," he finally confessed. "I am not a god. But then, neither am I a man. I am something . . . in between. The Sargasso too is something in between. Have my disciples done their work well? Has the human race been properly prepared to *see*, Lily? That's why we made it, you know. The fungus that carries the gift of the Sargasso back to the worlds and colonies of men. So that all might find the way."

"The way to what?" I asked, using my suit's own speakers.

Victor looked to me, annoyed.

"I did not give that one permission to speak," he said.

And the entire congregation got up from their benches and couches and surrounded me. Menacing in their demeanor. Not a one of them looked to be healthy enough to wrestle a child, much less a grown man in a full suit. I doubted that they could hurt me. But then I saw that there were pipes, and pieces of steel shaped for tool work. Grasped in each hand. The suit was built to withstand micrometeroid impact. But I doubted it could hold up for long against a sustained assault. Sooner or later the face bowl would crack or someone would damage something vital on the back pack, and that would be the end of it.

I held my hands up, trying to ward them off.

"Victor," Lily suddenly spoke, using a stern voice. "Is that any way to treat a guest? You know I always did hate it when you didn't show our guests proper hospitality. You should be ashamed of yourself."

Suddenly, the skeleton king's demeanor was crestfallen.

Tears sprang to his eyes and he clutched his forehead in one hand.

"I'm so sorry, Lily," he sobbed. "I'm so sorry I let you go."

The crowd around me gradually loosened, and began to disperse, eventually curling up in balls wherever it was comfortable, and weeping along with their master.

"It's okay, Victor," Lily said. "I'm here now. In fact, I've come to help! And so has my pilot. We need more fungus! Pure fungus. What's left on Earth has been polluted. It's not the same. People can't *see* what you want them to *see*, Victor. I want to take some of the spores back with us. To ensure that everyone sees. Can you do that, Victor?"

The skeleton king looked up, his skull-mask of a face grown hopeful.

"Only he will go? You will let him go back? *You* will stay?"

"I will stay," Lily said, placatingly. "I brought something to carry the fungus. I just need a little. My pilot will grow more, on the way home. But I will stay and be with you."

"You . . ." Victor said, then halted. His jaw quivered slightly. "You have always been with me. Even when hell itself had opened its womb, to birth pure evil into the universe—the faces, oh Lily, you didn't see the many faces—you were there. I built all of this for you, you know. Because I knew you'd come. I *saw* that you would come."

"Then you will take me—take us—to where the fungus is grown?"

"Yes, yes," Victor said.

For a man with practically no muscle on his body, he moved surprisingly fast. He swept away from his junkyard chair, and down one of the aisles. Lily and I trotted after him, trying to keep up. In the low gravity, we bounced more than we walked. Using our hands occasionally on the ceiling of the adjacent corridor, so that we wouldn't bump our heads.

Finally, we rounded a corner and came to a stop in a vestibule before a sealed door.

"Inside," Victor said, slapping his hand on the door.

"Good," Lily said. And reached to activate the mechanism that would open it.

"Not you," Victor said. "Only him. Let him get what he needs, and depart. You? I want you to take the whole suit off. Let me see you as I have always seen you—my perfect woman."

I saw Lily's shoulders sag, even through her suit.

I didn't move.

"What do we do?" I whispered suit-to-suit.

There was a long silence, then Lily said, "No matter what happens from here on out, just promise me you'll take care of Mateo? You, and O'Riley. You're the ones Mateo will need now. Tell him I love him very much."

Before I could tell her not to do it, she had reached to the collar on her helmet and undogged it from the ring. When her helmet came off, she began doing the same at her wrists, and then down the front of the suit proper, until the suit itself fell away and she was standing exposed to the light, wearing nothing but the form-fitting cooling garment underneath.

Victor was teary-eyed again.

"My angel, come to me again at last."

He reached for her, and she allowed herself to be taken in his embrace.

I felt my skin crawl, but also saw her turn her head toward me while Victor nuzzled at her neck.

What are you waiting for? Lily mouthed at me.

Right. I activated the door, and went through. It shut behind me.

I was presented with darkness. Flicking on my helmet lamps I suddenly observed vast vats of what could only be described as mildly undulating slime. The Rust—alive, almost liquid—was circulating in great, lazy ponds. Dozens of them. Some black, others red. I suddenly realized that it was a biological refinery, and that I was sitting on teracredits worth of the universe's most refined Rust. The kind of thing the Rust-runners back in the solar system would have given an arm and a leg for.

Lily had shown me how to work the catcher. I scooped up a little of the red, and a little of the black. Each in a separate chamber within the catcher. Then I went back out the way I'd come, wondering how long I was going to have to sit and be bleach-broiled in the decon cycle of my airlock, before I dared step foot inside my ship again.

When I came back out, Lily and Victor both seemed to be in

another world. Victor still held her, but loosely, and both of them were staring off into the air as if nothing real were around them. Lily's lips moved slightly, as if she were rhyming something, but no sound came. Victor too. They almost seemed to be repeating the same phrase, over and over again. Though I couldn't quite tell what the words were.

I chanced to grab at her wrist, to try to snap her out of it; or at least get her away from Victor. If they were both in a fugue state, perhaps I could drag her back to the hangar? Go get an emergency balloon from my ship. Load her into it, and get her off this ball, before Victor knew what was happening.

Alas, he seemed to sense me, and his grasp on Lily tightened.

"No!" he yelled. "I have seen her mind, at last. And now I have seen what you will do! Rat saw it too, but was stopped from speaking the truth—by her friend aboard your ship! You cannot destroy the Rust! I won't *let* you destroy the Rust!"

Carvahlo's people seemed to swarm on us from nowhere. Like ants. They must have followed behind, just far enough out of the way that we couldn't see them. Now they were clubbing at me, trying to mow me down.

The sample catcher in my hand was made of titanium and bullet-proof plastic. I began swinging it at heads. It came back covered in gore and blood.

"What the hell is happening in there?" O'Riley's voice shouted in my helmet.

"It's a nightmare!" I yelled at her. "A Rust-zombie nightmare!"

"How can I help?" she asked.

"Get ready to go," I yelled. "When you see me running, keep the ramp down—just enough to jump on. Then get us into the sky!"

"Copy that," O'Riley said firmly. Her pilot's voice was calm and controlled, just as mine would have been in the same situation.

I bulled my way through the crowd, hacking and swinging. I could feel the hits on my suit and helmet as I forged a path back into the corridor. Would the suit still be vacuum-tight by the time I needed it to be? Would a tell-tale crack mean I'd already been exposed, and wouldn't discover the problem until it was too late?

There, I saw an open lane between bodies.

I loped through it like a gazelle.

The path back to the hangar was not an easy one. Twice, I got lost, and had to fend off attackers. The disciples of Victor Carvahlo were practically single-minded in their determination to not let me leave with the sample catcher.

I found the throne hall, and the corridor our guide had originally used. At the very end of it, I found Rat.

"Please take me with you," she said. Her eyes were fighting towards lucidity. And I stopped myself from thumping the sample catcher squarely on her head.

"There isn't room," I said. "There's nowhere to quarantine you."

"The Other is strong here," she said. "The Other wants all of us. Everybody."

Turning around, I saw shadowy shapes coming down the corridor. Heard—through the external suit pickup—the cries of rage and anger.

"No time," I said, and shoved Rat aside.

"Mateo said he could help save me!" she shouted. "It's why I helped him come here!"

I stopped short, considered, then beckoned her to me. If she got out of line, I'd finish her the way I originally thought I'd have to.

Inside the airlock, I was shocked to see O'Riley—in a suit—on the other side of the window. She had an emergency balloon ready to go.

"How did you know?" I said over the helmet wireless.

"Mateo told me his friend would need one."

I decided not to argue the point, and ordered Rat to plug her nose, close her eyes, and hold her breath. She was about to get a first-rate taste of raw vacuum.

The Rust-zombies thudded against the inner airlock door just as the outer door came open, and O'Riley swept in. She was almost frantic in her effort to get Rat into the balloon, and seal it. And for good reason. O'Riley knew better than anybody what could happen to the human body if left exposed to the harshness of space.

Then we were trotting—the balloon suspended between us, and the sample catcher dangling at my waist from its tether. Up the ramp our boots went, and into the cockpit O'Riley charged. No time for the decon cycle now. Getting up and getting away was our only goal. I kept Rat's balloon behind me as I watched out the open ramp—the ship lifting over the frozen terrain.

And just like that, the dwarf moon was dropping away, back into the inky blackness of Sargasso Grid space.

★ ★ ★

It'll be weeks, getting back to Jupiter space. We think we've deconned the whole damn ship, but we can't really be sure. Hell with it. If the genetic synthesizer did its job, we'll know soon enough if the counter-virus works. We released it as soon as it was ready. For Mateo's sake, and for Jingfei's. They both lapsed into a coma not long after we crossed out of the Sargasso—a parting gift, from this Other Jingfei spoke of? Did it *know* we had escaped? Were those who'd previously been caught in its grasp, ever going to be made whole again?

Everything depends on the counter-virus now. And getting ourselves back to civilization in one piece.

We keep Mateo and Jingfei side-by-side, strapped to bunks in my cabin. O'Riley and I are taking turns sitting with them, while one of us pilots the ship. There hasn't been much to say along the way. I think O'Riley and I both feel it: a haunting sense of apprehension, for the fate of Lily. And a growing suspicion that—despite all that I'd seen inside—somehow, this wasn't the last of either Carvahlo, or his angel.

TWILIGHT ON OLYMPUS
★
by Eric Leif Davin

When the Ares *crash lands on the Martian surface, humanity's first mission to the red planet ends in death and destruction. But mission commander Phoenix Castillo still lives. And while she draws breath, she will never give up on her dream of touching the stars.*

ARES FELL IN FLAMES across the Martian sky. The spacecraft's braking aeroshell heated to a glowing white hot from atmospheric friction and began to melt like an ice cube left too long in the summer sun. Molten globs splattered and streaked the sides of the landing module as the vehicle plunged steeply into the thin air of Mars. Phoenix Castillo fired the braking jets, trying desperately to bring the craft up into a more horizontal descent. It wasn't working. They knew insertion into elliptical orbit would be a dicey maneuver. Come in too high and the *Ares* would have ricocheted off the Martian atmosphere into deep space like a stone skipped across a pond; too low and gravity's unforgiving embrace would bring the craft down too fast, ending *Ares'* six-month journey from Earth in fiery death. They came in too low.

Beyond the flaming port Phoenix could see the red Tharsis uplands mushrooming across the horizon, closer all the time. She burned the last of the craft's precious fuel, hoping to at least hit the surface like she'd tried to hit the atmosphere, a glancing blow at an oblique angle.

She heard her second in command yell in her helmet radio. She glanced left to where he was strapped in next to her. Frightened eyes behind his faceplate was the last thing she saw as the *Ares* slammed into the Martian surface and oblivion engulfed her.

It was April on Mars. Surface temperatures were beginning to climb and by high summer daytime temps would reach the low sixties, Fahrenheit. But it was still a hundred below zero along the north rim of the massive Valles Marineris canyon system. Named after the Mariner 9 probe of 1971 which first photographed it from space, Valles Marineris was a cleft in the side of Mars three miles deep and one hundred and fifty miles wide stretching for four thousand miles along the Martian equatorial region. It had been formed eons before by an updoming of this lowland region as Mars had split at the seams from some massive internal pressure, bulging and fracturing over an entire hemisphere. Just north of the jagged cliffs and serpentine valleys of the continent-long Marineris was Valles Marineris Base, the safe haven the *Ares* had been headed for.

Two years before a robot advance craft had set down in these lowlands where the scant Martian atmosphere was thicker, thus providing slightly more air to slow descending spacecraft. The robot lander had roughed out a camp site of several acres over the intervening two years and had been operating its one-hundred-fifty-horsepower nuclear reactor the entire time. Remote controlled by radio signals from Houston's Johnson Space Center, only twenty minutes away via radio, the lander had set up an air pump powered by that nuclear reactor. The Martian atmosphere is ninety-five-percent carbon dioxide; and for two years the air pump had been sucking in that carbon dioxide and combining it with six tons of liquid hydrogen it had brought from Earth. The resulting chemical reaction formed methane and water. The water was broken down into its component hydrogen and oxygen. The air pump thus continually built up supercooled stockpiles of liquid hydrogen, liquid oxygen, and liquid methane. Liquid oxygen and liquid methane are rocket fuels. During the long months this fuel factory had chugged away, sucking in the thin Martian air, it had synthesized well over a hundred tons of such rocket fuel, enough to get a small spacecraft off the Martian surface and back to Earth. Near the fuel factory sat that spacecraft, a small cone-shaped pod big enough for six astronauts. In anticipation of the *Ares'* arrival with those six astronauts, the robot had laid out a welcoming landing grid of twinkling lights to guide the *Ares* safely down.

But in unforgiving space, the best-laid plans can easily fail. The *Challenger* blew up. The robot *Mars Observer* of '93 simply disappeared as it prepared to go into Mars orbit. The *Galileo* probe to Jupiter malfunctioned. And the *Ares* never made it to Valles Marineris Base where the advance robot patiently awaited its arrival. Instead, it broke up over the Tharsis uplands, thousands of miles to the west across a vast, frozen, sand dune desert greater than any Earthly Sahara.

She awoke to a world of pain. But, she awoke. Phoenix Castillo was alive. She swam slowly upwards out of blackness and opened her eyes. She blinked in agony at the light of a distant sun. Vomit filled the interior of her helmet and its stench roiled her innards with a wave of nausea. She forced down the acid rain in her stomach and willed herself to be still, assessing her situation.

Her body was a massive bruise, but that she was alive at all indicated there were no immediately fatal injuries. And that she was alive at all on the Martian surface also meant that her spacesuit, battered though it might be, was intact. Any rips or tears would have meant rapid death from freezing and suffocation in the frigid, unbreathable Martian air. She seemed to be lying in a twisted pile of wreckage, all that remained of the *Ares'* landing module. She wondered how many times the module might have bounced and tumbled across the Martian landscape, spewing pieces of itself for how many miles before plowing into the sand all around her? Tentatively she moved her arms, feeling her torso. She was still strapped into her seat, its arms still wrapped around her in protective contours. No doubt she had its embracing shield to thank for the miracle of her life. She tried to lift her head and the movement shot bolts of crimson through her. She couldn't move her lower body. She managed to look down and saw that her legs were trapped under the crumpled metal of the module's control panel, bent back upon itself where the *Ares* had plunged into the final sand pile where it now rested. Her head fell back and once more blackness took her.

As consciousness slowly came to her, relief flooded over Phoenix Castillo. "Thank God!" she said. It was all a dream, like so many she'd had on this voyage, a nightmare of catastrophe and disaster, dire premonition of how the approach to Mars might end. But that's all it was, a horrible dream from which she was now awakening.

A slight frost covered her faceplate and again she was assailed by the stench of vomit. The familiar smell brought it all back to her. She wiped at her faceplate, her gloved hand clearing a swatch of visibility. She had no idea how long she'd been unconscious, but nothing had changed. She was still strapped into her seat. Her legs were still immobilized. She was still stranded on Mars.

She managed to raise her head and glance around to left and right. The movement brought more pain from her legs, entombed under the remains of the module's control panel. On her left was the mangled body of her second in command, also strapped into his seat, his faceplate shattered. To her right were the other members of the mission, still, broken, and lifeless. She alone lived, trapped on the Martian surface. Rescue was impossible. Death was near.

She lay back and stared up at the Martian heavens, calculating her chances. Her suit was a miniature spacecraft of its own. It had oxygen, water, a heating unit, emergency rations in paste form she could reach inside her helmet. But it wasn't designed for extended use. Her supplies were limited. And she couldn't move, anyway. And the pain from her legs told her something was broken down there. How long could she last? She envied her crew mates. At least they died quickly. She was going to slowly leak her life away here on Mars. Why not just crack open her helmet and end it now, at once?

"Fuck, no!" she said. Mars holds all the cards, she thought, but he hasn't beaten the *Ares* commander just yet. She gritted her teeth against the red mist of pain which flooded over her and unstrapped herself, sitting up amidst the carnage around her.

The *Ares* was a metal flower torn open, exposing its insides to the hostile skies. The wreckage lay on a long sloping incline. Below her and into the distance Phoenix Castillo saw a huge sandy plain littered with rubble to the horizon. On that horizon a procession of storms was stalking across her line of sight. They didn't seem to be part of some vast Martian dust storm which could blanket an entire hemisphere. Rather, they seemed to be a family of localized tornadoes skipping across the bleak surface, sometimes touching down and whipping up rocky debris into themselves and at other times retracting their funnels back up above the surface. And beyond them, Phoenix knew, thousands of miles beyond them to the east, was Valles Marineris Base and salvation. She knew she'd never make it.

Then she looked behind her and gasped. Reaching above her, stretching beyond her sight, vanishing into the distant skies above, was Olympus Mons—Mount Olympus—the largest mountain in the solar system. *Ares* had crashed on the sloping lower reaches of an extinct volcano three times higher than Mount Everest. Phoenix knew the geography of Mars well, having pored over photo montages of the Martian surface endlessly in preparation for the voyage. She'd studied Olympus Mons intimately, fascinated by this volcano formed by hundreds of millions of years of fiery eruption. But she'd always seen it from above, looking down. Now she was below it, looking up. It seemed beyond her imagination to take it all in. It was almost four hundred miles across at its base and seventeen miles high. At its peak, she knew, was an ancient caldera, a collapsed crater, about ten thousand feet deep, formed when Mount Olympus, like Mars itself, was still young and active. Huge above her, it reached for the heavens, reached for the stars, reached for Earth so far away. Phoenix clenched her jaw and began working at the ashes of wreckage all around her.

The sun had indicated it was about midday when Phoenix had first surveyed her circumstances. The Martian day is approximately as long as an Earthly day and twilight found her at last hobbling through the ruins of the *Ares*. She'd managed to grasp a long strip of fuselage and had used that as a lever to pry up the crumpled mass which had pinned her legs. Pain ripped through her anew as she slid her legs from beneath the pile and she discovered that her left foot had been crushed. The skin didn't seem to have been broken; rather, the whole foot had been compressed by the wreckage piled atop it. But, there was internal bleeding, the foot was swelling, and it was impossible to put any pressure on it. She gulped pain killers from her suit's rations and fashioned a rough crutch out of the same strip of fuselage she'd used as a lever. With its aid she managed to become mobile, searching over the debris of the *Ares*. Night fell, and so did the temperature. Her suit monitor told her external temperature was approaching two hundred and fifty degrees below zero. She turned up her heating unit all the way, oblivious to the energy expenditure, and fell into exhausted slumber.

In the morning she tossed away her oxygen tank and plugged in a reserve she salvaged from the *Ares*. She ate sparingly from her food rations, sipped at her water tube, bade her dead companions farewell, and climbed out of what remained of the *Ares*. She turned her face upward and began her ascent.

For a long time her climb was relatively easy, all things considered. The broad base of Olympus slopes gently upward at first, so that one is walking up an incline rather than actually climbing. Still, it was hard going. She was still physically shaken from the crash, her crushed foot throbbed relentlessly, the makeshift crutch dug into her armpit, and she had to work ceaselessly against her own spacesuit. An astronaut encased in a spacesuit is in her own private world of pressurized oxygen, heated underwear, and instruments monitoring every heartbeat. The external Martian atmosphere was a hundred times thinner than Earth's and her suit was like a tough balloon protecting her from it, pressurized with 4.3 pounds of pure oxygen per square inch. But that pressure had to be overcome each time Phoenix lifted her foot, bent an elbow, or grasped her crutch more tightly. She had to work against her suit in everything she did. Just moving in the suit was exhausting. This unceasing battle against her suit was somewhat mitigated by the lower Martian gravity, slightly over one-third of Earth normal. But even gravity only thirty-eight percent that of Earth's is still gravity, pulling constantly at one's leaden body, and her breath became ragged and harsh, sucking in more of the scarce oxygen from her tank. The interior of the suit was a dank swamp, filled with her sweat and the moisture from her exhaled breath. The air she breathed was itself reeking with blood, vomit, and the stale urine which soaked her diaper. But she had breathed the rank air for so long she was inured to it, obsessed only with climbing ever higher up the side of Olympus, ignoring her failing reserves of oxygen and strength.

Twilight found her among rocky outcroppings which presented a vertical climb. Her rate of ascent had slowed considerably. She pulled herself painfully up the ancient lava face of Olympus, dragging her crutch behind her. At last she reached an outthrust ledge which presented a welcome rest stop. Phoenix pulled herself up onto the ledge and braced her back against the side of Olympus, her legs splayed out before her.

Before and below her was an awesome sight of harsh beauty. Far below on the sloping outskirts of Olympus she could see a glint of metal as the setting sun reflected off the shards of what had once been *Ares*. Her gaze passed beyond the ruins of her spacecraft to the ruddy sand dunes and sinuous rills of the vast arctic desert below. The wind which had spawned the family of tornadoes was rising and more of them marched like an army across the horizon, over hill and valley, touching down and lifting up as they went. And beyond the horizon was the darkening night sky of Mars, the myriad stars stabbing down their sharp untwinkling light. Somewhere out there among the stars was Earth, a mere twenty minutes away by radio. But where she sat now, Phoenix knew, was the closest she'd ever again get to Earth. Olympus was the furthest Mars reached into heaven. It was the best she could do.

She was gasping, and not just from exertion. She was sucking in the last dregs of her oxygen tank. It wouldn't be long before she suffocated. Her heating unit was failing and she could feel the terrible cold seeping into her limbs. She'd long ago ceased to feel anything from her crushed foot.

As twilight fell on Mount Olympus, Phoenix stretched out one hand toward the distant shining light of Earth and cracked open her helmet with the other. What remained of her oxygen gushed out and vaporized immediately in the frigid Martian air. Phoenix Castillo froze instantly, hand reaching up toward home, an icy human statue frozen forever on the face of Olympus.

THE TROUBLE WITH TELEPATHS

★

by Hank Davis

Sergeant Zinman may be the least telepathically capable soldier in the United States Armed Forces, but that's just fine with him. He has no desire to go rummaging around in other peoples' minds, and he'd prefer the military peepers afford him the same courtesy. But Sergeant Zinman is no ordinary noncom. He's got a very special talent—one not even he knows about—and it might just be the key to humanity's salvation . . . or its doom.

THE TROUBLE WITH TELEPATHS is that they're all officers.

That'll do for starters.

At least, they're mostly not *serious* officers, or there'd be even more trouble. Most of the peepers are just second or first louies. A few make captain. They tend to be unstable, and don't really make good officers, and a lot of them wash out for mental reasons after a couple of years.

The highest ranking one I ever saw was a lieutenant colonel. That was a few years ago when I was a buck sergeant, but I doubt that he ever made full bird, since at the time he was talking about retiring. It was common knowledge that he wasn't much of a peeper, barely scoring above the minimum on the Rhines. His main thing was being an officer with all the usual officer stuff; maybe an officer with a little extra. Very little. Being good at poker might have been as useful to his career.

Not that anybody plays poker with a telepath. Even other telepaths don't.

Fortunately, I don't have a trace of telepathic ability. Back when I joined and was run through a day's worth of tests, I scored random noise on the Rhines. Pure chance on the nose. The score was so dead on, that one of the testers suspected I was cheating, trying to hide being a peeper, so he called in a card-carrying, officially certified peeper to buzz around in my skull and see if I had cheated. I hadn't, of course.

It was the first time I had been this close . . .

"You've never been this close to a telepath, Zinman," he said. It was a statement, not a question.

He was a captain, so . . .

"Yes, I'm very good at it," he said.

I had been wondering if . . .

"No, you can't feel me reading you. You'd have to be another telepath, and you still might not notice anything unusual."

I was getting a little worried . . .

"No need to worry, Zinman, what you're thinking doesn't count as insubordination."

I had heard that . . .

"You heard right. It's covered by the Revised Code of Military Justice. Like the song you just thought about says."

I'd thought of a line from an old song: *You can't go to jail for what you're thinking.* Or even if I'm thinking . . .

"Not that either. You might even be right that I wouldn't be giving you the creeps if I weren't commenting on things going through your mind. Ask me if I give a shit. You know that telepaths aren't volunteers." Again, it was a statement, not a question. "We're drafted as valuable weapons. Or valuable something. But you can think the word 'peeper' with impunity. Just don't say it out loud where a telepath can hear you. Saying it is still insubordination." He stood up, said to the test administrator, "He didn't cheat. He's a complete post."

"Post" was what the peepers called non-telepaths. It came from the phrase "deaf as a post."

He turned to leave, muttering, "Damned waste of my time. Damned . . ."

And then I flickered.

The captain turned around and walked back to me. "What did you just do?" he said.

"It's—"

"Never mind, I see that you don't have any control over it. I just asked you to bring the subject to the surface of your mind. That really felt weird. Yes, I know, you think telepaths are weird. But for an instant, your mind wasn't there anymore, and the place where it had been felt funny. Like I had stepped out of daylight, into an enormous dark cave, with odd noises echoing. Just for an instant, then you were back, just a regular post again."

That's how he described it. To me, it was like something dark passed over my eyes and was gone again in a fraction of a second. Doctors who had examined me had no idea of the cause—no sign of brain abnormalities—but it didn't prevent me from doing anything. Even the U.S. Army didn't think it was anything serious.

The peeper turned to the tester and said, "So that's the mini-seizures you were thinking about. Are you sure he belongs in the Army?"

"He's been examined—" the tester started to say, then the captain cut *him* off.

"I see. They're too short to worry about, and they have no after-effects. Not a problem unless they get longer or have side effects. No worse than an occasional sneeze." Then he did leave, muttering, "Good enough for government work," as he walked off.

The whole thing gave me a weird feeling. A damned peeper calling me a post, as if there was something wrong with *me*.

That was several years, two more stripes, and a couple of rockers ago, and I'd gotten used to peepers, and wasn't nervous anymore. There aren't a lot of them, they're not really around much, and since they're kicked up to officer rank automatically, they don't fraternize with the enlisted troops and NCOs. In fact they don't fraternize with *officers* any more than they can help.

So I was as used to peepers as a non-peeper (or post, if you insist) can get, and wasn't thinking about them the day that I got the odd assignment.

I should have guessed that something was up when I saw the First Sergeant standing nearby, watching the morning formation, obviously

waiting for it to be over. Actually, I did figure that something was up—
I just didn't figure that the something had anything to do with me.

As soon as the word "Dismissed" echoed across the field, the First
Sergeant headed over to me.

"Good morning, Sergeant," she said.

"Good morning, Top. Something up?"

"Something's up, all right. Tell Malone to take your platoon today,
then report to Lieutenant Minteer at the chopper pad at oh-eight
hundred."

This was not a good start for the day. Minteer was a real prick, even
if he wasn't a peeper. "Report to Minteer, okay. And do what, Top?"

"You'll have to ask him that," she said. "You now know as much as
I do about it."

Her eyes could look warm, the way brown eyes are supposed to,
usually if she'd heard a good joke (preferably a dirty one), but they were
hard now. Something was going on, and she was annoyed that she
didn't know much about it. At least she wasn't annoyed at me.

I told Malone to take charge of the platoon, then told PFC Moriko
to follow me to the motor pool. "I need one each chauffeur, O.D. in
color, Joe, and you just volunteered. So let's go get a limo." The mini-
seizures might be hazardous if anyone actually drove cars anymore,
but my own car, like any civilian car, did all the driving. I could have
used one of the Army buggies with no risk, either. They looked ugly,
their shock absorbers didn't do much absorbing, and their seats were
minimally comfortable, but they drove themselves, too. However, the
Army was still the Army, and my med profile required that I have a
driver, human-type, with me in the car, even though he wouldn't be
doing any driving.

"What's up, Sarge?" Moriko asked, once we were on the way to the
chopper pad.

"Damned if I know," I said, "but Lieutenant Minteer is supposed to
be there, so watch the language. 'Always perform your duties in a
military manner,' " I said, mimicking Minteer's eastern accent.

Minteer was there, all right, along with a full bird private. I told
Moriko to stay with the car until I knew what was going on, then walked
over to Minteer. We exchanged salutes and good mornings, then the
PFC told me, "The chopper should be here in five or less, Sarge."

Minteer scowled and said, "Did I hear you address this man as

'Sarge,' soldier? 'Sarge' is what sergeants get called in comic books. Do you think you're in a comic book, *Mister* Luigi?"

The PFC looked surprised, with a deer-in-the-headlights expression. He must not have run into Minteer before. "Uh, no sir. Sorry, sir."

Moriko was behind me where I couldn't see him, but I hoped he was managing not to smile. Looking inscrutable wasn't his strong suit.

Minteer wasn't through. "And the vehicle that's on its way here is a Field Drive Transport Vehicle, not a 'chopper.' You can call it a FDTV, if that's too big a mouth full for you, but it's not a 'chopper.' 'Chopper' is what helicopters were called because of the noise they made, and it's ridiculous to call an FDTV a 'chopper.' Have you ever seen a helicopter outside of a museum?"

Luigi said he hadn't, but fortunately for him, the chopper was now in sight, and approaching rapidly. From past experience, I knew that Minteer was just getting started.

The egg-shaped vehicle came to a stop, humming, then settled to the pad on its runners. The door on the side opened, and a captain stepped out and walked over to us. Then I noticed that his uniform had the stylized brain with an eye in the center of it that was the patch of the telepath corps. I noticed that before I got a good look at his face . . .

Flicker.

. . . and realized that I had seen him somewhere before, but couldn't remember where . . .

Flicker.

. . . but mostly I was wondering why I had just had two mini-whatsits less than a minute apart. That had never happened before.

He returned our salutes and said, "Good morning, gentlemen. Nothing like starting off the day with a chopper ride." Somehow, I was sure he did that on purpose. Peepers have an advantage when it comes to getting under someone's skin. Fortunately for Luigi, he was already showing a poker face, and kept it up. Minteer wasn't as successful at suppressing the sour look on his mug. "I'm glad you brought transportation, Sergeant Zinman. Let's go." He nodded to Minteer. "Thank you for meeting me here, Lieutenant," then headed for the car, without waiting for a salute or further pleasantries. Minteer looked like he'd just been handed a maggot sandwich.

"We need to go to building D-12," the captain said, then got into the back of the car. Moriko and I climbed into the front. Moriko said, "Sir, that building is off limits . . ."

"Not to me, Mr. Moriko. Let's go." He could have told the car where to go himself—its A.I. pays attention to rank—but kept up the polite fiction that Moriko was actually driving the vehicle.

We rolled along and I still had no idea why I was here. I didn't know what went on in D-12, but it must be restricted, since there was a fence around it with concertina on top, and an armed guard at the only gate, and I had a feeling that if the captain had clearance to go inside, I'd have to wait outside. Then I realized that I'd been trying to remember where I'd seen the captain before, and hadn't looked at his name tag.

Of course, he read me.

"Sergeant Zinman, my name is Carpenter, and I'll answer your questions once we get inside the building," the mystery officer said.

I flickered twice while he was talking. I was more puzzled by that than anything about Carpenter's business. Usually, months would go by without one of the micro-seizures, but I'd had a string of them just now. Maybe I'd be getting a medical discharge soon.

Carpenter had Moriko park the car outside the fence. "Wait for me," he told him.

"Just wait for you, sir?" Moriko asked.

"Sergeant Zinman may be coming back later," he told him, then, "Come with me, Sergeant," to me.

Carpenter was expected, which didn't surprise me, but I was on the guest list too, which was surprising. Inside the building, we walked down hallways with the usual drably painted walls, and came to a door that slid open when Carpenter put his ID in the reader.

The room wasn't large, and just had a conference table with a few chairs around it and a flatscreen on one wall. No windows, just the one door.

Carpenter sat down and gestured toward a chair on the opposite side of the table. "Have a seat, Sergeant."

I did . . . after I had flickered a couple of more times. I wondered . . .

"No, Sergeant, I'm not making you do that. Or maybe my presence is making you do it, but I'm not deliberately using any influence on you."

The flickering seemed to have stopped, but it felt different than usual, repeating that way. It was like I was building up a vague image of something that I had never noticed with the separated single flickers.

"Sergeant, what do you think of the Russian civil war?"

That stopped me from thinking about the flickers. "What? Uh, what do you mean, sir?"

"Don't you think it odd that the country broke apart like that, fighting against each other, even using a couple of tactical nukes, for no obvious reason at all?"

Well, everyone seemed to think it was odd. And it had caught all the Kremlin-watchers by surprise. "Yes, sir, I think it was odd." I decided to paraphrase Will Rogers. "But all I know about it is what was in the news." I wondered if . . .

"No, Sergeant Zinman, I don't suspect you of having gotten hold of any classified information about it. There's no classified information of importance, anyway. Just a lot of after-the-fact guessing. Actually, it was a trial run. Worked very well, too, and it didn't spread to other nations."

"You mean the U.S. started it somehow, sir?" And why was he . . .

"I'm telling you this, Sergeant, because we need to know just what you are. We need to know that before we start the main event."

"Main event, sir? You mean you're going to do the same to China?" And what did he mean, "What you are?" Surely he could see . . .

"Yes, I can see in your mind that you don't know anything about all this. Incidentally, we *are* going to do the same to China, but not just China; and when I say 'we'4rrrrr5r, I don't mean this country. But first, I needed to see about your odd flickering. You're a piece in the game that doesn't fit, Sergeant. Actually, that's not right, because you don't seem to be part of the game. But we don't know exactly what you are, and we can't take any chances."

Now I remembered where I had seen him before. Last Saturday, I had been in civvies, about to leave the fort and go into town. I had noticed the base C.O. talking with a captain, and just then I had flickered. And the captain had suddenly ignored what the general was saying and stared intently at me. It had been Carpenter. I had gone on and forgotten about it.

"Yes, you caught my attention that day. I had to find out what that flickering meant. Suppose I told you that the U.S. and China are about to have a nuclear exchange?"

I didn't understand, but I was feeling scared. Telepaths do go psycho, more often than, well, us posts. But I didn't think he was insane.

"Interesting. I expected that to make you flicker. How about this?"

Carpenter wasn't there anymore. In his place was a Chinese officer, a member of their telepath corps from the patch on his uniform. It, too, had a stylized brain, but with a dragon coiled around it. I started to get up.

Sit down, someone said to me. It wasn't a voice, but it was in my head. I sat down, not that I had any choice.

The Chinese officer was gone. Now a Russian officer was sitting across the table. "You know that a telepath can't lie to another telepath?" he said.

I didn't say anything, but I thought about how often I'd heard that.

Now, there was a different Russian officer talking to me. "I'm going from a double agent to a quadruple agent, Sergeant Zinman. When a Russian officer who happens to be a telepath tells another Russian officer who also happens to be a telepath that there's a group of traitors who are going to launch a tactical nuke at Moskva, he is believed. When the same officer tells another high-ranking telepath officer that traitors have taken over the missiles in Moskva and are about to attack the missile emplacements in the rest of the country, he also is believed. It worked. And it will work on the United States and China, too."

Somehow, I wasn't scared now. I should have been, but . . .

"Yes, it is odd that you're suddenly so calm. And I really expected you to start flickering again. Maybe we should take you apart to see if there's something different about your brain, but there isn't time. I guess you'll have to commit suicide." He took a small laspistol out of his uniform—I hadn't seen any sign of it before—and put it on the table. "Don't touch it until I tell you to."

I tried to reach for it, and nothing happened. "You wanted to know what I was—" I began.

"I still am curious, but as I said, there isn't time to satisfy that curiosity right now."

"What are *you*?"

"The name wouldn't mean anything to you. Nor would the number of the star of the planet I come from. Your astronomers have cataloged it and given it a designation, but I see that you, Sergeant, have only the most elementary knowledge of astronomy. Our telepaths are much stronger and more talented than any of yours, and I *can* lie to another telepath and be believed. Pick up the pistol now."

Flicker. "You're invading us? Won't the radiation poison—?"

"We are just eliminating possible competition. Pick up the pistol. Besides, we have ways of neutralizing radiation. *Pick up the pistol!*"

Flicker. He was looking nervous, and his face seemed to waver. Maybe he was close to reverting to his natural appearance.

He told me to pick up the pistol again, and got another flicker response. He started to reach for the pistol, and stopped. I could see he was trying to reach for it, but couldn't make his hand move.

And the flicker started and kept on going. It was like a color filter had dropped over my eyes, but it had nothing to do with color. I was standing up, now, though I didn't remember getting to my feet. And there was something in front of me, barely visible out of the lower part of my vision. I was looking straight ahead and had the feeling that I shouldn't try to look down.

Carpenter—or whatever his (its?) real name was—was staring at the middle of my chest. His human face looked terrified, and I somehow knew it wasn't an illusion.

Then something started speaking.

It wasn't using any words I knew. Most of the sounds wouldn't turn into anything like words, though some of them came into my head as nonsense syllables: *Ia! Frthgr! Nghall! Ia!* It made no sense to me, but I wasn't the intended recipient of the message. And somehow I could see into Carpenter's brain and hear what he was hearing. Not in words, but something more basic. *We have plans for this planet. You shouldn't have interfered with the property of others older and stronger than you. I see into you. I see where your pathetic little empire is located. We'll have to turn our attention to you vermin so that you won't interfere with us again.*

Carpenter was exerting all his concentration, I could tell. It was like I was a telepath, but I knew the other—*thing*—was doing all that and I was just picking up the overflow. He managed to get to his feet, and took a step toward the door while trying to reach for something in his pocket. Then he sat back down and picked up the laspistol. *In ten minutes*, the voice that wasn't a voice told him.

Then, the flicker closed back up. *I* closed back up. Somehow, it was like I had doors in my front and something had opened them and come partly out. It had kept me from looking down at it. I got the impression that seeing what it looked like would not be a good idea. I had a glimpse of its appearance darkly reflected in the flat screen on the wall, and started to scream, but something made me look away and somehow I forgot what I had seen, and wondered why I thought I needed to scream. The last thing I sort of heard was *close portal.* Then, I was leaving the room, and walking down the hall. I had the feeling that I had just had a talk with Carpenter, but couldn't remember anything about it. Or why he wasn't with me now.

I had an odd thought, about being chosen to be a portal to something else—sounded weird, like some kind of screwball religion or cult—then I forgot some more and wondered why I was thinking of the word "portal." Like I was trying to remember a joke I had heard long ago.

I went out through the gate. The guard asked me if Captain Carpenter was still inside, and I said . . .

Flicker.

I don't know what I said, but it satisfied the guard. I got back in the car. "Back to the platoon, Joe," I said.

"Is the captain staying behind?" Moriko asked, as he told the car where to go.

Flicker.

"What captain, Joe?"

Joe looked confused. "Did I say something about a captain? I must have been thinking of something else."

"Didn't you ever hear that you're not paid to think, soldier?" I said, imitating Lieutenant Minteer's accent so that Joe would realize it was a joke. For some reason, I was thinking about telepaths and how much trouble they were.

I must have been thinking out loud, because Joe said, "Look on the bright side, Sarge. Suppose Lieutenant Minteer was a telepath. That would be scary."

"I can't think of anything that would be scarier," I said.

We drove on.

THIS IS THE WAY THE UNIVERSE ENDS: WITH A BANG

★

by Brian Dolton

At the end of time, only ninety-two sentient entities remain in the universe. Titus is seven. She belongs to a cadre known as the Conclave of Those Who Will Pass Through, a group that believes life does not have to end just because the universe does. The Galasphere was another member of the Conclave. But now the Galasphere is dead, possibly murdered, and it falls to Titus to find out why. But she'll have to hurry— time is literally running out!

1: The Shock of the New

Titus is seven.

This is a relative, not an absolute measure of age. There are ninety-two definably sentient entities remaining in this weary old universe. Titus is the seventh oldest. She habitually consists of a condensate cloud of fluxing energy, a lattice of flickering quantum-state conversions (we will call Titus "she", "it" is simply too impersonal for a protagonist).

Titus is hanging in space, marveling that she has found something new.

The universe, at this point, has existed for so long that its end point is more than four thousand times closer than its beginning. The great majority of it is cold and dead, a wasteland of husked stars and expended energy.

To find something new is remarkable.

It appears to be a construct of some kind; a machine. It is built of twisted strings, recursively deforming its own structure in twelve dimensions. Titus builds new sensory structures in order to analyze it. There are thin skeins of hyperdense matter here and there, serving as anchors for all the additional dimensions it has bent to its mysterious purpose.

Certain components of the machine appear familiar, but her individual memories are insufficient to categorize them. Shared Memory would tell her, so she hives off a mindclone and sends it burrowing through underspace to fetch the information.

The structure does not exhibit any sign of sentience. Titus prods at it with a variety of energies. It does not respond.

At least, not to her.

She is still inspecting it when the attack comes. The attacker does not show itself. Ghost structures burst from underspace, filaments and vortices that whirl against Titus, attempting to tear her apart. She responds immediately. Attack is unprecedented, almost unthinkable. Titus therefore, in an instant, creates sentient subcomponents for which attack is not only thinkable, but purposeful. Attack, and also of course defense. She is not, after all, immortal. Anything and everything can be destroyed. In a near-dead universe, the Ninety-Two know this all too well.

Battle is costly. With time winding inexorably down, energy is a precious commodity, not to be squandered. Were Titus a member of the Faction of the Inevitable, she might simply bow her metaphorical head and accept death. But Titus is not such a fatalist. Titus is one of the eldest amongst the Conclave of Those Who Will Pass Through.

Titus fully intends to live beyond the end of this universe. She will not yield.

She shreds the ghost structures, wrecking them, absorbing from them all she can to replenish her expended energies. More ghosts well up against her. She needs to know who is attacking her. Her substructures fending off the attacks, she tears a hole in reality and drags her opponent out from underspace.

It is the Galasphere.

The Galasphere is five.

Long ago, some forgotten member of an almost-forgotten species developed the concept of a structure that could encompass an entire star, able to utilize all its energy. The idea was considered outrageous in scope.

Ah, the naïveté of a younger universe. The Galasphere is a shell habitat that encloses not a star but an entire galaxy. Most galaxies have long since burnt out, their matter exhausted by the voracious singularities that have consumed them, and which themselves have become old and choked. But the Galasphere trawls the dying universe, harvesting what it can find, pouring dead matter down the spiraling infinity of the balanced singularities at its core, sucking off the energy they emit.

The Galasphere is very powerful.

Titus has no idea why it is attacking her. The Galasphere is a fellow member of the Conclave of Those Who Will Pass Through. There should be amity between them, not enmity.

The Galasphere does not offer any form of communication beyond violence. Titus tries, and is ignored. Titus does not wish to fight back.

"So few of us are left," she pleads. "Why reduce our numbers further?" It is a plea to logic, but the Galasphere does not respond, only continues its assault. Titus is hard-pressed. She has not fought for eons. She knows, of course, all the necessary theories, but theory and practice have a learning curve between them.

Even as she hauls herself up that curve, she is being diminished. Parts of her are torn into their components, uncountable fermions and hadrons scattered to the void. She finds herself panicking, so she creates a specific substructure to indulge such an unproductive reaction. Spared from distraction, she analyzes the Galasphere.

Its weakness becomes clear.

Singularities are such unstable things.

She creates the necessary components and folds them into underspace. It costs almost a quarter of her mass. It is a gamble. If she succeeds, she will be able to replenish herself, even grow. If she fails . . .

She does not fail. The complex ten-dimensional structures emerge precisely where she calculated they would. The resulting deformation of space froths the surface of the event horizons into fractal chaos. The singularities cough and splutter.

They vomit. They have been gorging themselves for untold ages. They spew up a fountain of unchecked mass and energy, born at the heart of the Galasphere.

After that, it should only be a matter of time. The Galasphere is crippled. Desperate, it attempts to stem the explosions at its heart, to fold back space and twist it off in a secure knot. Titus withdraws, showing that she is prepared to be merciful.

"Why did you do this?" she asks. "Tell me. You do not need to die."

The Galasphere offers no answer; only, astonishingly, a further assault. Titus's response is to hurl herself into the core of the much larger Galasphere, to place herself where it can only attack her by attacking itself. There she hangs, defensive shells coiled around her.

"Why won't you explain?" she asks.

There is still no answer. But the Galasphere changes its approach. It directs its remaining energies to one purpose. Not to stem the crippling tide of chaos at its heart; not even to encompass Titus and drag her with it into oblivion.

It disassembles its core memory, turning data into ghosting neutrinos that scatter on the soft, tired winds of an ancient universe. Titus gazes, uncomprehending, as the sentience of the Galasphere evanesces before her.

As it does so, it destroys the mysterious construct as well. Hyperdense matter folds in on itself. The delicate balance of forces is disrupted and the deformed dimensions spring free, correcting themselves, uncoiling and rippling out, smoothing the fabric of reality into calm emptiness.

Titus emerges from the wreckage of the Galasphere and watches it, sad and confused.

"Now we are six," she thinks.

2: Six and One

Titus sends a mindclone message to Kabachi. There is a protocol that must be followed in the rare instance of a death amongst the Ninety-Two. The Ninety-One, now.

Kabachi is one.

Kabachi could be whatever it wanted. Kabachi was the first machine intelligence—whatever biological form it might once have possessed has long been deemed irrelevant and thus forgotten, not even stored in Shared Memory. As a species, the Kabachi forged new meanings for the very concept of identity. Capable of merging or splitting at will into algorithmic individuals as simple or complex as desired, they eventually grew tired of novelty. Now there is only Kabachi, a swarm of superfluidic computinos numbering in the octillions.

Titus is still hanging in the void, digesting what it can harvest from the wrecked Galasphere and musing over the information her mindclone retrieved from Shared Memory, when Kabachi arrives.

Titus expresses contrition, pouring out both informational and emotional content, explaining what she has done, and why. Kabachi devours both streams, chewing up the morsels of data. It creates and runs simulations, testing Titus's account for plausibility even as it joins Titus in plundering the vast, broken corpse. Resources. The dead are nothing but resources at the end of time.

The simulations are born and die in closed artificial universes, their time scales compressed so that eons run in mere millennia. These are immensely powerful entities, after all, to have survived so late in the universe's life. Reality has become a flexible concept.

But it can only flex so far. The universe is still going to end, and that end draws inexorably closer. Time is the simplest thing, and the most precious, for it cannot be made.

Kabachi is a member of the Faction of the Inevitable. Kabachi, longest lived of all, has nevertheless no desire to outlast the cosmos itself. Kabachi believes in death as an inevitability; a necessity, even. It defeated the last of the Schen Ko, so very long ago, after they had all but eradicated the Murr and the Humans and so many other species. Kabachi has dealt death and now accepts the approach of its own end without anything resembling passion.

This is not to say it does not grieve for the Galasphere, in its way.

Alongside Titus, it analyses the vortex echoes of the twelve-dimensional structure. They commune, sharing every scrap of data, every fragment of information. They inspect. They extrapolate. They conclude.

"So you agree?" Titus asks. Some part of her would like Kabachi to have found an alternative explanation.

"92-Designate-7-Titus : conclusion : confirmed. 92-Designate-5-Galasphere : action purpose (subcategory : initial) : machine defense. 92-Designate-5-Galasphere : action purpose (subcategory : final) : machine destruction. 92-Designate-1-Kabachi : conclusion : machine purpose (subcategory) : universal destruction. 92-Designate-1-Kabachi : conclusion : machine purpose (subcategory) : universal creation. 92-Designate-1-Kabachi : conclusion : machine purpose (subcategory) : bridge."

"It doesn't make sense," Titus says. The Galasphere was a member of the Conclave. The Galasphere would have passed through to the next universe, alongside Titus and the other thirty-two members. The creation of the machine made no sense; the destruction of it and the Galasphere's suicide even less.

"92-Designate-7-Titus : incorrect : logic."

Titus reorganizes her thought processes to more closely align with those of Kabachi.

"Designate Titus : logic accepted," she communicates. "Designate Galasphere : actions undisputed. Designate Galasphere : motive. Designate Titus : incomprehension."

A substructure retained her own preferred method of communication for her own memory files. *I understand. I'm not disputing that's what the Galasphere did, what the machine was for. But I don't understand why.*

"92-Designate-1-Kabachi : concurrence. 92-Designate-1-Kabachi : additional data requirement."

"Designate Galasphere : unavailable to supply data."

"92-Designate-1-Kabachi : analysis : machine structure : conceptual framework : triplicate."

That was a surprise. She asked for the data. Kabachi parceled it up and fed it to her, allowing her to draw her own conclusions.

The traces were slight. She might not have noticed them had Kabachi not pointed it out, but they were there.

The Galasphere had not built the machine alone. There had been three entities involved.

"A new faction?" Titus asked.

"92-Designate-1-Kabachi : agreement. 92-Designate-7-Titus : correct."

She considered the ramifications of that for a long time, even as she continued to graze on the digestible remains of the Galasphere, carefully avoiding the unstable singularities that wrestled with each other, deforming space around them as they fought for dominance.

A conspiracy. Secrets. The Ninety-Two had long since dispensed with secrets; the waning resources of the universe had demanded that. It was why they had created Shared Memory: the great data repository that all could access, saving each individual from the burden of storing such a cornucopia of information.

"We must inform the others. You invoke the Faction of the Inevitable. I'll address the Conclave of Those Who Will Pass Through. Afterwards, you and I will meet again. This is our course of action?"

"92-Designate-1-Kabachi : agreement," Kabachi confirms. There is a pause as it surveys the last few drifting scraps of the Galasphere, the frothing singularities. "Adjustment. 91-Designate-1-Kabachi : agreement. 91-Designate-6-Titus : advice : caution."

"Be careful yourself," Titus answers.

And so she departs, folding her slow way across the dying cosmos. As she travels, she analyzes herself. She has changed. She has new mental substructures in place, as well as new physical ones still being assembled from the wreckage of the Galasphere. She was attacked; she came close to death; she has uncovered a conspiracy to pervert the natural death of the universe.

Titus concludes that, for the first time in countless cycles, she is excited. Or perhaps scared. It is hard to tell which.

3: The Conclave of Those Who Will Pass Through

There are thirty-four members of the Conclave of Those Who Will Pass Through. No; correction. There are thirty-three now the Galasphere's existence has come to an end.

They convene, most physically adjacent, a few by telepresence or mindclone. Titus explains, slowly and in great detail, the events that have led to this meeting, providing packets of data from her experience, from Shared Memory, and from Kabachi's closed-universe simulations. The Conclave listens gravely.

Death is an old, old thing that has been made new once more. There are those who remember the stories of the Schen Ko: the species that attempted to erase all other life from the universe in order to hoard the vast but limited resources only for themselves. In that time, death spread its shadow over the universe and only a tiny handful survived.

But the stories of the Schen Ko are only stories. They are long dead.

"But the Galasphere was one of us!" =/= wails. "It would have passed through to the new universe along with the rest of us! It had no need to do this!" =/= is eighty-six, a fraction of the age of the likes of Titus, let alone Kabachi.

"And yet its actions are as they are, and thus must have a motive," Titus, now the oldest amongst the Conclave, chides =/=. It is only as she answers that Titus realizes with something resembling amusement that she is chiding =/= for expressing precisely the same reaction that she herself experienced. She sends a pulse of contrition. "In discussion, perhaps we can determine that motive."

Hapax Legomenon makes a proposal, doing so in a way that requires the other members of the Conclave to devote significant processing power to understanding it. Hapax communicates rarely, and only does so when it has something new to convey, something that has never before been said. The idea is expressed in complex mathematical sets, given color by allusive expressions in a language created especially for the purpose. Hapax kindly provides subset mindclones that can be absorbed by fellow members of the Conclave. Without them, comprehension would take eons.

It is possible, Hapax conveys, that the Galasphere felt it undesirable to share this new universe with quite so many others. It is possible that some small number of the ninety-two have decided that their status would be enhanced in some paradigm of their own creation if they were much fewer in number. Three, perhaps, instead of thirty-four.

Hapax Legomenon, Titus acknowledges on a private subchannel between them, is responsible for most of what little beauty remains in a dying universe. Hapax Legomenon does not respond. Titus does not consider this rude.

The Conclave falls into chaotic subchannel argument for a while. Titus permits it, watching closely. Her new substructures of suspicion are hard at work, parsing and teasing through layers of nuance. She is not entirely sure what guilt would look like, but she hopes she is learning.

She feels as if she is, in some way, diminished by this.

"I blame the Returners," Only and Always Forward suddenly broadcasts through its telepresence. "I always said their theories were untenable. This is their real plan. They're not going back to the start of this universe like they claim. They're planning to trigger the birth of a new universe and pass over and leave the rest of us to die in the wreckage of this one."

"The seven members of the Cabal to Loop Through the Infinite," Titus answers, "have presented their case clearly enough. The data is available to all. Their plan isn't entirely implausible." Formality, to Titus, is important in these trying times. She abhors the slang term "Returners" as she would loathe "Jumpers" for her own group, or "Fatalists" for the Faction,

"Travelling into the past is impossible." Only And Always Forward is adamant; perhaps not a surprise, given its name. "I have always said this. They cannot live on through infinite iterations of the same universe. It is patently absurd, since no such thing happened at the beginning of this universe, and there is no reason to believe ours is the first of all possible universes."

"We've debated this before," Titus offers, remaining calm with only a little effort. "Numerous possibilities exist. Their return to the early moments of the universe may simply diverge an alternate reality. Similarly, it may overlay this one, but without invalidating our experience—that we will never have existed in a restarted universe hardly means we did not exist in this one. Besides, the same argument can be leveled against our plan. There is no evidence that this universe was initially populated by entities from a previous iteration."

"There is strong evidence to suggest that each universe lasts longer than its predecessor," Infinite Recursion points out. Infinite Recursion changed its name when the Conclave was first formed; it has always been one of the most enthusiastic members.

"There are such theories," Titus corrects. "Let us hope we are able to test them."

"Hope? If there is a conspiracy, we need to do more than hope!" =/= flares in the night of the cosmos, wasteful and immature. "Forward is right! It's the Cabal!"

"If you've got evidence, present it. I've given you all the data I have. It's entirely possible that I've overlooked something." Titus allows a more patient substructure to speak for her. Expressing frustration, tempting though it is, would surely be unproductive. "But we shouldn't accuse the Cabal without evidence."

"What evidence do you need?" Infinite Recursion asks. "The Faction are happy to just die. We will pass across the gap and live on. Only the Cabal—"

"You're forgetting," Titus interrupts, an anger substructure bubbling up within her, "that the Galasphere wasn't one of the Cabal. The Galasphere was one of us."

"A spy," Only and Always Forward snaps back, but there is an undercurrent of doubt rippling out from others. Titus is privately pleased.

"Let us be clear," Titus says. "We face a threat to our existence, to everything for which we've worked so long. We wait for the final moments of the universe; only from that point may we fold ourselves through into the universe to come and thus survive. This conspiracy plans to create the next universe . . . ahead of schedule, if you will. In doing so, it appears they—and only they—intend to cross over. It is a betrayal, we cannot doubt it. Specifically, it's a betrayal of both us and the Cabal, since the only difference to the Faction is the precise time of their ending."

"Then perhaps some of the Faction are to blame!" Only and Always Forward suggests. "They may have pretended to accept death and be planning this in secret—"

"Kabachi has summoned the Faction. They meet now, even as we do," Titus says. There is something unbecoming, she thinks, about Only and Always Forward's eagerness to accuse. Only and Always Forward has always preferred to keep to itself. Perhaps, Titus's substructure muses, it has grown paranoid.

Paranoia can be forgiven. These are, after all, testing times.

"We must hunt," Titus continues. "There are other conspirators. If they will not reveal themselves, we must uncover them. Seek, all of you. Somewhere there will be other devices such as the one the

Galasphere destroyed. We must find and destroy them, and we must uncover their creators."

There is silence, for a time.

"And must we destroy them, too?" Champion asks. Champion is thirty-two—no, thirty-one now—and rarely emerges from a simulated environment in which it tests the martial techniques of a thousand dead species.

It is Hapax Legomenon who answers, with a complex mixture of infinite sadness and absolute necessity.

Nobody argues.

4: One and Six

The universe is dying, but it is not yet dead. It is not yet, perhaps, even capable of death. But soon . . . soon.

Titus meets with Kabachi as planned.

"90-Designate-1-Kabachi : conspiracy : confirmation," Kabachi announces without preamble.

Kabachi's self-reference tells Titus more than she wanted to know.

"Who?" she asks.

"Undesignate-(∞)(∞)," Kabachi continues. It presents a construct of the Faction's meeting for Titus to digest. As she absorbs the data, she in turn passes on her recording of the Conclave's meeting, including even Hapax's temporary language.

The Faction meeting had, apparently, been surprisingly brief. (∞)(∞) had offered scorn, defiance, mockery. It had laughed in the face of its supposed allies.

And it had died as the Galasphere had died, shredding its own mind to destroy any further information about the conspiracy.

There is silence in the void for a time, as Titus and Kabachi mull over each other's recordings.

"90-Designate-6-Titus : suggestion : additional input : 90-Designate-9-The Sum of All That Never Was."

The Sum of All That Never Was, the leader of the Cabal. Titus weighs advantages and disadvantages. Evidence suggests three conspirators. One from the Conclave has been eliminated; one from the Faction, likewise. It is possible that the Cabal contains the third conspirator.

The Cabal also contains only seven members. Which places the likelihood of The Sum of All That Never Was being a conspirator higher than Titus is comfortable with.

Besides, she has never actually liked him.

"Before we call on The Sum," she says, deliberately avoiding the correct form of address to underline her concerns, "we should theorize further. The behavior of the Galasphere and of $(\infty)(\infty)$ concerns me. The conspiracy appears designed to ensure their survival, yet both destroyed themselves when exposed. Indeed, $(\infty)(\infty)$ exposed itself for no clear reason. Their actions are inconsistent with their apparent motivation."

"90-Designate-6-Titus : agreement. Undesignate-$(\infty)(\infty)$ + Undesignate-Galasphere : action : factual/inarguable. 90-Designate-1-Kabachi : conclusion : Undesignate-$(\infty)(\infty)$ + Undesignate-Galasphere : motivation : undetermined."

"If their actions and their motivations are incompatible, there are certain possibilities," Titus mulls. "Perhaps we have erred in our analysis of their motivations. Or maybe their motivations were not their own. A conspiracy is, by definition, about betrayal. Perhaps, just as the conspiracy betrayed us, they in turn were betrayed."

"90-Designate-1-Kabachi : agreement. Unknown-Designate : conspirator (secret) : Undesignate-$(\infty)(\infty)$ + Undesignate-Galasphere : manipulated."

"Just so. But to what ends? The third conspirator must have needed them for some purpose, yet also have benefited from their being revealed. How could such an advantage arise?"

"Unknown," is Kabachi's only answer. "Insufficient data for simulation."

The bleakness of the statement horrifies Titus. She has never heard Kabachi communicate without designations. She flails for some shred of hope.

"But we know there must be a third conspirator. The true conspirator. If we can find them . . ."

There is a pause. She can almost see Kabachi collect itself.

"90-Designate-1-Kabachi : agreement. 90-Designate-6-Titus : query : alternative approach : subject : machine analysis." Kabachi accompanied the suggestion with detailed schematics. It was a polite though unnecessary touch; although Titus had pushed the information to Shared Memory, she had retained all the data in her own storage.

The machine the Galasphere had destroyed was similar to the machine the Conclave intended to use to cross the infinitely small yet infinitely vast gap between the end of one universe and the beginning of the next. That was the source of the nagging sense of familiarity. But the creation of the bridge into the next universe was only a part of its function. Its greater purpose—or the purpose, at least, of the greater part of the machine's structure—was to terminate the current universe.

Terminating the universe is not something that Titus has ever thought to contemplate.

"I need to access Shared Memory," she said. "There must be theoretical information stored—"

"90-Designate-6-Titus : futility. Undesignate : Shared Memory : relevant data : purged."

Titus is stunned into silence. If there is one single thing that is the ultimate taboo for the Ninety-Two (no, the Ninety: so hard to adjust to the re-emergence of death after so long), it is the deletion of data from Shared Memory. Shared Memory is sacrosanct, neutral ground no matter what conflicts might arise between the wildly disparate entities that wander the barren twilight of the universe. Once an experience, a fact, even an opinion has been downloaded into Shared Memory, it is supposed to remain there for the rest of time—and beyond, since the intention is for Shared Memory to be transferred by the Conclave into the newborn replacement cosmos.

"One of us has deleted all the data about this? Doubtless to make our task more difficult—"

"90-Designate-6-Titus : implementation : reverse extrapolation : theory."

"It's possible. But . . . it will take time."

"90-Designate-1-Kabachi : search : final conspirator and/or machine/device. 90-Designate-6-Titus : theoretical analysis."

She might have preferred it to be the other way around, but Kabachi is already swarming out into the void, fragmenting itself for the first time in countless eons to comb the vast emptiness. It can, she has to accept, search far more quickly than she.

Which leaves her to contemplate the machine. She examines its dataghost, hanging there in informational space.

The destruction of the universe. She does not want to think about it.

She has no choice. Not if she, and all of her Conclave, are to survive.

5: That Which Is New Is Not Always That Which Is Desired

The death of the universe is inevitable. All of the Ninety-Two had known this, eons past. They had analyzed and discussed and argued, and so the three groups had come about: the Faction, who intended to die with the universe; the Cabal, who intended to return to its beginning and live through the next iteration (and potentially over and over again); and the Conclave, who intended simply to leap across the momentary gap from the old into the new. Some of the arguments had been impassioned, others coldly logical, but after a time, the three groups had agreed to coexist, had agreed that none of their plans— not even those of the Cabal—impacted one another.

There had been harmony. But that harmony is over. Distrust now stalks the dying cosmos. Acceptance in the face of the inevitable, so hard-won over so many eons, has been broken.

This is a new thing. New things in an old universe should be precious, should be cherished.

But Titus cannot bring herself to cherish this.

She approaches her analysis from two directions. Firstly, there is the nature of the machine itself. She needs to know—without the benefit of the information stolen from Shared Memory—how such a device could trigger the premature end of this universe and the concomitant start of the next. But equally important, if more frustrating, is her attempt to analyze how the Galasphere and $(\infty)(\infty)$ could have been manipulated into their illogical actions.

And by whom.

Her analyses run side by side, with her core identity monitoring both, filtering conclusions, adjusting parameters, sliding data and philosophical frameworks from one to the other and back again.

The machine, she concludes, is viable. It is possible to trigger the end of the universe, subject to certain criteria. She sends to Shared Memory to fetch additional data.

She needs a map of the universe, and that, surely, has not been purged. It would be far too noticeable.

Her other line of enquiry is less fruitful. The Galasphere could have destroyed the machine without attacking her and thus kept its part in the conspiracy secret. $(\infty)(\infty)$ had no detectable reason to reveal itself during the meeting of the Faction. Her only conclusion is that they were not, in fact, the Galasphere or $(\infty)(\infty)$. Physically, they may have retained those forms; but in terms of their core sentience . . .

They had been destroyed already, hollowed out by the final conspirator, made puppets. It is the only explanation, and yet it remains inadequate; for it still does not explain why, even as puppets, they should reveal the existence of the conspiracy.

And it does nothing to identify the true enemy.

Back, then, to the machine. The machine exploits certain weaknesses in the underlying plane of two-dimensional space from which the other dimensions are extrapolated. The chaotic nature of the Big Bang, the first moments of the universe's creation, left that two-dimensional membrane imperfect. There are subtle folds and creases.

Weaknesses.

She needs the map. With the map, she can determine possible locations where the device—the machine to end all things—would best be operated. With the map, she can hunt her enemy. She finds the prospect delightful. She can correlate a list, plan the most efficient search strategy, eliminate possibilities one by one until her enemy has no place left to hide. She can eradicate it. She can exterminate everything that opposes her. She can—

There is something inside her, she realizes suddenly. Something that is not her. Something that is rewriting her substructures. Subverting her consciousness.

This, she realizes with horror, is what happened to the Galasphere, and to $(\infty)(\infty)$. They were hollowed out from within, their very sentience rewritten, slaved to senseless lusts and illogical desires.

But she is forewarned. She can do what they did not. She fragments herself, severing structures. Divide and conquer. She reframes her consciousness, building new mental processes even as she sends out mindclones to separately inspect each disparate element, determining whether it is safe to reattach. She shrinks to a point and then expands outward once more, renewing herself, reabsorbing the disparate elements individually, rewriting their corrupted mindlets afresh. She analyzes herself repeatedly. There can be no room for error, no allowance of doubt. The infection of her personality structures must be eliminated. Every last trace of it must be purged.

When she is done, she is whole again. But she still has no clue as to the identity of her enemy; only a new respect for their capabilities.

She needs the map. It is her only chance now. Time is running out—even without the map, she knows that. As the universe winds down, the flaws grow. With each passing eon, there will be more and more opportunities for the enemy to carry out its final act.

While she waits, she constructs eighty-nine small mindclones. They contain little; a warning of what the Enemy tried to do to her. She sends them out, each clone targeted to one entity.

She is aware that one of those entities will already know everything. She is aware that she exposes herself to another attack by doing this. But it is not just her own survival at stake. And the very act is one of defiance against the enemy. She will not think only of herself, no matter the danger.

She watches the mindclones flicker into underspace and begin their journeys. As she does so, something bubbles into reality alongside her.

It is the information from Shared Memory.

6: There Is a Crack In Everything

She studies the map of the universe in its final moments. She spreads it out in all its dimensions and studies its cracks and fissures, its points of weakness. She thinks for a moment of perfection, then dismisses it. Perfection, unblemished order, is dull. It is the subtleties of difference that give the universe its wonder and variety, even though so much to wonder at is gone and lives only in memory or simulation.

It is not easy to kill a universe, even one that is dying. It requires immense energy, and it requires that energy to be applied with absolute precision.

Each fissure is a possibility. There are too many. She rolls the map backwards through time, towards the now. Weaknesses evaporate. Fissures repair themselves.

If only, she thinks, reality could be reverted so easily. Mistakes could be corrected; regrets erased; missed opportunities taken; the dead restored . . .

The dead cannot be restored. They can be remembered. They can be mourned. But they are still dead.

And if the enemy is not stopped . . . even that will not be possible. For one thing is certain: the enemy, whoever it is, does not mourn for those it has already destroyed, and it will not mourn for the rest.

The rollback is completed. The map has become the territory. She identifies the weakest point in the universe, drills down into it, analyzing it minutely. At the moment, there is barely enough energy left in the entire universe to break it asunder. But with every passing age, the activation energy shrinks.

And who knows how long the enemy has been preparing for this? Who knows what secret stores of energy have been cached for this wickedness?

She folds herself into underspace and bubbles through the underlay of the universe, railing at the laws of physics and their indifferent limits. Reality can be bent, but it will not break.

Time passes.

Titus frets.

When she arrives, she bursts out of underspace, bristling with defenses.

The first thing she perceives is the machine. It bridges the invisible fissure, ready to pour energies into it, ready to widen an insignificant crack into a yawning gulf, a whirling vortex of chaos that will swallow the universe whole and vomit a new one in its place.

"You are persistent," Only and Always Forward says. It emerges from within the machine. Titus begins to perceive that the machine— as well as Only and Always Forward—are equipped with an unimaginable range of weaponry. She feels very small.

"You do not have to do this," Titus says. More defenses are building around her. But there have been needless deaths already; she would avoid more, if she can. Especially her own.

"This is our destiny. This has always been our destiny. We could not eliminate the other from this universe, but we will ensure that it does not pass on to the next. There will be only us, as it should be."

"Us?" Titus is puzzled. "The Galasphere is gone. $(\infty)(\infty)$, too. Are there yet more conspirators? Or . . ."

And the substructure of suspicion she created flares bright with the dawning realization.

"Just so," comes the answer. "There is no purpose in hiding. Not any more. We are not Only and Always Forward. We are the Schen Ko. We have always been the Schen Ko."

There is a smile in the undercurrent of emotive communication. It is the smile of a predator about to strike.

7: The End Of All That Is

Titus does not know how this is possible. Long ago, somehow, the last of the Schen Ko must have evaded the Kabachi. But from that assumption, the rest follows logically. Weakened, their plans to erase all other life in the universe were made untenable.

But where an outright assault had failed . . . perhaps stealth might succeed. It was the way of predators. Faced with their weaponry, you could easily forget their guile.

So they had hidden; and, somehow, had survived, and made themselves into something that aroused no suspicion. Waiting, all those countless eons, for the end to come, and for the chance to leap into a new universe all their own, free of opposition. A universe they could rule. A universe where they could snuff out any life aborning. A universe from which, again, they could leap on to the next, and the next.

An infinite future, universe after universe after universe, with the Schen Ko as the only form of life.

Even as her substructures analyze the Schen Ko's plan, Titus is defending herself. She has to. The assault is vicious, unrelenting. If she could, she would run; but to run would be to permit the Schen Ko to activate the device, to succeed. To run would be to die.

She realizes she may die anyway. The Schen Ko are older and more ruthless than any enemy she had envisaged.

"The others were fools." She tells the Schen Ko this in the hope of distracting it in some way, of dulling the ferocious concentration of its assault. "You would never have shared the future with the Galasphere, or with $(\infty)(\infty)$."

"We are the Schen Ko. We are sufficient. There is no *need* for any other life. They were necessary to assist with our design of the machine. Once their expertise was harvested, they served no other purpose."

Its assault is not weakened by its reply. Titus flails for a moment, her outer protections excoriated. She was strengthened by all she harvested from the Galasphere. She learned much about defense and attack. But in the arts of violence, she is still a child against the sleek brutality of the Schen Ko.

She tries. She launches attack substructures, building them as fast as she can, hurling them at the enemy. The Schen Ko envelop each of them in fractal membranes, sucking them through excess dimensions, stripping them of coherence.

She sends out mindclones to call for help. She fears it is futile, expecting them to be destroyed, too, but the Schen Ko do not even appear to care. It may be with good reason; her analytical submind informs her that survival probabilities are steadily dropping.

The Schen Ko continue their attack.

She tries to fight back. It is futile. The Schen Ko, in the far-distant past, destroyed countless civilizations, sterilized entire clusters of galaxies. They were masters of eradication when they were far, far less than they have become.

The Schen Ko laugh. Unimaginable, immeasurable energies flare around Titus. The Galasphere's attack, in comparison, was the ineffective flailing of a child.

She is going to die. She can withstand the assault for a time, but she is going to die. Unless help comes . . .

Help comes.

Champion is suddenly there. She could ask for no better companion to fight alongside her.

And he is not alone. Singular arrives, too, a peculiar entity she has never entirely understood, a mind shrouded in philosophical knots. And more; more of the ninety-two (no, the ninety . . . soon, perhaps, to be fewer . . .) are heeding her call, coming to her aid, coming to defeat the Schen Ko . . .

She is wrong.

She remembers being at war with herself. She remembers the

Galasphere: a mindless slave once its knowledge had been subsumed by the Schen Ko.

This is the end of all things. This is chaos beyond imagining. Some, such as Champion, fight alongside her. Others, such as The Closure of the Gap, fight alongside the Schen Ko; dead inside, hollow puppets of a monomaniacal species. Others appear to be at war with themselves as the Schen Ko's infection tries to take hold.

Incalculable energies whirl around the machine. It vibrates, subtly, absorbing power . . .

And this, Titus realizes with sudden horror, was the last part of the Schen Ko's plan. They did not *happen* to be found; they *wanted* to be found. For the energy expended in this battle is far, far more than the Schen Ko alone could possibly have marshaled. It is enough to widen the crack in the universe.

It is this, this last war, which provides sufficient energy to operate the machine.

It is unfolding, twisting. It is tearing open a hole in the universe, a crack that will widen and split and into which all reality will tumble. The laws of reality shudder under the strain.

Titus almost cowers under the roiling decoherence. All that the Conclave had hoped for lies in ruins. The device has been triggered. The universe is about to end. The Schen Ko are laughing amongst the raw chaos.

But then instinct—an instinct Titus did not even know she possessed—kicks in. Survival instinct. The Schen Ko are exulting in the madness around them, in their imminent triumph. They are laughing in the ruins. And in doing so, they have made one mistake.

Titus lets her defenses evanesce. With the little energy she has left, she twists underspace around a tiny core of self and hurls what remains of her down, ahead of the suddenly screaming Schen Ko, into the heart of the machine.

She, not the Schen Ko, enters the bridge.

Behind her, the universe dies.

8: All Is Once More Made New

Titus lives.

She doubted it, for a moment. A riot of energies blazed around her as she dove into the machine. An even greater riot of energies surrounds her now. A new universe is blossoming, condensing its laws into solidity. She gazes on the coalescent flux, the collapsing dimensions. She marvels at the complex particles, the wavelengths, the very rules of existence writing themselves as she watches. It is a glorious thing.

She grieves, for all those of the Conclave who should have lived on alongside her. Hapax Legomenon. Champion. The Closure of the Gap. Singular. =/=, even. So many, so many who would have lived on but for the Schen Ko. She feels a terrible guilt, which she cannot even name, for Shared Memory has been lost as well. She has only her own memories now. She has only herself. The others are gone, and she is alone in a newborn universe.

For now. But life will come. Life is glorious and persistent and inevitable. It will arise, in time, and she has so much of that, so very much.

She settles down to watch, and grow, and waits to greet intelligences as they arise in this brave new universe.

Titus is one.

THE TUMBLEDOWNS
OF CLEOPATRA ABYSS

★

by David Brin

Since the time of the Founders, Thumps have come at regular intervals, shaking the bubble-habitats of Cleopatra Abyss. Only now the quakes have become erratic—and deadly, threatening humanity's tenuous foothold deep under the oceans of Venus. Jonah will have to use a "rascal's" cleverness, adaptability and courage to save himself and his new wife. Even if that means doing the unthinkable.

★ 1 ★

TODAY'S THUMP was overdue. Jonah wondered if it might not come at all.

Just like last Thorday when—at the Old Clock's mid-morning chime—farmers all across the bubble-habitat clambered up pinyon vines or crouched low in expectation of the regular, daily throb—a pulse and quake that hammered up your foot-soles and made all the bubble boundaries shake. Only Thorday's thump never came. The chime was followed by silence and a creepy let-down feeling. And Jonah's mother lit a candle to avert bad luck.

Early last spring, there had been almost a *whole week* without any thumps. Five days in a row, with no rain of detritus, shaken loose from the Upper World, tumbling down here to the ocean bottom. And two, smaller gaps the previous year.

Apparently, today would be yet another hiatus . . .

Whomp!

Delayed, the thump came *hard*, shaking the moist ground beneath Jonah's feet. He glanced with concern toward the bubble boundary, more than two hundred meters away—a membrane of ancient, translucent volcanic stone, separating the paddies and pinyon forest from black, crushing waters just outside. The barrier vibrated, an unpleasant, scraping sound.

This time, especially, it caused Jonah's teeth to grind.

"They used to sing, you know," commented the complacent old woman who worked at a nearby freeboard loom, nodding as gnarled fingers sent her shuttle flying among the strands, weaving ropy cloth. Her hands did not shake, though the nearby grove of thick vines did, quivering much worse than after any normal thump.

"I'm sorry grandmother." Jonah reached out to a nearby bole of twisted cables that dangled from the bubble-habitat's high-arching roof, where shining glowleaves provided the settlement's light.

"*Who* used to sing?"

"The walls, silly boy. The bubble walls. Thumps used to come exactly on time, according to the Old Clock. Though every year we would shorten the main wheel by the same amount, taking thirteen seconds off the length of a day. After-shakes always arrived from the same direction, you could depend on it! And the bubble sang to us."

"It sang . . . you mean like that awful groan?" Jonah poked a finger in one ear, as if the pry out the fading reverberation. He peered into the nearby forest of thick trunks and vines, listening for signs of breakage. Of disaster.

"Not at all! It was *musical*. Comforting. Especially after a miscarriage. Back then, a woman would lose over half of her quickenings. Not like today, when more babies are born alive than warped or misshapen or dead. Your generation has it lucky! And it's said things were even worse in olden days. The Founders were fortunate to get any living replacements at all! Several times, our population dropped dangerously." She shook her head, then smiled.

"Oh . . . but the music! After every mid-morning thump you could face the bubble walls and relish it. That music helped us women bear our heavy burden."

"'Yes, grandmother, I'm sure it was lovely," Jonah replied, keeping a respectful voice as he tugged on the nearest pinyon to test its strength, then clambered upward, hooking long, unwebbed toes into the braided vines, rising high enough to look around. None of the other men or boys could climb as well.

Several nearby boles appeared to have torn loose their mooring suckers from the domelike roof. Five . . . no six of them . . . teetered, lost their final grip-holds, then tumbled, their luminous tops crashing into the rice lagoon, setting off eruptions of sparks . . . or else onto the work sheds where Panalina and her mechanics could be heard, shouting in dismay. *It's a bad one,* Jonah thought. Already the hab-bubble seemed dimmer. If many more pinyons fell, the clan might dwell in semi-darkness, or even go hungry.

"Oh, it was beautiful, all right," the old woman continued, blithely ignoring any ruckus. "Of course in *my* grandmother's day, the thumps weren't just regular and perfectly timed. They came in *pairs*! And it is said that long before—in *her* grandmother's grandmother's time, when a day lasted so long that it spanned several sleep periods—thumps used to arrive in clusters of four or five! How things must've shook, back then! But always from the same direction, and exactly at the mid-morning chime."

She sighed, implying that Jonah and all the younger folk were making too much fuss. You call *this* a thump shock?

"Of course," she admitted, "the bubbles were *younger* then. More flexible, I suppose. Eventually, some misplaced thump is gonna end us all."

Jonah took a chance—he was in enough trouble already without offending the Oldest Female, who had undergone thirty-four pregnancies and still had *six* living womb-fruit—four of them precious females.

But grandmother seemed in a good mood, distracted by memories . . .

Jonah took off, clambering higher till he could reach with his left hand for one of the independent dangle vines that sometimes laced the gaps between pinyons. With his right hand he flicked with his belt knife, severing the dangler a meter or so below his knees. Sheathing the blade and taking a deep breath—he launched off, swinging across an open space in the forest . . . and finally alighting along a second giant bole. It shook from his impact and Jonah worried. *If this one was weakened, and I'm the reason that it falls, I could be in for real punishment. Not just grandma-tending duty!*

A "rascal's" reputation might have been harmless, when Jonah was younger. But now, the mothers were pondering what amount Tairee Dome might have to pay, in dowry, for some other bubble colony to take him. A boy known to be unruly might not get any offers, at any marriage price . . . and a man without a wife-sponsor led a marginal existence.

But honestly, this last time wasn't my fault! How am I supposed to make an improved pump without filling something with high-pressure water? All right, the kitchen rice cooker was a poor choice. But it has a gauge and everything . . . or, it used to.

After quivering far too long, the great vine held. With a brief sense of relief, he scrambled around to the other side. There was no convenient dangler, this time, but another pinyon towered fairly close. Jonah flexed his legs, prepared, and launched himself across the gap, hurtling with open arms, alighting with shock and painful clumsiness. He didn't wait though, scurrying to the other side—where there *was* another dangle vine, well-positioned for a wide-spanning swing.

This time he couldn't help himself while hurtling across open space, giving vent to a yell of exhilaration.

Two swings and four leaps later, he was right next to the bubble's edge, reaching out to stroke the nearest patch of ancient, vitrified stone, in a place where no one would see him break taboo. Pushing at the transparent barrier, Jonah felt deep ocean pressure shoving back. The texture felt rough-ribbed, uneven. Sliver-flakes rubbed off, dusting his hand.

"Of course, bubbles were younger then," the old woman said. *"More flexible."*

Jonah had to wrap a length of dangle vine around his left wrist and clutch the pinyon with his toes, in order to lean far out and bring his face right up against the bubble—it sucked heat into bottomless cold— using his right hand and arm to cup around his face and peer into the blackness outside. Adapting vision gradually revealed the stony walls of Cleopatra Crevice, the narrow-deep canyon where humanity had come to take shelter so very long ago. Fleeing the Coss invaders. Before many lifespans of grandmothers.

Several strings of globelike habitats lay parallel along the canyon bottom, like pearls on a necklace, each of them surrounded by a froth of smaller bubbles . . . though fewer of the little ones than there were in olden times, and none anymore in the most useful sizes. It was said that, way back at the time of the Founding, there used to be faint illumination overhead, filtering downward from the surface and demarking night from day: light that came from the mythological god-thing that old books called the *sun,* so fierce that it could penetrate both dense, poisonous clouds and the ever-growing ocean.

But that was way back in a long-ago past, when the sea had not yet burgeoned so, filling canyons, becoming a dark and mighty deep. Now, the only gifts that fell from above were clots of detritus that men gathered to feed algae ponds. Debris that got stranger, every year.

These days, the canyon walls could only be seen by light from the bubbles themselves, by their pinyon glow within. Jonah turned slowly left to right, counting and naming those farm-enclaves he could see. *Amtor . . . Leininger . . . Chown . . . Kuttner . . . Okumo . . .* each one a clan with traditions and styles all their own. Each one possibly the place where Tairee tribe might sell him in a marriage pact. A mere boy and good riddance. Good at numbers and letters. A bit skilled with his hands, but notoriously absent-minded, prone to staring at nothing, and occasionally putting action to rascally thoughts.

He kept tallying: *Brakutt . . . Lewis . . . Atari . . . Napeer . . . Aldrin . . . what?*

Jonah blinked. What was happening to Aldrin? And the bubble just beyond it. Both Aldrin and Bezo were still quivering. He could make out few details at this range, through the milky, pitted membrane. But one of the two was rippling and convulsing, the glimmer of its pinyon forest shaking back and forth as the giant boles swayed . . . then collapsed!

The other distant habitat seemed to be *inflating.* Or so Jonah thought at first. Rubbing his eyes and pressing even closer, as Bezo habitat grew bigger . . .

. . . or else it was rising! Jonah could not believe what he saw. Torn loose, somehow, from the ocean floor, the entire bubble was moving.

Upward. And as Bezo ascended, its flattened bottom now re-shaped itself as farms and homes and lagoons tumbled together into the base of the accelerating globe. With its pinyons still mostly in place, Bezo colony continued glowing as it climbed upward.

Aghast, and yet compelled to look, Jonah watched until the glimmer that had been Bezo finally vanished in blackness, accelerating toward the poison surface of Venus.

Then, without warning or mercy, habitat Aldrin imploded.

★ 2 ★

"I was born in Bezo, you know."

Jonah turned to see Enoch leaning on his rake, staring south along the canyon wall, toward a gaping crater where that ill-fated settlement bubble used to squat. Distant glimmers of glow-lamps flickered over there as crews prowled along the Aldrin debris field, sifting for salvage. But that was a job for mechanics and senior workers. Meanwhile, the algae ponds and pinyons must be fed, so Jonah also found himself outside, in coveralls that stank and fogged from his own breath and many generations of previous wearers, helping to gather the week's harvest of organic detritus.

Jonah responded in the same dialect Enoch had used. Click-Talk. The only way to converse, when both of you are deep underwater.

"Come on," he urged his older friend, a recent, marriage-price immigrant to Tairee Bubble. "All of that is behind you. A male should never look back. We do as we are told."

Enoch shrugged—broad shoulders making his stiff coveralls scrunch around the helmet, fashioned from an old foam bubble of a size no longer found in these parts. Enoch's phlegmatic resignation was an adaptive skill that served him well, as he was married to Jonah's cousin, Jezzy, an especially strong-willed young woman, bent on exerting authority and not above threatening her new husband with casting-out.

I can hope for someone gentle, when I'm sent to live beside a stranger in strange dome.

Jonah resumed raking up newly fallen organic stuff—mostly ropy bits of vegetation that lay limp and pressure-crushed after their long tumble to the bottom. In recent decades, there had also been detritus of another kind. *Shells* that had holes in them for legs and heads. And skeleton fragments from slinky creatures that must have—when living—stretched as long as Jonah was tall! Much more complicated than the mud worms that kept burrowing closer to the domes, of late. More like the fabled *snakes* or *fish* that featured in tales from Old Earth.

Panalina's dad—old Scholar Wu—kept a collection of skyfalls in the little museum by Tairee's eastern arc, neatly labeled specimens dating back at least ten grandmother cycles, to the era when *light* and *heat* still came down along with debris from above—a claim that Jonah still deemed mystical. Perhaps just a legend, like Old Earth.

"These samples . . . do you see how they are getting more complicated, Jonah?" So explained old man Wu as he traced patterns of veins in a recently gathered sea weed. *"And do you make out what's embedded here? Bits of creatures living on or within the plant. And there! Does that resemble a bite mark? The outlines of where teeth tore into this vegetation? Could that act of devouring be what sent it tumbling down to us?"*

Jonah pondered what it all might mean while raking up dross and piling it onto the sledge, still imagining the size of a jaw that could have torn such a path through tough, fibrous weed. And everything was pressure-shrunk down here!

"How can anything live up at the surface?" he recalled asking Wu, who was said to have read every book that existed in the Cleopatra Canyon colonies, most of them two or three times. *"Did not the founders say the sky was thick with poison?"*

"With carbon dioxide and sulfuric acid, yes. I have shown you how we use pinyon leaves to separate out those two substances, both of which have uses in the workshop. One we exhale—"

"And the other burns! Yet, in small amounts it smells sweet."

"That is because the Founders, in their wisdom, put sym-bi-ants in our blood. Creatures that help us deal with pressure and gases that would kill folks who still live on enslaved Earth."

Jonah didn't like to envision tiny animals coursing through his body, even if they did him good. Each year, a dozen kids throughout the bubble colonies were chosen to study such useful things—biological things. A smaller number chose the field that interested Jonah, where even fewer were allowed to specialize.

"But the blood creatures can only help us down here, where the

pinyons supply us with breathable air. Not up top, where poisons are so thick." Jonah gestured skyward. "*Is that why none of the Risers have ever returned?*"

Once every year or two, the canyon colonies lost a person to the hell that awaited above. Most often because of a buoyancy accident; a broken tether or boot-ballast sent some hapless soul plummeting upward. Another common cause was suicide. And—more rarely—it happened for another reason, one the mothers commanded that no one may discuss, or even mention. A forbidden reason.

Only now, after the sudden rise of Bezo Bubble and a thousand human inhabitants, followed by the Aldrin implosion, little else was on anyone's mind.

"*Even if you survive the rapid change in pressure . . . one breath up there and your lungs would be scorched as if by flame,*" old Scholar Wu had answered, yesterday. "*That is why the Founders seeded living creatures a bit higher than us, but beneath the protective therm-o-cline layer that keeps most of the poison out of our abyss . . .*

The old man paused, fondling a strange, multi-jawed skeleton. "*It seems that life—some kind of life—has found a way to flourish near that barrier. So much so, that I have begun to wonder—*"

A sharp voice roused him.

"Jonah!"

This time it was Enoch, reminding him to concentrate on work. A good reason to work in pairs. He got busy with the rake. Mother was pregnant again, along with Aunts Leor and Sosun. It always made them cranky with tension, as the fetuses took their time, deciding whether to go or stay—and if they stayed, whether to come out healthy or as warped ruins. No, it would not do to return from this salvage outing with only half a load!

So he and Enoch forged farther afield, hauling the sledge to another spot where high ocean currents often dumped interesting things after colliding with the canyon walls. The algae ponds and pinyons needed fresh supplies of organic matter. Especially in recent decades, after the old volcanic vents dried up.

The Book of Exile says we came down here to use the vents, way back when the sea was hot and new. A shallow refuge for free humans to hide from the Coss, while comets fell in regular rhythm, thumping Venus to life. Drowning her fever and stirring her veins.

Jonah had only a vague notion what "comets" were—great balls drifting through vast emptiness, till godlike beings with magical powers flung them down upon this planet. Balls of *ice,* like the pale-blue slush that formed on the cool, downstream sides of boulders in a fast, underwater current. About as big as Cleopatra Canyon was wide, that's what books said about a comet.

Jonah gazed at the towering cliff walls, enclosing all the world he ever knew. Comets were so vast! Yet, they had been striking Venus daily, since centuries before colonists came, immense, pre-creation icebergs, pelting the sister world of Old Earth. Perhaps several million of them by now, herded first by human civilization and later by Coss Masters, who adopted the project as their own—one so ambitious as to be nearly inconceivable.

So much ice. So much water. Building higher and higher till it has to fill the sky, even the poison skies of Venus. So much that it fills all of creatio—

"Jonah, watch out!"

Enoch's shouted warning made him crouch and spin about. Or Jonah tried to, in the clumsy coveralls, raising clouds of muck stirred by heavy, shuffling boots. "Wha—? What is it?"

"Above you! Heads up!"

Tilting back was strenuous, especially in a hurry. The foggy faceplate didn't help. Only now Jonah glimpsed something overhead, shadowy and huge, looming fast out of the black.

"Run!"

He required no urging. Heart pounding in terror, Jonah pumped his legs for all they were worth, barely lifting weighted shoes to shuffle-skip with long strides toward the nearby canyon wall, sensing and then back-glimpsing a massive, sinuous shape that plummeted toward him out of the abyssal sky. By dim light from a distant habitat-dome, the monstrous shape turned languidly, following his dash for safety, swooping in to close the distance fast! Over his right shoulder, Jonah glimpsed a gaping mouth and rows of glistening-huge teeth. As sinuous body from some nightmare.

I'm not gonna make it. The canyon wall was just too far.

Jonah skidded to a stop, raising plumes of bottom muck. Swiveling into a crouch and half moaning with fear, he lifted his only weapon— a rake meant for gathering organic junk from the sea floor. He brandished it crosswise, hoping to stymie the wide jaw that now careened out of dimness, framed by four glistening eyes. Like some ancient storybook *dragon,* stooping for prey. No protection, the rake was more a gesture of defiance.

Come on, monster.

A decent plan, on the spur of the moment.

It didn't work.

It didn't have to.

The rake shattered, along with several ivory teeth as the giant maw plunged around Jonah, crashing into the surrounding mud, trapping him . . . but never closing, nor biting or chewing. Having braced for all those things, he stood there in a tense hunker as tremors shook the canyon bottom, closer and more spread out than the daily thump. It had to be more of the sinuous monster, colliding with surrounding muck—a long, long leviathan!

A final ground-quiver, then silence. Some creakings. Then more silence.

And darkness. Enveloped, surrounded by the titan's mouth, Jonah at first saw nothing . . . then a few faint glimmers. Pinyon light from nearby *Monsat* bubble habitat. Streaming in through holes. *Holes* in the gigantic head. Holes that gradually opened wider as ocean-bottom pressure wreaked havoc on flesh meant for much higher waters.

Then the smell hit Jonah.

An odor of death.

Of course. Such a creature would never dive this deep of its own accord. Instead of being pursued by a ravenous monster, Jonah must have run along the same downdraft conveying a corpse to its grave. An intersection and collision that might seem hilarious someday, when he told the story as an old grandpa, assuming his luck held. Right now, he felt sore, bruised, angry, embarrassed . . . and concerned about the vanishing supply in his meager air bubble.

With his belt knife, Jonah began probing and cutting a path out of the trap. He had another reason to hurry. If he had to be rescued by others, there would be no claiming this flesh for Tairee, for his clan and family. For his dowry and husband price.

Concerned clicks told him Enoch was nearby and one promising gap in the monster's cheek suddenly gave way to the handle of a rake. Soon they both were tearing at it, sawing tough membranes, tossing aside clots of shriveling muscle and skin. His bubble helmet might keep out the salt-sea, but pungent aromas were another matter. Finally, with Enoch tugging helpfully on one arm, Jonah squeezed out and stumbled several steps before falling to his knees, coughing.

"Here come others," said his friend. And Jonah lifted his gaze, spying men in bottom suits and helmets, hurrying this way, brandishing glow bulbs and makeshift weapons. Behind them he glimpsed one of the cargo subs—a string of mid-sized bubbles, pushed by hand-crank propellers—catching up fast.

"Help me get up . . . on top," he urged Enoch, who bore some of his weight as he stood. Together, they sought a route onto the massive head. There was danger in this moment. Without clear ownership, fighting might break out among salvage crews from different domes, as happened a generation ago, over the last hot vent on the floor of Cleopatra Canyon. Only after a dozen men were dead had the grandmothers made peace. But if Tairee held a firm claim to this corpse, then rules of gift-generosity would parcel out shares to every dome, with only a largest-best allotment to Tairee. Peace and honor now depended on his speed. But the monster's cranium was steep, crumbly and slick.

Frustrated and almost out of time, Jonah decided to take a chance. He slashed at the ropy cables binding his soft overalls to the weighted clogs that kept him firmly on the ocean bottom. Suddenly buoyant, he began to sense the Fell Tug . . . the pull toward heaven, toward doom. The same tug that had yanked Bezo colony, a few days ago, sending that bubble-habitat and all of its inhabitants plummeting skyward.

Enoch understood the gamble. Gripping Jonah's arm, he stuffed his rake and knife and hatchet into Jonah's belt. Anything convenient. So far, so good. The net force seemed to be slightly downward. Jonah nodded at his friend, and jumped.

★ 3 ★

The marriage party made its way toward Tairee's bubble-dock, shuffling along to beating tambourines. Youngsters—gaily decked in rice-flowers and pinyon garlands—danced alongside the newlyweds. Although many of the children wore masks or makeup to disguise minor birth defects, they seemed light of spirit.

They were the only ones.

Some adults tried their best, chanting and shouting at all the right places. Especially several dozen refugees—Tairee's allocated share of threadbare escapees from the ruin of Cixin and Sadoul settlements—who cheered with the fervid eagerness of people desperately trying for acceptance in their new home, rather than mere sufferance. As for other guests from unaffected domes? Most appeared to have come only for free food. These now crowded near the dock, eager to depart as soon as the nuptial sub was on its way.

Not that Jonah could blame them. Most people preferred staying close to home, ever since the thumps started going all crazy, setting off a chain of tragedies, tearing at the old, placid ways.

And today's thump is already overdue, he thought. In fact, there hadn't been a ground-shaking comet strike in close to a month. Such a gap would have been unnerving, just a year or two ago. Now, given how awful some recent impacts had been, any respite was welcome.

A time of chaos. Few see good omens, even in a new marriage.

Jonah glanced at his bride, come to collect him from Lausanne Bubble, all the way at the far northern outlet of Cleopatra Canyon. Taller than average, with a clear complexion and strong carriage, she had good hips and only a slight mutant-mottling on the back of her scalp, where the hair grew in a wild, discolored corkscrew. An easily overlooked defect, like Jonah's lack of toe webbing, or the way he would sneeze or yawn uncontrollably, whenever air pressure changed too fast. No one jettisoned a child over such inconsequentials.

Though you can be exiled forever from all you ever knew, if you're born with the genetic defect of maleness. Jonah could not help scanning the workshops and dorms, the pinyons and paddies of Tairee, wondering if he would see this place—his birth bubble—ever again. Perhaps, if the grandmothers of Lausanne trusted him with errands. Or next time Tairee hosted a festival—if his new wife chose to take him along.

He had barely met Petri Smoth before this day, having spoken just a few words with her over the years, at various craft-and-seed fairs, hosted by some of the largest domes. During last year's festival, held in ill-fated Aldrin Bubble, she *had* asked him a few pointed questions about some tinkered gimmicks he displayed. In fact, now that he looked back on it, her tone and expression must have been . . .

evaluating. Weighing his answers with *this* possible outcome in mind. It just never occurred to Jonah, at the time, that he was impressing a girl enough to choose him as a mate.

I thought she was interested in my improved ballast transfer valve. And maybe . . . in a way . . . she was.

Or, at least, in Jonah's mechanical abilities. Panalina suggested that explanation yesterday, while helping Jonah prepare his dowry—an old cargo truck that he had purchased with his prize winnings for claiming the dead sea serpent—a long-discarded submersible freighter that he spent the last year reconditioning. A hopeless wreck, some called it, but no longer.

"Well, it's functional, I'll give you that," the Master Mechanic of Tairee Bubble had decreed last night, after going over the vessel from stem to stern, checking everything from hand-wound anchor tethers and stone keel-weights to the bench where several pairs of burly men might labor at a long crank, turning a propeller to drive the boat forward. She thumped extra storage bubbles, turning stop-cocks to sniff at the hissing, pressurized air. Then Panalina tested levers that would let seawater into those tanks, if need-be, keeping the sub weighed down on the bottom, safe from falling into the deadly sky.

"It'll do," she finally decreed, to Jonah's relief. This could help him begin married life on a good note. Not every boy got to present his new bride with a whole submarine!

Jonah had acquired the old relic months before people realized just how valuable each truck might be, even junkers like this one— for rescue and escape—as a chain of calamities disrupted the canyon settlements. His repairs hadn't been completed in time to help evacuate more families from cracked and doomed Cixin or Sadoul bubbles, and he felt bad about that. Still, with Panalina's ruling of seaworthiness, this vehicle would help make Petri Smoth a woman of substance in the hierarchy at Laussane, and prove Jonah a real asset to his wife.

Only . . . what happens when so many bubbles fail that the others can't take refugees anymore?

Already there was talk of sealing Tairee against outsiders, even evacuees, and concentrating on total self-reliance.

Some spoke of arming the colony's subs for war.

"These older hull-bubbles were thicker and heavier," Panalina commented, patting the nearest bulkhead, the first of three ancient, translucent spheres that had been fused together into a short chain, like a trio of pearls on a string. "They fell out of favor, maybe four or five mother generations ago. You'll need to pay six big fellows in order to crank a full load of trade goods. That won't leave you much profit on cargo."

Good old Panalina, always talking as if everything would soon be normal again, as if the barter network was likely to ever be the same. With streaks of gray in her hair, the artificer claimed to be sixty years old, but was certainly younger. The grandmothers let her get away with the fib, and what would normally be criminal neglect, leaving her womb fallow most of the time, with only two still-living heirs, and both of those boys.

"Still," Panalina looked around and thumped the hull one last time. "He's a sturdy little boat. You know, there was talk among the mothers about refusing to let you take him away from Tairee. The Smoths had to promise half a ton of crushed grapes in return, and to take in one of the Sadoul families. Still, I think it's *you* they mostly want."

Jonah had puzzled over that cryptic remark, after Panalina left, then all during the brew-swilled bachelor party, suffering crude jokes and ribbing from the married men, and later during a fretful sleep-shift, as he tossed and turned with pre-wedding jitters. During the ceremony itself, Mother had been gracious and warm—not her typical mien, but a side of her that Jonah felt he would surely miss. Though he knew that an underlying source of her cheerfulness was simple—*one less male mouth to feed.*

It had made Jonah reflect, even during the wrist-binding part of the ceremony, on something old Scholar Wu said recently.

The balance of the sexes may change, if it really comes down to war. Breeders could start to seem less valuable than fighters.

In the docklock, Jonah found that his little truck had been decked with flowers, and all three of the spheres gleamed, where they had been polished above the water line. The gesture warmed Jonah's heart. There was even a freshly painted name, arcing just above the propeller.

Bird of Tairee

Well. Mother had always loved stories about those prehistoric creatures of Old Earth, who flew through a sky that was immeasurably vast and sweet.

"I thought you were going to name it after me," Petri commented in a low voice, without breaking her gracious smile.

"I shall do that, lady-love. Just after we dock in Laussane."

"Well . . . perhaps not *just* after," she commented, and Jonah's right buttock took a sharp-nailed pinch. He managed not to jump or visibly react. But clearly, his new wife did not intend wasting time, once they were home.

Home. He would have to re-define the word, in his mind.

Still, as Jonah checked the final loading of luggage, gifts and passengers, he glanced at the fantail one last time, picturing there a name that he really wanted to give the little vessel.

Renewed Hope

★ 4 ★

They were underway, having traveled more than half of the distance to Laussane Bubble, when a *thump* struck at the wrong time, shaking the little sub truck like a rattle.

The blow came hard and late. So late that everyone at the wedding had simply written-off any chance of one today. Folks assumed that at least another work-and-sleep cycle would pass without a comet fall. Already this was the longest gap in memory. Perhaps (some murmured) the age of thumps had come to an end, as prophesied long ago. After the disasters that befell Aldrin and Bezo, then Sadoul and Cixin, it was a wish now shared by all.

Up until that very moment, the nuptial voyage had been placid, enjoyable, even for tense newlyweds.

Jonah was at the tiller up front, gazing ahead through a patch of hull-bubble that had been polished on both sides, making it clear enough to see through. Hoping that he looked like a stalwart, fierce-eyed seaman, he gripped the rudder ropes that steered *Bird of Tairee*, though the sub's propeller lay still and powerless. For this voyage, the old truck was being hauled as a trailer behind a larger, sleeker and more modern Laussanite sub, where a team of twelve burly men sweated and tugged in perfect rhythm, turning their drive-shaft crank.

Petri stood beside her new husband, while passengers chattered in the second compartment, behind them. As bubble colonies drifted past, she gestured at each of the gleaming domes and spoke of womanly matters, like the politics of trade and diplomacy, or the personalities and traditions of each settlement. Which goods and food items they excelled at producing, or needed. Their rates of mutation and successful child-raising. Or how well each habitat was managing its genetic diversity . . . and her tone changed a bit at that point, as if suddenly aware how the topic bore upon them both. For this marriage-match had been judged by the Laussane mothers on that basis, above all others.

"Of course I had final say, the final choice," she told Jonah, and it warmed him that Petri felt a need to explain.

"Anyway, there is a project I've been working on," she continued in a lower voice. "With a few others in Laussane and Landis bubbles. Younger folks, mostly. And we can use a good mechanic like you. "

Like me? So I was chosen for that reason?

Jonah felt put off, and tensed a bit when Petri put an arm around his waist. But she leaned up and whispered in his ear.

"I think you'll like what we're up to. It's something just right for a *rascal*."

The word surprised him and he almost turned to stare. But her arm was tight and Petri's breath was still in his ear. So Jonah chose to keep his features steady, unmoved. Perhaps sensing his stiff reaction, Petri let go. She slid around to face him with her back resting upon the transparent patch, leaning against the window.

Clever girl, he thought. It was the direction he had to look, in order to watch the *Pride of Laussane*'s rudder, up ahead, matching his tiller to that of the larger sub. Now he could not avert his eyes from her, using boyish reticence as an excuse.

Petri's oval face was a bit wide, as were her eyes. The classic Laussane chin cleft was barely noticeable, though her mutant-patch—the whorl of wild hair—was visible as a reflection behind her, on the bubble's curved, inner surface. Her wedding garment, sleek and close-cut, revealed enough to prove her fitness to bear and nurse . . . plus a little more. And Jonah wondered—*when am I supposed to let the sight of her affect me? Arouse me?* Too soon and he might seem brutish, in need of tight reins. Too late or too little, and his bride might feel insulted.

And fretting over it will make me an impotent fool. Deliberately,

Jonah calmed himself, allowing some pleasure to creep in, at the sight of her. A seed of anticipation grew . . . as he knew she wanted.

"What *project* are you talking about? Something involving trucks?" He offered a guess. "Something the mothers may not care for? Something suited to a . . . to a . . ."

He glanced over his shoulder, past the open hatch leading to the middle bubble, containing a jumble of cargo—wedding gifts and Jonah's hope chest, plus luggage for Laussane dignitaries who rode in comfort aboard the bigger submersible ahead. Here, a dozen lower-caste passengers sat or lay atop the stacks and piles—some of Petri's younger cousins, plus a family of evacuees from doomed Sadoul dome, sent to relieve Tairee's overcrowded refugee encampment, as part of the complex marriage deal.

Perhaps it would be best to hold off this conversation until a time and place with fewer ears around, to pick up stray sonic reflections. Perhaps delaying it for wife-and-husband pillow talk—the one and only kind of privacy that could be relied upon, in the colonies. He looked forward again, raising one eyebrow and Petri clearly got his meaning. Still, in a lower voice, she finished Jonah's sentence.

"To a *rascal,* yes. In fact, your reputation as a young fellow always coming up with bothersome questions helped me bargain well for you. Did you intend it that way, I wonder? For you to wind up *only* sought by one like me, who would *value* such attributes? If so, clever boy."

Jonah decided to keep silent, letting Petri give him credit for cunning he never had. After a moment, she shrugged with a smile, then continued in a voice that was nearly inaudible.

"But in fact, our small bunch of conspirators and connivers were inspired by yet another *rascal.* The one we have foremost in our minds was a fellow named . . . Melvil."

Jonah had been about to ask about the mysterious "we." But mention of that particular name stopped him short. He blinked hard— two, three times—striving not to flinch or otherwise react. It took him several tries to speak, barely mouthing the words.

"You're talking about . . . *Theodora Canyon?*"

A place of legend. And Petri's eyes now conveyed many things. Approval of his quickness . . . overlain upon an evident grimness of purpose. A willingness—even eagerness—to take risks and adapt in chaotic times, finding a path forward, even if it meant following a folktale. All of that was apparent in Petri's visage. Though clearly, Jonah was expected to say more.

"I've heard . . . one hears rumors . . . that there was a *map* to what Melvil found . . . another canyon filled with Gift-of-Venus bubbles like those the Founders discovered here in Cleopatra Canyon. But the mothers forbade any discussion or return voyages, and—" Jonah slowed down when he realized he was babbling. "And so, after Melvil fled his punishment, they hid the map away. . . ."

"I've been promised a copy," Petri confided, evidently weighing his reaction, "Once we're ready to set out."

Jonah couldn't help himself. He turned around again to check the next compartment, where several smaller children were chasing each other up and down the luggage piles, making a ruckus and almost tipping over a crate of Panalina's smithy tools, consigned for trans-shipment to Gollancz dome. Beyond, through a second hatchway to the final chamber, where sweating rowers would normally sit, lay stacked bags of exported Tairee rice. The refugee family and several of Petri's sub-adult cousins lounged back there, talking idly, keeping apart from the raucous children.

Jonah looked back at his bride, still keeping his voice low.

"You're kidding! So there truly *was* a boy named Melvil? Who stole a sub and vanished—"

"—for a month and a week and a day and an hour," Petri finished for him. "Then returned with tales of a far-off canyon filled with gleaming bubbles of all sizes, a vast foam of hollow, volcanic globes, left over from this world's creation, never touched by human hands. Bubbles just as raw and virginal as our ancestors found, when they first arrived down here beneath a newborn ocean, seeking refuge far below the poison sky."

Much of what she said was from the Founders' Catechism, retaining its rhythm and flowery tone. Clearly, it amused Petri to quote modified scripture while speaking admiringly of an infamous rebel; Jonah could tell as much from her wry expression. But poetry—and especially irony—had always escaped Jonah, and she might as well get used to that husbandly lack, right now.

"So . . . this is about . . . finding new homes?"

"Perhaps, if things keep getting worse here in Cleo Abyss, shouldn't we have options? Oh, we're selling it as an expedition to harvest fresh bubbles, all the sizes that have grown scarce hereabouts, useful for helmets and cooking and chemistry. But we'll also check out any big ones. Maybe they're holding up better in Theodora than they are here. Because, at the rate things are going—" Petri shook her head. And, looking downward, her expression *leaked* just a bit, losing some of its tough, determined veneer, giving way to plainly visible worry.

She knows things. Information that the mothers won't tell mere men. And she's afraid.

Strangely, that moment of vulnerability touched Jonah's heart, thawing a patch that he had never realized was chill. For the first time, he felt drawn . . . compelled to reach out. Not sexually. But to comfort, to hold . . .

That was when the thump struck—harder than Jonah would have believed possible.

Concussion slammed the little submarine over, halfway onto its port side and set the ancient bubble hull ringing. Petri hurtled into him, tearing the rudder straps from his hands as they tumbled together backwards, caroming off the open hatch between compartments, then rolling forward again as *Bird of Tairee* heaved.

With the sliver of his brain that still functioned, Jonah wondered if there had been a collision. But the Laussanite ship was bobbing and rocking some distance ahead, still tethered to the *Bird,* and nothing else was closer than a bubble-habitat, at least two hundred meters away. Jonah caught sight of all this while landing against the window patch up-front, with Petri squished between. This time, as the *Bird* lurched again, he managed to grab a stanchion and hold on, while gripping her waist with his other arm. Petri's breath came in wheezing gasps, and now there was no attempt to mask her terror.

"What? What was . . ."

Jonah swallowed, bracing himself against another rocking sway that almost tore her from his grasp.

"A *thump!* Do you hear the low tone? But they're never this late!"

He didn't have breath to add—*I've never felt one outside a dome, before. No one ventures into water during late morning, when comets always used to fall.* And now Jonah knew why. His ears rang and hurt like crazy.

All this time he had been counting. Thump vibrations came in sequence. One tone passed through rock by *compression,* arriving many seconds before the slower *transverse* waves. He had once even read one of Scholar Wu's books about that, with partial understanding. And he recalled what the old teacher said: that you could tell from the difference in tremor arrivals how far away the impact was from Cleopatra Canyon.

. . . twenty-one . . . twenty-two . . . twenty three . . .

Jonah hoped to reach sixty-two seconds, the normal separation, for generation after generation of grandmothers.

. . . twenty-four . . . twenty-f—

The transverse tone, higher pitched and much louder than ever, set the forward bubble of the *Bird* ringing like a bell, even as the tooth-jarring sways diminished, allowing Jonah and Petri to grab separate straps and find their feet.

Less than half the usual distance. That comet almost hit us! He struggled with a numb brain. *Maybe just a couple of thousand kilometers away.*

"The children!" Petri cried, and cast herself—stumbling—aft toward the middle compartment. Jonah followed, but just two steps in order to verify no seals were broken. No hatches had to be closed and dogged . . . not yet. And the crying kids back there looked shaken, not badly hurt. So okay, trust Petri to take care of things back there—

—as he plunged back to the tiller harness. Soon, Jonah was tugging at balky cables, struggling to make the rudder obedient, fighting surges while catching brief glimpses of a tumult outside. Ahead, forty or fifty meters, the *Pride of Laussane*'s propeller churned a roiling cauldron of water. The men inside must be cranking with all their might.

Backward, Jonah realized with dismay. Their motion in reverse might bring the *Pride*'s prop in contact with the tow-line. *Why are they hauling ass backwards?*

One clue. The tether remained taut and straight, despite the rowers' efforts. And with a horrified realization, Jonah realized why. The bigger sub *tilted* upward almost halfway to vertical, with its nose aimed high.

They've lost their main ballast! Great slugs of stone and raw metal normally weighed a sub down, lashed along the keel. They must have torn loose amid the chaos of the thump—nearly all of them! But how? Certainly, bad luck and lousy maintenance, or a hard collision with the ocean bottom. For whatever reason, the *Pride of Laussane* was straining upward, climbing toward the sky.

Already, Jonah could see one of the bubble habitats from an angle no canyonite ever wanted . . . looking *down* upon the curved dome from above, its forest of pinyon vines glowing from within.

Cursing his own slowness of mind, Jonah let go of the rudder cables and half-stumbled toward the hatch at the rear of the control chamber, shouting for Petri. There was a job to do, more vital than any other. Their very lives might depend on it.

★ 5 ★

"When I give the word, open valve number one *just a quarter turn!*"

It wasn't a demure tone to use toward a woman, but he saw no sign of wrath or resentment as his new wife nodded. "A quarter turn. Yes, Jonah."

Clamping his legs around one of the ballast jars, he started pushing rhythmically on his new and improved model air pump. "Okay . . . now!"

As soon as Petri twisted the valve they heard water spew into the ballast chamber, helping Jonah push the air out, for storage at pressure in a neighboring bottle. It would be simpler and less work to just let the air spill outside, but he couldn't bring himself to do that. There might be further uses for the stuff.

When *Bird* started tilting sideways, he shifted their efforts to a bottle next to the starboard viewing patch . . . another bit of the old hull that had been polished for seeing. Farther aft, in the third compartment, he could hear some of the passengers struggling with bags of rice, clearing the propeller crank for possible use. In fact, Jonah had ordered it done mostly to give them a distraction. Something to do.

"We should be getting heavier," he told Petri as they shifted back and forth, left to right and then left again, letting water into storage bubbles and storing displaced air. As expected, this had an effect on the sub's pitch, raising the nose as it dragged on the tether cable, which in turn linked them to the crippled *Pride of Laussane*.

The crew of that hapless vessel had given up cranking to propel their ship backwards. Everything depended on Jonah and Petri, now. If they could make *Bird* heavy enough, quickly enough, both vessels might be prevented from sinking into the sky.

And we'll be heroes, Jonah pondered at one point, while his arms throbbed with pain. This could be a great start to his life and reputation in Laussane Bubble . . . that is, *if* it worked. Jonah ached to go and check the little sub's instruments, but there was no time. Not even when he drafted the father of the Sadoul refugee family to pump alongside him. Gradually, all the tanks were filling, making the *Bird* heavier, dragging at the runaway *Pride of Laussane*. And indeed . . .

Yes! He saw a welcome sight. One of the big habitat domes! Perhaps the very one they had been passing, when the thump struck. Jonah shared a grin with Petri, seeing in her eyes a glimmer of earned respect. *Perhaps I'll need to rest a bit before our wedding night.* Though funny, it didn't feel as if fatigue would be a problem.

Weighed down by almost-full ballast tanks, *Bird* slid almost along the great, curved flank of the habitat. Jonah signaled Xerish to ease off pumping and for Petri to close her valve. He didn't want to hit the sea bottom too hard. As they descended, Petri identified the nearby colony as Leininger Dome. It was hard to see much through both sweat-stung eyes and the barely polished window patch, but Jonah could soon tell that a crowd of citizens had come to press their faces against the inner side of the great, transparent bubble wall, staring up and out toward the descending subs.

As *Bird* drifted backward, it appeared that the landing would be pretty fast. Jonah shouted for all the passengers to brace themselves for a rough impact, one that should come any second as they drew even with the Leininger onlookers. A bump into bottom mud that . . .

. . . that didn't come.

Something was wrong. Instinct told him, before reason could, when Jonah's ears popped and he gave vent to a violent sneeze.

Oh no.

Petri and Jonah stared at the Leiningerites, who stared back in resigned dismay as the *Bird* dropped below their ground level . . . and kept dropping. Or rather, Leininger Bubble kept ascending, faster and faster, tugged by the deadly buoyancy of all that air inside, its anchor roots torn loose by that last violent thump. Following the path and fate of Bezo Colony, without the warning that had allowed partial evacuation of Cixin and Sadoul.

With a shout of self-loathing, Jonah rushed to perform a task that he should have done already. Check instruments. The pressure gauge wouldn't be much use in an absolute sense, but relative values could at least tell if they were falling. Not just relative to the doomed habitat, but drifting back toward the safe bottom muck, or else—

"Rising," he told Petri in a low voice, as she sidled alongside and rested her head against his shoulder. He slid his arm around her waist, as if they had been married forever. Or, at least, most of what remained of their short lives.

"Is there anything else we can do?" she asked.

"Not much." He shrugged. "Finish flooding the tanks, I suppose. But they're already almost full, and the weight isn't enough. *That* is just too strong." And he pointed out the forward viewing patch at the *Pride of Laussane,* its five large, air-filled compartments buoyant enough to overcome any resistance by this little truck.

"But . . . can't they do what we've done. Fill their own balls—"

"Ballast tanks. Sorry, my lady. They don't have any big ones. Just a few little bottles for adjusting trim."

Jonah kept his voice even and matter-of-fact, the way a vessel captain should, even though his stomach churned with dread, explaining how external keel weights saved interior cargo space. Also, newer craft used bubbles with slimmer walls. You didn't want to penetrate them with too many inlets, valves and such.

"And no one else has your new pump," Petri added. And her approving tone meant more to Jonah, in these final minutes, than he ever would have expected.

"Of course . . ." he mused.

"Yes? You've thought of something?"

"Well, if we could somehow cut the tether cable . . ."

"We'd sink back to safety!" Then Petri frowned. "But we're the only chance they have, on the *Pride of Lausanne.* Without our weight, they would shoot skyward like a seed pip from a lorgo fruit."

"Anyway, it's up to them to decide," Jonah explained. "The tether release is at their end, not ours. Sorry. It's a design flaw that I'll fix as soon as I get a chance, right after re-painting your name on the stern."

"Hm. See that you do," she commanded.

Then, after a brief pause.

"Do you think they might release us, when they realize both ships are doomed?"

Jonah shrugged. There was no telling what people would do, when faced with such an end. He vowed to stand watch though, just in case.

He sneezed hard, twice. Pressure effects were starting to tell on him.

"Should we inform the others?" he asked Petri, with a nod back toward *Bird's* other two compartments, where the crying had settled down to low whimpers from a couple of younger kids.

She shook her head. "It will be quick, yes?"

Jonah considered lying, and dismissed the idea.

"It depends. As we rise, the water pressure outside falls, so if air pressure inside remains high, that could lead to a blow-out, cracking one of our shells, letting the sea rush in awfully fast. So fast, we'll be knocked out before we can drown. Of course, that's the *least* gruesome end."

"What a cheerful lad," she commented. "Go on."

"Let's say the hull compartments hold. This is a tough old bird." He patted the nearest curved flank. "We can help protect against blowout by venting compartment air, trying to keep pace with falling pressure outside. In that case, we'll suffer one kind or another kind of pressure-change disease. The most common is the Bends. That's when gas that's dissolved in our blood suddenly pops into tiny bubbles that fill your veins and arteries. I hear it's a painful way to die."

Whether because of his mutation, or purely in his mind, Jonah felt a return of the scratchy throat and burning eyes. He turned his head barely in time to sneeze away from the window, and Petri.

She was looking behind them, into the next compartment. "If death is unavoidable, but we can pick our way to die, then I say let's choose—"

At that moment, Jonah tensed at a sudden, jarring sensation—a *snap* that rattled the viewing-patch in front of him. Something was happening, above and ahead. Without light from the Cleopatra domes, darkness was near total outside, broken only by some algae-glowbulbs placed along the flank of the Pride of Laussane. Letting go of Petri, he went to all the bulbs inside the *Bird's* forward compartment and covered them, then hurried back to press his face against the viewing-patch.

"What is it?" Petri asked. "What's going on?"

"I think . . ." Jonah made out a queer, sinuous rippling in the blackness between the two submarines.

He jumped as something struck the window. With pounding heart, he saw and heard a snakelike thing slither across the clear zone of bubble, before falling aside. And beyond, starting from just twenty meters away, the row of tiny glow spots now shot upward, like legendary rockets, quickly diminishing then fading from view.

'The tether," he announced in a matter-of-fact voice.

"They let go? Let *us* go?" A blend of hope and awe in her voice.

"Made sense," he answered. "They were goners anyway." *And now they will be the heroes, when all is told. Songs will be sung about their choice, back home.*

That is, assuming there still is a home. We have no idea if Leininger Dome was the only victim, this time.

He stared at the pressure gauge. After a long pause when it refused to budge, the needle finally began to move. Opposite to its former direction of change.

"We're descending," he decreed with a sigh. "In fact, we'd better adjust. To keep from falling too fast. It wouldn't do, to reach safety down there, only to crack open from impact."

Jonah put the Sadoulite dad—Xerish—to work, pumping in the opposite direction, less frantically than before, but harder work, using compressed air to push out-and-overboard some water from the ballast tanks, while Petri, now experienced, handled the valves. After supervising for a few minutes, he went back to the viewing port and peered outside. *I must keep a sharp look out for the lights of Cleo Crevice. We may have drifted laterally and I can adjust better while we're falling than later, at the bottom.* He used the rudder and stubby elevation planes to turn his little sub, explaining to Petri how it was done. She might have to steer, if Jonah's strength was needed on the propeller crank.

A low, concussive report caused the chamber to rattle and groan. Not as bad as the horrid thump had been, but closer, coming from somewhere above. Jonah shared eye contact with Petri, a sad recognition of something inevitable. The end of a gallant ship—*Pride of Laussane.*

Two more muffled booms followed, rather fainter, then another.

They must have closed their inner hatches. Each compartment is failing separately.

But something felt wrong about that. The third concussion, especially, had felt deep-throated, lasting longer than reasonable. Amid another bout of sneezing, Jonah pressed close against the view-patch once again, in order to peer about. First toward the bottom and then upward.

Clearly, this day had to be the last straw. It rang a death knell for the old, complacent ways of doing things. Leininger had been a big, important colony, and perhaps not today's only major victim. If thumps were going unpredictable and lethal, then Cleopatra might have to be abandoned.

Jonah knew very little about the plan concocted by Petri's mysterious cabal of young women and men, though he was glad to have been chosen to help. To follow a *rascal's* legend in search of new homes. In fact, two things were abundantly clear. *Expeditions must get under way just as soon as we get back. And there should be more than just one, following Melvil's clues. Subs must be sent in many directions! If Venus created other realms filled with hollow volcanic globes that can be seeded with Earthly life, then we must find them.*

A second fact had also emerged, made evident during the last hour or so. Jonah turned to glance back at a person he had barely known, until just a day ago.

It appears that I married really well.

Although the chamber was very dim, Petri glanced up from her task and noticed him looking at her. She smiled—an expression of respect and dawning equality that seemed just as pleased as he now felt. Jonah smiled back—then unleashed another great sneeze. At which she chirped a short laugh and shook her head in fake-mocking ruefulness.

Grinning, he turned back to the window, gazed upward—then shouted—

"Grab something! Brace yourselves!"

That was all he had time or breath to cry, while yanking on the tiller cables and shoving his knee hard against the elevator control plane. *Bird* heeled over to starboard, both rolling and struggling to yaw-turn. Harsh cries of surprise and alarm erupted from the back compartments, as crates and luggage toppled.

He heard Petri shout—"stay where you are!"—at the panicky Xerish, who whimpered in terror. Jonah caught a glimpse of them, reflected in the view-patch, as they clutched one of the air-storage bottles to keep from tumbling across the deck, onto the right-side bulkhead.

Come on, old boy, he urged the little sub and wished he had six strong men cranking at the stern end, driving the propeller to accelerate *Bird of Tairee* forward. If there had been, Jonah might—just barely—have guided the sub clear of peril tumbling from above. Debris from a catastrophe, only a small fraction of it glittering in the darkness.

Hard chunks of something rattled against the hull. He glimpsed an object, thin and metallic—perhaps a torn piece of pipe—carom off the view-patch with a bang, plowing several nasty scars before it fell away. Jonah half expected the transparent zone to start spalling and cracking, at any second.

That didn't happen, but now debris was coming down in a positive rain, clattering along the whole length of his vessel, testing the sturdy old shells with every strike. Desperate, he hauled even harder, steering *Bird* away from what seemed the worst of it, toward a zone that glittered a bit less. More cries erupted from the back two chambers.

I should have sealed the hatches, he thought. But then, *what good would that do for anyone, honestly?* Having drifted laterally from Cleo Canyon, any surviving chambers would be helpless, unable to maneuver, never to be found or rescued before the stored air turned to poison. *Better that we all go, together.*

He recognized the sound that most of the rubble made upon the hull—bubble-stone striking more bubble-stone. Could it all have come from the *Pride of Laussane?* Impossible! There was far too much.

Leininger.

The doomed dome must have imploded, or exploded, or simply come apart without the stabilizing pressure of the depths. Then, with all its air lost and rushing skyward, the rest would plummet. Shards of bubble wall, dirt, pinyons glowing feebly as they drifted ever-lower . . . and people. That was the detritus Jonah most hoped to avoid.

There. It looks jet black over there. The faithful old sub had almost finished its turn. Soon he might slack off, setting the boat upright. Once clear of the debris field, he could check on the passengers, then go back to seeking the home canyon . . .

He never saw whatever struck next, but it had to be big, perhaps a major chunk of Leininger's wall. The blow hammered all three compartments in succession, ringing them like great gongs, making Jonah cry out in pain. There were other sounds, like ripping, tearing. The impact—somewhere below and toward portside, lifted him off his feet, tearing one of the rudder straps out of Jonah's hand, and leaving him to swing wildly by the other. *Bird* sawed hard to the left as Jonah clawed desperately to reclaim the controls.

At any moment, he expected to greet the harsh, cold sea and have his vessel join the skyfall of lost hopes.

★ 6 ★

Only gradually did it dawn on him—it wasn't over. The peril and problems, he wasn't about to escape them that easily. Yes, damage was evident, but the hulls—three ancient, volcanic globes, still held.

In fact, some while after that horrible collision, it did seem that *Bird of Tairee* had drifted clear of the heavy stuff. Material still rained upon the sub, but evidently softer items. Like still-glowing chunks of pinyon vine.

Petri took charge of the rear compartments, crisply commanding passengers to help each other dig out and assessing their hurts, in order of priority. She shouted reports to Jonah, whose hands were full. In truth, he had trouble hearing what she said, over the ringing in his ears, and had to ask for repetition several times. The crux: one teenager had a fractured wrist, while others bore bruises and contusions—a luckier toll than he expected. Bema—the Sadoulite mother—kept busy delivering first aid.

More worrisome was a *leak*. Very narrow, but powerful, a needle jet spewed water into the rear compartment. Not through a crack in the shell—fortunately—but via the packing material that surrounded the propeller bearing. Jonah would have to go back and have a look, but first he assessed other troubles. For example, the sub wouldn't right herself completely. There was a constant tilt to starboard around the roll axis . . .

. . . then he checked the pressure gauge, and muttered a low invocation to ancient gods and demons of Old Earth.

★ ★ ★

"We've stopped falling," he confided to Petri in the stern compartment, once the leak seemed under control. It had taken some time, showing the others how to jam rubbery cloths into the bearing and then bracing it all with planks of wood torn from the floor. The arrangement was holding, for now.

"How can that be?" she asked. "We were *heavy* when the *Pride* let us go. I thought our problem was how to slow our descent."

"It was. Till our collision with whatever hit us. Based on where it struck, along the portside keel, I'd guess that it knocked off some of our static ballast—the stones lashed to our bottom. The same thing that happened to *Pride* during that awful thump quake. Other stones may have been dislodged or had just one of their lashings cut, leaving them to dangle below the starboard side, making us tilt like this. From these two examples, I'd say we've just learned a lesson today, about a really bad flaw in the whole way we've done sub design."

"So which is it? Are we rising?"

Jonah nodded.

"Slowly. It's not too bad yet. And I suppose it's possible we might resume our descent, if we fill all the ballast tanks completely. Only there's a problem."

"Isn't there always?" Petri rolled her eyes, clearly exasperated.

"Yeah." He gestured toward where Xerish—by luck a carpenter—was hammering more bracing into place. Jonah lowered his voice. "If we drop back to the sea floor, that bearing may not hold against full-bottom pressure. It's likely to start spewing again, probably faster."

"If it does, how long will we have?"

Jonah frowned. "Hard to say. Air pressure would fight back, of course. Still, I'd say less than an hour. Maybe not that much. We would have to spot one of the canyon domes right away, steer right for it and plop ourselves into dock as fast as possible, with everyone cranking like mad—"

"—only using the propeller will put even more stress on the bearing," Petri concluded with a thoughtful frown. "It might blow completely."

Jonah couldn't prevent a brief smile. *Brave enough to face facts . . . and a mechanical aptitude, as well? I could find this woman attractive.*

"Well, I'm sure we can work something out," she added. "You haven't let us down, yet."

Not yet, he thought and returned to work, feeling trapped by her confidence in him. And cornered by the laws of chemistry and physics— as well as he understood them with his meager education, taken from ancient books that were rudimentary and obsolete when the Founders first came to Venus, cowering away from alien invaders under a newborn ocean, while comets poured in with perfect regularity.

Perfect for many lifetimes, but not forever. Not anymore. *Even if we make it home, then go ahead with the Melvil Plan, and manage to find another bubble-filled canyon less affected by the rogue thumps, how long will that last?*

Wasn't this whole project, colonizing the bottom of an alien sea with crude technology, always doomed from the start?

In the middle compartment, Jonah opened his personal chest and took out some treasures—books and charts that he had personally copied under supervision by Scholar Wu, onto bundles of hand-scraped pinyon leaves. In one, he verified his recollection of Boyle's Law and the dangers of changing air pressure on the human body. From another he got a formula that—he hoped—might predict how the leaky propeller shaft bearing would behave, if they descended the rest of the way.

Meanwhile, Petri put a couple of the larger teen girls to work on a bilge pump, transferring water from the floor of the third compartment into some almost-full ballast tanks. Over the next hour, Jonah kept glancing at the pressure gauge. The truck appeared to be leveling off again. *Up and down. Up and down. This can't be good for my old* Bird.

Leveled. Stable . . . for now. That meant the onus fell on him, with no excuse.

To descend and risk the leak becoming a torrent, blasting those who worked the propeller crank . . . or else . . .

Two hands laid pressure on his shoulders and squeezed inward, surrounding his neck, forcefully. Slim hands, kneading tense muscles and tendons. Jonah closed his eyes, not wanting to divulge what he had decided.

"Some wedding day, huh?"

Jonah nodded. No verbal response seemed needed. He felt married for years—and glad of the illusion. Evidently, Petri knew him now, as well.

"I bet you've figured out what to do."

He nodded again.

"And it won't be fun, or offer good odds of success."

A head shake. Left, then right.

Her hands dug in, wreaking a mixture of pleasure and pain, like life.

"Then tell me, husband," she commanded, coming around to bring their faces close. "Tell me what you'll have us do. Which way do we go?"

He exhaled a sigh. Then inhaled. And finally spoke one word.

"Up."

★ 7 ★

Toward the deadly sky. Toward Venusian hell. It had to be. No other choice was possible.

"If we rise to the surface, I can try to repair the bearing from inside, without water gushing through. And if it requires outside work, then I can do that by putting on a helmet and coveralls. Perhaps they'll keep out the poisons long enough."

Petri shuddered at the thought. "Let us hope that won't be necessary."

"Yeah. Though while I'm there I could also fix the ballast straps holding some of the weight stones to our keel. I . . . just don't see any other way."

Petri sat on a crate opposite Jonah, mulling it over.

"Wasn't upward motion what destroyed Leininger Colony and the *Pride?*"

"Yes . . . but their ascent was uncontrolled. Rapid and chaotic. We'll rise slowly, reducing cabin air pressure in pace with the decreased push of water outside. We have to go slow, anyway, or the gas that's dissolved in our blood will boil and kill us. Slow and gentle. That's the way."

She smiled. "You know all the right things to say to a virgin."

Jonah felt his face go red, and was relieved when Petri got serious again.

"If we rise slowly, won't there be another problem? Won't we run out of breathable air?"

He nodded. "Activity must be kept to a minimum. Recycle and shift stale air into bottles, exchanging with the good air they now contain. Also, I have a spark separator."

"You do? How did . . . aren't they rare and expensive?"

"I made this one myself. Well, Panalina showed me how to use pinyon crystals and electric current to split seawater into hydrogen and oxygen. We'll put some passengers to work, taking turns at the spin generator." And he warned her. "It's a small unit. It may not produce enough."

"Well, no sense putting things off, then." Petri said with a grandmother's tone of decisiveness. "Give your orders, man."

The ascent became grueling. Adults and larger teens took turns at the pumps, expelling enough ballast water for the sub to start rising at a good pace . . . then correcting when it seemed too quick. Jonah kept close track of gauges revealing pressure, both inside and beyond the shells. He also watched for symptoms of decompression sickness— another factor keeping things slow. All passengers not on-shift were encouraged to sleep—difficult enough when the youngest children kept crying over the pain in their ears. Jonah taught them all how to yawn or pinch their noses to equalize pressure, though his explanations kept being punctuated by fits of sneezing.

Above all, even while resting, they had to breathe deep, as their lungs gradually purged and expelled excess gas from their bloodstreams.

Meanwhile, the fore-chamber resonated with a constant background whine as older kids took turns at the spark separator, turning its crank so that small amounts of seawater divided into component elements—one of them breathable. The device had to be working—a layer of salt gathered in the brine-collector. Still, Jonah worried. *Did I attach the poles right? Might I be filling the storage bottle with oxygen and letting hydrogen into the cabin? Polluting the sub with an explosive mix that could put us out of our misery, at any second?*

He wasn't sure how to tell—none of his books said—though he recalled vaguely that hydrogen had no odor.

After following him on his rounds, inspecting everything and repeating his explanations several times, Petri felt confident enough to insist. "You must rest now, Jonah. I will continue to monitor our rate of ascent and make minor adjustments. Right now, I want you to close your eyes."

When he tried to protest, she insisted, with a little more of the accented tone used by Laussane mothers. "We will need you far more, in a while. You'll require all your powers near the end. So lie down and recharge yourself. I promise to call, if anything much changes."

Accepting her reasoning, he obeyed by curling upon a couple of grain sacks that Xerish brought forward to the control cabin. Jonah's eyelids shut, gratefully. The brain, however, was another matter.

How deep are we now?

It prompted an even bigger question: *how deep is the bottom of Cleopatra Canyon, nowadays?*

According to lore, the first colonists used to care a lot about measuring the thickness of Venusian seas, back when some surface light used to penetrate all the way to the ocean floor. They would launch balloons attached to huge coils of string, in order to both judge depth and sample beyond the therm-o-cline barrier and even from the hot, deadly sky. Those practices died out—though Jonah had seen one of the giant capstan reels once, during a visit to Chown Dome, gathering dust and mouldering in a swampy corner.

The way Earth denizens viewed their planet's hellish interior, that was how Cleo dwellers thought of the realm above. Though there had been exceptions. Rumors held that Melvil, that legendary rascal, upon returning from his discovery of Theodora Crevice, had demanded support to start exploring the great heights. Possible even the barrier zone where living things thronged and might be caught for food. Of course, he was quite mad—though boys still whispered about him in hushed tones.

How many comets? Jonah found himself wondering. Only one book in Tairee spoke of the great Venus Terraforming Project that predated the Coss invasion. Mighty robots, as patient as gods, gathered iceballs at the farthest fringe of the Solar System and sent them plummeting from that unimaginably distant realm to strike this planet—several each day, always at the same angle and position— both speeding the world's rotation and drenching its long-parched basins. *If each comet was several kilometers in diameter . . . how thick an ocean might spread across an entire globe, in twenty generations of grandmothers?*

For every one that struck, five others were aimed to skim close by, tearing through the dense, clotted atmosphere of Venus, dragging some of it away before plunging to the sun. The scale of such an enterprise was stunning, beyond belief. So much so that Jonah truly doubted he could be of the same species that did such things. *Petri, maybe. She could be that smart. Not me.*

How were such a people ever conquered?

The roil of his drifting mind moved onward to might-have-beens. If not for that misguided comet—striking six hours late to wreak havoc near the canyon colonies—Jonah and his bride would by now have settled into a small Laussane cottage, getting to know each other in more traditional ways. Despite, or perhaps because of the emergency, he actually felt far *more* the husband of a vividly real person than he would in that other reality, where physical intimacy happened . . . still, the lumpy grain sacks made part of him yearn for her in ways that—now—might never come to pass. That world would have been better . . . one where the pinyons waved their bright leaves gently overhead. Where he might show her tricks of climbing vines, then swing from branch to branch, carrying her in his arms while the wind of flying passage ruffled their hair—

A *twang* sound vibrated the cabin, like some mighty cord coming apart. The sub throbbed and Jonah felt it roll a bit.

His eyes opened and he realized, *I was asleep.* Moreover, his head now rested on Petri's lap. Her hand had been the breeze in his hair.

Jonah sat up.

"What was that?"

"I do not know. There was a sharp sound. The ship hummed a bit, and now the floor no longer tilts."

"No longer—"

Jumping up with a shout, he hurried over to the gauges, then cursed low and harsh.

"What is it, Jonah?"

"Quick—wake all the adults and get them to work pumping!"

She wasted no time demanding answers. But as soon as crews were hard at work, Petri approached Jonah again at the control station, one eyebrow raised.

"The remaining stone ballast," he explained. "It must have been hanging by a thread, or a single lashing. Now it's completely gone. The sub's tilt is corrected, but we're ascending too fast."

Petri glanced at two Sadoulites and two Laussaners who were

laboring to refill the ballast tanks. "Is there anything else we can do to slow down?"

Jonah shrugged. "I suppose we might unpack the leaky bearing and let more water into the aft compartment. But we'd have no control. The stream could explode in our faces. We might flood or lose the chamber. All told, I'd rather risk decompression sickness."

She nodded, agreeing silently.

They took their own turn at the pumps, then supervised another crew until, at last, the tanks were full. *Bird* could get no heavier. Not without flooding the compartments themselves.

"We have to lose internal pressure. That means venting air overboard," he said "in order to equalize."

"But we'll need it to breathe!"

"There's no choice. With our tanks full of water, there's no place to put extra air and still reduce pressure."

So, different pumps and valves, but more strenuous work. Meanwhile, Jonah kept peering at folks in the dim illumination of just two faint glow bulbs, watching for signs of the Bends. Dizziness, muscle aches and labored breathing? These could just be the result of hard labor. The book said to watch out also for joint pain, rashes, delirium or sudden unconsciousness. He did know that the old dive tables were useless—based on Earth-type humanity. *And we've changed. First because our scientist ancestors modified themselves and their offspring. But time, too, has altered what we are, even long after we lost those wizard powers. Each generation was an experiment.*

Has it made us less vulnerable to such things? Or more so?

Someone tugged his arm. It wasn't Petri, striving at her pump. Jonah looked down at one of the children, still wearing a stained and crumpled bridesmaid's dress, who pulled shyly, urging Jonah to come follow. At first, he thought: *it must be the sickness. She's summoning me to help someone's agony. But what can I do?*

Only it wasn't toward the stern that she led him, but the forwardmost part of the ship . . . to the view-patch, where she pointed.

"What is it?" Pressing close to the curved pane, Jonah tensed as he starkly envisioned some new cloud of debris . . . till he looked up and saw—

—light.

Vague at first. Only a child's perfect vision would have noticed it so early. But soon it spread and brightened across the entire vault overhead.

I thought we would pass through the therm-o-cline. He had expected a rough—perhaps even lethal—transition past that supposed barrier between upper and lower oceans. But it must have happened gently, while he slept.

Jonah called someone to relieve Petri and brought her forth to see.

"Go back and tell people to hold on tight," Petri dispatched the little girl, then she turned to grab Jonah's waist as he took the control straps. At this rate they appeared to be seconds away from entering Venusian hell.

Surely it has changed, he thought, nursing a hope that had never been voiced, even in his mind. *The ocean has burgeoned as life fills the seas . . .*

Already he spied signs of movement above. Flitting, flickering shapes—living versions of the crushed and dead tumbledowns that sometimes fell to Tairee's bottom realm, now undulating and darting about what looked like scattered patches of dense, dangling weed. He steered to avoid those.

If the sea has changed, then might not the sky, the air, even the highlands?

Charts of Venus, radar mapped by ancient earthling space probes, revealed vast continents and basins, a topography labeled with names like Aphrodite Terra and Lakshmi Planum. Every single appellation was that of a female from history or literature or legend. Well, that seemed fair enough. But had it been a cruel joke to call the baked and bone-dry lowlands "seas"?

Till humanity decided to make old dreams come true.

What will we find?

To his and Petri's awestruck eyes, the dense crowd of life revealed glimpses—shapes like dragons, like fish, or those ancient *blimps* that once cruised the skies of ancient Earth. And something within Jonah allowed itself to hope.

Assuming we survive decompression, might the fiery, sulfurous air now be breathable? Perhaps barely, as promised by the sagas? By now, could life have taken to high ground? Seeded in some clever centuries-delay by those same pre-Coss designers?

His mind pictured scenes from a few dog-eared storybooks, only enormously expanded and brightened. Vast, measureless jungles, drenched by rainstorms, echoing with the bellows of gigantic beasts. A realm so huge, so rich and densely forested that a branch of humanity might thrive, grow, prosper, and learn—regaining might and confidence—beneath that sheltering canopy, safe from invader eyes.

That, once upon a time, had been the dream, though few imagined it might fully come to pass.

Jonah tugged the tiller to avoid a looming patch of dangling vegetation. Then, ahead and above, the skyward shallows suddenly brightened, so fiercely that he and Petri had to shade their eyes, inhaling and exhaling heavy gasps. They both cried out as a great, slithering shape swerved barely out of the sub's way. Then brilliance filled the cabin like a blast of molten fire.

I was wrong to hope! It truly is hell!

A roar of foamy separation . . . and for long instants Jonah felt free of all weight. He let go of the straps and clutched Petri tight, twisting to put his body between hers and the wall as their vessel flew over the sea, turned slightly, then dropped back down, striking the surface with a shuddering blow and towering splash.

Lying crumpled below the view-patch, they panted, as did everyone else aboard, groaning and groping themselves to check for injuries. For reassurance of life. And gradually the hellish brightness seemed to abate, till Jonah realized. *It is my eyes, adapting. They never saw daylight, before.*

Jonah and Petri helped each other stand. Together, they turned, still shading their eyes. Sound had transformed, and so had the very texture of the air, now filled with strange aromas.

There must be a breach!

With shock, still blinking away glare-wrought tears, Jonah saw the cause. Impact must have knocked loose the dog-bolts charged with holding shut the main hatch, amidships on the starboard side—never meant to open anywhere but at the safety of a colonial dock.

With a shout he hurried over, even knowing it was too late. The poisons of Venus—

—apparently weren't here.

No one keeled over. His body's sole reaction to the inrushing atmosphere was to sneeze, a report so loud and deep that it rocked him back.

Jonah reached the hatch and tried pushing it closed, but *Bird of Tairee* was slightly tilted to port. The heavy door overwhelmed Jonah's resistance and kept gradually opening, from crack to slit, to gap, to chasm.

"I'll help you, Jonah," came an offer so low, like a rich male baritone, yet recognizably that of his wife. He turned, saw her eyes wide with surprise at her own voice.

"The air . . . it contains . . ." His words emerged now a deep bass. " . . . different gases than . . . we got from pinyons."

Different . . . but breathable. Even pleasant. Blinking a couple of times, he managed to shrug off the shock of his new voice and tried once more to close the hatch, before giving up for now. With the boat's slight leftward roll, there was no immediate danger of flooding, as seawater lapped a meter or so below. The opening must be closed soon, of course . . .

. . . but not quite yet. For, as Jonah and Petri stood at the sill, what confronted them was more than vast, rippling-blue ocean and a cloud-dense firmament. Something else lay between those two, just ahead and to starboard, a thick mass of shimmery greens and browns that filled the horizon, receding in mist toward distant, serrated skylines. Though he never dreamed of witnessing such a thing first-hand, they both recognized the sight, from ancient, faded pictures.

Land. Shore. Dense forests. Everything.

And overhead, creatures flapped strange, graceful wings, or drifted like jellyfish above leafy spires.

"It will take some time to figure out what we can eat," his wife commented, with feminine practicality.

"Hm," Jonah replied, too caught up in wonder to say more, a silence that lasted for many poundings of his heart. Until, finally, he managed to add—

"Someday. We must go back down. And tell."

After another long pause, Petri answered.

"Yes, someday."

She held him tight around the chest, a forceful constriction that only filled Jonah with strength. His lungs expanded as he inhaled deeply a sweet smell, and knew that only part of that was her.

CONTRIBUTORS

★

David Brin is a scientist and best-selling author whose future-oriented novels include *The Postman* and *Earth*. His Uplift-based Hugo Award winners include *Startide Rising* and *The Uplift War*. (*The Postman* inspired a major film in 1998.) Brin is also known as a leading commentator on modern technological trends. His nonfiction book *The Transparent Society* won the Freedom of Speech Award of the American Library Association. Brin's newest novel *EXISTENCE* explores the ultimate question: Billions of planets may be ripe for life, even intelligence. So where is Everybody?

★ ★ ★

Eric Leif Davin, Ph.D., is the author of "The Desperate and the Dead," from Damnation Books. This is his second appearance in this annual anthology.

★ ★ ★

Hank Davis is Senior Editor at Baen Books. He served in Vietnam in the Army and has a story in Harlan Ellison's® *The Last Dangerous Visions,* as well as stories in *Analog, The Magazine of Fantasy and Science Fiction*, and the *Orbit* anthology series. He is the editor of several popular anthologies, including *The Baen Big Book of Monsters, A Cosmic Christmas, A Cosmic Christmas 2 You, In Space No One Can Hear You Scream, Future Wars . . . and Other Punchlines,* and *Worst Contact*.

★ ★ ★

Seth Dickinson is the author of the epic fantasy *The Traitor Baru*

Cormorant and sixteen short stories. Born in 1989, raised in the hills of Vermont, he studied racial bias in police shootings, wrote much of the lore for Bungie Studios' *Destiny*, and threw a paper airplane at the Vatican. He teaches at the Alpha Workshop for Young Writers. If he were an animal, he would be a cockatoo.

★ ★ ★

Brian Dolton has ridden a camel in the Sahara, played volleyball on a sandbar in the Pacific Ocean, and stayed in a Zen Buddhist monastery on a sacred mountain in Japan. He recently moved from rural England to rural New Mexico, where he intends to continue writing until they pry the computer from his cold, dead hands. Anyone who knows who the "they" in question might be should get in touch via http://tchernabyelo.livejournal.com so that suitable preparations can be made.

★ ★ ★

David Drake was attending Duke University Law School when he was drafted. He served the next two years in the Army, spending 1970 as an enlisted interrogator with the 11th Armored Cavalry in Vietnam and Cambodia. Upon return he completed his law degree at Duke and was for eight years Assistant Town Attorney for Chapel Hill, North Carolina. He has been a full-time freelance writer since 1981. His books include the genre-defining and bestselling Hammer's Slammers series, the nationally bestselling RCN series including *In the Stormy Red Sky*, *The Road of Danger*, *The Sea without a Shore*, and most recently, with John Lambshead, the Citizen series entries *Into the Hinterlands* and *Into the Maelstrom*.

★ ★ ★

Brendan DuBois is the award-winning author of nineteen novels and more than one hundred and fifty short stories. His short stories have twice won him the Shamus Award from the Private Eye Writers of America, and have also earned him three Edgar Award nominations. A former *Jeopardy!* champion, he has recently appeared on—and won—the game show *The Chase*. His first science fiction novel *Dark Victory* was published in January 2016, by Baen Books. A sequel is in the works. He lives in New Hampshire.

★ ★ ★

Claudine Griggs is the Writing Center Director at Rhode Island College, and her publications include three nonfiction books about transsexuals along with a couple dozen articles on writing, teaching, and other topics. She has also recently begun writing fiction, publishing three stories, and hopes to draft more science fiction, her first-love genre as a teenager. Griggs earned her BA and MA in English at California State Polytechnic University, Pomona. She is a Vietnam Era veteran (USAF).

★ ★ ★

Champion Mojo Storyteller **Joe R. Lansdale** is the author of over forty novels and numerous short stories. His work has appeared in national anthologies, magazines, and collections, as well as numerous foreign publications. He has written for comics, television, film, newspapers, and Internet sites. His work has been collected in more than two dozen short-story collections, and he has edited or co-edited over a dozen anthologies. He has received the Edgar Award, eight Bram Stoker Awards, the Horror Writers Association Lifetime Achievement Award, the British Fantasy Award, the Grinzani Cavour Prize for Literature, the Herodotus Historical Fiction Award, the Inkpot Award for Contributions to Science Fiction and Fantasy, and many others. His novella "Bubba Ho-Tep" was adapted to film by Don Coscarelli, starring Bruce Campbell and Ossie Davis. His story "Incident On and Off a Mountain Road" was adapted to film for Showtime's *Masters of Horror*, and he adapted his short story "Christmas with the Dead" to film his ownself. The film adaptation of his novel *Cold in July* was nominated for the Grand Jury Prize at the Sundance Film Festival.

He is currently co-producing several films, among them *The Bottoms*, based on his Edgar Award-winning novel, with Bill Paxton and Brad Wyman, and *The Drive-In*, with Greg Nicotero. He is Writer In Residence at Stephen F. Austin State University, and is the founder of the martial arts system Shen Chuan: Martial Science and its affiliate,

Shen Chuan Family System. He is a member of both the United States and International Martial Arts Halls of Fame. He lives in Nacogdoches, Texas, with his wife, dog, and two cats.

★ ★ ★

Andrea M. Pawley's story "For the Love of Sylvia City" was inspired by the work of oceanographer Dr. Sylvia Earle and a government publication with one of Andrea's favorite titles: "The Shallow-Water Benthic Habitats of the Main Hawaiian Islands—2007." Follow her itinerant interests at www.andreapawley.com and on Twitter @andreapawley.

★ ★ ★

Sarah Pinsker's fiction has appeared in *Asimov's*, *F&SF*, *Lightspeed*, *Apex*, and numerous other magazines and anthologies. She won the Sturgeon Award for her novelette "In Joy, Knowing the Abyss Behind" and she is a two-time Nebula finalist. She lives with her wife in Baltimore, Maryland. Find her online at sarahpinsker.com and on twitter @sarahpinsker.

★ ★ ★

Brad R. Torgersen is a healthcare computer geek by day, a United States Army Reserve Chief Warrant Officer on the weekend, and a speculative fiction writer by night. Award-winning and award-nominated, he is a regular in the pages of *Analog* magazine, and has published numerous pieces of short fiction in other venues such as Mike Resnick's *Galaxy's Edge* magazine (where "Gyre" originally appeared) and *Orson Scott Card's InterGalactic Medicine Show* magazine. Brad's first novel, *The Chaplain's War*—which is based on the short *Analog* pieces "The Chaplain's Assistant" and the readers' choice award winning and Hugo award-nominated "The Chaplain's Legacy"—is currently out, from Baen Books. Brad also has two short fiction collections: *Lights in the Deep* and *Racers of the Night*, both from Wordfire Press. Happily married for 21+ years, Brad presently lives in Utah with his wife and daughter.

★ ★ ★

With over seven million copies of his books in print and seventeen titles on the *New York Times* bestseller list, **David Weber** is the science fiction publishing phenomenon of the new millennium. In the hugely popular Honor Harrington series, the spirit of C.S. Forester's Horatio Hornblower and Patrick O'Brian's *Master and Commander* lives on—into the galactic future. Books in the Honor Harrington and Honorverse series have appeared on fourteen bestseller lists, including those of *The Wall Street Journal, The New York Times*, and *USA Today.* While Weber is best known for his spirited, modern-minded space operas, he is also the creator of the Oath of Swords fantasy series and the Dahak saga, a science fiction and fantasy hybrid. Weber is has also engaged in a steady stream of bestselling collaborations including his Starfire series with Steve White, which produced the *New York Times* bestseller *The Shiva Option* among others. Weber's collaboration with alternate history master Eric Flint led to the bestselling *1634: The Baltic War,* and his planetary adventure novels with military science fiction ace and multiple national best-seller John Ringo includes the blockbusters *March to the Stars* and *We Few.* Finally, Weber's teaming with Linda Evans produced the bestselling Multiverse series. David Weber makes his home in South Carolina with his wife and children.